SEDUCED BY DESIRE

"Miss Moran," he spoke in a whisper, "you take my breath away."

"And you mine, Nate Laramie." Her lips covered his.

"You're not real, are you?"

"Oh, yes, and this is very real," she murmured as her soft hands played across his body.

He made one last half-hearted protest, which she silenced with another lingering kiss before he gave in completely to his overwhelming desire.

"Yes sir, my bandit, I know exactly what I'm doing." She didn't, not really, but she trusted in her newly awakened feminine instincts and Nate's loving tenderness to show her the way. "And I know exactly what I want."

"I believe you do, lady," he breathed.

Wrapped in the cocoon of his arms, Sadie knew she'd never felt so secure, so peaceful, so complete . . .

Let Sonya T. Pelton Capture Your Fantasies!

Captive Chains   (2304-9, $3.95/$4.95)

Shaina Hill had always yearned to be a teacher. Heading out for the remote area of Thunder Valley in the Washington Territory, she never dreamed her employer would be the rugged rancher Travis Cordell.

Inexperienced in the ways of the heart, Shaina was a willing and eager student when Travis took her in his tanned, powerful arms. When the virile, handsome rancher branded her with his kiss, Shaina knew she would be bound with Travis in love's *Captive Chains*.

Dakota Flame   (2700-1, $3.95/$4.95)

Angered by the death of his father at the white man's hands, Chief Wild Hawk wanted to lead his people to peace and obey the call of his dream vision: to capture the beautiful young girl who possessed the sacred talisman of the Dakota people. But Audrina Harris proved to be more of a captive than Wild Hawk had bargained for. Brave and fiery, she soon tempted him with her auburn hair and lovely fair skin. Each searing kiss and passionate embrace brought their worlds closer together. Their raging passion soon ignited into a fierce *Dakota Flame*.

Love, Hear My Heart   (2913-6, $4.50/$5.50)

Her mother wanted her to marry a wealthy socialite; her father wanted her to marry his business partner, the handsome river pilot, Sylvestre Diamond. But radiant Cassandra St. James needed to know what *she* wanted to do, so she slipped on board the *River Minx* for a trip down the Missouri River.

One moonlit night, she shared a passionate kiss with the one man she had sought to escape. The satiny kiss and powerful embrace of golden-eyed Sylvestre captured her desire, yet he knew it would be more difficult to claim the rebellious heart of his blue-eyed love.

BOUND BY ECSTASY

KRISTAL LEIGH SCOTT

ZEBRA BOOKS
KENSINGTON PUBLISHING CORP.

ZEBRA BOOKS

are published by

Kensington Publishing Corp.
475 Park Avenue South
New York, NY 10016

First printing: March, 1991

Printed in the United States of America

Chapter One

Arizona Territory, 1881

There it was again! The plaintive, wailing cry of hunger from a prairie wolf. For the fifth time in as many hours, Sadie Moran burrowed her head under an unyielding pillow, its stiff ticking and spiny stuffing scraping the back of her bare neck and shoulders. Some time passed before she edged out from under its flimsy protection, ear cocked for a repetition of the awful, eerie sound.

She heard nothing more. All was quiet within the square-cornered adobe house, and all was quiet outside on the grim and forbidding Arizona desert she already detested.

Her heartbeat gradually slowed and no longer thudded painfully in her chest. But she would sleep no more this night. With a shudder and a muttered curse, she abandoned the attempt and slid her narrow feet into homemade slippers. Her soft flannel nightgown fell to the floor as she stood, but not quickly enough to keep out the bone-chilling air seeping upward through the wooden planks of the floor.

For the thousandth time she wondered what she was doing here in this godforsaken land so very far from home. She was terrified that she might never see her father or her home again, and she trembled as much from fear as from the insidious cold.

A tear glistened in the corner of her eye and rolled down her cheek before she angrily brushed it away. She had neither the time nor the patience for tears. They were a sign of weakness, and that was something she could not tolerate.

Besides, soon *he* would be back.

Carefully, she had notched the wooden bolt in the door for each of the three blessed days of his absence. Over that span of time, she had meticulously made her plan. She was ready for his return.

Pacing the floor, she struggled to control her agitation. She knew what she must do and suspected she would have only one chance.

Sadie reached above her head and yanked the rifle down from its cradle over the brick fireplace. In her small hands it felt alien, so out of place she almost dropped it; but she held on tightly, resolutely checking its chamber to be sure it was loaded. She could not afford a mistake, though she'd certainly made enough of them in her twenty-three years.

Shouldering the firearm, she tested it, sighting down the long barrel toward the door. He would not be expecting anything and she would have him, shooting straight for his wide chest before he could reach for the lethal Colt he always kept in a holster strapped around his hips.

She had been practicing her aim ever since she'd discovered the weapon beneath a loose floorboard the day he'd left.

"Ha!" she'd exclaimed, scampering to get a stick

6

of wood to pry it out. "So you thought you had me flumboozled, and that I wouldn't have sense enough to find it, huh?" He really must take her for a total fool. Why, anyone with fairly good eyesight would have spotted the hump in the warped boards.

He was so obvious—she would just have to tell him *how* obvious when he returned . . . *if* he returned. Maybe he'd gone away and left her there to die. The thought troubled her greatly. But no, something about the man reassured her he would not have done that. He would be back, but he had said it might be a day or two, possibly three.

She probably still had time to take the gun and get away from him. But where would she go? She hadn't a notion where she was, much less which way to go to seek help! The nearest town was not likely within walking distance.

Frantically, she had tried to make a plan, figure a way out of her predicament. There just didn't seem to be one. She would have to wait for him to come back. But then, *then,* she did not have to remain his helpless captive any longer, for now she had a gun! She could make him take her back to civilization. Or could she?

With a shiver, Sadie recalled the rock-hard strength of the arms that had lifted her off the ground, and the solid muscular wall of his chest. Even with the gun, she would be no match for him. And there was simply no telling what he planned to do with her, or whether he would ever release her.

Another alternative had come to mind: she could shoot him! Then she would take his horse and ride as far as she needed to find help. The perfect solution! Of course, she wouldn't shoot to kill, and she would send help back for him—which was more than he'd done for her.

But I don't know how to use this thing! she had moaned, glancing down at the foreign-looking object she had unearthed. It was undoubtedly a rifle of some sort, but she had never seen one before, much less held or shot one.

And didn't one have to have bullets, or some such thing? Gingerly, she picked up the evil black thing and ran her hands over it, careful to keep the barrel pointed away from herself.

At first she could not see where ammunition would be kept in the gun, even if she had some. Her hands became a little more accustomed to the size and shape, and she noticed a crack that circled the gun at one point.

"Maybe it opens up," she said, thinking out loud. But she pushed and pulled for a long time before finally breaking it open. "So that's it!" she cried, but she examined the chamber and found it to be quite empty.

Was it possible some ammunition was hidden in the same place she'd discovered the gun? She flew back to the gaping hole and, falling to her knees, felt around in the dirt until she found a small box. When she opened it and saw shells inside, she almost shouted with joy.

Sitting on a three-legged stool with the gun precariously across her lap, she looked closely at the shells, then at the empty chamber, and decided there was only one way for them to go in. She dropped one in each side and closed the gun once more, narrowly missing catching the soft skin of her hand in the crack.

Carefully, she held the gun out in front of her, but she could tell it wasn't right. She would have to brace it on something. Somewhere she had seen a picture of a cowboy with one of these things resting against his shoulder. She tried it and though it felt awkward, decided it had to be the way to do it.

Then she had looked around for something to shoot at. "Wish you were here, Nate Laramie!" she said, pointing the weapon first at the door, then at his cot. She thought better of pulling the trigger indoors and, yanking the latch loose on the door, stepped outside, blinking in the bright sunlight. Her eyes eagerly sought an appropriate target, but at first found nothing she could feel comfortable about shooting.

When an unsuspecting cactus caught her eye, she grinned widely. She was so sick of the spiny, spindly things—one less would surely do the world no great harm! She planted her feet, hefted the weapon into position on her shoulder, and, squinting, looked down the barrel, which seemed much larger than it had before. The cactus, in the meantime, seemed to have grown ever so much smaller!

Oh, well, she had to try it sometime. Her finger squeezed, then squeezed harder, but nothing happened, nothing at all. What was wrong? Was the confounded thing broken? Or had she managed to put the shells in backward or something? Maybe it needed an adjustment of some sort. That funny looking little lever, perhaps . . .

Gently she pulled the lever back and jumped at the sound it made, but it stayed where it was. That had to be the problem. Once more she took aim and with two fingers, squeezed the trigger. This time a deafening boom was accompanied by a strong kick and a hard push against her shoulder that knocked her backward to the ground.

"Ouch! Damn it!" she cried, and commenced to spit out a stream of not very ladylike oaths. She'd had no idea such a thing could happen merely from shooting a gun. Her shoulder was already throbbing in pain.

Scrambling to her feet and retrieving her smoking weapon, she looked to see how much damage she'd done to the wretched cactus.

It stood there proudly, untouched, and if she hadn't known better, she'd have sworn it was sneering back at her.

Still muttering angrily, she rubbed her aching shoulder and lifted the gun again. It was heavier than ever and took all her strength just to hold it straight, or as straight as she could manage. Her eyes narrowed and she squinted at the cactus. She was coldly determined to hit it.

This time the noise made her ears ring and the force sent her toppling over onto her rump again. She decided it didn't matter at all, if only she had somehow managed to hit her target. But the cussed, fringe-topped thing stood there as straight as a tree, daring her to disturb a single one of its spines.

"Okay, you asked for it."

Sadie almost ran back to the shack for more shells. Pleased at how easy it was to load now that she knew how, she once more took aim, steadied herself, and fired.

Grinning happily, she saw from her reclining position on the ground that this time she had put a hole right through the broad base of the cactus.

But her thrill of victory was short lived when she discovered that, though she had indeed blasted the offending cactus to bits, the one underneath her with its spines sticking painfully into her bottom was definitely alive and well!

"Yeow!" she howled, and lurched to her feet. Thankful for the trousers that had offered some measure of protection, she twisted to look back over her shoulder and saw several wicked spikes sticking out. The burning pain told her they had pierced not only the thick material of her pants, but the tender skin on her rear end as well!

Most of that first evening was spent in the tedious and awkward job of removing the nasty things one by one, and soaking her fiery red rear in a tub of warm water. She slept on her stomach and did not sit much the following day.

Undaunted, she had practiced with the shotgun for long hours while he was gone, using nearly all of the precious ammunition. At last, her shoulder bruised and aching and her fingers burned, she had been able to hit a target—cactus or otherwise—from a distance of thirty feet or more.

Of the precious ammunition hidden with the gun, she'd reserved only two shells. One now rested in the gun's chamber and the other lay deep in the pocket of her nightgown.

She sank onto the narrow bed, tucking her cold feet up underneath her body, and leaning her back against the rough inner wall of the shack. Her muscles stiff and cramped, she waited without moving until the first faint flush of dawn peeked through the room's single slatted window.

Staring straight in front of her, she did not see the room's spartan furniture or the quarter-inch cracks in the walls.

This morning there would be no fire, no coffee, and no breakfast. Only a single blast from the gun that lay across her knees. She thought no further than that one deadly act. It was enough.

Wrapped in a fur-lined cowhide coat and sitting lean and tall in the saddle though he was bone weary,

Nate Laramie longed for a warming fire and a stout cup of hot coffee. The trip had been long and hard, but successful. He should not have long to wait for his answer.

Funny, how his thoughts had strayed so often to the spunky young woman he had left behind when he had ridden out across the desert a few days earlier. He nudged his horse into a lope, anxious to see how she had fared in his absence. He had taken every precaution when he'd had to leave her, but there had been no choice, none at all.

He smiled. From what he had seen thus far of Miss Sadie Moran, he was sure she would have little difficulty fending for herself. Though apparently unaware of it, she was an extremely self-reliant young woman. She had spoken up to him and yet had refused to put any of the other stagecoach passengers in jeopardy, even though it had meant relinquishing her own freedom.

In that moment he'd felt the stirring of a reluctant respect for the gently bred daughter of Lucien Moran. The sun-lined creases of his face curved downward in a frown as he considered that name . . . *Lucien Moran* . . . his enemy.

With a feeling of immense relief, Laramie topped the last rise and saw the cabin below him. Strangely, no welcoming smoke bellowed from the chimney. He knew she would be up by this time, and wondered at the lack of a fire in the room that must be ice cold.

What was wrong? Had something happened to her in his absence? Were marauding Indians that had maintained a silence over the past months once more on the rampage? A shiver shook his large frame as he imagined what they might have done to a helpless, beautiful woman. And then, in this part of Arizona, there were white men who were equally as dangerous as the red man. He had been an utter fool to leave her alone!

In grim haste, he spurred his tired mount across the sandy, cactus-dotted expanse between him and the adobe building.

He swung out of the stirrups, but as his feet hit the soft earth, he felt a vague prickling of fear, a sudden need for caution. He stood still and listened intently. Then he began to move, his booted feet making no noise as he crouched and loped in a zig-zag pattern to the side of the shack.

He could barely see between the slats of the window by rising up on his toes. When his eyes adjusted to the dim interior, he was so shocked by what he saw, he almost cursed aloud.

There sat the recent object of his concern — Sadie Moran, the refined young lady from St. Louis, with a heavy rifle braced against her shoulder, aiming straight for the unbolted door! Was it possible she intended to shoot him?

No. Surely something had spooked her and she hadn't realized who was riding in. She wouldn't have to worry now that he was back. He chuckled.

At the sound, she whirled, caught his eye, and fired. The shot went wild, but still might have hit him had he not ducked in a quick, practiced reflex.

The little firebrand had actually been planning to shoot him.

His grin was wide now, revealing brilliant white teeth beneath his trimmed mustache. He peeked through the window once more and watched her struggling to reload.

"Honey, open the door," he drawled, "and I'll do that for you."

"You . . . you . . . disreputable blackguard!" she shouted. "I won't let you in! You can rot out there—

13

or *freeze* in your Arizona winter, for all I care!"

"And how long can you go without fresh water, locked in your little fortress, my dear?" His voice was silken but deadly, and it began to work a subtle magic on her frayed nerves.

Her resolve was weakening, and she knew she had no choice—she would have to let him in, but perhaps not right away, she decided, letting the gun slide out of her hands onto the bed.

"Sadie, it's so cold out here, it'd freeze the whiskers right off a black-tailed jackrabbit. Now, let me in, honey, and we'll talk this over." His tone was cajoling as he crept around toward the front door.

Angry with herself for even listening to him, Sadie made all the noise she could throwing some logs into the fireplace and setting a match to them. Let him cool his heels awhile—it sure wouldn't hurt his cocky self-assurance. She would let him in only when she was good and ready.

Or so she thought, until the door slammed back on its hinges, reverberating against the wall. His hulking form filled the doorway, blocking out the early morning light.

"You forgot one little thing, Miss Moran," he said, his voice deceptively soft as he stepped into the room and closed the door behind him. "When you set a trap, be sure you're not caught in it yourself."

Sadie's eyes snapped with angry fire, revealing none of her fear, but she did not answer, knowing her quivering voice would give her away instantly.

He advanced toward her. The sun behind him cast his face in shadows. His spurs scraped over the rough wood of the floor. Otherwise, all was silent save for the early-morning serenade of a cactus wren outside the window.

Sadie was certain she could hear her own heart

hammering as he came nearer. He stopped just inches from her, towering over her. She caught her breath and bit her lip until she tasted blood. What would he do?

Nate Laramie was a dangerous man and deadly serious about whatever had brought them both to this place. Until now, he had not been cruel; instead, he had been almost kind at times. But she was no closer to discovering his reasons than she had been when he kidnapped her a few days before — nor was she any closer to escaping him.

And now she found herself trapped with this same desperate man in a one-room shack, an unloaded rifle on the bed beside her and his anger a very real third presence in the room.

He had to know she had meant to shoot him, and there was no telling how he would retaliate. The man was driven by a burning hatred and apparent desire for revenge, although why or against whom she had no idea. What part she played in the whole thing was the most puzzling thing of all.

"Before you kill me, would you at least tell me what this is all about?" she asked, her voice strong, though she was still reluctant to look him in the eye.

Her reasonable tone and request defused Laramie's anger as probably nothing else could have, and he turned away from her. "You needn't worry. I have my reasons, but I won't hurt you." His voice was flat and unemotional, and it revealed nothing of what he was feeling.

She did not find the promise comforting and watched him closely as he filled the coffeepot with water and used grounds and hung it over the fire. Some minutes passed before he turned back toward her, his face a mask devoid of emotion. He would tell her nothing. Whatever his reasons for kidnapping her, he would never tell her. If she found out, she'd have to discover it somehow on her own.

Sadie wondered what he thought as his striking blue eyes raked over her, lingering on the night-clothes she still wore and the way her breasts heaved beneath the rough fabric. He had made no advances in that way, but something in his eyes now warned her to beware, that he was not unaware of her as a woman.

As their eyes held, she noticed the growth of beard on his face, the shadows under his eyes, and the be-draggled condition of his clothing. In spite of her-self, she felt a burst of pity for him, driven as he was by some inner demon.

"You need food and rest," she said quietly. With-out understanding why she did it, she began to pre-pare a meager breakfast, and then she realized she was famished. He helped her by bringing out some battered tin plates and utensils and arranging them on the crude pedestal table.

"Looks good," he murmured as they sat down, the table effectively separating them physically, but do-ing nothing to distill the emotion-charged intensity that vibrated between them. They ate in silence and carefully avoided looking at each other. Though he would not allow himself to look at her again, the lush curves of her body scarcely hidden by the night-gown remained etched in his mind and tormented him.

When he was finished eating, he strode over to the door and dropped the bolt in place. He picked up the rifle, loaded it, and lay down with it across his chest. "I'm a light sleeper," he warned before his eye-lids closed. He was asleep almost immediately.

Sadie made no attempt to leave. She was not sure why. It could be that she had realized she would not know where to go if she were able to get away . . . it could be that she feared any attempt would wake him . . . it could be that her desire to run was not as strong as it had been earlier. She found that she was tired too; after she had cleared away the dishes, she stretched out on the cot next to his.

She slept dreamlessly and awoke refreshed to find him still sleeping. He looked younger in sleep, his features softer and more vulnerable. For the first time she really looked at Nate Laramie and observed how ruggedly handsome he was, even with the shadow of his beard and the dust that clung to his hair and mustache. High, aristocratic cheekbones spoke of an Indian heritage as did his dark hair and skin, but his features bore also the look of culture and refinement. Long, black lashes lay against his cheeks, and only the lines etched around his nose and mouth were evidence of the strain he had been under, the kind of life he must have led.

Once more she wondered what had driven this man to his desperate act and where it would lead them both before this was over. Careful not to disturb him, she rose and went to stare out the single window. Streaks of late afternoon sunlight revealed that she had slept longer than she'd imagined. It would soon be night, and the blackness that descended so quickly on the desert would be upon them.

A fierce loneliness and longing for home swept over her, the feeling so powerful she shivered and hugged her arms close to her. Would she ever see St. Louis again? Would she be returned safely to her father? Was he all right? After Laramie's threat, she suspected there was some involvement between the two men, but she hadn't a clue about what that might be. What must her father be thinking if he'd

17

learned of the kidnapping? Would he say, "I told you so?" For he had been adamantly opposed to her making the trip that had gotten her into this fix.

She could almost hear his voice. . . .

Chapter Two

St. Louis, Missouri

"Sadie Moran! Will you listen to me for once? I will not have you risking a stagecoach trip across that godforsaken country! It is absolute folly! I can arrange for a nurse to look after your Aunt Eunice. There is no need for you to think you have to be involved."

"Father, she's Mother's only sister, and I've never seen her. I owe it to Mother and to myself to go and do what I can for her." Sadie spoke in the self-assured voice of one long accustomed to having her own way.

"I am going to Tucson," she continued quietly.

"Balderdash! I will not have it, Sadie! I absolutely will not have it." Lucien Moran's voice softened, and he became even more difficult for his daughter to refuse. "Please, child. I couldn't bear it if anything happened to you. Don't go, Sadie."

A fire crackled in the hearth behind the elderly, balding gentleman, and evening shadows darkened the corners of the comfortable sitting room. Sadie's father pulled his footstool nearer his only child, pressing home his point, feeling his slight advantage.

This argument was not the first between a stubborn father and a headstrong daughter, but Sadie loved her father devotedly and smarted from the harsh things they had just said to each other. He was the only family she had left, since her mother had died giving birth to her, and she never enjoyed displeasing him.

Since his wife's death, Moran had raised his daughter alone, with a procession of housekeepers who came and went. Looking at her now, he felt great satisfaction in seeing the young woman she had become. Her plans to travel to Arizona had come as a harsh shock, and he was determined to find some way to stop her.

Over the course of the next few days, Moran reasoned with Sadie, played on her love and sympathy for him, enlisted friends to plead his cause, and did everything he could to dissuade her short of locking her in her room, an extreme possibility he'd briefly considered.

For her part, Sadie struggled with her conscience. It hurt her deeply to go against her father's wishes, but in the end she held firm in her decision. She could not live with herself if she didn't go to her aunt and do what she could for her.

An uneasy truce was called, and the subject was closed, though Sadie harbored no doubts about her father's unchanged position.

In addition to his disapproval, she found that she had some trepidation about leaving the only home she'd ever known. She had been born in the comfortable two-story house and loved every nook and cranny of each of its rambling rooms.

Though the current housekeeper Millicent tended to everyday chores, Sadie was active in the management of the household. She had sought out and acquired many of the beautiful furnishings and chosen the wall and window treatments with great care. Now she was not sure how long her errand of mercy would have her absent from her home: it could be months, perhaps even a year.

But she had meant it when she'd told her father she could not turn her back on Aunt Eunice, who had been the victim of a sudden serious illness and was now unable to care for herself. Her aunt had no one else, and Sadie was determined to go to her. She would do this for the mother she'd never known, but whose picture she had clutched tightly to her chest as a child when she toddled about, the same picture that even now commanded a revered position on her bureau.

As quickly as she could make the arrangements, Sadie prepared for her departure. She withdrew her small savings from the bank, purchased a few necessary items, gave careful instructions to Millicent for the care of the house and her father, and said goodbye to a few of her best friends.

At last she carefully wrapped her mother's picture in soft cloths and tucked it into her trunk. She was packed and waited only for her father to drive her to the stagecoach as he'd promised.

Once the decision was made, Moran was unusually quiet and took very little part in her preparations for the journey. This morning he had been closeted in his study, involved in a series of important meetings.

Impatiently, Sadie paced the wide hallway as the voices behind the closed door grew louder in disagreement. What was Father so angry about? she wondered as the door swung open and a tall, masculine frame filled the doorway, his shadow falling across the tiled entryway where she stood.

With the sun behind him, the stranger was

swathed in shadows. She could not see his face, but was instantly aware of a powerful aura of danger about him, and of something else, something that made her pulse race as she tried not to stare at him. She had never been so deeply affected by a man before. In her inexperience she could not begin to understand it, nor could she find words to speak for a moment.

The man whisked off his hat and inclined his head in her direction. When he spoke, his voice was deep and resonant, deadly serious, but he was not addressing her. Turning back, he said, "Mr. Moran, I beg you to reconsider . . ." The words apparently were difficult for the proud man. The subject of the discussion was of vital importance to him, that much was certain, Sadie thought as she looked with concern in her father's direction.

"I'm sorry, sir," came Moran's firm tones. "Our business is at an end. Good day."

That he was displeased with the meeting just ended was clear in the tension of the man's lean, athletic body as he moved in her direction.

"Good day, Miss Moran," he said in a rough whisper as he brushed past her and out the door. She still had not seen his face clearly, but had in some strange way been touched by his presence. Instinctively, she felt this was a man she would like to know, felt that he would have a kind, handsome face, though he was troubled and no doubt frowning as he left the Moran home.

Sadie answered politely, hoping the tone of her voice would not indicate the turmoil he'd aroused in her. "Good day, sir."

Turning back to her father, she continued, "Father, we really must hurry. The stage leaves in one hour, and there's not another one for Tucson for days."

"Yes, my dear," he agreed, apparently unruffled by the man's words or abrupt departure. He took Sadie's arm and helped her down the front steps and into the buggy, already loaded with her luggage. She was intensely aware of the stranger's eyes on their backs as they pulled away, but she did not dare turn back to look at him.

What could have occurred between the two men? Had her father's unease over the past week been due not merely to her upcoming trip, as she'd thought? She looked up at him for some clue, but none was forthcoming, as he sat looking stiffly forward. It would do no good to question him further. She knew him too well.

Neither of them spoke until they reached the station.

"And if you need anything," Moran assured his daughter as he told her good-bye, "I'm as near as the telegraph office. Let me know. I'll even come out there, Sadie."

His daughter knew that for Lucien Moran such would be a fate worse than death — to leave civilization for the distasteful world of the "wild West," as he liked to call anything beyond St. Louis.

With a catch in her throat, Sadie hugged him tightly and planted a kiss on his wrinkled cheek. In spite of their differences, she loved him and she knew she would miss him a great deal.

Sadie glanced up at the big sign on the coach office that proudly proclaimed, **BUTTERFIELD OVERLAND MAIL—OXBOW ROUTE.** The stage itself was gleaming with new paint in bright colors and was hitched to six fresh-looking horses. She thought the ornate scrollwork and landscape scenes painted on the doors a bit ostentatious, but if looks were any indication, perhaps this trip wouldn't be too bad.

The thrill of the adventure of seeing new places and people filled her, and she began to look forward to this change in her life. In vain she tried to control the flutter of excitement and anticipation that clutched at her stomach as the driver helped her up on the shiny black step that was set a good distance above the ground.

This particular coach was for six passengers rather than nine, and she was relieved to see that only three other passengers were aboard. Two were middle-aged women, and the third was a man who barely spoke to any of them, but snored constantly and loudly behind his newspaper. There was little discussion among any of them, for that matter. Though she tried several times to involve one or the other in some sort of conversation, their replies were monosyllables and she soon gave up.

Sadie learned later that every twelve miles on their route, they would reach a "swing" station, which was sometimes only a barn and corral presided over by a stock tender. Here, the stage paused only long enough to change horses, which could be done in under four minutes, and to grease the axles, before they were quickly under way again. She came to envy the tired team who remained behind for rest and fodder, for the trip was interminable and unbelievably uncomfortable.

Though everyone in St. Louis had raved about the wonderful Concord coach, she failed to see what was so wonderful about the thorough braces, leather straps that acted as shock absorbers. Personally, she was sure she would have preferred bouncing to the constant swaying motion that brought on persistent attacks of nausea among the other passengers.

Looking around inside the coach during the long

hours on the road, she had to admit that it *was* handsome, with its wood paneling, polished metal, and fine leather. But she spent a great deal of time with the leather shade raised so that she could watch the changing terrain as they tracked through the wilderness, leaving civilization far behind. She had never imagined so much space could be inhabited by so few people.

A sudden thunderstorm was even a welcome change of pace as the team of six horses was forced to slow its breakneck pace and the passengers made cursory remarks about the lightning display. Sadie watched wildly rolling dark clouds illuminated by vivid flashes of light. She caught her breath when she saw the outline of a lone rider atop a bluff not far from them.

"What do you suppose anyone would be doing out in weather like this?" she asked, not really expecting an answer.

The corpulent woman facing her did glance briefly out the window, but then looked back at Sadie with a puzzled frown. "Who?" she asked.

"Why, that man on the big yellow horse." Sadie motioned toward the rise where she had seen the rider, but apparently he had disappeared as quickly as he had come, for now with the latest flash of lightning Sadie saw that there was no one there.

"Humph!" said the fat woman, settling back into her seat, obviously miffed that she'd even made an effort to look.

But Sadie was sure she had seen someone, and she was troubled by the way he had seemed to be watching the coach. What other reason would a man have for being in such a wilderness on such a night as this? Sadie had a hard time dismissing him from her mind as the coach rolled on, picking up speed once the rains had stopped. The rain was gone as suddenly as it had appeared, the moisture quickly absorbed by thirsty ground. Before long it was impossible to tell it had rained at all.

"Home station up ahead!" yelled the driver, his voice full of the anticipation they all felt when arriving at these more elaborate stations situated every forty or fifty miles along the trail. Here they could rest and generally expect a good meal and perhaps some conversation before starting out again with a new driver and a fresh team.

Always glad to have someone to talk to, the stationmaster's wife chattered away to Sadie as she set out places for everyone in the big, open room that served as the dining room.

"It's so good to see a smiling face, I can't tell you, and a *female* one at that! Too many of the folks who come through here are the rough-and-tumble sort, tired of travelin' and sometimes even 'stage-crazy!' Why, oncet there was a man stopped here, calmly ate his dinner jest as polite as you please, then went high-tailin' it down the road on foot, screamin' his fool head off!"

Sadie smiled. "You can get an awfully closed-in, cramped feeling in that stage!"

"Yup—we do git some strange ones . . . oncet," her voice softened to a confidential whisper as she continued, "oncet I even met Jessie James hisself!"

"You didn't!" Sadie had heard of the too-handsome young bandit, but to think he might have been right there was unsettling.

"Yup, and jest as gentle and polite as the next one, he was. I din' know till he was long gone who it was that bragged on my cookin' so!"

"It must be very lonely out here." Sadie's eyes were soft with compassion for the woman, for she

26

couldn't imagine how one would survive in this wilderness without companionship, without even one other woman to talk to.

"That it does. But it ain' so bad, I reckon. I got my Jim, and that's enough fer me. Reckon I'd foller him anywheres, even if he went to . . ." She paused to think, then continued soberly and as though it were the end of the world ". . . to Or-e-gon!"

The love Sadie saw in the woman's eyes was such a surprise, she didn't know what to say. She had no idea how it must feel to love a man enough to be willing to follow him anywhere!

At that moment the object of their conversation entered, bringing with him the other passengers, their driver, and the relief driver who would be taking over from here. Introductions were made all around, and they all sat down to the delicious ham and fried potatoes, green beans, warm biscuits and gravy, and fresh coffee.

Jim was outgoing and friendly, and it was apparent he returned his wife's affections as he reached often to pat her hand and helped her serve the table and entertain their guests.

When they all complimented her cooking, he beamed at her, his pride obvious. "JoBeth *is* a good cook! Don' rightly know how I'd get along without her."

Sadie had never been around a couple who were so openly caring and she found it refreshing, but at the same time it filled her with longing. She realized how much she would like for a man to look at her like that with love in his eyes, how wonderful it would be to have someone so solicitous of her welfare, so proud of her accomplishments. She had to admit that the easy companionship and comfortable banter between the two married people made her more than a little envious.

The stranger she'd seen coming out of her father's study the day she left St. Louis jumped unbidden to her mind. How she could have been so deeply affected by him without ever seeing his face baffled her. But he'd caused a warm tingling to go through her, and something about him had drawn her like a magnet. She had wanted to touch him, to learn what troubled him so, and she had wanted to make it all right.

Sadie closed her eyes and could see the broad, athletic slant of his shoulders, the lean, tapering waist, and the graceful long legs. He was an exciting man — a dangerous man — and there had just been something about him . . .

"Sadie, more potatoes, hon? No? Well, we've got us a nice fresh fruit pie for dessert."

Too soon, the meal was over and Sadie heard the new driver's summons. "All aboard! Awaaay!"

They were under way again. She leaned out the window, waving to JoBeth, who stood by her husband in the shadow of the humble sod house. Sadie was sorry to leave the loving couple behind.

The worst part of traveling by coach was the impossibility of resting, much less sleeping; the coach kept rolling endlessly through the long nights. Naps could be caught while sitting upright, but they were too often interrupted by a bone-jarring bounce or by one's head falling to the side, or by a sudden movement or some noise from one of the other passengers. So fatigue became a factor as the coach rolled on across the long miles.

They passed through Indian territory without incident and without a sign of an Indian, for which Sadie knew she would be eternally grateful and, after crossing the wide and muddy Red River, were at last in Texas!

At first the countryside was green, with plenty of trees and rolling hills and Sadie thought it very beautiful. But after leaving Fort Belknap and moving farther and farther west, she noticed that the trees and green grasses disappeared and there was a terrible dreariness about the country. The flat, dry land was good for travel, though, and the coach made excellent time.

The terrain soon changed again, becoming rocky, with mountains in the distance peeking out from behind a blue haze. In a few hours more they would reach El Paso. The Guadalupes, off to their right, were breathtakingly beautiful, their craggy peaks cloaked in mysterious fingers of fog that refused to lift, even with the encouragement of the late morning sun. Sadie had always loved mountains and longed for the freedom to wander alone and unhampered through them.

Leaving Texas and El Paso behind, the coach rocked on through the deserts and mountains of New Mexico. These mountains were scruffier and had a wilder look about them, but were beautiful, too, in their own way. The driver told them only twelve to fourteen hours remained until they reached Tucson, and Sadie began to look forward to the end of the monotonous trip with great anticipation.

In the meantime, she continued her vigil, staring out the window at the sandy rolling hills, now dotted with dozens of varieties of cactus. One of the women passengers was absorbed in needlework and the other in the pages of a thick book, while the man snored away behind his paper, so Sadie was the first to see a solitary horseman galloping toward them, a cloud of dust almost obscuring him.

Aware of the continuing threat of highwaymen,

29

she felt her heart jump to her throat. She didn't have much money, but she would need every cent for her expenses and the return trip home.

Their driver, an easygoing sort who had taken over at the last home station, did not seem alarmed. He sawed on the three pairs of reins he held in his left hand, slowing to allow the mounted rider to overtake them.

"Howdy!" the stranger called out in friendly greeting.

"Howdy!" the driver replied, reining the six coach horses to a stop, prepared to take an overdue break for a stretch and grab a refreshing drink from one of the canteens.

Shock coursed through Sadie as she recognized the yellow horse of the rider she had seen watching them before during the thunderstorm. He must have been following them for days! She motioned to the driver, about to warn him that something was very wrong, but it was too late.

As the driver started to climb down, the stranger pulled a gun and ordered brusquely, "Stay where you are." He obviously intended to rob them—or worse!

His reddening face registering his dismay, the driver had no trouble following directions, knowing he could get himself killed by doing something foolish. He scrambled back up to his seat without argument, hands raised high over his head.

"Folks, if we just go along with him, nobody'll git hurt," he called out to his passengers, while his mind flew to the green strongbox under the front boot. Why couldn't he have someone like the famous Wyatt Earp for an escort? No robbers ever seemed to trouble the Wells Fargo stage when one of the Earps was along! But he was unfortunate enough not even to have a shotgun!

"Climb down, all of you," the mounted man ordered, his voice deep and implacable, his face shaded by a big black hat.

Sadie was the last to comply, her unwillingness obvious as she was helped to the ground by the overweight male passenger who was panting in terror, fanning his face with a wadded newspaper and trying hard not to faint. She looked up into the eyes of the dark-skinned man on horseback.

"Sadie Moran?" he asked, his eyes trained on her as though he already knew who she was, regardless of what anyone might say.

"I am Sadie Moran," she answered clearly. "What do you want with me?"

His amazingly light blue eyes glittered, whether with anger or humor it was impossible to tell. But his reply was smooth and brooked no argument. "Well, then, ma'am, you will come with me."

"What?" Sadie gasped, unable to believe what was happening to her. What could this arrogant stranger want with her? She glanced hopefully toward the coach driver but immediately saw she would get no assistance from that quarter as he lowered his eyes and looked away uncomfortably.

The other passengers shrank back as well, apparently willing to allow her to be sacrificed in order to protect themselves and their valuables.

"Well, I won't go." Sadie did not put her hands on her hips, but she might as well have. Her defiance was clear. If he took her, it would have to be by force.

A raised eyebrow met her words. She squared her shoulders and stared right back at him. He could not intimidate her, gun or no gun! Before she knew what was happening, the man reached down with one strong arm, seized her around the waist, and hauled

31

her up on the horse in front of him. She was held so tightly against him that the breath was expelled from between her parted lips and she was unable to argue further.

Slipping the big revolver back into its holster, the man wheeled his horse and galloped off in the direction from which he'd come, Sadie sputtering and struggling uselessly in his arms.

Even with the double weight, the big buckskin horse he rode quickly covered the miles, leaving the coach far behind. At the pace they traveled, Sadie was unable to voice the questions that ran unchecked through her mind: Where was he taking her? Would he hold her for ransom? It was true, her father made a comfortable living in his riverfront mercantile business, but surely others had much more. Which brought her back to the question of how he had come to pick her, how he'd known her name and what she looked like. And why was there something so familiar about him? She hadn't been able to see his face clearly, yet she felt almost as though she knew him. Did she?

The next few hours passed in a confusing blur of soreness and aching and unchanging scenery. She was sure she could develop a real dislike for this rocky, treeless land, uninhabited by any human as far as she could tell.

Choking red dust clung to Sadie's bare skin and blanketed her clothes. Her initial fear edged more toward anger with each jolting step taken by the big animal beneath them.

"How can anyone bear to live out here?" As usual, she spoke without considering the consequences.

Nate Laramie glanced down at the beautiful, petulant face, his own anger building. "It's good country," he argued. "Nobody says you gotta like it, lady.

32

I don't understand what possessed me to kidnap a coddled, spoiled little brat like you anyway."

This flame-haired woman was pure *loco* and had been nothing but trouble since he'd first pulled her into his arms off that stage! Purposefully, he turned his mind from the tempting feeling of her lush curves as he'd held her nestled in front of him for the first part of the trip.

"You're not exactly a charmer yourself, you know." She spoke through gritted teeth, becoming very impatient with the crude cowboy.

"Huh!" He was so mad he didn't trust himself to speak. She was impossible, absolutely the most troublesome female he'd ever come across. He lowered her to the ground. "We'll spend the night here."

"That's impossible!"

"Not at all. Hold this." He untied the laces holding the bedroll and saddlebags and dropped them into her arms. Sliding effortlessly to the ground, he turned to unsaddle his horse. When he heard the thump of her burden hitting the ground, he whirled on her.

"Miss Moran, you can choose to help and see to your own comfort, or you can continue to act stubborn and sleep on the ground. I really don't care. But that is the extent of your choices, for we *will* stay here for the night, with or without your approval."

Sadie stared back at him and didn't answer. However, when he again offered her a blanket, she took it without comment and spread it out on the ground. He turned his attention to building a fire and warming a can of beans, the aroma bringing a rumble from her hungry stomach. She didn't see his smile. When he held a portion of the food out to her, a sober look had replaced the smile. They ate in silence, but she helped him clean up afterward without saying another word.

She breathed a sigh of relief when he walked away from her and stretched out on the other side of the fire.

"Go to sleep, Miss Moran. Maybe you'll wake up in a better frame of mind."

But she didn't.

"How do you sleep out on the ground like that?" she complained the next morning, rubbing her stiff and aching limbs as she folded her bedroll. "It's hard as a brick and I hate to tell you, but that saddle is no feather pillow."

"I wouldn't know. I slept without a saddle or anything else for a pillow!"

His remark apparently sailed right over her oblivious head. Did she have cotton for a brain? He hadn't slept any too well himself, but he didn't have any intention of letting her know that! His lack of sleep hadn't been caused entirely because of his discomfort. He had had a hard time dismissing from his mind the way she'd felt snug against him as they rode, and the tempting fresh smell of roses. But how could he possibly be attracted to her when he didn't even *like* her?

"And I felt things *crawling* all over me!"

He chuckled. "There are some mighty friendly spiders out here, a few scorpions as big as your hand, and a wide variety of snakes, too."

He was gratified to see her shiver. She was a soft, city-bred woman, all right, just the type he'd come to despise. The fact that she was so damned beautiful and desirable made his job a little harder, but it didn't change anything.

"My father will have posses all over this state hunting for me. There will be a bounty on your head so big, men will come thousands of miles just for the chance to put a bullet in you!"

"Then I'd better warn you not to ride too close to me, Miss Moran. You might make a soft target for a stray bullet."

Her eyes were huge, and the most intriguing shade of honey-brown. Laramie knew he was saying too much, but she goaded him so badly he couldn't seem to stop.

"Ride!" she exclaimed in alarm, rubbing her rear, bruised black and blue, and knotted by tight, over-strained muscles. "Oh, I really don't think I can ride any further." She looked up at the saddle resting on his horse. She wasn't even sure she could get up there again if she wanted to—and she knew good and well she didn't want to.

"Oh, but you must, Miss Moran . . . you really must." His voice had a deadly, quiet authority that brooked no argument, and Sadie saw she had no recourse. "I'll help you up." He had noticed her rubbing a sore bottom and his voice was a bit gentler. "Give me your foot."

She stepped in the stirrup fashioned of his hands and allowed him to lever her up into the saddle. She winced but made no further complaint, catching up the reins he handed to her.

All she had to do was kick her mount and gallop away while he was unprepared and still on the ground. She *might* just be able to get away from him.

But then what?

A vast sea of sand, sprinkled with some spindly cactus and a few sprigs of hardy grass, spread out from them endlessly on every side. The only life for hundreds of miles consisted of swooping buzzards, the nocturnal crawling things she'd felt as she slept, the two of them, and his horse. Common sense cautioned her this was not a good time to make a break for it. Besides, she saw in her mind how quickly he had vaulted into the saddle. He could easily stop her before she could get going. And he had a very mean-looking gun strapped to his hips. She was not sure he would shoot her if he had to, but she wasn't willing to take the chance.

It went against her grain to see herself so helpless, but for the moment she had to accept the fact that she was the captive of a man who looked as much Indian as white and who could no doubt ride and shoot as well as the most noble savage.

But there would come a time, an opportunity, for escape, and she would not miss it. He might even provide her with her chance. *Be watchful and keep your eyes open, Sadie,* she admonished herself, careful to keep her emotions from being revealed on her all-too-expressive face. Her father had often said he could see her very soul through her eyes.

Even as she considered her options, he leaped up behind her and she no longer had any.

"We have a long day ahead of us before we get where we're going," he warned her. He didn't look forward to her first reaction to the shack where he planned to keep her prisoner. It was a long, long way down from the accommodations someone like her would be used to, he thought. She probably slept every night on silken sheets perfumed with lilac and rose water and had servants to tend to her every whim.

"Never done a lick of work in your life, have you, Miss Moran?" What business of his was it what she'd done or not done, and why should he care?

"I most certainly have. I supervised our household staff, and once or twice I've done the marketing." Her answer sounded vain and hollow, even to her

36

own ears. She bit her tongue and wished she'd kept quiet.

He mocked her, his cruel, biting words stinging. "My, my, my! Aren't we the busy ones!" He reached for her tiny white hand and turned it palm up. "Born to a life of leisure. These hands have never known a blister or labored over hard work!"

"That is true, but I fail to see how that makes me a bad person, Mr. Laramie." Why was he treating her so harshly? She had done nothing to him. *He* was not the injured party here — no one had kidnapped *him!*

"I owe you no apologies," she said, snatching her hand back.

He had the grace to be chagrined at his less-than-gentlemanly behavior, but he was too stubborn to say he was sorry. He couldn't remember the last time he'd said those words.

They rode in silence until he signaled that it was time to stop and stretch and eat lunch.

"Are you hungry?" he asked, not unkindly.

"No, not really." But she was desperately tired and not far from collapse. Still, her pride kept her from admitting her condition. She wanted no pity from him . . . not that she thought she'd get any.

Her thoughts almost made her laugh. She wanted very badly to fling them at him, but the forbidding scowl on his face and the powerful, threatening slant of his shoulders convinced her to use discretion for once.

How had he brought out such an about-face in her attitude in the few short hours they'd spent together? She couldn't explain it and was too tired to think about it any more.

For a hot, soapy bath and a warm, comfortable, *clean* bed, she would give a king's ransom. Sadly, her fortune at the moment consisted of the few coins she'd had in her pockets when he abducted her. Her trunk and reticule were probably safely in Tucson by now and more than likely she'd never see either again. The dust-laden clothes on her back were all she had to her name, with no prospects of getting new ones. A bath was no good without clean clothes.

"Oh, hang the bath, then!" she fumed, not realizing she'd spoken until she saw Laramie's puzzled frown.

"What? What bath?"

"Nothing! I was talking to myself. There's no need for you to fret. Just go on with whatever it is you're doing." Her big brown eyes didn't miss a single thing as he moved around, preparing them something to eat.

Late that afternoon they finally arrived at a disreputable-looking adobe shanty without having seen a single soul or exchanged another word. Sadie had only the vaguest notion of where they were, except that it was a long way from Tucson!

"We'll stay here," he told her in his economical way of speaking, without further explanation, and without apology.

"Where are we?" she demanded to know, but he refused to give her any more details.

"Don't worry. It won't be for long."

"What won't be for long?" The man was infuriating, so nonchalant and so cool, while inside her everything rolled around wildly like the loose baggage in that blasted Concord stage!

But she heartily wished she were still aboard the coach. By now she would have reached her Aunt Eunice in Tucson but for this man's rude interference! What would her aunt do when Sadie failed to arrive as planned? Would there be anyone else there to help her? Maybe Sadie's father would secure a nurse for her aunt as he'd offered when he had tried to talk her out of making the trip. But how long would it be before word reached him of her disappearance? Surely he already knew. He would have checked to be certain she arrived at her destination safely. He was probably looking for her right this very moment. She hugged that comforting thought to herself as she studied her surroundings more closely.

The shack was at least of a respectable size, and the thick walls, except for a few wide gaps, provided some insulation against the harsh extremes of weather she had already experienced in their trek across mountains and desert. Sadie had seen nothing to like about Arizona and was amazed at her captor's apparent affection for the land.

"You have an advantage over me, sir." She spoke firmly as she eyed the big man moving about the sparsely furnished room, setting some coffee on to boil over a fire he'd coaxed to life in the brick fireplace.

He turned abruptly, his hands on trim hips, and smiled widely. "Do I, now?" he asked, humor lightening his blue eyes. "And what might that be?" He was so handsome without the perpetual scowl that Sadie's heart did an unexpected flip. With his rugged, tanned features and vivid blue eyes, he was the best-looking man she'd ever seen. Sadie tried desperately not to reveal the direction her thoughts had taken, knowing he'd only take advantage of any weakness on her part.

"You know my name."

"So I do," he agreed, still smiling.

"But it seems I do not know yours."

"No."

"Well?"

"Well."

"Don't you think I'm entitled to know the name of the villain who pulled me bodily from a stage and brought me across miles and miles of godforsaken land to this . . . this . . . this shack?"

"It's really not much, is it?" He looked around him as though seeing it for the first time. "But my friend Pete was comfortable here." He seemed a bit puzzled as he continued, "It's no place for a lady, though."

Lazily his eyes moved over her dusty, disheveled clothing, lingering with interest on her flowered straw hat, askew atop a riot of vivid auburn curls. His eyes made the briefest of apologies as he knelt and pulled a trunk from under one of the two crude cots. The lid creaked when he pulled it open as though it had been neglected for a long time.

He pawed through the clothing, his big brown hands out of place among the feminine trappings. "Should be something here that might work since we had to leave your things behind." He held up first a nightgown and then a pair of trousers and a woolen shirt. Eyeing her closely and bringing a blush to her cheeks, he said in a low voice, "Yeah, these ought to be about right."

Sadie stood and brushed dust from the folds of her skirt. She'd had on the same clothing for much too long, and it would feel good to change. But it would feel even better to bathe.

"Is there water for a bath?"

She was pleasantly surprised when he not only nodded, but set about to drag out a wooden tub and put some water on to heat. He was rough and lawless, but she had glimpsed signs of a kindness in him that surprised her and made her wonder about her kidnapper and what had motivated him to take such drastic actions. With a start she remembered the strongbox on the stage. Surely he'd known about it, but he hadn't demanded it and had seemed single-mindedly interested only in her. Why? She longed to ask the question of him again, but knew he would refuse to explain.

Thoughtfully he turned his back while she undressed and settled luxuriously into the warm, soapy water.

"Surely you can tell me your name?"

"Laramie. Nate Laramie."

The name had a nice, strong sound. She repeated it and liked the way it rolled off her tongue. She thought he wore his name well.

Sadie was completely mystified by her response to Nate Laramie. By all rights, she should hate him for taking away her freedom, but she acknowledged that what she felt for him was a long way from hatred. She was puzzled and yes, she admitted, even concerned about this stranger. She really didn't believe he was a violent man, but he was a desperate one.

He had, for the most part, treated her with respect and tried to make her as comfortable as he could. If they'd met under other circumstances she could have felt something for this brooding, mysterious cowboy. She thought back to the unique relationship between the stationmaster and his wife. But they *hadn't* met under different circumstances, and this man *had* kidnapped her, whatever his reasons might be. She had to find a way to get away from him.

Chapter Three

Sadie's father had been right about the dangers of the trip, and she should have listened to him. But no, had gone on in her own hardheaded way, as usual. Look what a fix she'd gotten herself into this time!

Surely her father would have the law searching for her by now, and would do everything he could to find her. But what chance did he have? She had not seen a soul since her abrupt departure from the stage; she felt completely isolated. She had the sinking feeling it would be up to her if she were ever to leave this place. No one would come for her, of that she was nearly certain.

The sleeping man murmured, and she turned to look at him once more. She hated to admit it, but even his hateful presence was better than being alone, as she had been during his unexplained absence.

Sadie had probably never been alone for more than a few minutes in her whole life, and she had been miserable while he was gone. The only thing that had kept her going was her plan to shoot him when he returned, and in that she had failed completely! But she could not be sure she was sorry as she watched the steady rise and fall of his wide chest in sleep.

Sadie thought of the way he'd looked after she'd discharged the gun. His response had been unexpected, and she wondered if he hid his true feelings beneath that mocking smile and deadly calm exterior. She would have been less surprised if he'd been furious with her.

He stirred in his sleep and threw one muscled arm above his head as though to ward off some real or imagined threat. A frown creased his brow, and he muttered unintelligibly.

"Laramie." She walked toward him, speaking softly, wanting to summon him back from the dark world of his dreams.

"Laramie," she repeated, as she placed a hand on his arm. "It's nearly dark, and you need to tend to the animals."

He cursed, his hand grasping hers where it lay on his arm. He pulled her down until she lay across him. Sadie's heart pounded fearfully, but she did not struggle. She had entered his dream. He would surely release her in a moment if she stayed still and did nothing further to upset him.

His other hand buried itself in the luxuriant hair on the back of her neck and forced her face toward him, though his eyes were closed and he still breathed evenly. She could feel the steady rhythm of his breathing and the strong beat of his heart beneath her breasts. Their bodies were melded together, and she could feel the muscled length of his thigh and the whisper of his breath across her mouth.

"My love," he murmured, before his lips slanted across hers possessively. The kiss was inescapable because of the way he held her, and there was a gentleness in it she could neither fathom nor resist. It was full of yearning and passion and aroused a powerful response deep inside her. The masculine scents of tobacco, sweat, and dust were not unpleasant, and Sadie's mind whirled as she found to her dismay that she was kissing him back and enjoying the feeling of his arms around her!

Her response frightened her and she struggled in his arms, as much against herself as against his hold on her. Her hands on his chest, she pushed, but his arms tightened around her.

"No!" he cried out, but whether in pain or fear or anger, she couldn't be sure. She stilled her movement, and he quieted, one hand tenderly stroking her arm. Sadie trembled, and a tear rolled down her cheek and dropped onto his face.

"What?" his eyes blinked open, and, for long moments, stared deep into hers. Before the mask dropped back into place, she glimpsed suffering such as she had never seen before and a tender longing that moved her heart.

"What are you doing here, Miss Moran?" His softly mocking tones marked his return to consciousness and to the role she was more familiar with than the gentle, loving man he had been in his sleep. Whoever he had been caressing so lovingly in his sleep was not his captive, but someone from his past life, long before she'd entered it.

Sadie found that she was much more able to deal with this Nate Laramie and pulled herself stiffly to her feet, smoothing her skirt. "I was only trying to awaken you," she explained, attempting to bring her emotions under control.

"I noticed," he said. "And quite an effective way, I might add." His wicked smile transformed the swarthy face, making it incredibly handsome, and her breath caught in her throat. It occurred to her that this stranger, her kidnapper, might be dangerous to her in more ways than one and that she couldn't afford to let her guard down with him.

"No! you don't understand. It wasn't that way at all," she argued.

"Well, then, perhaps you would like to tell me what way it was." His eyebrow arched again as he waited for her to continue.

"You . . . you were dreaming . . ."

"Too bad, and it seemed so real, too." He was still smiling, but there was a softer light in his eyes as he looked at her.

Unable to bear his scrutiny any longer, she turned away. "When you go out, Laramie, you might bring some water for a bath. You appear to need one."

He got slowly to his feet, yawned, and stretched lazily, chuckling as he strode toward the door. "Outspoken little thing, aren't you?" he challenged as he disappeared outside.

She gathered the soap and homespun toweling and put a kettle on for hot water while he was gone. A round wooden tub stood in a small alcove of the room that afforded some privacy to the bather. He pushed the door open, his arms loaded with wood which he laid on the fire, before going back out for the bucket of water he would add to what she'd already heated.

"Thank you," he said to her without further comment and began stripping out of his dusty clothing. She turned away, but not before she'd caught a glimpse of his muscled chest covered with a dusting of dark hair. Carefully, she turned her attention to another part of the room. He had done the same for her during her bath the night before, except the one time she had suspected that his eyes had strayed in her direction and lingered. She flushed at the thought.

Sadie had never seen a naked man before, as her father was always scrupulous about not undressing in front of her, and she'd had no experience at all with any other men. The kiss she'd shared with the sleeping Laramie was her first real kiss, and still set her heart pounding when she thought of it. It had been so real and so full of passion and tenderness! She had to keep telling herself he'd been sleeping and hadn't even known who was in his arms. And that thought disappointed her more than she ever imagined.

Laramie watched her putter about with her back to him, smiling as though he could read her thoughts and knew exactly what troubled her. Humming as he scrubbed himself, he enjoyed her discomfort almost as much as his bath, which was a great deal, indeed! He splashed noisily, trying to get her to look in his direction, and began to sing a ditty he'd once heard on a trail drive in Texas.

"Must you make all that racket?" she asked peevishly. "Why can't you take a bath like ordinary folks?"

"And just how do 'ordinary folks' bathe?" he asked. "I suppose you have watched a lot of them, to make a such a judgment?"

"No!" she snapped, flustered by his suggestive question. "I've never. . . .Oh! just shut up!"

"Yes ma'am!" But he continued to hum as he stood up, the water dripping from him, and reached for the towel.

"I can't reach it."

"What?" she turned and whirled back around when she saw that he stood there naked! He was not ashamed of it, had even goaded her into turning

46

around! And she would never be able to get the sight of that magnificent body out of her mind. She'd really had no idea! A collage of bronzed skin, rippling muscles, and dark, curling hair crowded other thoughts out of her mind.

"I can't reach the towel," he continued reasonably, "and I don't want to track water all over the floor. Could you hand it to me, please?"

How in the world was she supposed to do that without looking at him? The towel was somewhere behind her on a stool. He could surely reach it if he tried!

As she hesitated, he said, "Oh, well, I'll just have to get it myself," and started to step out, water running off him onto the floor.

"Oh! just a minute, Laramie! I'll get it." She backed toward him, careful not to turn around, feeling for the towel. Though he was quiet, she knew his eyes were laughing, and as her hand fell on the towel, she started to laugh, too.

His hand brushed hers as he reached for the towel, and their laughter died away abruptly. Sadie hastened away from him.

Through the long night she wrestled with her troublesome feelings for Laramie. He was quicksilver, sliding so easily into a role and out again that he was impossible to fathom. One minute he was the harsh, ruthless man who kidnapped her, and the next he could be impossibly gentle and she found herself a victim of his warm sense of humor. Then he could be so wickedly charming and handsome. At rare, unguarded moments, she was sure she caught the flicker of pain in his blue eyes.

The first narrow shaft of sun through the slatted window found her still lying with wide-open eyes and filled with a new sense of urgency. Her weakness where he was concerned made it even more vital that she get away from him soon.

But how? She would not get far on foot. She had to have his horse, not an easy task. Perhaps during the coming night, while he slept . . .

Nate Laramie awoke to the rattling of pots and pans, sounds which should have been pleasant precursors of morning, the evidence of breakfast being prepared. But Sadie's dainty feet were making decidedly undainty noises as she trod back and forth, and her treatment of the utensils was something less than gentle. He quirked an eyebrow in amusement. Something had her more riled than usual. He supposed her bad humor could be the result of lack of sleep; she'd had a restless night.

Laramie hadn't slept well himself and he yawned widely, rubbing the rough bristle on his face as he threw his long legs over the side of the bed and hastily pulled on his pants and shrugged into the coarsely woven shirt he'd worn the day before. With a chuckle, he remembered her wide brown eyes when they'd make a quick survey of his nakedness during his bath. He had seen a glimmer of admiration in them that pleased him to an uncomfortable degree. Was that what was troubling the fiery Sadie Moran this morning?

To avoid an early and unpleasant confrontation, he would give her a wide berth, he decided, as he fastened his gunbelt around his hips and grabbed his hat from a nearby nail.

He had learned a surprising amount about Sadie Moran in the short time she'd been his captive. In the beginning, he had expected her to be spoiled and haughty, and had been fully prepared to hate his enemy's daughter. What he had not been prepared for was the soft, tender look in her big brown eyes, or

48

the graceful way she carried herself, even in the rough homespun clothing. And he definitely had not been prepared for the single dimple that showed itself only when she smiled that certain, rare smile that did such odd things to his stomach. He'd have to watch his blind side, or she would sneak up on him sure and that was not at all in his plan.

Stealing a glance at her, he reassured himself she would not be smiling that particular smile today. Her lips were compressed to a thin line and her eyes were a dark amber and snapping with anger.

What was eating her today, Laramie wondered, his eyes narrowing as he continued to watch her slamming about in the kitchen. He couldn't afford to feel sympathy for Sadie Moran. He was as sure of that as he'd ever been of anything in his life, and he hardened his resolve to resist the effect her presence was having on him.

"What are you staring at, Laramie?" she barked at him, raising that stubborn chin. But she blinked rapidly and if he hadn't known better, he might have thought she choked back tears as she went on. "Don't you have anything better to do than stand there gawking at me?"

A smile swept over his strong features and lighted his eyes as he moved swiftly in her direction. Involuntarily she backed away, watching him. But he stopped and reached a suntanned hand toward her face. With a feather-light touch he brushed away a smudge of flour that decorated her upturned nose.

"I can't think of anything better—to look at, that is," he said softly.

A frisson of fear mingled with another emotion she couldn't name, walked up Sadie's spine as she looked into his startling blue eyes.

Abruptly she turned away and swiped at the

49

wooden table with a cloth she still clutched in her hand. For long seconds there was no sound in the small room. Then she thought she heard the deep rumble of a chuckle before he also turned away, moving with long strides toward the front door.

"Think I'll go watch the sunrise, then," he said, his voice expressionless, though she suspected that mirth lay just below the surface of the quiet, unoffensive words. The man was completely exasperating!

A smile curved his full lips as Nate ducked and stepped outside the shanty into the brisk Arizona morning, a smile that widened as his eyes took in the familiar terrain he'd come to love so passionately. An ocotilla cactus stood starkly silhouetted against the brilliant colors of the early-morning sun, and the sight took his breath away. God, this country was harsh at times, but so beautiful! He found even the biting air of autumn more invigorating than cold as he filled his lungs with it. Next to sunset, he loved this time of day best.

A hard look chased away his earlier good humor. His shoulders straightened, and he flexed the muscles in his arms, eyes fixed on some faraway scene, his pleasure in the sunrise displaced by a fierce anger. Dark brows knitted together, and a muscle worked in his jaw. Though he was unaware of it, his teeth clamped together and his hands balled into tight fists. His lank body tensed like a coiled spring and all at once, he was a lethal weapon, ready to react violently at the slightest provocation.

Sadie, who had been watching him from the window, felt her heart jump to her throat at the sudden, disturbing change in the man. The small fear she'd experienced earlier was multiplied tenfold. She never wanted to face his wrath, or the anger that was suddenly evident in every line of his taunt body, and she pitied anyone who had to face it.

The sun slipped up from behind the shelter of a nearby mountain, a brilliant orange ball, and Sadie found that she dreaded the day to come.

Soon after daybreak, Laramie rode off on his big dun-colored horse, telling her only that he would return in time for dinner.

The long day crawled by. As afternoon shadows lengthened, Sadie began to worry that he might be away for days on some unexplained mission, as he had been before. Something haunted and controlled Nate Laramie that she could not fathom, and whatever it was, it scared her. It had to be connected to the reasons for her kidnapping, but she was still very much in the dark about that.

After Sadie had swept the floor for the third time, scrubbed her single change of clothing, and hung it before the fire to dry, there was little to occupy her time. The minutes and hours dragged wearily by.

She found some dried beans and soon had them bubbling in an iron pot suspended over the fire, but there was little else to eat. She hoped Laramie would at least come back with some venison, or rabbit, or something good to eat for his efforts.

Had he, indeed, gone hunting for wild game for their dinner, or had something else drawn him away?

Sadie told herself she should have shot him when she had the chance. She should have been ready for him when he returned. It was true, he'd caught her off guard at the window and her firing had been in the way of a reflex action, but had she consciously pulled her shot to the left? A niggling doubt filled her as she thought about it. If she had purposely missed her target, why had she done so? Because he was a man, a living human being, and because she had been taught the sanctity of life? Or was there another, more compelling reason?

Was it because he was Nate Laramie? Was it because she felt a soft fluttering in her heart when he was near, a vague heaviness in other parts of her body when they touched, as they had when she'd reluctantly handed him the towel for his bath? Her body had flared wildly in response to the brand-like feeling of his hand brushing hers. And when she'd watched him sleep and been aware of his unsuspecting vulnerability, she'd almost felt tenderness, along with some other bothersome emotions.

How was it possible she could feel that way when the man had, kidnapped her in a cold-blooded, calculated way, and was holding her here against her will? What kind of body—what kind of mind did she have, to feel these treacherous longings where he was concerned? She was a fool, certainly, and she resented the reactions of her heart and body to Nate Laramie.

More than one young man back in St. Louis had tried and failed miserably to stir such a response in her. What was there about this dark, intense cowboy that moved her so?

The need for caution where he was concerned filled her with a new urgency. She could not allow these disturbing feelings for him to rule her head and hamper her efforts to escape. Instead, they were all the more reason for her to be free of him, and it must be soon.

At sunset, Sadie saw riders approaching from the west. Her pulse quickened. Could she dare to hope help was about to arrive? Perhaps she would soon be on her way back home to her father. She could not control the desperate hope that filled her heart as she watched them ride nearer.

Sadie rushed out into the yard and stood there in

the chilly air, straining her eyes in an attempt to see who the riders might be. If only they would hurry, they could all be on their way away from there before Laramie returned and discovered her missing. The thought of Nate Laramie in pursuit of her was not a pleasant one, but anything was better than waiting to see what he might do next.

Shading her eyes and hardly daring to breathe, Sadie stared into the distance. The mounted men were in no hurry. There appeared to be three of them, two mounted on dark horses. But the one in the middle . . . the one in the middle rode a yellow horse!

Laramie rode toward her, and he was not alone! She did not think he had seen her yet, so she moved along in the shadows toward the barn, which was closer to her than the house.

A rough-looking, bearded man and an Indian rode in with Laramie, one on either side, mounted on almost identical blacks. The three men stopped and dismounted near the well, and Laramie pulled up a bucket of water for their horses. Sadie could see that a brace of rabbits had been thrown over his horse's rump, the blood from one dripping onto the hard-packed dirt.

She stood shivering, just inside the barn, about ten feet away from the three men. Breathing heavily, but listening unashamedly, she remained hidden by the heavy, hinged door. He would never have to know she'd been there, and maybe she could learn something useful, something that might help her escape. For escape she would . . . somehow. Perhaps tonight.

"Laramie." The gruff voice of the heavier-set man carried to her ears as he absently scratched his graying beard. "Somethin's up back in town. I don't know jest what, but you'd best come in and find out."

No answer filled the void of silence for long minutes. The Indian nodded in agreement.

"I'll be in when I'm ready." Laramie's voice indicated his position of leadership and his self-confidence. "But," he continued with a calculated smile, ". . . but I think it may be soon."

Both men showed their relief, the set of their shoulders relaxing as they shared a glance.

Who, Sadie wondered, were these strange men, and what was Laramie's connection with them? Did they know about her? Whatever was about to happen sounded serious, and she was desperately afraid that it might involve her.

While the men shared a few parting words, Sadie made her way back into the shanty without being seen. Grateful for that good fortune, she awaited Laramie's return. He spent much too long tending to his horse, before she finally heard his heavy footsteps approaching, the thump of his boots equipped with Mexican silver spurs rattling the loose boards of the porch.

Chapter Four

The two of them ate a simple supper of the rabbits he'd skinned, the beans she'd cooked, and some potatoes they'd found in a tiny cellar. He did not mention the visit of the two men and she did not want him to know she had eavesdropped, so there was little conversation during the meal or afterward as they prepared for the night. He had been careful not to touch her or come near her since the episode in his sleep. He said goodnight and stretched out on his bunk.

"You're going to kill me, aren't you?" Her soft voice cracked, revealing the intensity of her new fear.

Sadie remembered how calmly he'd told her his name and allowed her to see his face. Did that mean he intended to kill her? That he would never let her go?

His eyes lingered on her quivering lips and his heart stirred at the sight of a single tear as it made its way down her cheek.

"Go to sleep, Miss Moran. It's been a long day."

Hell's bells! Why hadn't he at least told her he didn't plan to rape and murder her in her sleep? What kind of man had he become, anyway?

"I won't hurt you," he muttered, but not loud

enough for her to hear. When there was no response, he slapped his hat down over his eyes and said nothing more.

Sadie satisfied herself that he slept deeply by listening to his regular breathing for long minutes before she carefully eased her legs over the edge of her cot. This time when her feet met the icy floor she was prepared and stifled her natural tendency gasp.

Feeling around in the dark, she located one slipper and gratefully slipped her foot inside. Dropping to her knees, she groped blindly with both hands under the makeshift bed, trying to find the other, knowing she would not get far in the chilling night air with only one shoe! Her hand brushed something soft and her fingers eagerly closed around her second shoe, but as she dragged it toward her, it made a loud scraping sound.

Sadie did not move, nor did she breathe while she waited, expecting at any moment to hear his feet hit the floor and his strong voice boom out into the silence. But there was no sound except for his regular breathing. She snatched up her pitiful stack of clothing and crept toward the door, knowing she would have to change her clothes in the meager shelter afforded by the barn rather than risk wakening her captor.

Her hand fell on the rough chunk of wood that bolted the only door firmly in place. She tugged hard, but nothing happened. Then she pulled once more, much harder, but it still refused to budge. She had opened it before, without much difficulty, and she hadn't expected any now.

Quick, angry tears sprang to her eyes as she breathed a prayer, "Please God, not now." Setting her clothing down so she could work with both hands, she pushed upward until she felt the heavy object move and begin to slide until it was free and the door swung open slightly.

The streak of moonlight that fell across the floor was so bright she was certain it would wake him. She looked, anxious, unsure what she'd do if he did catch her. Relieved, she saw the strip of yellow light laying across his ankles rather than his face, as she had feared.

As quickly as she could, she retrieved her clothes, slipped through the small opening, and pulled the door softly shut behind her. She headed for the barn, making as little noise as possible. Sharp stones pressed into her tender feet through her thin-soled shoes. Her progress was slow and uneven, and once she almost danced with a tall cactus whose limbs waved in the soft night breeze.

Even inside the barn it was freezing. She shivered violently when she threw off her nightdress and slippers to get into the britches and soft woolen shirt. They fit surprisingly well, and she now had cause to be thankful Laramie had provided her with such sensible garments, even if they left something to be desired in appearance. They would be perfect for riding.

"Riding!" she whispered. "Oh my God!"

It dawned on her she would not only have to ride Nate's big buckskin, but she would also have to—somehow!—get a saddle and bridle on the beast! Everything she knew about doing that came from the miserable trip she had made with Laramie when most of the time she had ridden behind him, clinging to his sturdy body for dear life.

Her first impression of riding horseback was far from pleasant, and she did not look forward to any extended time in the saddle. She remembered how Laramie had saddled and bridled his horse with ease, but she admitted to herself that she hadn't watched him very closely. She had only a vague impression of what needed to be done.

Could she do it? She had to, didn't she? She couldn't very well ask him to come out and do it for her! She smiled as she thought of his reaction to such a request. Thankful for the light of the moon, which made her task a bit more manageable, she looked around for the gear she would need. Hanging on a nail outside Shorty's stall was a funny leather contraption, but as she walked over and lifted it off the wall, a frown furrowed her forehead. The frown became a scowl the closer she looked at the strange piece of equipment. She held it up, first one way and then another, the leather straps flapping wildly in the air.

Shorty nickered, but whether in panic or in encouragement she couldn't tell. "Well, old boy," she said to him, "I think this is supposed to fit over your head somehow." She spoke softly as she held it up toward him. For some reason, it never occurred to her to be afraid of the animal that towered over her and looked down on her with wide, interested brown eyes.

"Now, you just stand still . . . whoa! just a minute and we'll have this thing on you!" She had pulled on Laramie's fur-lined jacket on the way out, but her teeth still chattered from the cold, and it was hard to keep her hands from shaking uncontrollably.

"Easy now, just open your mouth a little more . . . there!" She had the shiny metal part in his mouth, but how was she to get the rest over his head so high above her? Holding the bottom of the bridle in one hand and what she assumed to be the top in the other, she felt behind her with her foot for a rail and stepped up without turning to look. The horse shifted, and she leaned against him at a precarious angle while she pulled at his ears and finally managed to settle the leather piece over one of them.

The whole thing sat rakishly to one side and was decidedly not right. Sadie clambered to the ground and looked at him from the front.

"Aha!" she said and, reaching as far as she could, pulled a thin strap of leather behind his other ear. The reins fell straight down and she left them hanging there, not sure what else to do with them.

She turned her attention to the saddle seated over the top rail of the stall. It was so big! Too bad she couldn't just walk him under it! She wondered if she might be able to stay on him without it? Looking at his wide back and the distance to the ground, she shook her head. There was no help for it, no way around it — she had get it on him somehow.

Gingerly, she walked around the big horse and grasping the saddle with both hands, pulled as hard as she could. It slid a little toward her. She yanked at it again.

"Oof!" The heavy saddle swung free and caught her off balance. She sat down hard with the saddle planted in her lap.

"Don't laugh!" she admonished the horse who swung his head in her direction. "I know *you're* the one who's supposed to wear the thing! Just wait a minute."

She scrambled out from under the saddle and grabbed for it again. Heaving for all she was worth, she got the saddle no more than halfway up to where it needed to be, and it fell back, pinning her against the side of the stall.

"Oh, yeah," she muttered, heaving it up in the air in the general direction of the horse. This time, Shorty seemed inclined to help and took a sidestep toward her. She heard, more than saw, the ridiculous leather seat land with a thud on the horse. She had done it!

Dusting off bits of hay and stepping back, she smiled and put her hands on her hips. But the self-satisfied smile slowly faded from her lips when she looked more closely at the horse.

She could not believe what she saw! It was true — she had gotten it on with only two tries, but it now appeared to her astonished eyes that horse and saddle were going in opposite directions!

"Oh no!" When she started to giggle, she had cause to be glad the barn was at a distance from the house and that Laramie could not possibly hear the commotion.

Holding her sides, she leaned against a post until she could quit laughing. "Laramie, if you could only see me now," she whispered, still hiccupping.

But Laramie had awakened instantly as the door slid shut behind her. He had followed her out as soon as he'd pulled on his pants and shirt. Curious to see what she would do and how far she might get, he'd been watching her silently through a crack in the wall of the barn, but was barely able to keep his laughter subdued watching the city girl wrestling with a horse and saddle many times bigger than she.

He knew he had to stop her before she got far and he knew how angry she would be, but there was no help for it. For now, he was enjoying himself as he hadn't in a long time. Thinking back, he could hardly remember smiling, much less laughing, since Jeff was murdered, at least not until the remarkable Miss Sadie Moran came into his life.

The thought that she was good for him was a new and unsettling idea and he tucked it away for later consideration.

He stared intently through the slit in the wall as she pulled the saddle off, spied the blanket and threw it on before struggling with the saddle again until she had it back in place, this time facing the right direction!

He almost laughed out loud when he saw her trying to decide what would keep it from slipping off. Then her wide smile as she discovered the cinch made his knees go weak with the dawning of a new admiration for her spunk.

She had done it! God! but the little minx was stubborn and possessed a quick intelligence that filled him with wonder.

Shorty snuffed quietly as she led the huge horse out the door and faced the momentous task of how to get on top of him! The stirrups were too high off the ground for her to reach. She tried jumping for them, but couldn't quite get a hold and slid back to the ground several times.

An inspiration came to her as she remembered seeing pictures in school books of people climbing up on boxes or being lifted into the saddle. Since no one stepped forward to give her a hand up, she searched for a box or something she might stand on. There was nothing in sight.

She had to find a way—she hadn't come this far for nothing. She noticed with alarm that the first light of dawn was streaking the sky behind the nearby mountains. Laramie would be up soon and would be less than happy to find his horse saddled and ready to ride! Especially when he learned *who* had saddled him and *why*, she thought with a wry grin.

The fence! Of course! As her eyes lit on the wide railing of the corral, she knew she was as good as on top of the patient animal. Pulling him in that direction, Sadie had to make several awkward attempts before she positioned him in just the right place. Quickly, she climbed the railings until she was on an even plane with the horse's back. With the reins still tightly clutched in one hand, she launched herself across the saddle, belly first.

Painfully, she struggled to right herself so that she was straddling him. But then she realized the horse was only willing to go in a tight, left-handed circle. Holding on for dear life as he turned, she leaned way out over his neck and somehow got the reins split with a thin leather strap on either side of his neck and the ends clasped firmly in her small hands.

Her feet dangled uselessly, not even nearly reaching the stirrups, but it would just have to do. There was no more time. She nudged him with her knees, the only thing she dared to do at this point and the big horse stepped out with long strides, causing her to lurch backward and almost drop the reins.

She would have to hold onto something, she thought frantically as she grasped the leather straps in one hand and with the other reached for the silver horn. There! She was no longer in immediate danger of falling, at any rate, and was beginning to feel a bit pleased with herself once more.

But which way to go? She had watched Laramie ride off through a pass in the mountain west of the cabin, so that must be the way to the nearest town. She urged Shorty in that direction, unaware that someone followed them closely on foot.

As Laramie trailed them, confident that he could stop his horse with a whistle, if necessary, he felt a mixture of reluctant admiration along with consternation and concern for her safety. Had she no idea what she might be getting into? Of the dangers she faced on the perilous ride to town? No, of course not, how could she know? She knew nothing of the wild and lawless land into which he'd brought her.

For the first time, he doubted his own motives and the necessity of his actions. Surely there had been another way to reach Moran. He had been a hard-headed and selfish fool. His self-reprimands did nothing to improve his steadily worsening temper. With every step he was becoming more and more angry with himself.

Ahead of him, the horse steadily climbed the craggy mountain pass. He kept quiet but stepped up his pace. He had been a fool to let her get so far. Why hadn't he stopped her in the barn? He had to admit it was because of the respect he'd felt for her courage and cleverness.

He had known all along he could not let her go, even as he watched her ride away. But he had wanted to — some part of him had cheered her valiant efforts and postponed putting an end to it.

He whistled. Shorty stopped in his tracks. It was then that he saw something that made the hair stand up on the back of his neck. He raised his rifle and fired, Shorty bolted, and Sadie fell in a heap on the ground.

Her last conscious thought was that her escape attempt had failed and it had been all his fault! She was not aware when he checked her over carefully for injuries or when he gently picked her and carried her all the way back down the hill in his arms. Shorty trailing along behind them.

"I will *not* go back in there! Nothing you can do will persuade me!" she stormed at him when he deposited her back on the porch of the shanty.

"Perhaps not," he said, his voice soft and thoughtful. In two steps, he reached her and fastened his arms around her midriff so her feet dangled uselessly off the ground. In one lithe movement, he slung her over his shoulder and one muscled arm wrapped snugly around her upended bottom!

"Oof!" was the only reply she was capable of making as the blood rushed crazily to her head and her small hands pounded ineffectually against his broad back.

He set her feet on the floor none too gently once they were inside, his fury barely restrained.

"That was a stupid thing to do," he told her, his voice gruff with emotion and his blue eyes angrily raking her slowly top to bottom and back up again. The little fool could have gotten herself killed out there, almost had, in fact. His heart had stopped when he saw the snake and then her lifeless body on the ground. If he'd killed her, or let something happen to her, he didn't know how he would live with himself. If he hadn't been there . . .

"Oh, and I suppose *you* are the one with all the good sense, *Mister Laramie!* Why, I was just fine until you frightened the horse with your precious . . . six-shooter!" She spat out the hateful word and looked up at him triumphantly.

"Well, *Miss Moran*," he spoke slowly, as though choosing his words carefully. "That 'precious six-shooter' saved your pretty little neck and quite possibly your life, too."

Her eyes flew open and she brushed back strands of the reddish-brown hair flecked with gold that he found so remarkable. Her pink lips made a rounded "O" of shock or displeasure as she stared back at him.

"What are you talking about?" she demanded. "You *shoot* at me and then claim to have saved my life?" The more Sadie thought about it, the more hotly indignant she became, and her breath came in

64

short bursts.

Fascinated, he noticed her eyes snapping and her head toss with anger, and he could not keep his eyes from lingering over the lush breasts that rose and fell provocatively with each tortured breath. He remembered the way his hands had so easily spanned her waist and the rounded softness of her bottom and, damn it, he even remembered the clinging fragrance of wild roses that had drifted about them while he held her over his shoulder.

What was happening to him? The more he thought about it, the angrier he became, until the fire in his blue eyes matched that in her amber ones.

"My dear young lady," he said, intentionally drawing out his words and filling them with a mocking threat she couldn't ignore, "what I shoot *at,* I always hit."

An unexpected twinkle in his eyes softened his face and a wide smile curved his lips upward. "Not in the fashion of someone we both know whose skill with a rifle leaves something to be desired, eh?"

With utmost effort, Sadie controlled the desire to stomp her foot and throw herself at him. No, she would show him she could be as reasonable as anyone.

"And what, pray tell, were you shooting at, if not at me?" Let him try to get out of this, she thought smugly. Of *course* he had been shooting at her, and the great Nate Laramie had missed! If the horse hadn't shied at the loud noise and dumped her unceremoniously to the ground, practically at his feet, she would still be going and would soon be in Tucson — or somewhere, anywhere besides here!

"The diamondback rattler sunning itself a few inches from your elbow."

At his quiet answer to her question, Sadie shivered. "A . . . a . . . rattler?" Could that rustling noise she had heard only seconds before the gunshot spooked her horse have been made by a rattler preparing to strike?

"Oh, my!" Sadie's hand flew to her mouth, and her eyes widened even more.

Laramie thought the flush on her cheeks very attractive, but was glad to see he'd gotten the best of her at last. Even though she was supposedly his captive, he admitted to himself that there were times he wondered who was really in control of whom.

Sadie returned his stare, angry at the off-handed, casual way he had put an end to her desperate bid for freedom, but intrigued by the man who stood before her, in spite of herself.

Nate Laramie was tall, well over six feet, and his frame was solid and muscular, but his wide shoulders tapered to a narrow waist and his widespread legs were long and lean, encased tightly in the buckskin he always wore. He was big, bold, and masculine, a man to be reckoned with.

The weathered skin of his face made it difficult to judge his age, but she guessed him to be nearly thirty. His fierce, terrible beauty spoke of an almost certain Indian heritage, but that was something he had never mentioned and didn't seem likely to. Actually, she knew almost nothing about him and was surprised at how much she wanted to know him better. Was there something familiar about the man? Could they have met before?

Her lips quivered and curved into a tiny smile as she thought, "Well, Miss Moran, you certainly have a chance to get better acquainted now. It seems you are right back where you started."

Without moving a muscle, Laramie studied her and the self-mocking smile on her lips brought back that quivering feeling he had felt while watching her in the barn. She was really something! But she had no idea what she was doing to him, that was clear. It was important that she never find out. The blood pounded in his ears as he stood there thinking how soft and pliable she would be in his arms and how sweet and delicious she would taste with his lips covering hers.

He looked down to be sure his feet were still firmly planted where they had been and battled with his senses. He would not touch her! He must not! She'd probably bite him and punch him, anyway, he realized with a wide grin. What could he be thinking of? He was ten kinds of a fool! Pivoting, he strode out the door, slamming it behind him.

"C'mon, Shorty!" he said, untying his big buckskin horse that was anything but short. "Let's get you some oats. You've had a big mornin'!"

His hoot of laughter carried inside to Sadie, who had not moved, but who could not stop her answering smile.

Laramie's shadow filled the doorway when he returned from tending to his horse. "You want to go to town so bad, Miss Moran? I'll take you." The words fell like stones in the quiet room. Laramie's expression told her nothing as he stood with legs spread apart, as though expecting argument. Hope surged up in Sadie as she thought of civilization and the chance of getting someone to help her, perhaps even getting word to her father.

Dark blue eyes that missed nothing were riveted on her face, and his expression showed that he read her thoughts.

"No, Miss Moran, do not think of escape. I will

be watching you every minute we're in Tombstone. There will be no opportunity."

Sadie's mobile, expressive face showed her keen disappointment so clearly his heart jumped painfully, but his face remained outwardly unchanged. On this trip into town, he could not leave her behind, but he meant what he said to her. He would see to it that she had no chance to get away from him. The stakes in the deadly game he played were much too high.

Chapter Five

In the early 1880s, Tombstone was a boom town that had quickly blossomed to a population of several thousand. This number included a cross-section of people, from the unscrupulous drifter and bounty hunter to the few honest men who wanted only a decent home and a decent living for their families.

For the most part, Tombstone was young, brash, and undisciplined, much like the vast, unsettled Arizona territory in which it rested. Its main streets, Allen, Tough Nut and Fremont, were lined with mostly one-story businesses and houses of frame, brick, and adobe. The sidewalks were sheltered by projecting roofs, supported by posts at the curbs.

Broad streets constantly teemed with traffic that included wagon trains bringing lumber from the mills, stages setting out for Benson, Bisbee, and Tucson, and heavy wagons gouging deep ruts into the limestone of the roadbed. Over one hundred saloons and gambling halls did as much business at noon as at midnight. It was truly a town that never slept, and a night's entertainment could be bought for a quarter. Men with composure and blazing six-shooters kept order, men the likes of Wyatt Earp and his brothers and Doc Holliday.

Since 1863, Arizona had been an organized territory and considered not ready for statehood or for entrance into the Union. The Federal government exercised direct control over it and many of its officials were appointed rather than elected as in other states. Congress could even take away its land, as shown by the so-called "lost county" of Pah-Ute, which had been reassigned to Nevada in 1866.

A "federal clique" controlled politics in the territory as late as 1878, when John C. Frémont, called "the Pathfinder" because of his explorations in the West, used his connections with President Hayes to be appointed governor of Arizona in order to rescue himself from financial difficulties. In conjunction with the prestige of the governorship, he was also privy to opportunities for successful business ventures, especially in mining and land acquisitions, on the side. Apparently caring little for the country he was charged to oversee, Fremont was absent for long periods, when he would travel back East on "business."

Tombstone's sheriff, Dan Potts, owed his appointment to the "absentee" governor, whom he considered his mentor, if not his friend. Potts was not popular in the town, and was known to have a quick, undiscerning trigger finger. "Boot Hill" was populated with victims of his smoking Colt, both the guilty and the innocent, according to those who knew him and his methods of law enforcement.

"Now, Sheriff, will you stop that danged fidgeting?"

"Lil, you know I can't stand it! I never could stand to wait!" Lily Delgado leaned toward one of the most feared sheriff in the territories, straightened his stiff collar and reknotted his thin tie with a soft smile on her lips.

"It ain't ever' day you get to see the *governor* hisself, now, is it?" she asked, acknowledging the cause of his frustration.

"No." He winced at her poor grammar and turned away, but not before she discerned the cause of his withdrawal. With a steady hand and eyes that refused to look away, she handed him his white hat.

"I'm sorry, Lil," he blurted out, "but I've put a lot into this reception and there's a lot riding on it."

Her eyes showed how much she did understand, sometimes too much for her own good. The pain he'd caused her lay buried below her ready smile, and with a final, gentle shove, she pushed him out the door.

"You jest get over there and show them what a real man looks like, Sheriff!"

He smiled and kissed her soundly on the lips before turning on his heel. Lily stood there, looking after him. Dan Potts felt comfortable with her and it was understood she was his "woman," but he never escorted her to public functions. He had his image to maintain.

The tall sheriff trod through a town built in large part from the quick, easy money that flowed through the less-than-savory establishments lining the main streets. The Crystal Palace Saloon and Bird Cage Theater were popular places of entertainment frequented by miners, ranchers, and trappers, but respectable ladies never went near them. Of course, there were precious few of that category who called Tombstone "home," at any rate.

One such lady was Rachel Foster, who stood watching the sheriff as he neared her house. An unpredictable string of circumstances had brought her into these environs and left her here, alone, to fend for herself and her two small sons. She did not fit in, and the locals wondered why she hadn't high-tailed it back East after her husband's sudden death. Rachel had her reasons.

The lovely old Victorian-style home she and husband Jeffrey had built together in the first flush of new wealth from their mine, foolishly called the "Silver Lining," stood near the northern edge of town as a monument to their love and a painful reminder of a future that might have been.

The only person Rachel felt she could trust, the only person who still cared about her and Christopher and little Timothy, was Nate Laramie, who had once been her husband's partner in the mine. And she hadn't seen him in several weeks now. What could have kept him away for so long? Rachel worried about Nate and his obsessive hatred for Sheriff Potts; she dreaded the showdown that was inevitable between them.

Lately the sheriff had been overly solicitous of her and her boys, and she knew he had an ulterior motive. He was up to something, for sure. If she kept her eyes and ears open, perhaps she could help Nate get the proof he needed of Potts' involvement in the death of her husband and of his theft of their mine. Neither she nor Laramie had any doubt of the sheriff's guilt; they needed irrefutable evidence, the kind that would stand up in court.

For this cause, she had reluctantly accepted the sheriff's invitation to the reception for Governor Frémont, being held in the town hall that very evening. Her heart beating faster than usual, Rachel watched Dan Potts stride up her long front walk, confidence showing in every line of his body, his white hat at a rakish angle. He obviously looked forward to the evening with an anticipation she did not share.

When she opened the door, he greeted her with a wide smile that somehow didn't reach his eyes. His icy eyes never seemed to glow or darken with emotion. Cool eyes . . . lizard eyes, she realized with a shiver that had nothing to do with the chilly weather.

His hand grasped hers even as she rigidly controlled her impulse to recoil from his touch. It was important that he not be allowed to see her aversion to him. He might be using her, but she would use him as well, to find out something that might help Nate.

As he placed her wrap around her shoulders and his hands lingered overlong, her heart cried out to her dead husband for help he was no longer able to provide, and for forgiveness for the things she might be forced to do.

The governor's reception was as splendid as an event could be, so far removed from the fashionable East Coast. The townspeople had dragged out their finest attire in an attempt to impress the visiting politician and his entourage. Spirits flowed freely, and a magnificent feast was spread out on long buffet tables, overseen by employees of the local taverns, dressed in matching uniforms. A hastily assembled musical ensemble played surprisingly well, and the large center of the room was cleared for dancing.

Rachel was grateful the sheriff was too preoccupied in awaiting the governor's arrival to demand a dance. The thought of his arms around her, his breath on her neck, was almost more than she could bear. She prayed for something to rescue her from that fate.

As the handsome pair strolled through the crowded room, they were greeted courteously by many who would have liked to turn their noses up at her, but didn't dare as long as she was in the company of the powerful sheriff.

Rachel visited with the wife of the town's doctor, Elizabeth Connors, as they waited for the governor's entrance, when the party would be in full swing.

"And how are your two dear young ones, Mrs. Foster?"

"Oh, Christopher and Timothy are thriving. They're such wonderful boys, so much like their father . . ." Her voice trailed off, but she continued, "And please call me Rachel."

"Of course, my dear, and you must call me Elizabeth." The older woman's kind words and smile warmed Rachel's heart, and she felt she might have found a friend at last in Tombstone. Until that moment she hadn't realized how she'd missed having someone to talk to.

"Oh, look! Here comes our esteemed governor!"

Elizabeth announced with a mocking smile that revealed all too clearly her opinion of the striking man just entering the room and who immediately became its center of attention.

The governor bestowed handshakes and words of greeting on the important citizens of Tombstone who rushed forward to greet him. Much time passed before he made his way to the side of Tombstone's impatient sheriff, who strove to conceal his irritation at not being singled out earlier.

"Well, Dan . . . Dan Potts! How are you, my good man?" The sheriff obviously did not notice the condescending tone of his voice that was so evident to Rachel. She responded politely to her introduction to the governor, and saw the flicker of interest in the man's eyes as he looked her over.

"Well, well, well, a fine-looking young woman, sheriff, fine-looking indeed."

Rachel acknowledged his compliment with a tight smile, but her attention did not linger on him for just behind the governor, towering above him, stood one of the most handsome young men she had ever seen. Tall and slender, he had sandy brown hair and the merriest brown eyes.

When her eyes met his, she could have sworn he winked at her impudently! Though intrigued, still she diverted her eyes, noticing the emergence of several couples onto the dance floor.

"And this is the 'eyes' of the Federals, sent out to keep me in line." The governor laughed loudly, but without humor, as he presented to them the tall man who stood behind him.

"Jonathan Lee, meet Sheriff Dan Potts and his lovely companion, Rachel Foster."

With a contagious chuckle, that young man returned their greetings and shook hands, first with Rachel and then with the sheriff. Rachel's palm tingled long after his hand was taken away.

Looking straight into her eyes, he said, "I haven't danced with a pretty lady in such a long time. May I have this dance, ma'am?" A hint of challenge in the depths of his eyes and her desire to escape from Dan Potts made her acceptance a foregone conclusion. Before her escort could protest, she swept by him and was out on the dance floor, Jonathan Lee's strong arm fitting easily about her trim waist. The two of them moved into the steps of a slow dance.

"I certainly didn't expect to find anyone so beautiful buried out here in this godforsaken country, if you'll excuse my boldness, ma'am."

"Well, I'm not exactly *buried* yet, Mr. Lee," she pointed out, but her voice was soft and her answer no real rebuke.

He laughed heartily. "No, ma'am, and that's a fact!" He thought her the most bewitching creature he'd ever seen — light as a feather in his arms, and a long, long way from dead and buried!

Recalling who had escorted her to the dance, though, he tightened his arm reflexively, and his step faltered. She simply did not seem the sheriff's type, certainly not someone to be found willingly in the company of Dan Potts! Jonathan knew enough of Tombstone's sheriff to know the man was less than honest and possibly even dangerous.

"Something wrong, Mr. Lee?"

"Why, no, ma'am. Nothing, that is, if you will agree to call me Jonathan."

"I will, and you may call me Rachel, Jonathan."

"Is there a Mr. Foster, Rachel?"

"No . . ." she hesitated, throwing a hard glance at Potts, who danced with the mayor's wife, ". . . not anymore."

He wisely sensed she didn't want to talk about it and let the matter drop. He was surprised at how glad he was to know she wasn't married and his steps quickened with the changing tempo of the dance.

"Have you and the sheriff been friends long?"

"We're not friends." Her comment was brief, and she explained no further, but her opinion of the lawman was so clear that his mind was set at ease.

"May I cut in?" drawled a husky, self-assured voice.

"Oh, Nate! It's so good to see you!" Rachel's eyes lit with pleasure and Jonathan's heart dropped to the vicinity of his knees as he looked into the harshly handsome features of Nate Laramie.

"Thank you for the dance, Jonathan," Rachel dismissed him politely but abruptly, almost flying into the arms of the other man, who hugged her and gave her an enthusiastic kiss before sweeping her away.

"Damn!" The curse was rare for Jonathan Lee, but he muttered under his breath as he practically stalked off the dance floor in the direction of the punch bowl, hoping it had been liberally spiked.

Governor Frémont stood nearby and watched the events with some humor. "So she dropped you for the first handsome cowboy to come along, eh? Not your usual luck with women, my young fellow."

Lee flashed the governor a quelling look. His feelings were still smarting, and he did not need it

77

rubbed in.

But Frémont continued, "Perhaps Dan here could tell you more about the young lady in question."

At first, the sheriff seemed unwilling to discuss Rachel Foster, but soon he warmed to his subject, and filled them in on her history since her arrival in Tombstone. He glossed over the violent death of her husband as the "inevitable outcome" of the man's greed, and did not mention his own company's acquisition of the Silver Lining as a result.

"And so, she's been a widow for some months now—" the governor raised his eyebrows at his companion, "and eligible, I would assume?"

The sheriff, who sensed trouble brewing, decided he needed to put a quick end to the young man's interest in the attractive widow. "I wouldn't advise getting involved with her just now. Laramie was her husband's best friend, and he's very protective of her, having taken her under his wing, so to speak, since her husband's tragic and untimely death."

His words were suggestive and carried a thinly disguised warning. "I don't think he'd look kindly on any interference, or outside interest of any kind, for that matter."

"Interference is never a good idea, sheriff." Jonathan's words made their point, and without another word he walked away. The sheriff watched him go, a murderous look on his face.

"Fine young man," he said sarcastically.

"Yes," agreed the governor. "He's been sent out here to spy on me. I'm almost sure of it. Those vultures back East are just waiting for me to make a mistake."

78

"You never make mistakes, governor."

"No, of course not."

But Dan Potts realized he had made a mistake by letting the young widow out of his sight and into the arms of his enemy. As he watched Nate Laramie dancing with Rachel, the sheriff felt his usual surge of envy, though he was at a loss to explain it or understand it.

Since Laramie had lost the Silver Lining and his partner, the drifter had nothing that should make anyone envious of him. He had no home, no roots, and no apparent source of livelihood. But he certainly did seem to have the affections of the young widow.

"I have Moran's daughter." The quiet statement sent a shiver through Rachel as she followed Laramie's lead across the crowded dance floor.

"What?" she asked, hoping she had not heard correctly.

"You heard what I said, Rachel. It's the only way I can get the mine back for you and the boys. I owe that to Jeff." His arms tightened around her protectively, and she found it hard to question his motives.

"Where is she?" she asked softly.

"At Mabel's."

"Of course. Well, she'll be safe and looked after there. What do you plan to do with her, Nate?"

"Keep her until I get what I want."

"How long do you think that will be?"

"I sent a cable to Moran the other day. We should hear something soon."

"You're not getting involved with the association, are you, Nate? I know they mean well or Wyatt wouldn't be involved, but violence isn't the way to work this out."

"No, not unless I have to, Rachel. I don't agree with their methods, either, but a man has a right to fight for what's his."

"Did you hear they pulled down Murphy's barn in the middle of the night and set fire to his pastures?"

"None of that was his, Rachel. He stole every bit of it from Rufus Brown and his brothers."

"I know, but that still doesn't make it right."

Across the room, Wyatt Earp stood surrounded by the other impressive-looking Earp brothers and the always dapper Doc Holliday. The group were part of the Citizens' Safety Commission, a vigilante group formed to combat lot jumping and land scams that were rampant in the town filled with money-hungry men.

Under cover of darkness they meted out "justice" to the rustlers who did the dirty work for the Townlot Company. Many of their number had been putting pressure on Laramie to join them as he had suffered as much at their hands as any one of them. The two men he'd met up with the day before had told him about the reception and had encouraged him to join up with them, knowing he had a score to settle.

"I can work this out by myself," he assured the troubled widow.

"You seem pretty sure of yourself." She smiled.

"It will work, Rachel. It has to. Moran will come across."

"Take me to her, Nate."

"What?"

"I want to see Sadie Moran. I think she probably needs a friend."

80

"Right now?"

"Right now."

"Talk about someone used to getting her own way . . ." he muttered, but he had already given in. As soon as the music stopped, they began to move toward the door, and he was soon settling her wrap around her shoulders.

As they turned toward the exit, a loud, belligerent voice halted them. "Just where do you two think you're going? The lady came with me."

Sheriff Potts stepped between them and the door and reached to put his hand on Rachel's arm in a proprietary fashion. Nate knocked his arm away.

"That was a mistake you'll live to regret, Laramie." The sheriff's voice was cold and too calm, unnatural. He uttered a threat not to be taken lightly. "You're a troublemaker and no longer welcome in Tombstone. You have until noon tomorrow to get out of town. And there will be a warrant waiting for your arrest if you should be foolish enough to return."

"A warrant? For what?" Nate's voice was also soft, but deadly. Rachel's hand rested on his arm, and her presence beside him was the only thing that restrained him from giving Potts the drubbing he deserved.

"For the murder of your poor unfortunate partner, of course."

"Oh!" Rachel gasped and her hand flew to her mouth. "No! That's not true, and you know it, Dan Potts!" she exclaimed. "What is the meaning of this?"

"I have a witness who will swear he saw your good friend here kill your husband, Mrs. Foster."

His black eyes slid over her like the caress of a serpent.

"Come on, Nate, let's go. I've had enough of this party, anyway. It's gotten stuffy in here." She looked pointedly at the sheriff, who seemed uncertain whether he should pursue the confrontation any further. Out of the corner of his eye he could see the governor staring at them from across the room.

"Out of my way, Potts, or you'll be sorry."

"All right, Laramie. But I mean what I say . . . noon tomorrow."

Without another word, Nate ushered Rachel out the double doors and into the clean, cool night air.

"He's not worth it, Nate, not worth you losing everything you've been working for. And you can do me and the boys no good inside a jail cell, or in a coffin! You must do as he says. Get Sadie and leave. Or better yet, leave her here with me, and get yourself out of town. I'll keep an eye on things here and get word to you if anything happens that you should know. All right? Please, Nate."

"I never was able to resist a pretty woman with a reasonable request," he said, smiling a crooked, endearing smile that warmed Rachel to her toes. She did care for this man, and the sheriff's words had filled her with a new fear for his safety.

He continued slowly, "But Sadie goes with me."

Rachel always seemed to know when it was best not to argue with Nate Laramie, and she decided this was one of those times. "Now, let's go see your lady-friend," she said, hooking her arm in his.

"I'm afraid that's not at all true," he said ruefully. "I don't think you could say she's very fond of me at the moment."

"No," she laughed, "but that's only because she doesn't know you as I do."

Chapter Six

Sadie fumed and paced, acutely aware of the festivities occurring only a few blocks away, festivities Nate Laramie was attending while she was once more locked away from the world in this cell of a room in a tawdry boarding house. He had not seen fit to tell her of his plans for the evening, but the gossipy landlady, Mabel had willingly filled her in with details of the governor's reception.

The lady was kind and friendly, and Sadie at first had hopes she might seek help from her until she glimpsed the older woman's devoted loyalty to Laramie. It was clear she would do exactly as he asked, which was obviously to keep Sadie securely locked away in the upstairs bedroom.

Restless, Sadie walked to the room's only window and threw it open, admitting a burst of cold air. She found its brisk chill pleasant and breathed in gratefully.

A small balcony overlooked a deserted dirt roadway. Looking down, she judged the distance to the ground: it was much too far to jump without breaking a leg, or perhaps her neck! And there was nothing on the smooth wall on which to get a grip to climb down.

No one seemed to be abroad, and she assumed they were either cavorting at the reception or drowning their sorrows at one of the local taverns. There were enough of those lining the thorough-fares of the town, she thought, remembering what she had seen on their arrival earlier that after-noon.

That morning, Laramie had hitched his horse to the rickety wagon stored in the back of the barn.

"We're going to Tombstone, and you're going to be a good girl and keep still. I can't leave you here alone again. But if you try anything, and I mean *anything*, I have a man in St. Louis who will see to it that your father pays for your mis-take."

"How do you know . . ." she sputtered, wanting to question him about his connection with her family, wanting to know what he knew about her father, but he cut her off.

"Doesn't matter. Just remember that I know plenty about you and about him. One word from me and Lucien Moran is a dead man. Do you understand?" Laramie hoped that if he kept his face expressionless, she might believe him and not guess it for the big bluff it was. He had no man in St. Louis and he did not plan to kill her fa-ther; the man was much too valuable to him alive, at least for now.

"All right, Laramie. I'll do what you say. But don't let anything happen to Father, please." So, she thought, there was something between her father and this outlaw and she had to find out what it was in time to help him, in time to help herself.

On the long trip in to Tombstone he had sat close to her, his leg occasionally brushing hers, one arm thrown casually along the wooden seat behind her. She had sat stiffly, uncomfortably, beside him, unwilling to relax, and was immeasurably glad when they pulled up in front of the boarding house. Climbing down, she cast her eyes about for someone she might call out to but there was no one close at hand and Laramie had a firm grip on her arm as he hurriedly escorted her inside.

Then, to her disappointment, she'd discovered they would be sharing a room. Later, she had watched as he prepared for the evening. She had never dreamed he could look so elegant, so heart-stoppingly handsome, in his best suit and freshly starched white shirt. Only a slight, suspicious bulge revealed the six-shooter riding on his narrow hips beneath his coat, as usual.

Did he expect trouble? Nothing in his expression or demeanor suggested that, but still she sensed the tightly drawn tension in the muscles of his body, in the way he carried himself, in the depths of his dark blue eyes.

"You will be all right." It was a statement, not a question, spoken softly and she might have thought with some concern had there been any softening in the lines of his face.

She did not answer, but rather exchanged a long look with him.

"I may be late." It was no apology, but there could have been regret underlying his soft tones.

She had an impulse to shrug her indifference, but the gesture was so alien to what she was feeling that she couldn't bring herself to do it.

Glancing toward the narrow window and then in the direction of the heavy door that opened directly into the facing apartment of the landlady, Sadie could not resist a small smile and a barbed response, "I'll be here."

A brilliant smile washed over his craggy features, and he cast a look of grudging respect her way, in recognition of her spirit, her wry humor.

"Take me with you, Laramie." The words, unbidden, were out of her mouth before she had time to reconsider. It was the first request she had made of him. But she wanted so desperately to be among people again.

He was aware of the cost to her pride, and for a moment something warred in him, darkening his eyes. His strongest impulse from a personal standpoint was to grant her request. He would actually like to take her, would be pleased to escort this delicate beauty to the ball. Though he hated to admit it, her company was far from unpleasant most of the time, and much to be preferred over the majority of the Tombstonians he would see this night.

"No!" His denial was harsh, gruff.

Sadie, certain there would be no arguing with it, fought to conceal her disappointment and turned from him, taking a step away.

The strong hand that fastened on her shoulder, halting her flight, was firm, but not ungentle. Slowly, he turned her so that she was once more facing him.

He had seemed about to speak as his eyes searched her face, but with a muffled curse, he released his hold on her and pivoted away, striding across the room to the door. His hand lingered on the knob for brief seconds before he twisted and yanked the door open. It slammed after him abruptly, and she clearly heard the rasp of the key in the lock.

Now what was she supposed to do, she wondered, while her kidnapper was out enjoying himself? She spent the long, lonely hours of the evening alternating between nervous pacing and staring absently up and down the quiet street. She hoped someone might come along so she could cry out for help, but then she remembered too clearly Laramie's warning and knew that at least for now that was not a solution she dared to use.

Laughter from the street below reached Sadie's ears where she stood on the balcony. With a start she realized that the sounds of merriment came from a couple walking along the street. Looking more closely, she recognized Nate Laramie. A beautiful woman walked close beside him, her arm linked possessively in his.

An unwelcome jealousy swept through Sadie while she watched the two laughing and talking companionably as they approached the boarding house. Who was that woman? And what did she mean to Laramie? These questions were quickly followed by another: Why should she care who held his arm, who walked beside him, who laughed with him?

Hurriedly, Sadie reentered the room and took her place in an overstuffed chair to await their arrival, for she assumed they were coming up, though for what purpose she could not imagine. A half hour passed, however, before she heard anything more.

"Hello, Mrs. Morrell." A soft, friendly voice spoke just outside her door, and Sadie heard the landlady's high-pitched, friendly answer.

The key turned in the lock, and the door swung open. Sadie jumped to her feet but did her best to appear unconcerned as the attractive couple entered the room, still arm in arm.

"Rachel, this is Sadie Moran. Sadie, Rachel Foster."

"Hello, Sadie."

"Hello," Sadie answered shortly, determined not to be overly friendly, although Rachel Foster had one of the prettiest and kindest faces she'd ever seen and Laramie's lopsided grin was contagious, too.

Sadie was acutely aware of Laramie's close scrutiny of her. What did he expect from her? That she would throw her arms around this stranger in welcome? Well, he could just think again. As far as she was concerned, she had met no one who cared anything for her since she boarded that wretched stagecoach and bid *adieu* to her dear father. She owed these people nothing, certainly not friendship! They seemed to have enough of that between the two of them, at any rate.

Rachel caught the play of emotions across Sadie's mobile face and sympathized with this lonesome, lovely young woman who was so far from home.

"Sit here, Rachel," Nate invited in a solicitous

tone he had yet to use with Sadie, and it infuriated her.

"Sit here, Rachel," she muttered, as she flounced down on the edge of the bed and eyed them both warily. Did she imagine Laramie's lips quivering in response to her petulance? So he thought she was funny, did he?

"Sadie, I'm sorry for what's happened to you." The sincerity in Rachel's voice sounded so real Sadie was strongly tempted to believe what she said, before she reminded herself that this was Laramie's friend, someone who had probably been in on the whole thing from the very beginning!

"I didn't realize what Nate was planning to do, but I can promise you that he means you no harm." Rachel smiled warmly at Nate, and a spasm of unhappiness coursed through Sadie. There was more than mere friendship between this man and woman. There had to be.

He walked over to stand in front of Sadie. "It's true, you know. You're safe with me. And it will only be for a short while longer. Then you can return home and resume your life as though all this were a bad dream." The apology was clear in his rich voice.

Why did the thought of going back home leave her bereft? Damn it, what did she want, anyway? Surely not this outlaw! How was it possible she found herself so attracted to the likes of him? Of course, it was purely physical — he was strikingly handsome, wasn't he? But as soon as he was out of her sight, she would forget all about him, and wouldn't she have some story to tell her grandchildren? She smiled in spite of herself.

"A bad dream," she repeated, standing and looking straight at Laramie, whose eyes held an emotion she couldn't fathom.

After long seconds, he turned back to Rachel. "Satisfied?" he questioned softly.

"Yes, thank you, Nate." She rose, but turned once more toward Sadie. "God be with you, Sadie. Please be careful, and remember what I've said."

Sadie did not answer, watching the other woman move gracefully toward the door. Laramie escorted her out, closing and locking the door behind them, leaving Sadie alone with her thoughts. A long time passed before he returned.

When he did, he entered the room quietly, and Sadie decided to pretend she was sleeping. In the dark, he began to undress, and she realized with a start that he planned to share her bed! Why had she not considered that before? But even if she had, there would have been little enough she could have done about it.

If she wrapped in a blanket and slid to the floor, would he stop her? She heard him unbuckle his gun belt and drop it over a chair. His weight eased onto the edge of the bed and the musky aroma of rum and tobacco wafted over her. His boots fell with a soft thud to the floor.

Sadie held her breath, remembering her reaction to him as he'd slept the day before, troubled by his nightmares. She had been moved to an emotion she hadn't ever expected to feel for her abductor. She had wanted to comfort him, to find out what haunted him in his dreams. And, she had to admit, she'd felt a strong attraction to the

91

ruggedly handsome man and wanted nothing so much as to curl up and stay in his arms.

Sadie remained motionless as long as Laramie sat still as a statue on the mattress beside her. What was he thinking? Did he have thoughts about ravishing her where she lay? He had had opportunities before and had never moved to take advantage of her. But she was sure, at least she *hoped* she was sure, that he'd been just as affected as she when they touched.

Did he think of his sweetheart perhaps, or Rachel Foster, or even a wife he'd left behind somewhere?

Finally he swung his legs on top of the bed and lay back on top of the covers, his hands behind his head.

"Laramie?" she whispered.

"Yes."

"Is . . . is something wrong?" she asked softly, thinking of his disturbing nightmares. Unbidden came thoughts of the kiss they'd shared while she'd been a part of whatever vision had plagued him in his dreams before. Even now she fought an urge to stroke the length of his arm where it lay, almost touching her.

"It doesn't concern you." His response was not impersonal, nor unkind, but indicated his reluctance to discuss his problems with her.

"Perhaps not," she murmured, then asked abruptly, "Are you married, Laramie?"

"No."

"Never?"

"No."

"What about Rachel Foster?" Sadie asked, her

voice still hushed, cushioned by the cozy darkness of the room.

"What about her?" he turned the question back to her, the tone of his voice not giving her the slightest clue.

Sadie rushed on, "Are you in love with her?"

A soft chuckle and then a long silence met her impetuous question, and she wished she'd never asked.

"I suppose, in a way, I do love Rachel," he answered as honestly as he could.

"Oh." The small sound brought a wide smile to his lips in the darkness. She was disappointed.

"Her husband was my closest friend, and we all spent a lot of time together."

"You said "was". Did something happen to him?"

"Jeffrey Foster was murdered." One arm had been thrown over his forehead, and his voice was muffled, but unmistakably full of pain.

Sadie didn't know what to say. When she questioned him further, he refused to discuss the details of his friend's death.

"Why did you bring me here, Laramie? Does it have something to do with my father? Promise me you won't hurt him. I've done what you asked, haven't I?"

Surely it couldn't be the first time she had asked the question that plagued her, yet she couldn't remember having asked so directly before.

"Yes, you *have* done well. Your father is safe, and so are you. I took you from the stage because I had to. I'm sorry; it was the only way. You ask too many questions, Sadie Moran," he said, abruptly ending the conversation. Turning away from her, he sought relief from his pain in sleep that, as always, seemed to claim him quickly. But he had made promises she wouldn't soon forget, and he'd actually said he was sorry. There *was* good in this man. But he was nevertheless a man driven by a terrible mission, and he was very determined and had the potential for violent action, if provoked.

Chapter Seven

Tombstone, a young city that had stormed to life practically overnight with the discovery of a vast wealth in silver mines, slumbered as the first pale streaks of dawn lit its streets with an unearthly glow. A solitary figure watched nature's decoration from the second floor front bedroom of Mrs. Morrell's boarding house.

Somehow Nate Laramie had managed to sleep soundly for several hours beside his beautiful captive before the troubled dreams he had come to expect awoke him long before dawn. Restless, he had walked out onto the balcony and lit one of the black Mexican cigars he reserved for just such a situation. He puffed lazily, and with his hands thrust deep in his pants pockets, he revealed none of the frustrations that chased through his mind.

He had promised Rachel he would leave, but now he rebelled at the thought of being run out of town by the likes of Sheriff Dan Potts, who knew he had done nothing wrong! Damn it to hell! Potts was the one who should be railroaded out of Tombstone, or better yet, hanged for his crimes! Laramie seethed, his already virulent hatred for the lawman fueled even more by their unpleasant encounter the night before.

Nate had gone to the reception in hopes of speaking to the governor about recovering the Silver Lining, but he would have been a fool not to have seen how thick the two of them were. The governor and the sheriff—how cozy! He had not even been able to get close to Frémont all night. It had been a fool's errand that drew him there, anyway. There seemed to be no peaceful solution to his problem.

In passing, he wondered about the young man who had been dancing with Rachel when he cut in. Apparently Jonathan Lee had come to town with Frémont, but the governor did not seem to welcome his presence. It might bear looking into further, Nate thought with a slight smile. He could surely use an ally, especially one in the governor's own camp.

He had hoped to keep Sadie safely in Tombstone at Morrell's Boarding House until he heard from her father, but now because of the sheriff's ultimatum, he would have to drag her back out to that godforsaken shack! Nothing was working out as he planned, in spite of what he'd said to Rachel. Given his current run of luck, Moran would never receive his telegram or, when he did, would bring the entire U.S. militia with him to Tombstone, although Laramie had taken pains to warn him against such an act.

Nate chuckled. If he hadn't been such a damned fool, he would have realized he was biting off more than he could chew when he kidnapped Sadie Moran. The girl's presence was like a splinter under a fingernail—a throbbing ache that wouldn't be ignored was too deeply embedded to be extracted easily. She was starting to get under his skin in more ways than one, he thought, remembering how badly he'd wanted to take her in his arms last night and make long, passionate love to her. She did something to all his senses that became almost unbearable when she got too close. And sleeping in the same bed definitely qualified as too close!

He felt that she was beginning to soften toward him, to feel something other than fear or revulsion, and that frightened him, even though it also made him glad. He couldn't take advantage of her, though. She was much too young and innocent.

On the street below, Tombstone stirred, coming slowly to life. One by one the doors of businesses swung open to welcome the day's customers, and proprietors began arranging their wares and sweeping off their walks. The sun grew brighter, snaking its way down the dusty street, filling every crack and crevice with its soft, golden light.

A drunken cowboy weaved his way along, his hand occasionally on the wall to steady himself as he stumbled. A loser, from the look of him, at the all-night faro or poker tables at one of the crowded saloons. Words from the off-key ditty he sang drifted up to Nate's ears, and he smiled at the familiar song.

A rooster hopped to the top of a fence on a corral near the end of the street and lifted its voice in another greeting to the morning. The robust aroma of coffee and the tantalizing smell of frying bacon brought an answering rumble from Nate's stomach. Mrs. Morrell, bless her heart! He had almost forgotten what a good cook she was, and his mouth watered as he thought of her homemade corn muffins.

In the bed behind him, Sadie stirred restlessly, her soft murmurs drawing him back into the room. For long minutes he stood looking down at her, admiring her innocent beauty and remembering her plucky, if foolhardy, courage. In spite of himself, he was drawn to his captive and intrigued by her.

Shaking his head wearily, he buckled on his gun belt and hurried out of the quiet room, closing the door firmly behind him. He would let Mrs. Morrell wake her! Meanwhile, he would check on the horses and make preparations for leaving town soon after breakfast.

When he returned from the stables, Sadie was sitting down to the bountiful table set by a frowning, blustering Mabel Morrell.

"Bless, my soul, chile! You set yourself down here and eat hearty! You could sure use some more meat on them bones!

Nate thought with a wide smile that Sadie's "bones" looked pretty good to him, but he never dared to disagree with Mabel—never had, never would. The woman was a treasure and had been like the mother he'd never known, ever since she'd taken in both him and his partner, Jeffrey when they hadn't had enough money between them to buy a second mule to make a span.

She had given them free room and board without question until they'd found an investor and had been able to pull together their stake. When they'd made a big strike and established the Silver Lining, they'd paid her back every penny and more, though she had never asked for a cent. She was an angel and a real friend. He had known she would take to Sadie and would not ask him any embarrassing questions.

"What about me, Mabel?" he asked, seating himself at his usual place at the head of the table.

"Law! What *about* you, Nate Laramie?" she retorted, passing big bottles of freshly churned, melted butter and deep purple jam for their steaming muffins. "Ain't you somethin' though, showin' up like this and with a pretty little thing like her, too?" Just then, Mabel noticed his wagon waiting out front and wailed, "Now, you cain't possibly be leavin' me already!"

"I'm afraid so, Mabel. But I'll be back soon. Don't worry."

"Don' worry, indeed! I ain' done nothin' *but* worry 'bout you, Nate Laramie, from the first day you showed up in Tombstone!"

Sadie quietly watched the friendly exchange, surprised to see Laramie relaxed and smiling so easily and to see the honest affection he shared with the older woman.

More surprises awaited her when they stopped at the Foster home to tell Rachel and her boys goodbye.

"Uncle Nate! Uncle Nate!" both young boys yelled with delight and ran full-tilt down the long walk leading to a spacious Victorian-style house with its wraparound screened-in porch.

"Hey! You two hooligans! Slow down there!" But Laramie was smiling widely as he lifted a boy in each arm and hugged them soundly. "Christopher, Timothy, this here is Sadie Moran. Say hello." After they did as he directed and Sadie had spoken to each of them in turn, he continued, setting them back on the ground, "Now which of you two ruffians will run tell your mama we're here?"

"I will! I will!" they both shouted at once, obviously anxious to please their Uncle Nate.

Sadie was feeling a little overwhelmed by their exuberance, having never spent much time around little boys, but she noticed the soft affection in Laramie's eyes and read between the lines of his quiet words when he said to her, "They're good boys."

He reached to open the gate that had slammed shut behind the mad dash of the boys, and the two of them strode up the walk side by side, surrounded by the fragrance of late-blooming flowers and the greenery of a well-cared-for lawn.

"Well, hello there!" called a friendly voice from the shaded front veranda. "Nate! Sadie! Do come in. I've made some fresh tea and some of your favorite cookies, Nate."

With something less than pleasure, Sadie saw that Rachel looked more beautiful than she had the night before, even though she was clad in a simple cotton skirt and blouse and her buttercup-yellow hair was caught up off her neck with a ribbon that matched the green of her smiling eyes. Rachel was petite, with a tiny waist and feet, and she had to rise up on her toes as Laramie lowered his head to receive her affectionate kiss. Her two sons stood on either side of her full skirt, and Laramie ruffled the two towheads as he passed them and entered the wide foyer with Sadie's hand still securely in his.

Sadie had not expected such understated elegance in the West — and especially not in a wild and woolly place like Tombstone. "It's lovely," she couldn't resist saying in praise of the tastefully furnished house.

Rachel laughed and the sound was contagious. "Not quite what you'd expect out here, is it? But Jeff was so set on giving the boys and me the very best of everything." Her voice caught on the emotions the mention of her husband brought, but she went on, "He felt bad for taking me away from my home and family and vowed to build me a dream house we could be proud of. And he did." Her voice was soft and full of love, but laced with regret. "But he got to enjoy it for such a short time. And now . . . now . . . well, we may not have it much longer."

"No one is ever going to take this house away from you and the boys, Rachel. I promise you that." The deep timbre of his voice, gentle with Rachel but filled with deadly menace toward anyone who threatened her, sent an involuntary thrill through Sadie. What must it feel like to have someone care that much about what happened to you? She knew even as he spoke that he did not make the promise lightly and that he would do whatever might be necessary to carry it out. She would not want to be the one standing in his way.

Rachel led her guests into the parlor, saw that they were seated comfortably, and then left, returning with a tray containing a silver tea service and china cups.

"Christopher, you go and get the cookies for your Uncle Nate and Miss Moran now."

"Yes, Mama." The youngster pulled nervously on his overalls because of the unaccustomed company, but sped off to do as his mother directed.

"And, Timmy, you can help your brother."

"Yes, Mama," he answered proudly, scurrying out of the room.

"They're fine, polite boys, Rachel. You've done a good job with them."

"Yes. I think Jeff would be proud of them."

"He sure would." Chuckling, he added, "Why, I remember the day you told him he was going to be a father. He was the goldarned proudest man I'd ever seen. That's when I started smoking those awful Mexican cigars. He insisted and I couldn't refuse. And he was just as excited about young Timothy's birth, too, if I remember right."

"Yes, he was." A smile lit up Rachel's jewel-tinted eyes and her whole face.

Sadie was feeling left out of the conversation until Rachel, noticing, included her.

"Where is your home, Sadie?"

"St. Louis."

"Ah, yes, Missouri, the 'gateway to the West,' it's called. Jeff promised to take us all East sometime, but we never seemed to have the chance."

"Where are you from?" Sadie asked.

"Minnesota. Duluth. Quite different from Arizona, for sure. But I've come to love it here, too. It's our home now."

How could someone as refined as Rachel find anything to love in the sand, the cactus, the saloons and bordellos in Tombstone? Sadie wondered, but was too polite to ask aloud. Personally, she couldn't wait to get home to the soft green hills and valleys of Missouri. If she never saw another cactus, it would be too soon.

The tea was delicious, sprigged with mint leaves, and the cookies light and tasty. "This is really wonderful," she said honestly.

"Yup! Rachel is the greatest cook in the West — outside of Mrs. Morrell, of course," Laramie said, laughing. "And she makes all of her own clothes and the boys' too. Bet you'd never guess she's also an excellent horsewoman and a pretty good shot with a Winchester, now, would you?"

When he mentioned marksmanship, he shot a mocking glance at Sadie, in reference to her bad aim when she'd tried to shoot him. Would he never let it drop? And she wasn't sure she could listen to any more praise of his precious Rachel Foster! If he thought she was so terrific, why didn't he marry her himself?

But maybe that was a part of his plan.

"It doesn't hurt to have a few unwomanly skills in these parts," Rachel answered with a chuckle. "Do you ride, Sadie?"

The twinkle in Laramie's eye didn't stop Sadie from responding. "I'm learning," she said, making up her mind that she was going to do that very thing. She would show the high and mighty Nate Laramie a few things about what she could and couldn't do!

"Shorty was a little too much for her to handle," he said, daring her to reveal more about her one attempt at riding horseback.

"Yes, he was," she agreed, "but he won't be the

103

next time."

He acknowledged her threat with a slow nod of his head. "We'll see," he said. "We'll see."

"Nate, it's almost noon," Rachel noted, pointing to the grandfather clock at the far end of the large room. "You'd better be going."

"He has no right to order me out of town." His voice was calm, but deadly.

"I know, Nate, but he has the badge, and the power to have you hanged or sent away to Yuma."

Nate knew that a ten-year sentence to the Yuma territorial prison was a fate almost worse than death by hanging and didn't relish the thought of either end for himself. "He has the upper hand for now, but I'll get him, Rachel. I'll make him pay for what he did to Jeffrey."

The fierce light in Laramie's blue eyes chilled Sadie, and she sensed the extent of his hatred for Tombstone's sheriff and wondered if he could be the one responsible for Jeffrey's death.

"I've packed you a lunch," Rachel put in, hoping to cool his anger and hurry their departure. "Come with me, please, Sadie, and we'll get it." Rachel led the way toward the kitchen, which spanned the width of the house all the way across the back. They passed by a library on the left of the central hallway and a guest bedroom on the right.

Glancing in, Sadie was surprised to see a beautiful quilt in the popular Star of Bethlehem pattern. When she remarked on its loveliness, Rachel told her it had been stitched by Lily Delgado, a woman with a good heart, though she lacked a good reputation in a town that was sometimes too quick to judge. She did not mention Lily's friendship with

Sheriff Dan Potts.

"Nate's a good man, Sadie. He's just had a rough time lately."

Sadie didn't quite know how to respond to that, so she didn't say anything.

Rachel continued, "I wish you could have known him before all this happened. He wasn't bitter or hard back then. He was warm and caring, and he had such dreams for himself and for the territory! But then everything went bad and he seemed to change, not that anyone could blame him for that!"

From the tone of Rachel's voice and the clear affection she held for Nate Laramie, Sadie knew she would never listen to one bad word about him, so she didn't mention the very obvious fact that he was now an outlaw who had held up a stage and kidnapped someone.

But Rachel, aware of her unspoken protests, answered them. "Don't be too hard on him, Sadie. He's only doing what he thinks he has to do."

"But why me?" Sadie asked, needing to know.

"I can't answer that. But I'm sure he'll tell you himself in time."

Sadie was not so sure, but she would learn nothing more from the very devoted Rachel Foster about Nate Laramie's reasons for abducting her.

"Here now," Rachel said, changing the subject, "I've made you both some fried chicken, and there's fresh bread and a fruit pie. It's a long way back through the mountains to Pete's place. You'll need more than beef jerky." She wrinkled her pert nose at the thought of the cowboy's staple diet.

"That's very kind of you, Rachel," Sadie said,

holding the basket as Rachel continued to pile it high with good food. She could hear Laramie whistling off-key as they walked back toward the parlor. Rachel carried canteens filled with clear, fresh water from a spring behind her house. It seemed she'd thought of everything, and Sadie was once more bothered by a surge of unreasonable jealousy.

Rachel was thoughtful, capable, self-sufficient — and she was also so pretty! Sadie was certain she herself was none of those things and that it showed all too clearly when she was in the older woman's company. And Nate Laramie even seemed like a different man when he was with Rachel — softer, gentler, and not at all the tough, range-hardened man he had been with her.

Sadie found to her surprise that she was actually anxious to leave civilization and the presence of the ever-perfect Rachel Foster behind, even if it meant being back in the wilderness, alone with Laramie. That thought brought a shiver to her spine, but it was not of fear, but more of anticipation, of excitement. What was happening to her, anyway? She should be thinking of ways to escape, not looking forward to being alone with this man!

A few minutes later, the picnic was stowed on the wagon and Sadie and Laramie climbed aboard and waved good-bye to Rachel and her two sons, who stood by the gate.

"Be careful, Nate," Rachel called after them.

Laramie avoided the main streets of Tombstone on their way out of town. Let the sheriff wonder if he'd left on time. He sure wasn't going to make it easier for him.

The wagon rolled along the dirt-packed back

106

streets of town before Laramie turned it eastward, toward the mysterious Dragoons looming up ahead, but separated from them by a vast expanse of flat terrain.

Sounds of rowdy laughter and frantic squawkings reached their ears at the same time. "A cock fight," he said, by way of explanation, but swinging wide to avoid the spectacle and its boisterous crowd. Still, Sadie was able to see over their heads into the dusty ring where two bloody roosters battled valiantly until one lay twitching on the earth.

A roar went up from the crowd, and moans were heard from the losers as money quickly exchanged hands.

"How awful," she murmured, having never seen anything like it before.

"Out here it passes for entertainment. Gives men something to do besides kill each other."

"Maybe." As she spoke, though, she saw two men arguing angrily and wondered if money wasn't responsible for some of the fights among the men. An unruly bunch had chosen Tombstone to be their home. Sadie thought the rough, unformed character of the town matched the brawling, six-shooting, hard-drinking men who'd settled there to make their fortunes.

Was Nate Laramie one of them, as she'd first assumed? Or could it be there was more to this man, as Rachel claimed, and as she herself thought she'd glimpsed in him on a couple of occasions?

The two men were shouting now and one shoved the other, knocking him down, and reached for his gun. The man on the ground whipped out a six-shooter from a holster at his belt and fired once.

The standing man dropped, a hole in his chest, and lay in the dirt, unmoving. Someone handed the murderer, who was now on his feet, a bottle of beer, and two others grabbed the dead man by his feet and began hauling him up a sloping hill.

Though Laramie had kept the wagon moving steadily away from the scene, Sadie saw the shooting and heard someone say, "A right proper candidate for Boot Hill." She glanced to the top of the hill, her eyes sweeping over several rocky mounds, marked with crude white crosses. A cemetery!

"They're going to bury him, just like that?"

"Mos' likely," he said, without further comment, and urged the horses into a trot as they left the last dwellings of town behind them.

Though the sheriff had not personally witnessed their departure, three of his men watched from a shadowed alleyway. After a hushed conversation, they hurried away to round up their horses from the livery. In less than an hour they rode out of town in pursuit of the wagon.

The trio appeared to be in no particular hurry to overtake them, but neither would they allow them to have too much of a lead. Clearly, they could see the wagon moving across the desert on its approach to the mountains, and were not worried about losing sight of Laramie and the woman. The men had their orders, and they didn't want to botch this job — they dared not.

Chapter Eight

The weather worsened. As they neared the rocky face of the Dragoons, Laramie began to fear that they faced the first real storm of winter. Such weather had never bothered him before, but he was sure Sadie was unaccustomed to being out in the elements. They could turn back and wait out the storm, but he'd noticed the rising dust from riders behind them. He was sure they had but one alternative: to press on.

If a storm developed, he would try to find shelter for them in the mountains. He turned the team toward the north and a biting wind greeted them, stinging their faces and bringing tears to Sadie's eyes.

Reaching under the seat, Laramie pulled out a tattered quilt and swung it around her shoulders, tucking it under her legs.

Sadie protested, "Here, you take some of it." He refused, turning up the collar of his jacket to protect his ears. "Will it snow?" she asked.

Looking at the boiling gray clouds wrapping themselves around the peaks of the mountains that surrounded them, he nodded.

"Will we be able to get through?"

He nodded again, but qualified it by saying, "If it doesn't snow too much or too fast."

"Oh."

He looked at her. She was shivering, and her turned-up nose was already red from the cold air. She looked up at him, surprised to see concern in his eyes, and smiled.

"I'll be okay," she said, teeth chattering. "I . . . I'm just not used to such c . . . c . . . cold weather. I thought Arizona was s . . . supposed to be hot."

"Only in summer." He laughed, putting an arm around her and dragging her up next to him. She made an attempt at laughing too, but gave up when her teeth chattered uncontrollably and snuggled against his side, grateful for the warmth.

They had traveled only a few miles further when Laramie realized with some satisfaction that she was sleeping peacefully, her head resting against his shoulder. Her shivering had stopped.

It troubled him how unexplainably happy this made him feel. He was filled with the sudden overwhelming need to protect her from harm, and his hand moved of its own accord to stroke the fiery silk that was her hair. She murmured in her sleep and snuggled even closer.

His body reacted to her nearness and the memory of the kiss they'd shared when her lips had been so soft, warm, and caring moving against his. But it had been in the midst of a dream, and he'd caught her unawares, he tried to tell himself. She was not interested in returning his kisses, awake or asleep. The feisty Sadie Moran cared only about

110

getting away from him, and the sooner the better.

And he only cared about getting the mine back and getting his revenge. No dainty red-haired girl, no matter how winsome, was going to deter him from his purpose.

A loud noise disturbed the silence, echoing back from the rocky hillside. "Damn!" he cursed, immediately recognizing the report of a rifle. Someone was shooting at them, probably one of the riders he'd noticed earlier, who had followed them all the way from town, biding their time, waiting for the right opportunity. He hadn't really thought the sheriff would go so far as to ambush them.

Laramie reached for his rifle even as his eyes scanned the rocks for a place to take cover. He knew of a cave further up the mountain, but he wasn't sure they could make it that far.

Sadie had been in the middle of a pleasant dream and didn't want to wake up, but the loud noise and Laramie's answering curse brought her out of it much too abruptly.

"Wha's goin' on?" she asked sleepily, straightening up, trying to get her bearings.

"Get down!" he ordered harshly, and pushed her to the floor. "Fool girl! Wanna get yourself killed?" He whipped up the team, knowing he had to put some distance between them and whoever was taking potshots at them. Rifle fire still ricocheted all around them, even as the first big flakes of snow began to fall.

"That's just great!" he muttered, getting off a backward shot with his left hand while they lurched around the side of a mountain, barely missing a collision with an outcropping of rock.

111

The winding, climbing road gave him a slight advantage, but he didn't dare slow their speed and knew he took the chance of sending wagon, team, and passengers careening over the side.

Sadie's eyes were huge as she watched the stumpy trees and rocky hillside flying by in front of her face. What in God's name was he doing, trying to kill them both? She held onto a sideboard to keep herself from catapulting up and out of the wagon, and felt a new bruise form with every wild, bucking bounce.

Had the noise she'd heard earlier been gunfire — and was that the reason for this hell-bent speed? Who could be shooting at them? The sheriff? Did sheriffs really shoot at innocent people?

Maybe he'd sent a posse to rescue her and Laramie was trying to outrun them. Yes, that was probably it. And that was more than likely the real reason for his hasty departure from town. She would soon be rescued and back home with her father.

But what would they do to Laramie? She didn't understand why she cared, but at that moment she found, to her surprise, that she did. She cared very much. If the sheriff hated Laramie as much as Rachel seemed to think, he wouldn't stop short of the hanging he'd already threatened, with or without a fair trial. Laramie had kidnapped her, that was true, but he didn't deserve shooting — or hanging!

The gentler swaying motion of the buggy alerted her to a distinct change of pace. They were slowing down. But only when the wagon had completely stopped, did she dare raise her head.

The first thing she saw was blood dripping onto

the floorboards. Was it hers? Pulling herself to her knees, she examined herself, reassured to discover she had escaped injury, but one look at Laramie and she was aware of exactly what had happened. His left hand was flat against his left shoulder, and blood was seeping through his fingers.

"You've been shot!" she exclaimed, jumping up to sit beside him once more. She snatched the quilt up from the floor and pressed it against his chest to stanch the frightening flow of blood. "What can I do?" She had no other thought at that moment except how she could help him.

"We . . . have . . . to . . . get . . . to . . . that . . . cave." His voice was thin and raspy. She knew they had to move fast before he lost consciousness. She jumped down and reached up to help as he slid to the ground and leaned heavily on her. Her foot slipped on a loose rock and they both nearly went down, but with a valiant effort she managed to keep them going. It seemed to take forever, but they finally made it. Stooping down, they entered the dark cavern.

"Now . . ." he directed her, though he was breathing and speaking with difficulty, "go back . . . get my gun . . . food. Send . . . wagon . . . down . . . other . . . side. They . . . may . . . not . . . think . . . to look in here. Hurry!"

Sadie scampered to do as he'd said, giving no further thought to the possibility of her rescue by the sheriff. Those men had been shooting to kill—and they didn't seem to care who they hit! Somehow, she knew she was safer with Laramie. She would take her chances with him.

She climbed back into the wagon, grabbed his rifle and ammunition, and tucked it under one arm. Scooping up the picnic basket and an extra blanket in the other, she lowered herself to the ground, which was now covered with a thin layer of snow.

Running, she dumped her load inside the cave and then hurried back to the wagon, slipping and sliding in her haste. She made sure the reins were secured inside, picked up the whip, and snapped it at the horse, yelling "Giddap!" as loud as she could until Shorty was galloping away up to the top of the hill and out of sight down the other side.

Looking back down the rutted trail, she was relieved to see and hear nothing. The men chasing them were not yet in sight. Thank God! Before she went back inside, she took a tree limb and carefully obscured their footprints leading up to the mouth of the cave, feeling very satisfied with herself for having thought of that extra precaution.

"How did we lose them?" she asked Laramie, crawling back inside, pushing the gun and picnic lunch in front of her.

"A . . . y . . . in . . . road. They . . . took . . . other. Back . . . soon."

"The wagon and the horse are gone," she told him. "Maybe they'll follow it."

"Maybe."

He was slumped against the dirt wall of the cave, his face growing paler by the minute.

"Tell me what to do, Laramie," she demanded. While she waited for him to gain the strength to speak, she heard the thundering of hooves as their pursuers passed by the mouth of the cave without slowing down. Breathing a sigh of relief, she listened intently to his breathy instructions.

At his bidding, she gathered sticks and, with matches from his pocket, started a feeble fire. But she blanched and almost lost her nerve when he told her she would have to dig the bullet out and sear the wound with a heated stick.

His head slumped down to his chest and Sadie knew he was unconscious and could die if she didn't move fast.

"Don't you die on me, Nate Laramie," she muttered, even while she worked frantically to save his life. His directions had been very specific, leaving no doubt as to what had to be done.

Diligently, and without stopping once to reconsider, Sadie worked, digging in the inflamed skin until, after several long minutes, the bullet popped free. Alarmed, she saw the blood spurt out along with it. A trembling hand reached for the stick with the red-hot end. Trying not to think, she applied the smoking end of it to the wound, heard a sickening sizzling, and smelled burned skin. She forced herself to breathe deeply and held the stick there for several seconds, even when he began to moan and thrash about with his free hand.

"You asked for this. Now you just be still," she commanded, and moved to sit across his lap to be sure he obeyed. She leaned to reach for the strips of her petticoat she had already torn and her breasts brushed his chest, causing a reaction deep inside her.

Grabbing the strips hastily, she moved back and looked down at him closely, assuring herself he was still unconscious. She remembered all too clearly when she'd been in almost this same position before and he had kissed her so thoroughly, even though he'd been dreaming. She half expected to see his eyes blink open any minute and light up with that same mocking humor. But he was still now, so still she found herself wishing he would look at her, make fun of her, yell at her, anything but this pallor and lifelessness.

She had done exactly as he told her, but maybe it had been too late, or not enough. Hesitantly, she reached her fingers to his neck just below his ear and felt the faint pulse of his life. He lived! She was unaccountably glad but knew she could not be certain of his recovery yet. Gingerly she crawled off him and settled the quilt over him before she turned to build up the fire.

Shadows and light played over the interior, and she saw that the cave was much larger than she'd originally assumed. It was a perfect place to hide, if only the horse would keep up its wild running and lead their pursuers far astray.

Sadie hobbled over to the entrance, her foot still smarting from the run-in with the rock. Snow fell, soft but heavy, and showing no signs of letting up. It was much darker now, but she couldn't tell if the darkness was caused by the snow or the passage of daylight hours. She had no idea how long she had worked on Laramie's wound but supposed it could be evening by now.

Her muscles cried out from the unremitting stress of the day. She realized how very tired she had become, and her eyes grew heavy watching the falling snow.

With some effort she walked back to where Laramie lay sleeping. He seemed to be resting, and she could only hope she'd done the proper things. Placing the back of her hand to his forehead, she was relieved to find he had no fever.

The small fire had taken some of the chill from the air, and she took off the coat she wore, spread it out not far from her patient, slumped down on it, and was quickly sound asleep.

Laramie's thrashing and moaning woke her abruptly, and she hurried to his side. His cheeks were unnaturally bright, and when she touched his skin, she was alarmed at how hot he felt. What had gone wrong? She rebuked herself for sleeping when she should have been watching him.

The wound must have become infected, and Sadie knew how serious that could be. But what could she do now? Somehow she had to cool the raging fever, bring it down. If she didn't, he might die.

At a loss, she looked around her and spied the canteen. Soaking another strip from her petticoat in the still-cool water, she applied the cloth to his forehead and gently rubbed it over his face and neck, trying to stay out of the way of his flailing arms. He mumbled and muttered and seemed very uncomfortable and troubled. Then he began to shiver uncontrollably.

Sadie reached for the quilt and once more tucked it in around him. Still, he was shaking so hard, she pulled back the cover and lay next to him, her body half-covering his but careful not to touch his wound. She pulled the quilt around them both and snuggled as close as she could, willing to share the warmth of her body with him. She couldn't help it that her own body reacted in ways quite unfamiliar

117

to her, but she knew she'd never felt more comfortable or more exactly in the right place than she did at that moment. Desire was building in her and was matched by a tender protectiveness for the helpless outlaw. She continued to bathe his face with the cool cloth until the fever began to abate. For long hours she lay next to him, trying to anticipate what he needed and supplying it without thought or question, until she almost dropped from fatigue.

Toward morning, his fever showed signs of lessening and he slept peacefully at last. Sadie breathed more easily and eased away from him. After checking the fire, she curled up in a corner of the cave and fell into a deep sleep. Neither she nor Laramie heard the rumble of horses' hooves as their pursuers passed by again, going in the other direction.

Laramie's delirious dreams tormented him, replaying terrible scenes from the past he had tried to forget.

"No!" he cried out, but it was too late to help his partner. He opened his eyes and looked around, slowly taking note of his surroundings. It looked to be some kind of cave, but he couldn't remember how he'd gotten there, or why. Gradually, consciousness returned completely, and he remembered the snow, the shots, and his run for cover with Sadie.

Where was she? The complete silence around him convinced him that he was alone now. Of course, at her first opportunity she had run straight back into the arms of the sheriff and as far away from him as she could get! But he really couldn't blame her, could he? His mind said no, but his heart said otherwise.

Coming to grips with the fact that his captive had escaped for good this time, he started to get up, but was stopped by a blinding pain in his shoulder that shot through his arm and upper body. In surprise, his hands reached to the crude bandage that covered the wound.

As his fingers probed gently, he recalled the searing pain of the bullet that had hit him. But he'd been unconscious and unable to dress it himself. Who, then? Had Sadie done it before she'd taken off?

He didn't think so, but then he remembered the gentleness in her brown eyes and in her touch, was reminded of her kindness and her innocence. Yes, he supposed she was the kind of woman who would help a man, even a man who had kidnapped her, even a man she would later turn over to the sheriff. Now she was gone, and he had to find her.

With his good arm he pushed himself away from the wall to a sitting position. His eyes searched the cave for his gun before it dawned on him that she would most likely have taken it with her. It wouldn't occur to her, or it wouldn't matter if it did, that she didn't know beans about shooting it.

Amazed, he saw his rifle leaning against the opposite wall, and right beside it, a tiny shape, curled in sleep. She hadn't run away! His heart sang; he was more pleased than he would ever have imagined he would be. She had nursed him and then deliberately chosen to stay there with him, when she could have gotten away, could have left him there in his sleep.

119

Looking at her more closely, he saw that she herself was deep in an exhausted sleep, her beautiful russet hair tangled and in disarray around her pale face. He noticed bright purple bruises on her fair skin and scooted a little closer. Was she all right? Had she too been wounded in the sporadic gunfire that had chased them into this hiding place? His own heart raced with fear while he watched her chest, anxious to see whether she still breathed.

A great, overwhelming relief swept over him when he saw the slight rise and fall of her chest. It had been a horrendous and terrifying episode for one so gently bred as she, and she had no doubt fallen into an exhausted and much-deserved sleep.

He hated to admit it, but his respect for his captive had just escalated a few more notches. She must be strong and courageous, to do what she had done for him. And he vowed that he would allow nothing to happen to her. As soon as he had what he wanted from Moran, he would see that she was returned home safely. "Hah! You've done a class job of keeping her safe so far, Laramie!"

"What did you say?" she asked, rubbing her eyes and sitting up beside him. "Oh!" she added in surprise, seeing him conscious and alert and apparently somewhat recovered from his injury. "You're all right?"

"Yes, I think so." He smiled at her. "And you?"

"Yes, I'm fine. Or I think I am." She moved slightly and her sore muscles complained vigorously. A hesitant smile on her full lips answered his. "We fooled them," she said, her smile widening and honey-brown eyes twinkling.

"We sure did." He honestly didn't know what to

make of her most of the time. "I don't think they'll be back for some time. At least not until this storm has blown over." *And not until they've gotten some help,* he thought, but didn't want to frighten her by mentioning that. It must have been the sheriff's thugs, and Laramie was almost sure that the sheriff had not been with them. But next time he would be. Sheriff Potts was a vengeful man who would stop at nothing.

Sadie scrambled to her feet and replenished the fire with the few remaining sticks she found inside the cave. The light reflected off the walls, its soft, yellow glow filling the interior, keeping the cold air at bay. Outside the door, the snow swirled, and it was almost impossible to determine whether it was night or day. But what did it really matter? They were safe and almost cozy near the crackling fire. And there was food, she remembered, reminded by the hungry rumblings of her stomach.

"Look!" She hauled the picnic basket over in front of them and opened it, pulling out the bag of cold fried chicken. "Doesn't this look wonderful?!" she exclaimed.

They ate the chicken greedily, stopping only to lick their fingers, before moving on to the potato salad and finishing off with a thick slice of homemade fruit pie. Rachel had been generous and there was plenty left for another meal or two. They shared the water, wishing for hot coffee, but grateful for the liquid, in whatever form.

"That was a thoughtful thing for Rachel to do," Sadie said appreciatively, repacking the remaining lunch.

"Yes, it was," he answered.

121

"She's lucky to have two such handsome, well-mannered boys."

"Yes." But as he spoke, a shadow passed over Laramie's face, and Sadie knew that his thoughts had turned again to the father of the two boys she'd mentioned. "Little Timmy is the image of his dad." The pain was evident on his face. "Christopher looks more like his mother."

"Uh-huh. She's very beautiful, don't you think?"

"Rachel? Yes, she is. Jeffrey claimed she was the most beautiful woman in the territory—and he was seldom ever wrong about anything. They had been married for several years, but they had a very special relationship." The regret was clear in his voice, along with a touch of envy, perhaps?

"What happened?" she asked softly. "You loved someone once, didn't you?

Laramie's eyes took on a haunted, faraway look. After a while, he spoke slowly. "I thought she cared about me, about Jeff, too. But it was all for show, all a clever act. She never meant any of it, not a word, not a single gesture of affection. But I bought it, oh yes—hook, line, and sinker. I made it so easy for her. She crawled into our lives and spun her web of deceit and treachery around us both so tightly we had no idea what hit us until it was much too late."

At first, Sadie wondered if he might be talking about Rachel Foster, but the hatred gleaming in his eyes could in no way be directed toward that woman for whom he felt such high regard. If not Rachel, who was he describing? She dared not interrupt for she truly wanted to know the story he was revealing to her.

"She was so beautiful and her voice was that of an angel." His eyes were distant now, as though seeing things again as they once were. "It was not just the two of us, but the whole town was captured by her magic. Scheffelin Hall was sold out and every seat filled for the few nights of her performances there. I've never heard applause like that — when she sang, it was as though she held the hearts of her audience captive in her very hands."

The fire flickered and diminished, throwing longer and darker shadows about the cave's interior. Sadie said nothing and did not move. It was almost as though she had entered his troubled dreams again, but this time his vivid blue eyes were wide open. He didn't look at her but continued speaking.

"After the show, we walked and talked. It was spring, and the air was crisp and cool, the night dark but silvery with stars. She laughed happily and took my hand in her excitement that was like a child's."

" 'There's someone I want you to meet," she said, and pulled me along into the Oriental saloon, though I would have much preferred to keep walking alone with her.

"Josiah Matthison was his name. And the whole thing, the meeting, the romance, *everything* was a setup, pure and simple. He had money, he said, and power and influential friends, including the sheriff, who would like to help us get our mine on 'substantial footing' and showing a 'healthy profit.' He also claimed to be a mining engineer and a lawyer, though most of what he said to us was unadulterated lies. He'd never been near a silver

123

mine—until we welcomed him into the Silver Linings with open arms! We never saw the money or the people he claimed to know, but when the smoke cleared and the ink dried on a bogus contract, he and his beautiful songbird were long gone, Jeff was dead, and the Silver Linings had mysteriously changed hands!"

The bare bones of the tragic story shocked Sadie into continued silence. Now Laramie, too, had lapsed into silence, but his anger and despair vibrated through their shelter.

At last she spoke. "I'm so sorry, Laramie. I . . . I . . . don't know what to say. It's so awful."

"Yes, it was awful, all right," he snarled, as if directing his wrath at her. "Should have known there were cheats and liars in the world, shouldn't I? And murderers!"

"These people killed your partner?"

"Someone sure as hell did! It's greed, not love that makes the world go round, Miss Moran."

"No, I don't think that's . . ."

"What do you know about life—from your vast experience with it?" The sarcasm was heavy in his voice, mingled with the pain.

"Not much, I suppose," she answered softly, "But I do know that love is—*has* to be—more important than greed. If it's not, what good is life?"

"Yes, what good indeed?" His eyes clouded with a weary hurt she had seen in them before, and the fight seemed to ebb out of him.

Sadie moved closer, changing the subject. "Let me check your bandage."

He acquiesced without saying anything more. Her fingers moved lightly over his skin. Satisfied that the bleeding had ceased and everything seemed to be in order, she shifted back, putting a more comfortable distance between them.

"I think I'll see if I can find more wood to build up the fire." She rose and disappeared into the dark interior, returning after a few minutes with an armful of twigs and limbs. "This should last through the night, at least."

Wearily, his eyes closed. She stoked up the fire and then stretched out not too far away from him. They both slept soundly until well after dawn.

The snow had stopped during the night. When Laramie awoke, he appeared refreshed and much improved, but it was obvious he wouldn't get far without doing damage to his wounded shoulder.

They shared more of the food from the picnic lunch, this time being careful to reserve as much as possible, not knowing how long they might have to depend on it. Sadie collected some snow from just outside the opening and set it near the fire to melt for drinking water to replace what Rachel had sent with them.

Unspoken were their shared doubts about how long they might be confined in this hiding place, how far they could stretch the remaining food, how they would travel without the wagon, and when the sheriff would return for them.

Chapter Nine

Rachel paced. Laramie had had that closed look on his face before he had left with Sadie, the one that always worried her so. Troubled, she walked out onto the front porch, peering out over the desert flatness that separated Tombstone from the Dragoons. Several trails were visible leading out toward the mountains.

As long as they were in sight, she watched the wagon carrying Laramie and his beautiful captive away. Sadie was too gentle, too fragile, and too much of a lady, and she didn't belong in this wilderness. Desperation had driven Laramie to the actions he'd taken; he could not have been thinking clearly. She had always known him to be a warm and caring person, but the events of the past months had hardened and toughened him.

It was painful to watch what he was doing to himself. He no longer seemed to trust anyone, except perhaps, her. And he hadn't even confided in her his plans for kidnapping the daughter of Lucien Moran until the act was completed.

Sheriff Potts was a cruel and selfish man, impressed with his own importance, and he possessed a driving ambition for power and wealth. He would not let Laramie stand in his way, and he, along with his powerful friends, had the resources at his fingertips to wipe out anyone he chose.

The wagon grew smaller, having covered a lot of ground while she'd been lost in thought. The two figures in it were barely discernible now. A cloud of dust billowed up two or three miles behind them. At first, Rachel thought it was a dust devil stirred up by the increasing wind of an approaching storm.

From her vantage point where her house sat on the eastern slope of a hill on the outskirts of town, she could clearly see the smoky blue and purple of the Dragoons. She often sat on her porch to watch storms intensify there and move across the almost treeless expanse of land between the mountains and the town. Sunrises over those same ramparts could be breathtaking.

But now her eyes focused on the swirling dust, and her concern increased when she realized it was caused by horsemen rather than the storm. She sensed trouble. Riders had followed Laramie out of town and were trailing him. Should she get her buggy and go after them? No, chances were she could never catch them in time, and anyway, she could not leave her boys, nor could she take them with her into certain danger.

"Christopher! Christopher!" she cried. When the lad appeared, she shouted to him, "Run quickly to the blacksmith shop. Tell Mr. Nester I need Indian Joe right away. Hurry now!"

"Yes, ma'am!" His short legs churned as he ran off down the street, and Rachel turned back into the house. She couldn't even think what she would do if Laramie's Indian friend could not be located quickly.

The small boy ran headlong down dirt-packed Fremont Street in the direction of the blacksmith shop. He loved to go there to visit and to watch Mr. Nester working the hot furnace and the glowing irons over the fire. He liked the musty, acrid odors and even enjoyed the intense heat and the way it made sweat pop out on his forehead. It made him feel like a man, somehow. And he liked that. He was the oldest and it was up to him to take care of his mother as the man of the family, now that his father was gone.

But today he didn't have time to stop and listen to the yarns Mr. Nester liked to spin. No. His mother had told him to hurry, and she'd seemed awful worried about something. He ran through the dark doorway without slowing down and crashed into something that felt like a brick wall.

Two strong arms fell on his shoulders, steadying him. "Whoa there, lad. Where are you going in such a hurry?" The soft laughter he heard eased his mind about the stranger being angry with him, and Christopher backed off and looked up into warm, smiling brown eyes.

"I'm mighty sorry, sir. It's just that my mama, she told me to git down here fast and see Mr. Nester."

"Well, we wouldn't want to keep you from doing what your mother sent you to do, now would we? Mr. Nester! There's a young man out here to see you," he called over his shoulder.

Young man! Christopher stiffened and stood up

a little straighter. No one had ever called him a young man before. Wow! He stared at the stranger, noticing how tall and thin he was, and how the sandy hair fell in an unruly way over his forehead. But most of all it was the kind, dark eyes that he liked — and the wide smile.

"Christopher Foster, sir," he said, holding his hand out in what he thought was a very grown-up manner.

"Well, it's nice to meet you, Christopher Foster. I'm Jonathan Lee."

Mr. Nester came out of the shadows, wiping his hands on his leather apron. "Your horse is as good as new, Mr. Lee. Just about threw a shoe, it did. But it's all fixed now and ready to go!"

"Thank you, Mr. Nester, but I believe Christopher has important business with you. I can wait."

"Christopher. How are you? Your mother and Timmy are all right now, aren't they?"

"Yes, sir!" he blurted out. "At least I think she's okay, but she sure seemed awful worried about something."

"What's wrong, boy?"

"I don't know for sure, Mr. Nester. But she wanted me to find Indian Joe. Is he here with you?"

The Indian whom Christopher was looking for sometimes did odd jobs for the blacksmith and could often be found hanging around the shop.

"Nope. He ain't been here yet today. I'm not sure he's back yet from his last trip out to the Huachucas. You know he's got folks out that way."

The truth was that Indian Joe went down to the range of mountains behind the fort of the same

129

name when he needed money for whiskey or to settle a gambling debt.

"Tell your pretty ma that he may not be back till evenin'. Ask her if there's anything I can do for her though, hear?"

"Yes, sir." The boy's face had fallen at the news, and his shoulders drooped as he turned away. He didn't like to disappoint his mama. When she sent him on an errand, he never let her down.

Remembering his manners, he turned back. " 'Bye, Mr. Nester, Mr. Lee. It was nice ta meet ya."

"Sure thing, son. 'Bye now."

When the boy was gone out the door, Jonathan turned to the blacksmith. "Any idea what could be wrong?"

"No. But Rachel Foster is a lady and a fine person. Hope nothin's wrong out there. Maybe I should close up here and go see for myself, just in case."

"I met Mrs. Foster at the governor's reception last night. Why don't I just offer my services in your stead? I know how hard it is for you to leave here, and I'm sure she'd understand. Like you say, she is a nice lady." *And beautiful!* he thought, more eager than he wanted to let on to see her again.

"Well, if you're sure you don't mind. I'd feel a lot better."

"No trouble." Quickly, Jonathan put a gold piece in the man's big hand and retrieved his horse. Swinging into the saddle, he rode out through the door and down the street in time to see the boy vanish around a corner.

"Wait up!" he called. "Christopher!" But the boy hadn't heard and was in the middle of the next block before he caught up with him.

"Can I give you a ride home?"

Christopher's eyes brightened, and he grinned. "Well, sure. I don't suppose Mama would mind that, would she?"

"No, I don't think she'd mind at all. And maybe I can do something to help her with her problem since you couldn't find Indian Joe, huh?"

A load lifted from the boy's thin shoulders, and he chattered happily as they cantered to the outskirts of town.

"Over there," he said, pointing to a large white house. His mother saw him and waved to them from the porch.

"Christopher! Oh, Mr. Lee . . . Jonathan! It's good to see you again. But how . . ?"

With a helping hand from the man who had brought him home, Christopher slid to the ground. Barely able to contain his excitement and sense of importance, he ran up to his mother, who was now halfway down the walk.

"I ran as fast as I could, Mama. And I ran smack into Mr. Lee. But he wasn't mad! And Mr. Nester hasn't seen Indian Joe, said he mightn't be back till tonight. And Mr. Lee here caught up with me on my way home, and he gave me a ride and he said maybe he could help!"

Jonathan, with a smile on his face, had dismounted, wrapped the reins around the top rail of the fence, and trailed the boy up the walk. "I hope you don't mind, Rachel. Mr. Nester couldn't get away just now, and he was concerned about you. I told him we'd met and that I'd be glad to look in on you and see what was wrong here."

"Well, that's very kind of you. Nothing is really wrong here, but there's a good friend of mine who may be in a lot of trouble. I was hoping Indian Joe could take a couple of his friends and help him out."

Jonathan knew without asking that she spoke of the man who'd cut in when he'd danced with Rachel the night before. That man had certainly seemed more than able to take care of himself. But now Jonathan knew he'd been right when he'd suspected that the Widow Foster cared for Nate Laramie, whose identity he'd learned later.

"What can I do, Rachel?"

"I don't know. He and Sadie left town in a wagon, heading for Middlemarch Pass through the Dragoons earlier today. I watched them go." She pointed toward the string of sharp peaks that stretched from north to south in a natural barrier to the desert prairies leading into them. "Then I saw a storm coming, and I'm almost sure I saw two or three men following them. I'm afraid someone means to hurt them."

Rachel didn't mention her suspicion that the men had been sent out by Sheriff Potts, or that Sadie was, in truth, Nate's captive.

"And you'd like somebody to ride out and warn them, or try to help them?"

"Yes," she said, but she thought, *if it's not already too late*. "But not you, Jonathan. You don't know the territory, especially the mountains. You couldn't go out there alone. Indian Joe knows them like the back of his hand. He was once part of Cochise's band of renegades who used the Dragoons as their hideout from the military. Wait! I know somewhere else we can look! Maybe Joe is at the Oriental. He spends a lot of time at that saloon when he's not helping Mr. Nester."

Quite a town, where men start drinking before breakfast, Jonathan thought, but he said only, "I'll go see if I can find him. You don't worry now. Your friend will be all right." He squeezed her shoulder gently before mounting and wheeling his horse away in the direction of the strip of saloons that lined Allen Street. He knew the Oriental would not be hard to find, and that an Indian should stand out among the cowboys and townsmen.

The saloon was neither as busy nor as rowdy as it would be later in the day, but a few men lounged at the bar, nursing drinks, and one poker game was in full swing at a back table. No one paid much attention as the stranger entered and looked around, seeking the Indian. He saw no one who fit that description, but he strolled up to the bar and slapped down a coin.

"Have you seen someone called Indian Joe today?" he asked the bartender.

The man behind the wide, polished counter apparently found him harmless looking, and he grinned. "Nah, not this mornin'. What'll ya have, mister?"

"Just information," said Jonathan. "Any idea where I might find him?"

The other man swept the coin Jonathan offered off the bar and into his pocket. "If he's in town, he's here, at the smithy shop or at the Eagle Brewery."

That only left one place to look, Jonathan thought, thanking the man with another coin. He

133

walked quickly out the door and down the walk. The second saloon was darker but more elegant than the first, sparkling crystal twinkling in the huge mirror behind the ornate mahogany bar. Two bartenders in freshly starched white shirts were already at work and were efficiently serving the needs of their clientele, who looked a little more respectable than those in the Oriental. Jonathan suspected the whiskey here would be of the finest quality and not watered down.

But was Indian Joe here? As his eyes grew used to the dark, he took in the few well-dressed citizens and cowboys a caliber above those who frequented the Oriental.

From where he sat on a stool at the far end of the bar, a wide-shouldered man stared at Jonathan. The man had his back to the light, and Jonathan could tell little about him, but he felt strongly that he just might be the man he was looking for. He walked toward him and sat down a couple of barstools away. Now he could see that the big, muscular man was indeed an Indian and, most likely, the very same Indian Joe he had come to find.

"You Indian Joe?" he asked quietly.

"Who wants to know?" The man's voice was gruff, not angry but noncommittal. Men who strode the streets of Tombstone and lived were careful men.

"I am Jonathan Lee. Rachel Foster sent me to find a man called Indian Joe. She has a friend who is in trouble and in need his help." Jonathan kept his voice low enough that no one else could hear. "Are you Indian Joe?"

"Yes."

"Good, then if you'll come with me, maybe we can help the lady—and her friend."

The Indian followed him on his own horse. He said nothing further while they rode back out toward Rachel's house.

When they got there, Rachel told him how happy she was to see him, explained the dilemma, and asked for his help.

With a nod, Indian Joe indicated his willingness, but all he said was, "Laramie, my friend." And to Jonathan, who wanted to go along with him, "Joe ride alone."

"Of course." Even as he spoke, Jonathan knew there would be no arguing with the Indian, though he would have liked to go along.

After the Indian rode out, he encouraged Rachel, "I'm sure he'll find them in time. Don't you worry."

"I hope so, Jonathan. Thanks so much for your help."

"It was nothing. Guess I'd better be going. Christopher, you look after your mother now."

"Yes, sir!"

Sadie watched Laramie's chest rise and fall in sleep, the rhythm of it less uneven than it had been before. He was getting better, she felt sure of it. A momentary gladness and a reluctant feeling of pride for her part in his recovery moved through her. He was strong, and his body had fought hard to heal itself, but without her he would probably have bled to death.

Still, he was far from being as good as new. He'd lost a lot of blood and been weakened a great deal by it. He would need lots of rest before he was truly well. And food, she thought, with some dismay, looking at the few scraps they had left. They couldn't wait until he felt well enough to do something about it, or they would both starve.

What could she do? Snow had piled into two-to-three foot drifts around the cave's entrance. She could manage to get out through that, but then what? The road would be covered as well, and hard to follow. Besides, it was much too far back into town on foot.

Was there anything near at hand she could scavenge for them to eat? She had heard of people eating—or drinking—from cactus. But the last cactus plant she'd seen was far down the other side of the mountain. Game or birds, then? She smiled when she imagined Laramie's reaction to her notion that she might actually shoot something they could eat. Even if she could find something and get close enough to it, she would never be able to hit it! But, she thought, easing the rifle away from where it lay near his head, *I just might get lucky!*

She had to do something. If she failed, they wouldn't be any worse off. But she was very quiet putting on her boots and coat and pushing the snow away from the mouth of the cave, knowing he would object strongly if he awoke and saw what she was doing.

"Bye, Laramie," she whispered, leaving with the rifle up over her shoulder.

It felt so good to be outdoors, to breathe in the fresh air again. Her step was light, her hopes high as she strode away from the cave and the sleeping Laramie.

136

The snow had stopped, but not before it had blanketed the trail and left a glistening coating on all the trees and bushes. She caught her breath at its beauty as she looked out across a valley to other snow-covered peaks. The snow made everything new and beautiful. Maybe Arizona was not so awful as she'd thought, she admitted, walking farther and farther away, unsure what it was she was looking for—or what she might find.

She looked behind her occasionally to be sure she could still see her footprints in the soft snow. Reassured that she would be able to follow them back if necessary, she kept on going. A hawk swooped by overhead, throwing its shadow over the snow, but otherwise nothing stirred.

Her aching muscles and the position of the sun sinking lower in the sky alerted her that more time than she'd thought must have gone by. She'd gone much further from the cave than she'd ever intended, and she was still empty handed.

Just when she was ready to turn back, a bright color in a snow bank caught her eye. Flowers peeking out of the snow? Intrigued, she walked closer and brushed away the snow, revealing beautiful buttercup-shaped red flowers. She broke one off and lifted it, entranced by its beauty and curious about the incongruity of where she'd found it. If she gathered a few more and took them back; maybe they would cheer Laramie up.

"Berries!" she exclaimed, when she squatted and looked more carefully. Greedily she ate a few, enjoying their icy sweetness and then stuffed more into her pockets. With a small bouquet of the colorful flowers still clutched in her hand, she started back, trying to retrace her footprints.

"That's far enough, I reckon, my beauty!"

Sadie whirled. She had been so sure she was completely alone. Where had the three menacing-looking men come from? Who were they? She and Laramie had both been so sure the sheriff's men had given up and turned back.

She did not move as her eyes took in the motley group of men. Surely the sheriff wouldn't choose men like these as his deputies. Her eyes remained expressionless with a great deal of effort, for inside, her heart pounded with fear, her lungs were finding it hard to get air, and her knees felt like jelly.

Laramie awoke slowly, stretching as much as his sore shoulder would allow. He was stiff and his wound still throbbed, but he felt much better than before.

Something was wrong . . . An unnatural silence filled the cavern. Sadie was gone, really gone this time! Of course, now that he was getting better, her humanitarian heart would allow her to leave him.

Where would she go? Back the way they had come—but in the snow, on foot? He had begun to think she was smarter than that. Well, he would have to find the little fool before she got herself killed.

Either she would make it back to town—something he could not permit—or she would get lost in the snow and freeze to death or starve, possibilities he could not face.

Laramie knew and respected these mountains. More than one person had disappeared into them never to be seen again. The thought of her lying still and cold in a snowdrift someplace was enough to get him moving.

He gingerly pushed himself away from the wall and tried to stand, but the throbbing pain in his shoulder combined with a furious pounding in his head dropped him back to his knees. Dizziness swept over him, and he was afraid to move again. But he knew he had to—he would just take it a little slower. Damn that woman, anyway. Why couldn't she just stay where she was? In the cave she would have been safe until he figured out their next move.

He remembered the gentle hands that had cared for him while his fever raged. He had been lulled into trusting her, and where had it gotten him? He should have learned long ago never to trust a woman, no matter how soft her hands, how sweet her voice, how beautiful her face.

Still on his knees, and careful not to move too fast, he belted on his gun and reached for his rifle. Damn it! She had taken it! He should have known. Though she'd come nearer shooting herself in the foot with it than anyone else, she was dangerous with a weapon. He knew that from experience. He would have to be careful—a man could end up just as dead from an accidental shot as from an intentional one!

Her footprints in the snow were as clear and easy to follow as a well-marked trail. Being careful to jar his shoulder as little as possible, he haltingly started off after her, cursing her foolishness under his breath with every painful step. "Damn woman! Stupid tenderfoot! Sneak thief!"

When he found her, he might just be angry enough to leave her there in the blasted snow to freeze! She didn't deserve to be rescued for doing such a foolhardy thing. But he kept walking steadily, following the tiny set of footprints, hoping desperately that he would find her soon, before it grew dark, before it was too late.

Sadie's eyes swept over the clearing where the men had her cornered and were now moving apart in an attempt to surround her. They looked mean and tough and were a lot stronger than she, but she didn't think they were very smart. If they had been, they would have discovered the cave already. And if they had the least bit of intelligence, they would have sneaked up behind her, overpowered her and taken the rifle she now held tightly in both hands. Slowly she backed away from them, preventing any of them from moving around behind her.

Each of the three had a gun pointed straight at her, and they were not the type who would hesitate to use a gun even on a woman. These were bad men, these sheriff's mercenaries, men not interested in law and order, but in earning the bounty they'd no doubt been promised. But they were cowards and not the least bit interested in getting themselves shot.

The one nearest on her left was the one who had first shouted at her. He was so big, the rifle in his hands looked like a toothpick. His pockmarked face was partially covered with a red, matted beard, and when he leered at her, there were gaping holes where his teeth should be.

He spit a stream of brown tobacco onto the snow and motioned to the small man to his left. "Cactus," he said with a low chuckle. "Take the lady's gun."

"Humph!" snorted the wiry little man, who was all angles and sharp features. "Take it yerself, Lucas!"

"Be reasonable, miss," spoke up the third, whose plaid shirt peeked out from under a heavy ragged coat. "We don't want to hurt you, but our orders is to bring ya back. Now, if we don't do that, we's in big trouble. You can understand our little problem, now, cain't ya?"

Sadie swung her gun to point it directly at him. He seemed to be the real leader of the small band, if there was such a thing. Though he spoke in measured, reasonable tones, Sadie suspected he was the meanest of the bunch, the one she should worry about most. His lecherous eyes had examined her so closely Sadie felt as if she'd been stripped naked by his stare.

"Now see if you can understand my problem, *gentlemen*. I'm only one person and I have only one gun, but I'm a good shot," she lied, "and I'm going to kill at least one of you. So," she swung the gun from one to the other as she continued, "which one will it be?"

"We can cut you down so fast you won't know what hit you," bragged the small one, the one they called "Cactus."

"But I will take one of you with me, won't I?" She pointed both barrels straight at him and her face said she meant business.

"Wally?" asked the big man.

"Jest a minute, Lucas. I'm sure we can work this thing out. All we really want is Laramie. So, if you'll jest tell us where he's hid, we'll let you go on your way, little lady. We'll jest round him up and take him back to the sheriff."

But Sadie knew what they had planned for Laramie, and she was almost certain she knew what her own fate would be in their hands.

"Laramie's dead," she bluffed. "And it serves him right, too."

"Wall now, ain't that somethin'! Laramie a candidate for Boot Hill, and this little gal here all alone," growled Lucas, his hands itching to wrap themselves around her creamy flesh until she cried out for mercy.

But Wallace wasn't buying. "Now jest hold on, Lucas. What makes you think she's tellin' the truth? She might be protectin' him, coverin' up. Yeah, I think thet's jest what she's doin'."

Before Sadie had time to react, he was upon her, wrenching the gun from her grasp, his hulking body propelling hers to the ground.

She had the breath knocked out of her by the fall, and the weight of her attacker crushed her body into a snow bank. She struggled, but he was a dead weight, pressing against her. Her lungs screamed for air, and dizziness swept over her. Rancid breath blew across her face, and she wrenched her head away as fat, damp lips tried to claim hers — then slid in a wet smear across her cheek.

Blackness threatened to engulf her, and with horror she felt his big paw pulling at her skirt.

"Hey, boss!" whined the bearded one. "What about us?"

"You'll get yer turn," he gritted between clenched teeth, shoving a heavy leg up between Sadie's thighs. "There's plenty here to go round."

Chapter Ten

"Back off!" called a blessedly familiar voice from among the trees surrounding the clearing.

Sadie felt the weight on her diminish when the man lifted himself on his forearms and turned his head to see who threatened him.

"I said move! Right now! Or those will be the last words you'll ever hear." Laramie stepped into the clearing, both pistols cocked and one aimed at the head of the man who pinned Sadie to the ground. His voice was tempered steel and so angry it vibrated like a whiplash through the still, cold air.

The man called Wally scrambled to his feet and backed away a couple of steps. Lucas, thinking Laramie's attention focused on the other man, made a fatal mistake and pulled off a shot that missed. Laramie turned one of the pistols on him and fired. The man fell backward into a snowbank and did not move.

Wally had dropped his gun in the scuffle with Sadie and now shoved himself to his feet and made a running dive for Laramie, his body striking him viciously.

Laramie's shoulder exploded in pain, and blood soaked the bandage again. Stars flashed in front of his eyes, and a heavy blackness threatened to over-take him. But he couldn't let it, not this time. Sadie would be at the mercy of these two, and he couldn't bear to think what they'd do to her, what they'd al-most done to her already.

With a loud bellow of rage, he threw the heavier man off him. With his good arm, he threw a solid punch to his jaw, backing him up. Laramie had a driving need to punish the man who'd been on top of Sadie. He landed another bruising blow to the man's head, slamming him back against a tree.

Staggering, the big man came at him yet again, but Laramie smoothly ducked wild punches of the man's beefy fists, feinting and then striking back with lethal, killing fury. Blood poured from Wally's nose and one eye puffed up, nearly closed.

Still Laramie was not satisfied. This man would have viciously raped Sadie and then he would have killed her coldly and without compunction. Laramie struck a savage blow to the man's corpulent midsec-tion and followed with a punishing uppercut to his jaw.

The mountain of a man who had been so brave while pushing up a lady's skirts now howled in pain and terror and threw up his hands to protect his head from further injury.

"You go back . . ." Laramie gritted between clenched teeth, "and you tell that skunk of a man who sent you out on this dirty little errand . . . that he should come after me himself. And if I ever," he threatened, moving closer to the cowering man, "if I *ever* see you anywhere near this lady again—you'll wish I *had* killed you today."

Fear gave speed to the man's big clumsy feet, and he turned tail and ran off through the thick woods,

leaving horse and gun and his two companions behind in his haste.

While the two men battled with their fists, Cactus
had moved around, trying to get a good shot off at
Laramie without hitting Wally in the attempt. His attention strayed from Sadie, since he didn't consider
her a threat, just long enough for her to roll over
and grab Laramie's rifle.

She saw Cactus, with his rifle trained on Laramie's
back, jumped to her feet, and swinging as hard as
she could, brought the butt of the rifle down on
back of the small man's neck. He slumped to the
ground.

When Laramie turned to see if Sadie needed his
help, his vivid blue eyes took in the sight of her
standing over the inert form of the man she'd struck,
as though daring him to move. He laughed, but the
expression on his face was more one of wonder than
of humor. She was all right! Sweet relief swept
through him but was followed just as quickly by a
burning rage.

Sadie felt a sick weakness when she realized how
close Laramie had come to being shot in the back.
Her heart revolted at the vision of him lying in the
snow, his blood staining the pristine whiteness. It
had been so close! If she hadn't struck Cactus when
she had, the shot that had gone off wildly by the reflex action of his finger on the trigger would have
found its mark in the very middle of Laramie's solid
back.

Grinning happily that they had both somehow sur-
vived, she looked over at him. At first, she was sure
she saw in his eyes the same relief, the same joy, and
perhaps even a bit of respect for her and gratitude
that she'd stopped Cactus from shooting him in the

146

back.

But if those feelings had been revealed briefly, they were quickly squelched. What she saw now was a formidable, bitter anger twisting his handsome face. What had she done to make him so angry? Her heart, which had been filled with soaring happiness moments before, now plummeted. He was not glad she lived, nor glad she'd saved his life, nor even aware that together they'd fought off a common enemy. He looked at her for all the world as though she herself were that enemy and his job not completed until she was taken care of as well. He advanced a couple of menacing steps toward her, his eyes changed to a deep shade of indigo and snapping with an anger she couldn't begin to understand.

Sadie straightened her shoulders and stared back at him, her eyes wide now with dawning comprehension. He was angry because she'd left, because she'd done something on her own without his approval, and because he'd been forced to come after her. He cared nothing about her or her safety; he was only protecting his investment in her as his hostage. Her brown eyes turned cool, assessing, but an answering anger was now seething inside her. She didn't trust herself to speak.

"Fool woman!" he shouted at her. "Almost got us both killed, didn't you?"

"How dare you . . . !"

"Come on! We'll freeze to death out here." He grabbed her hand and pulled her over to where the horses belonging to the men who'd attacked her were hobbled. Without another word he gave her a hand up into the saddle. He threw the inert body of Cactus and the lifeless Lucas over the saddle of one horse, wrapped a rope around them to hold them securely, and slapped its rump, sending horse and baggage galloping down the hill.

When Sadie moved out onto the trail leading back up the mountain to their hideout, he followed her quickly on the remaining horse. Neither spoke another word until they found themselves alone again in the cave, but tempers were boiling. Laramie was furious with her, and she with him for his inexplicable attitude.

"Since you can't hit the broad side of a barn, you use my rifle like a club? How inventive, Miss Moran."

"I saved your worthless neck, didn't I?"

"If you hadn't gone traipsing off alone like that, there wouldn't have been any need for me to save you — or for you to save my 'worthless neck,' as you so sweetly put it."

His voice was getting louder and louder, and he couldn't seem to help himself, he was so thoroughly, unreasonably furious with her.

"And I suppose it never occurred to you in that thick head of yours that I might, just *might*, have had a very good reason for doing what I did?"

Sadie had never resorted to name-calling before, but he was making her so mad she couldn't think straight. Here, she'd gone off looking for the food they desperately needed — and found some, too, and all he could do was shout at her for endangering *him!* She supposed he had not given a thought to being a little grateful to someone who'd bandaged his wounds and looked after him, probably saved his life?

Alarmed, she noticed a spreading bright red stain on his bandage, and her anger dissipated. "Be quiet and sit down, Laramie."

148

His mouth dropped open and he stared at her, not moving from his spread-eagle stance.

"I said sit down. And you can close your mouth, too."

His jaws snapped shut. He eyed her warily as she set aside the rifle and strode purposefully over to him. "You stubborn, hardheaded, thick-skinned outlaw! Will you *please* sit down and let me see what you've done to my bandage?"

This was a side of her he'd not seen before. Without another word he sat down and obediently opened his shirt, his eyes never leaving her face. Tension still crackled between them, but now a new dimension had been added to the anger.

When her fingers touched his bare skin, he jumped.

"Cold?" she asked.

"No," he muttered. Not cold, but something like fire had gone through his veins from her touch.

"Does it hurt?" Her fingers were so gentle and her touch so welcome that he had to be reminded of the renewed pain in his wound.

"Damnit! Of course it hurts!"

"I'm sorry."

She did not flinch at his curse, but he felt like a heel anyway. "I'm sorry, Sadie."

His head was reeling. He wasn't sure why, but he knew that her touch was driving him crazy. He wanted to ask her to stop or at least to hurry, but didn't trust himself to speak. Either he'd be shouting at her again, or he would be pulling her into his arms and tasting those tempting lips for himself. And if he ever held her, he was very much afraid he'd never let her go.

Finally, she finished and sat back on her heels, her

149

face flushed. "There. That should take care of it," she said.

Oh no, it won't, he thought. *That won't take care of it at all.*

He saw the concern on her face almost simultaneously with the black film that settled over his eyes before he lost consciousness.

When the darkness began to recede, he felt the familiar cool touch on his forehead and gratefully sipped the water she offered to him.

"You have to quit leaving me this way, Laramie." She smiled at him. "I never get to finish an argument with you."

He smiled back, feeling more than a little foolish. "I think that may be the only way I'm ever able to win one."

"That's about the smartest thing I've heard you say today." She laughed and offered him some of the berries she'd gathered.

Berries! The truth hit him between the eyes! Now he felt like a bigger fool than ever. She hadn't been running away at all! Instead, she'd been trying to help—in the only way she knew how. His anger at himself for misjudging her gave way to a grudging admiration for her, to be followed by confusion over his hopelessly tangled emotions where she was concerned.

"You found berries," he laughed softly.

"Of course. You didn't doubt I would, did you?" She laughed too. He was unaccountably thrilled at the sound of that laughter and to see the sparkle of life return to her eyes.

"No, not for a minute," he assured her, his eyes lingering on her face.

She plopped one of the juicy berries in his mouth

while he was still grinning stupidly at her. How could he ever have doubted her, he wondered.

Fascinated, he watched her delight at the taste of the berries, wondering how she would taste, knowing it would be far better than berries! Her luscious soft skin drew him like a magnet.

She had stood up to those men, putting herself in jeopardy — and all to protect him! The thought would have been enough to knock his legs out from under him if he'd been standing, he was sure. He had to admit, he'd never in his life known anyone like her. Maybe there was one other good woman besides Rachel in the world . . . a woman who wouldn't use a man, then turn her back on him when he needed her most. A woman who'd be loyal, who'd stick by a man in thick or thin.

"Thanks," he said.

"For what?" she asked, sitting cross-legged on the floor facing him and generously sharing her berries with him.

"For what you did out there."

She felt again the crunch of the man's skull as she'd struck him with the rifle as hard as she could. She shivered. "It was nothing."

"No, it was a lot more than that. It was brave, and," he grinned, "very effective."

"Yes, it was, wasn't it?" She was smiling again. "He crumpled like a rag doll. Not so tough as he thought."

"Nope. Or maybe you're just tougher."

"Yup!"

He laughed out loud, thumping his leg and wincing from the answering pain in his shoulder.

She eyed him suspiciously. "What's so funny, Laramie?"

151

"You! I guess if you can't shoot 'em — you can whack 'em to death!"

"You'll eat those words, Nate Laramie. I will learn to shoot, and when I do, you'll wish guns had never been invented!" She had picked up his revolver and was waving it around.

He held up both hands. "I already do. Please, Miss Moran, have mercy. I'm an unarmed one-armed man. Sadie, put that thing down. You're making me nervous. I'll teach you myself if you'll promise me not to pick up another gun until I do."

He breathed a sigh of relief when she returned the gun to his holster.

"Make you nervous, Laramie?"

"You bet!"

"You don't really think I'd shoot you after I went to so much trouble to save your life, now do you?"

"Not on purpose."

They both laughed, but when their eyes met in new understanding, the laughter died away.

"You were pretty good out there yourself!" She recalled her joy at seeing him arrive in the clearing just in time, and her respect at the way he'd handled the three ruffians. He had really been something and had done it all with only one good arm. She shuddered to think what would have happened to her if he hadn't come looking for her.

He had been angry at her for leaving, sure, but she suspected much of his anger was caused by his fear of what might have happened to her. Did he really care about her — other than as his hostage, a means to an end? Something in his actions and in his eyes today told her he did. A new closeness wove its way around them. They had shared a common enemy and fought it out together. It felt good.

The stash of firewood Sadie had found in the cave had dwindled until it was almost gone. A small fire still burned, but as darkness fell, the cave grew colder.

"I'm afraid it's going to be hard to stay warm tonight," she said, adding another small piece of kindling to the fire.

"Maybe not. We still have the quilt. It's big enough for two, and it's very warm under here." His tone of voice and his eyes challenged her as he innocently tucked the quilt around himself.

Sadie considered her options—crawling under a quilt with Nate Laramie was a most unsettling idea, and not her first choice. She tried for a while sitting huddled up near the fire, but she couldn't keep that up. There was her coat, but she wouldn't be able to sleep on it and under it, too. The bare ground looked distinctly cold and uninviting. She glared at Laramie, who looked toasty warm and comfortable under his quilt.

"You could offer me the damned quilt, you know."

"Yes, I know, but you wouldn't want the fever to come over me again now, would you?"

"You look all right to me." Her eyes narrowed. "Is this a trick, Laramie?"

"I am merely offering a lady the comfort of my quilt and the warmth of my body on a cold night."

Her eyes flew open. But his face looked innocent of lascivious intent. And it was not as if he hadn't had plenty of opportunities before to compromise her, if he'd wanted to.

Sadie shivered and decided she was being hardheaded and stupid. He wasn't going to attack her, certainly not now.

It was only after she'd spread her coat on the ground and slipped under the edge of the quilt with him that she realized what she had been most afraid of: herself . . . and the response of her body to the proximity of his.

Warmth from the quilt and the masculine form stretched out beside her stole over her pleasantly, and she soon stopped shivering and sighed with contentment.

He smiled into the darkness and edged a little closer, gratified to feel her leg along the length of his before she jerked it away.

"The closer we are, the warmer we'll both be. And it will get much colder in here as the fire dies out."

I'll bet! she thought, stubbornly refusing to budge or to move closer to him.

Laramie, for his part, fought a raging battle with his senses. He wanted nothing more than to pull her to him, cover her soft mouth with kisses, and warm her skin with his hands and his body. It was a painful longing that hurt every bit as much as the wound in his shoulder.

He lay awake for hours, even after her even breathing told him she slept. Only with the strength of his will was he able to control arms and legs that wanted nothing more than to wrap themselves around her and never let her go.

The firelight dancing on the opposite wall dimmed, and he felt her tremble beneath the covers. He slipped his good arm underneath her and ever so gently urged her into the shelter of his body, drawing her close. She snuggled, seeking the warmth he offered. His arm around her ribs moved with the gentle rhythm of her breathing, and her soft curves meshed with his strong length in an immeasurably satisfying

154

way. After a long, long time, he slept.

Sadie awakened first before dawn, comfortable and warm in the circle of his arms. It was something one could easily get used to, and she wondered what it would feel like to make love to him. He would be gentle and would never force her to do anything she didn't want to, for Nate Laramie was more of a gentleman than he wanted anyone to suspect. And he was intelligent and strong. A woman could lose herself in a man like that.

She sighed and sleepily snuggled closer to his warm protective body, her heart singing with contentment. He threw his good arm over her, and it rested just beneath her breasts. A longing she didn't understand started building inside her, and she ached to feel his touch, his big, gentle hand stroking her bare flesh. She wanted his strong body as close to hers as she could get. Yes, she admitted, she wanted the two of them to be one. She wanted . . . she wanted Nate Laramie!

She turned toward him on her side, his arm still over her, and studied his handsome face. She'd never known what it was like to want something so desperately and he was sleeping contentedly through it all. She smiled.

He blinked and opened his eyes, surprised to find himself nose to nose with a bewitchingly beautiful woman.

"Sadie . . ." he began, about to remove his arm, thinking he might have offended or frightened her. "I'm sorry."

"No."

"No?"

"No, don't be sorry, and don't you dare move your arm. I think it's about time you kissed me for real,

155

outlaw."

"Sadie, have you lost your mind? You're not serious . . . are you?" He hardly dared to breathe while he waited for her reply.

"Oh, yes, I'm very serious." Warm, honey-brown eyes told him everything he needed to know.

"Oh, God! Sadie. You can't know . . . How much I've wanted you. Come here."

"No, wait. You'll hurt yourself."

"Doesn't matter. Besides, I'll for sure hurt myself if you *don't* come here! Nothing matters but this."

He kissed her, drinking in the essence of her, tasting her unbearable sweetness. His good arm stroked the length of her back, warm beneath the shared quilt, but his other arm was useless and they both knew it.

"Do you think you could. . . ?"

A long silence made him tremble while she considered his request. She had no doubts about what he was asking her to do. As much as she wanted to, Sadie wasn't at all sure she could.

"Laramie . . ." she began.

"No, it's all right," he said softly. "It's too soon. You don't even know . . ."

"Hush." She scrambled out from under the covers, turned her back to him, and as quickly as her fumbling fingers would allow, removed her shirt, then dropped her trousers and pantaloons to the floor and stepped out of them. He was treated to only a quick glimpse of a strikingly beautiful body and skin almost the same honey-gold as her eyes before she was once more beside him and hesitantly working loose the button on his pants, her other hand sliding up under his shirt to tentatively stroke the thick, curling hair on his chest.

"Miss Moran," he spoke in a whisper, "you take my breath away."

"And you mine, Nate Laramie." Her lips covered his. She pushed his shirt, now unbuttoned, off his shoulders and down his arms slowly. Her bare breasts moved temptingly against his chest.

"You're not real, are you?" he asked, sure that anything so wonderful could never be real.

"Oh, yes, and this is very real," she murmured as her soft hands played across his body. Her satiny flesh moved over him and he felt every inch of her, from those tempting breasts to her flat stomach and long, silky legs.

He made one last half-hearted protest which she silenced with another lingering kiss before he gave in completely to his overwhelming desire. If he couldn't make her his and soon, he might just die from it.

"Yes sir, my bandit, I know exactly what I'm doing." She didn't, not really, but she trusted in her newly awakened feminine instincts and Nate's loving tenderness to show her the way. "And I know exactly what I want."

"I believe you do, lady," he breathed as he pulled her over him and was rewarded with the welcoming tightness of her love around him. She was molten fire, and he was burning out of control. They moved together, slowly at first, then faster, in a rhythm as old as time, and cried out their mutual fulfillment as they reached heights of ecstasy neither of them had ever imagined was possible.

He fell back, breathing hard. Concern filled her eyes when she looked up at him, her eyes going to his bandage. "Are you all right?" Her hand reached to check the wound, but he caught it and brought it to his lips, where he kissed it, tasting the sweet flesh of her hand.

"I don't think I've ever been more all right."

"Me, too." She practically purred as her hand traced the rugged, handsome planes of his face, suddenly so dear to her.

"You sure? No regrets?"

"Absolutely not."

"It was your first time."

"Yes."

"Thank you." And he felt so grateful, so humble as though she'd given him the best imaginable gift and she had.

"You're welcome."

He pulled her head to him and again explored her face with his lips, kissing her eyes, her nose, her cheeks, and finally her lips.

"You taste delicious."

"It's the berries."

"I doubt it."

Surprised at himself, Laramie realized he was aroused again and his loins aching for her sweet response. He had to have her again, only this time he was determined to orchestrate the lovemaking, bad arm or no.

"Come here."

She did.

After he'd taken her breath with a very thorough kiss, he rolled her gently to her back and his hand moved over the tempting softness of her breasts, savoring their fullness, then slid down along her ribs, her tapering waist and lower still, to explore all the mysteries she held for him. With a surprised gasp, she arched her back and moved into his caress, urging him on, delighted by the intimate touch of his hands and his fingers. As he stroked, she moved in unison with the motion, wanting him so desperately it drove all else from her mind.

"Please, oh, please, Nate," she begged, pulling him over on top of her.

"Whoa . . . I said I was in charge this time, little one. Now, you just be patient." He held his body back from her, but his hands continued to torture her toward a mindless yearning.

"Oh, yes!" she cried as he entered her at last.

"Now, my beloved, now."

Her cries were voiceless but rapturous as she rose to meet him stroke for stroke and they climaxed near the top of this mountain of their own making.

Wrapped in the cocoon of his arms and body, Sadie knew she'd never felt so secure, so peaceful, so complete.

Laramie was experiencing the same, but his joy in her was tempered by escalating feelings of guilt. What had he done? He'd taken her innocence and he had nothing to give her in return, nothing but his driving lust for revenge and the heartache of knowing the truth. When she knew, when he had carried out his plan and she knew everything, she would never forgive him. So, he was leading them both into a box canyon full of hurt with no way out, except back the way they'd come. There could never be a future for a city girl and a drifter.

He pulled away and reached for his shirt. "I'm sorry. I shouldn't have done that."

"What? That's the *stupidest* thing you've ever said, Nate Laramie and you've said a lot of stupid things. Here, let me help you."

She pulled his shirt on over his wounded shoulder gently and buttoned it up. Then she worked his feet and legs into the trousers with the help of his one good arm, deliberately not looking at him.

Her heart crying out against his unexpected rejection, she dressed quickly and turned away. She had given herself to him willingly and with all her heart, and now he was apologizing? All he could say was that he was sorry? His apology hurt her more than any other response she could have imagined. Why couldn't he just be happy and share the joy she'd been feeling, the joy he'd felt too, if only for a few minutes? She'd been a fool, and she could see it all too clearly now. Her new feelings toward him had blinded her to the truth.

"Well, then, I guess I'm sorry, too," she said with a note of finality in her voice. He obviously didn't want a woman, a commitment, someone who might get in the way of his precious revenge, so that's the way it would be. He would be her kidnapper and she his captive until she found a way to be free.

Nate Laramie could never be the man for her. He harbored too many secrets and nurtured too many grudges. He was rough and unfettered, as different from her as night from day. She needed a home, a family, and security, things he probably would never want or need.

She thought of Rachel, who had left everything and everyone for the man she loved, and who seemed to have no regrets, even now. But her husband had been murdered. *Is that the way you want to live?* questioned her logical mind. *Maybe even on the run from the law?*

No, Sadie knew she couldn't live that way. She admired many things about Nate Laramie, and she responded to him in ways she couldn't understand. She cared about him, and the feelings she had for him, whatever they were, were getting stronger. In her heart, though, she knew it could never work. He would never let it work, and she would not allow it to go any further. She had to rein in her feelings before they were even more out of control.

She walked slowly away from him and stood looking out the door of the cavern. Shame coursed through her at the thought of how wantonly she'd behaved with him — what she'd allowed him to do — what she'd done herself. Surely none of this was real. This couldn't be happening to the daughter of Lucien Moran.

Oh, father, she cried out silently, *what is happening to me?* She wasn't sure what it was that caused her to tremble as she stood there feeling completely alone.

Sheriff Dan Potts sauntered through one of the three sets of double doors of the Bird Cage Saloon, intent on finding an evening's pleasure there. He felt good and in a mood to celebrate. Soon business with Laramie would be settled.

"Where's Lil?" he demanded of the bartender.

"Now, Sheriff," laughed One-Eyed Jake, "you know she's right where she always is — and a'waitin' fer you, er I miss my guess!"

The sheriff grinned, slapped down a handful of coins, and said, "Well, you just send us up some drinks on the double, then!"

"Yes, sir! Good as done!"

Jake reached for a dumbwaiter used to ferry drinks up to the birdcage compartments. The saloon had gotten its name from fourteen of these cribs, suspended from the ceiling. Each sported red velvet drapes and had a view of the casino and dance hall below. In these boxes, the ladies of the night entertained their customers for twenty-five dollars a night.

The sheriff's spurs jingled as he pushed open the door to the back portion of the saloon. He eyed the gambling tables, crowded with rowdy men, each sure this would be his night to get rich. He couldn't wait to try his own hand at faro or high-stakes poker. Loud, rollicking music, smoke, and raucous laughter filled the large room. On the dance floor, painted women wearing brightly colored ruffles danced with rough-clad cowboys and some of the town's leading citizens dressed in dapper black suits and ties.

Glancing up at Lily's box, he saw her waving at him and made his way upstairs and into her waiting arms. He could always count on Lil!

"I've missed you, Sheriff." No recriminations, no questions. Her ability to accept him without question was one of the things he liked best about Lily Delgado. Of course, there were other things, he thought, his arms spanning her ample but pleasing girth and pulling her to him. She was round and firm and womanly. She felt terrific in his arms.

"Me, too, Lil." He swatted her playfully on the rump and said, "Now, let's have a drink — and a good time!"

"Sure thing." She helped him off with his coat and seated him on the brocaded settee, where he had a good view of the activity below. She filled their glasses and settled herself next to him. "I thought you might not come. You've been so busy lately."

"Yeah. But that's all over now. Everything is taken care of. Now I can relax."

Lily thought he did seem relieved about something, but there was an undercurrent of excitement

162

running through him. He looked far from relaxed, his fingers drumming on the wooden arm of the settee, his foot tapping nervously on the floor.

What was up? she wondered but dared not ask. He never shared his business with her. She could only hope he would mellow with another drink or two.

The house lights dimmed and the lively tinkling of the piano grew louder, signaling the beginning of the show. Heavy curtains moved apart on the stage, and the comedian of the evening stepped forward to loud hoots and catcalls.

The Birdcage was not an easy audience to play, and many of the higher-caliber acts passed it up entirely in favor of the more respectable Scheffelin Hall. Sometimes a patron here even got a little crazy with a six-shooter and started shooting up the place, attested to by dozens of holes in the walls and even a few in the stage itself.

But this entertainer was funny and soon had the rambunctious crowd eating out of his hand, though their behavior was still unruly and their appreciation shown in unorthodox ways. Lily watched happily as the sheriff laughed and hollered right along with the rest of them. When he was like this she enjoyed being with him, and she looked forward with anticipation to the night ahead.

The stand-up routine was followed by a colorful and bawdy can-can dance that really livened up things in the primarily male audience. Men stomped their feet and applauded loudly, eager for more of the same. The girls on the stage made their way down the steps, and stirred up the crowd by sidling up to some of the men, sitting on their empty laps, enticing them to get up and dance with them. More and more joined in until almost everyone was making some effort to dance, though some were untaught and their movements resembled mauling more than dancing.

"C'mon, Lil! You haven't danced with me in a long time."

"That's cause you ain't asked me in a long time," she laughed.

They were both smiling and out of breath when the music stopped. "That was sure fun!" she exclaimed, eyes shining. "Can we go again?"

"In a few minutes. I need another drink first." Lily would have slowed his drinking, knowing that the times when he was fun and carefree, as now, were usually followed by periods when he would be mean and ugly with too much drinking. Finally, if he kept drinking, he would fall into a stupor. She desperately wanted to find a way to prolong the early, pleasant part of the evening, and sometimes had Jake water his drinks so that his good mood lasted a little longer. But tonight, she had forgotten to mention it.

Another alternative would be to keep him dancing, but she was not usually successful in that. If he ever started gambling, she might as well go on home alone, especially if it was a big game and he was winning, even just a little. Faro was one of his consuming passions, though she failed to understand the hold that silly game of chance had on him.

The entrance of the sheriff's man Wally, bruised and battered and complaining loudly, abruptly put an end to whatever plans she might have had for the evening.

"What are you doing back here, Wally?" the sheriff asked in a deceptively calm voice. "You were sent out to do a job for me."

164

"Yeah, I know boss, but . . ."

"I can see you've done a right fine job of botching it up. Should have known better! I knew I should have gone myself. Bungling idiots! Where's Cactus and Lucas? Never mind, we can't talk here. Come outside."

Turning to Lily, he made the briefest of apologies before turning to grab the sullen Wally by the arm. He hauled him out of the place without another word to anyone.

Chapter Eleven

Laramie awoke, but lay with his eyes shut, thinking. He could still see the hurt in Sadie's eyes that she'd tried so hard to cover with her anger. Why had he let things get so out of hand? He was the one with experience, the one who should have put a stop to the lovemaking and left her with her innocence intact. He'd never done anything like that before. The women he'd had in his life had all known what they were getting into, until now.

But she'd seemed so willing and had even been contented afterward, at least until he'd been dumb enough to say he was sorry. That had been a lie, anyway. Nothing had ever been so wonderful, so right, in his whole life, as the love they'd shared and he'd tried to put it behind him, pretend it never happened, with an apology. No wonder she was hardly speaking to him. He was ten kinds of a fool. If there was still a God in Heaven, maybe He'd find a way to make it up to her and make everything right again . . . if the sheriff's men didn't get them first!

Why had the sheriff sent his bullies after him instead of simply arresting him while he was in Tombstone? Probably because he knew he didn't have enough evidence to try Laramie for Jeff's murder. It had only been talk, its sole purpose to get him out of town.

166

Potts could have locked him up for several days, but then he would have had to let him go. So, it had been much easier for the sheriff just to run his enemy out of town and send his hired killers after him.

Laramie chuckled. Sheriff Potts could have chosen better. The men he'd sent had been easily routed by a woman and a man with the use of only one arm! But he had to admit, Sadie Moran had been something . . . definitely someone you'd want on your side in a squabble!

He envisioned the scene between Wally and the sheriff when that man limped back into town to tell his boss how they'd failed. Potts would be livid. Unquestionably, he would decide to handle Laramie himself and would set off after him without further delay. The sheriff knew about Pete's cabin and that Laramie used it on occasion. It would be dangerous to take Sadie and go back there. But they could not stay much longer in the cave, even though he admitted to himself with a smile, it had not been an unpleasant time in spite of his reservations about getting close to her.

With particular relish he remembered the previous night, when he'd tricked her into sharing his quilt. She had felt so damned good snuggled in his arms as she slept. And that didn't begin to compare with the satisfying lovemaking that had followed. But this morning he would join her in pretending it hadn't happened, for he was sure she would be determined to see that it never happened again.

They had both been swept up in the passion, but no words of love had been spoken. Someone like Sadie Moran could never love the likes of him. And even if she could, what did he have to offer her? A life on the run, a meager existence — no permanent home or family. He had nothing, nothing except his overwhelming need for revenge.

167

"Sadie," he said.

She whirled around from where she'd been standing staring out at the snow.

"Yes, Laramie?"

He started to say something, but the only thing that came to mind was another apology. She was looking up at him and he had to say something, so he muttered, "We have to leave here. There's no more firewood or food, and the sheriff will be sure to look here first thing. He's a bit smarter than his hired guns."

She nodded her head, agreeing, but said nothing, waiting for him to continue.

"We can't go back to the shack. He knows about it, too." She watched him intently while he considered the possibilities.

"Going back to Tombstone is out of the question, at least for now. We need a place that is secluded, known to very few people, but where we can find shelter and food."

"Sounds like a travel advertisement for a first-class hotel." She smiled, suddenly longing to chase the somber look from his face.

"Yeah!" he laughed, glad she seemed ready to put the past behind them, at least for now. "That's the idea, Miss Moran. Any suggestions?"

"Well, there is one elegant, discreet hotel in downtown St. Louis. It has the most wonderful restaurant, too. European cuisine." Her eyes were dreamy and her lips curved into a wide smile. "But I don't suppose you've brought your best suit with you, have you, Laramie?"

Although he looked wonderfully masculine in his buckskins, which hugged his muscular legs, and the snowy white shirt that set off his swarthy skin to such advantage, she couldn't imagine anyone with sense turning him away. Even the new growth of whiskers

168

stubbling his face only added to the aura of male mystery that clung to him. She was finding it very difficult to hold onto her anger and her promise to herself that she wouldn't get in any deeper.

There was something boyishly vulnerable and appealing about the way he was grinning at her now, and it wasn't helping her feelings any. She loved it when he let this other side of himself slip out and reveal itself, even for the briefest moment. It convinced her there was another aspect of his personality, one he kept carefully concealed, but one she was more and more anxious to uncover. Something told her it would prove to be worth her while.

Even as she thought along these lines, the controlled mask slid over his features and hooded his blue, blue eyes. Easily he made the transition back to tough and dangerous outlaw, a man in control of his own destiny, and hers as well.

"I know a place that's not too far from here. Let's go."

Doubt flickered in Sadie's eyes before she bent to gather up the quilt and the few other items they might need. He strode out the door of the cave and soon had the horses saddled and ready. They rode off together without exchanging another word, the world around them a wonderland of white.

Down the trail from them, Indian Joe had just discovered the clearing where a deadly struggle had taken place. He looked carefully at the signs, his black eyes missing nothing. He could see that Laramie and his woman had fought their attackers together. But one of them had been hurt. The blood on the tree and in the snow around it could have belonged to either one of them. He was not sure.

There had been three men: heavy footprints showed that one had gotten away in a hurry, leaving his horse behind. Two men, one of whom could still be alive, had apparently left on one horse. He suspected correctly that Laramie and the woman had taken the other two horses. So it must be they no longer had the wagon. He would see if he could find Laramie's horse later.

He followed the two sets of hoofprints to the mouth of the cave. Sharp eyes and the finely honed tracking instincts of an Indian filled in for him what had happened here. One had been wounded and cared for by the other. Their firewood and food gone, they had moved on. And they hadn't been gone long: the fire was still warm and their tracks fresh. He mounted and followed their trail farther back into the mountains. If they stopped for the night, he would catch up with them then.

The deserted mine shack looked, if anything, worse than the cabin where he'd first taken her, Sadie thought. Its weathered, blackened boards leaned against the mountain, as if without that support it might come crashing down. The door hung open, and the one hinge that held it in place creaked loudly in the snowy silence.

It looked cold and inhospitable and made Sadie wish for the cozy cave where they'd spent the last few days. But at least it would be a sheltered place to escape the new storm that had been threatening for the last couple of hours. Sadie watched the dark storm-clouds sweeping down on them and felt the new assault of the howling, frigid winds when the storm struck with all its wintry fury.

"I'll take care of the horses. You get on inside,

170

quick! Storm's upon us!"

Sadie could hardly hear him for the roaring of the wind, but she jumped from her horse, threw the reins to him, and ran for the shack, which was beginning to look a lot better to her by the minute!

Inside, though, it was little better than it had seemed from the outside. A lumpy, narrow bed with two flattened pillows filled one corner. A sink, a small wooden table, two chair, and a couple of crates made up the cooking area.

The most welcome sight in the place was a big stack of firewood and a smoke-blackened potbellied stove.

When Laramie entered, stomping snow off his boots and yanking the door into place with a bang and an angry curse, she had rubbed some of the feeling back into her fingers and was piling wood and kindling into the stove.

"Here, let me help." In no time he had a very welcome fire crackling in the stove, and they stood close together, warming their hands over it, soaking up the pleasant warmth.

The glow from the fire warmed the room, making it look a little less unappealing. Sadie discovered some dried foods, flour, and salt in one of the crates and happily set about cooking their dinner. Beans and drop biscuits cooked on top of the red-hot stove had never tasted so good.

"Better than berries, huh?" she asked, glad to see the hard look had gone from his eyes again.

"Sure enough," he answered. "You're a pretty good cook."

"Really? As good as Mrs. Morrell? or maybe even Rachel?" she demanded, holding more biscuits just out of his reach.

"Better!"

She laughed and handed him two more of the big,

flat biscuits.

"You're a smarter man than I gave you credit for, Laramie."

"Thank you, Miss Moran. You're not so bad yourself."

"Why, that's just about the nicest thing you've ever said to me, Laramie. Watch yourself — you're getting soft, outlaw."

"Never!"

"Oh no? You are actually smiling, Laramie. See?" Her fingers touched his upturned lips.

"It's just an act, Miss Moran — another trick to get you under my quilt."

"So! You admit that was a trick?" She snatched her fingers away.

"It was all for your own good," he teased.

He was still smiling, and she found herself wishing her fingers were back on his lips, or that her lips were there instead. She had an almost overwhelming urge to fall into his arms and kiss those lips until he cried out for mercy. How she loved his eyes when they were warm and happy as they were now, such a soft, deep blue that she feared getting lost in them forever. She knew in that moment she would go to great lengths to keep him as he was now, smiling, relaxed, and happy.

"Sadie . . ." he started to say something, but his voice trailed off, his eyes never leaving hers.

"Laramie . . ." she responded, wishing she were brave enough to cross the distance that separated them, but knowing much more than a matter of inches or feet kept them apart. They were separated by what they were, by where they came from, and even by where they planned to go from here.

"I . . . I . . . think I'll just put these things away. Have you had enough?" she asked.

Enough! Would he ever have enough of her? What

in God's name was happening to him? What kind of spell was she weaving over him?

"Yes," he said slowly. "I'm finished."

He watched her move around, her skirt falling over slender hips, whispering around trim ankles and that incredible bronzed red of her hair that made him want to sink his hands into it, have it spill over him. . . .

Angrily, he turned away, his movement so quick and violent it sent a blinding pain searing through his shoulder and he moaned. Instantly it seemed, Sadie was standing behind him, her hand on his arm stroking softly, her voice gentle and husky with concern, asking, "Laramie? What is it? Does your wound trouble you still? Here, let me see."

"No!" He moved away from her, unable to bear either her touch or her concern. Realizing he was being unkind and unreasonable once again, he apologized. "I'm sorry, Sadie. I know I seem to growl at you all the time. But it's nothing." Still, he didn't dare turn to look at her or allow her to come any closer. "I'll check on the horses. Sounds like that storm is about to become a blizzard." Before she had a chance to reply, he had slammed his way out the door.

Sadie stood looking after him for long minutes, her face quizzical and concerned. She would never understand this man. But the room had become so empty, so lonely after he'd left her. She turned her attention to other matters, not wanting to think about him anymore. They would need to sleep soon, and the accommodations were not of the best.

She looked at the single, lumpy bed. It was big enough for two, but only barely. "And it's definitely not big enough for you and me, Laramie," she said with a smile, suddenly understanding what had troubled him earlier.

With the insight of a woman, she saw clearly that he

was a man bothered by rampant desire and perhaps other feelings that he didn't understand as well as he did the needs of his body. Was he starting to feel something for her, then? Maybe she would just have to find out. He probably had felt obligated to apologize for making love to her. She might just show him there was nothing to be sorry for.

Sadie shook out the covers that covered the small bed, replaced them, and spread the quilt over them, plumping up both pillows at the head of the bed. She turned back the covers invitingly, then put out the lantern. The only light was the cozy glow from the stove, the only sound the crackling of the kindling.

She peeled off her travel-worn clothes and pulled one of his extra shirts over her head. Then she climbed under the quilt and slid as far as she could against the wall, leaving barely enough room for Laramie. There was no place else for him to sleep, she assured herself as she looked around the spartan room. Unless he chose to sleep sitting up in that hard, wooden chair! She couldn't wait to see his face when he saw what she'd arranged.

But by the time he came back in, covered with snow and shivering, chilled to the bone she was sleeping contentedly, her slender arms and legs stretched out across the whole bed. He frowned, then stood staring at her for long minutes while melting snow puddled around his feet.

God! Why did she have to be so damned beautiful? Why couldn't he have kidnapped some homely little urchin? Sadie Moran was a complication he could easily do without, he told himself. But could he really? She was starting to get under his skin in the strangest ways, ways he couldn't begin to fathom. And the more he felt himself reacting to her, the angrier it made him.

Anger had become his weapon, his refuge, the only

174

way he could hide from her, the only way he might be safe from her. So he pulled it out now and fired it up, to keep himself from running his hands over those enticing curves, to keep his hands out of the red silk of her hair, to keep his lips off hers, to keep from losing himself in her.

"Excuse me, Miss Moran. But do you think you could spare at least one pillow?" he growled as he snatched a pillow from beneath her arm.

Sadie's eyes flew open and widened as she watched him stomp across to the chair and throw the pillow down onto it. He ripped off his sodden coat and dumped it on the floor. Sitting down on top of the pillow he'd thrown in the chair, he yanked his boots off and left them where they fell. Miraculously, his shirt and pants had stayed dry, but he pulled off the belt with the nickel-plated buckle and dropped it on the heap of clothing beside the chair.

Sadie was intrigued and found herself wishing he would take off the shirt so she could see the mat of dark hair that she knew covered his chest, that he would drop his buckskin trousers so she could see . . .

Good grief, Sadie Moran! What is wrong with you? A tension of a sexual nature had been building right along with the anger between the two of them, but neither wanted to admit it, and they fought desperately against doing anything about it. If anything, they countered it with their anger whenever possible.

The question was, what was wrong with that goldarned man? Here she'd made him a nice, cozy place on the bed and he'd come back in fighting mad, had even snatched one of the pillows away from her and was apparently planning to sleep sitting up in the chair.

"Here, Laramie! Why don't you have both pillows?" She hurled the second pillow at him, accidentally hitting him in the face.

175

"Now I have both pillows," he said quietly, a bit too patiently, holding the second pillow in his lap.

The gleam in his eyes should have warned her.

He sent the pillow sailing back across the room. It hit her with a decided whack. Scrambling to her knees, she said through clenched teeth, "I believe this is *your* pillow, Laramie!" Sadie threw the flimsy pillow as hard as she could, but in the meantime, he had sent the other one hurtling her way. It hit so hard, it caught her off balance, and she fell back on her bottom. Quickly, she recovered the pillow and resumed her previous stance on her knees.

Calculating, she waited, watching him. When he threw the pillow he held, she ducked neatly and picked it up. "Now I have both pillows," she mocked him, her voice low and threatening, but a smile in her eyes.

"So you do." He had risen to his feet and took a step in her direction. "So you do."

"Laramie," she warned, brandishing the pillows, one on either side of her.

His eyes had strayed to her heaving bosom, thinly covered by his shirt. He moved closer.

"Laramie."

"Yes, Miss Moran? Was there something you wanted to say to me?" He was smiling widely now, but he looked no less dangerous.

Sadie sidled away, backing up against the wall behind the bed.

"Stay away from me."

"Why? It seems you have the advantage here. You have all the ammunition, the only weapons in this battle." He moved closer and was so near she could almost reach out and touch him.

With a crafty smile, she recovered. "So I do," she said. "So I do."

She swung one of the pillows at his head, and it

176

came apart with a flurry of feathers that drifted down over him. With a swift movement he intercepted her wrist and took what was left of the pillow out of her grasp. He tossed it back at her and she, too, was covered with the floating, tickling feathers.

Not giving up, she drew back and flung the remaining pillow at him. It sailed by him ineffectually and fell with a thump on the floor.

He paid it no attention. His eyes were riveted on her, watching the path of the feathers as they fluttered down, landing in the most godawful places. One trembled on a pert breast, moving with her every breath, and one landed on a smooth, trim thigh that was bent back underneath her. One tried to perch on her upturned nose, but she blew it away impatiently.

"You don't look so good yourself," she countered, misinterpreting his expression. *But he did, God help her, he did!* He looked wonderful!

Feathers dusted his dark hair and more than one had landed on his wide, muscular shoulders. A few hardy ones clung to the tight cloth that encased his tapering hips and long legs. Most of them had fallen to his feet and covered them in a fine, white layer.

"Duck feet!" she giggled helplessly, pointing.

"Insults don't become you, Miss Moran. But since you have chosen to play that game," he said, stomping his feet in a flurry of feathers, "I must say that plucked, you would make a nice, plump goose for Sunday dinner!"

"Plump, indeed! At least, I'm not some stringy, tough old bird that no one could get a tooth into!" She had pulled herself up straighter and glared at him, daring him to better her in the war of words.

At almost the same moment, they both seemed to realize what a comical, ludicrous sight they made, slinging pillows and then insults at each other, and covered with feathers. One of them started to chuckle. Then the other joined in. Soon they were shaking uncontrollably with laughter.

Tears streamed from Sadie's eyes and Laramie clutched his aching stomach. Doubled up, she rolled off the bed into a downy blanket of white feathers that covered the floor. When he reached to help her up they were taken with spasms of unrestrained glee once more, and they rolled on the floor until their laughter was spent.

When it was over, they found to their mutual dismay that they lay in each other's arms, as naturally as if they'd been born there. A quiet settled over the room He reached to brush a feather off the tip of her nose. She remembered that other time, when he'd first brought her to that other cabin and he'd gently brushed a smudge of flour off her nose. She had been afraid of him then, hadn't known him at all. But now . . . now did she really know him any better? Most of the time, she did not fear him, but there were still times when that guarded, hooded look came over him and she was careful to keep her distance.

But now . . . those vivid blue eyes had a vulnerable, warm glow that knotted her stomach, made her want to stroke his cheek, run her fingers through his thick, black hair. Alarmed, she felt herself sinking under his spell. The touch of his big, but now strangely gentle, hands on her arm and then her waist turned her limbs into soft butter. She was incapable of moving.

In response to the soft, seeking look on her face, his hand on her waist began a gentle assault, sliding up and down ever so lightly.

Laramie was finding himself equally spellbound and unable to move, or to stop what he was doing. "Do it, Sadie," he said, his voice husky. "I can see you want to touch me, too."

178

Tentatively, her hand moved in answer to his voice. Lightly, her fingers played down the sharp planes of his high cheekbones and over the taut skin of his neck. Eagerly, they slid up into his hair and buried themselves there.

With a muttered curse and a groan, he lowered his head and his lips covered hers. The kiss was soft and sought a response from her. When her fingers tightened on the back of his neck, pulling him closer, his arm swept around her, molding her body tightly against him. His lips plundered, taking what she offered so willingly. His kiss was an exploring, a questioning at first, but with her response it deepened and intensified until both of them breathlessly sought to come up for air.

Once again, their eyes met and held, delving into mysteries of the heart, making promises they had no assurance they could keep. Something blossomed between them there on the hard, rough, feather-covered floor of that cabin. And it was more, much deeper, than the building physical desire that buffeted them. It was scary and frightening and more wonderful than anything they'd ever known.

"You could have left me there, in the cavern, when I was wounded. Why didn't you?" he asked, wanting to know, needing to know.

Sadie thought about it. Why hadn't she? "I couldn't leave anyone to die, Laramie."

"I know that. No, I mean later. After you knew I would be all right. That I could probably make it out on my own. Why didn't you go, then?"

"Let's just say I had an investment in you by then." She smiled.

He smiled back, but he wasn't going to let her off that easy. "Tell me," he commanded.

"All right, if you must know. There's something

about you when you're asleep. You looked like a little boy who was in trouble, and I couldn't leave you." She hoped that would satisfy him, for his questions were making her look into herself in a way she would prefer to avoid.

He grinned. He was beginning to understand that she was trying desperately to hide her feelings for him from herself. "Admit it, Sadie Moran. You care for me just a little." His lips teased her, moving across hers briefly, before he backed off to look into her eyes again.

"Why would I care for a renegade outlaw like you?" she bantered, trying to keep from having to answer his question, to herself as well as to him.

"I swear, I really don't know," he said softly.

"I had your bed all ready."

"What? You mean you . . ."

"You didn't think I planned to keep that whole bed to myself, now, did you, Laramie?"

"You sure looked awful comfortable spread-eagled across it when I came in."

"You stayed out too long."

"I know. I'm here now."

"Yup."

"And there's the bed and what's left of the pillows."

"Yup."

He looked into her eyes for a long time, seeking the answer her heart willingly gave.

"Take me to bed, Laramie."

"Always willing to oblige a lady."

He kissed her in a leisurely way, his hands lingering on her waist, then stroking tenderly upward until his thumbs grazed the sides of her breasts, savoring the rediscovery of tempting curves and hidden warmth and softness. She matched his pace, in awe of his potent strength. When he pulled away and stood to take off

180

the rest of his clothes, she watched. His long, lean frame was as familiar to her as an old friend, but always new.

The demands of their bodies became more insistent when he joined her, though, and his arms tightened around her as though he feared someone would snatch her away. Still, his passion was tempered by a tenderness that spoke more loudly than words of his feelings for her.

Her hands played over the hot, smooth flesh on his arms, his shoulders, then lingered on his chest, where she felt his thundering heartbeat.

"I have to have you now, my love."

Sadie opened herself to him lovingly, gladly, as anxious as he to cross the last barrier that separated them, wanting him, needing him, and hungrily accepting all he had to offer her. She could not seem to get enough, and yet when it was over and they lay spent in each other's arms, she was more completely satisfied than she'd ever been in her life. His arms did not leave her, nor did either of them stir.

No words were necessary. Side by side they slept.

During the pillow fight earlier, Indian Joe had stood outside the single window of the cabin, looking in. He had watched the crazy behavior between the cowboy and the lady, shaking his head in disbelief. He did not understand what was going on between them. What he did understand, however, was that his presence was not needed there, nor would it likely be welcome. "They okay," he said to himself, as he trudged away through the falling snow. "They no need me tonight. I go find Shorty."

Chapter Twelve

"Good evening, Rachel. May I join you?" The warm, masculine voice was a welcome interruption of her troubled thoughts and Rachel Foster smiled cordially at Jonathan Lee, motioning for him to join her where she sat alone on her front porch.

The evening air was chilly, but a shawl wrapped snugly about her shoulders kept Rachel comfortable. She loved sitting outside and watching the sun sink below the distant mountains. But tonight she'd gotten little pleasure from the spectacle, so worried was she about Laramie and Sadie. Had Indian Joe been able to reach them in time to help? Where were they now?

Sensing her distress and its cause, Jonathan patted her hand reassuringly. "I'm sure they're safe," he said. "Laramie seemed the type who could take care of himself."

She smiled. "He is that, all right!"

"Who was the woman with him? I don't remember seeing him with anyone at the dance."

As much as she was coming to like Jonathan Lee and even to trust him, Rachel wouldn't jeopardize Laramie by revealing Sadie's identity.

"No, she wasn't feeling well that night. She's just a

friend from back East." She hoped desperately he would let it go at that, not liking the feeling of lying to him, but unable to tell him the truth without breaking Laramie's confidence in her. She breathed easier when he seemed content and changed the subject.

"Where are the boys?"

"Timmy is asleep, and Christopher's still out back tending to Gopher. That's his new horse and his very special friend."

"Every boy needs one of those, a special friend." His voice was deep but soft, and when their eyes met, she realized with a jolt that his words had a double meaning.

"I'd like to be your friend, Rachel, if you'll let me, yours and the boys'," he continued.

Her heart sank. She wanted that very much, too. There had been no one but Nate since Jeff's death, and he'd seemed so far away most of the time. She had been lonely—she'd never understood just how much until this moment—with this handsome man's offer of friendship. But would it be disloyal to the memory of her husband to reach out to Jonathan? Deep in her heart, she knew Jeff would be pleased.

"Jeffrey would have liked you," she said in answer. "And Christopher has talked of nothing else since he bumped into you and brought you back here. Yes, Jonathan, I think we can be friends." Her decision made, she was surprised at how good, how relaxed and happy she felt.

"He's a fine boy, Rachel." Jonathan's heart pounded in gladness and relief. He'd been afraid she wouldn't want anything to do with him, and he admitted to himself how important it was to him that she welcome his presence, his friendship. He'd never known a woman so beautiful both outside and inside. She was a fine woman, a good mother, and he knew without really knowing that she'd been a loving, devoted wife to her dead husband. The brief stab of pain he felt at that thought shook him.

"Have you been alone long?"

"Over a year. And you, Jonathan. Are you married?"

"No!" he exclaimed, anxious to reassure her there was no one in his life. "But I'd very much like to be some day, with the right woman. And I'd love to have fine sons like Timothy and Christopher."

She blushed prettily, not quite knowing how to answer his very personal remark.

He found that he couldn't seem to take his eyes off her. And he wanted nothing so much as to put his arms around her and kiss her until she was breathless. He was taken aback by the notion that he wanted a lot more from Rachel Foster than mere friendship. But she was a lady, a widow, and he knew he had to move slowly, one small step at a time. Still, he vowed he would make her his wife and he wouldn't leave Tombstone until he did!

She needed someone. She was so vulnerable and alone, and her boys needed a father. He had to admit Christopher had already charmed the socks right off him, and Timothy was a sweet, handsome child, too.

Though he tried to hide these tumbling, troublesome emotions, Rachel was very perceptive. She sensed the direction his thoughts had taken. She was unaccountably glad to see Christopher come charging around the corner of the house at a dead run, as usual.

"Hey, Mom! Mr. Lee!" He grinned and halted, out of breath, at the bottom of the porch stairs.

"Hi, Christopher. How's Gopher?" Jonathan

asked.

"How'd you know . . . oh, Mama told you, didn't she? Gopher's great! He's just great! Mama, you should have seen him just now. He came when I whistled. And he found the carrot I had in my pocket. He's the most wonderful horse in the whole world! Thanks, Mama!" He launched himself at her and threw his small arms around her neck.

"You know you're very welcome, Chris. A boy needs a horse on his ninth birthday. And you've certainly shown you know how to care for Gopher and how to train him, too!"

"I will always take care of him, Mama. And I'll learn him good, too, you'll see!"

"*Teach* him, Christopher, not *learn* him."

"Sure, Mama, I'll *teach* him, too!"

His mother laughed softly and set him back on his feet. "Why don't you run on in to bed now, son?"

"Sure, Mama. Goodnight. Goodnight, Mr. Lee."

"Goodnight, Christopher. Maybe you and I could ride together sometime?"

"I'd like that. Could I, Mama? Could I?"

"Of course you can. Now be sure and wash up before you get into bed. I'll see you in the morning, sweetheart."

The boy was gone in a flurry of scuffling feet and slamming doors. A quietness settled over the couple on the porch.

"He's terrific," Jonathan said after a long silence.

"Yes, he is," she answered. "He's a good boy."

"You're pretty terrific yourself." He couldn't believe he'd said that! What was wrong with him, anyway? He was acting like a schoolboy!

"Thank you."

She hadn't laughed at him or moved away, or asked him to leave! His heart soared. He felt warm

185

and happy, and he was utterly amazed at himself. He'd never felt or acted this way with a woman before. He'd always had a way with them and had flirted and enjoyed their company, but this was something else.

"I think I'd better go." He stood.

"Would you . . . would you like to have lunch with the boys and me tomorrow? It's Sunday and we usually have something special. And we do like to have company, all of us." She was chattering like a magpie, she thought, and reminded herself that she hadn't intended to encourage him, to invite him back. But the words had spilled out before she could stop them. Nevertheless, she was glad when he accepted, promising to be there promptly at noon.

"Goodnight, Rachel," he said, backing down the walk.

"Goodnight, Jonathan. See you tomorrow."

It sounded almost like the way she'd said goodnight to Christopher. Had he imagined the caress in her voice? For a brief, startling moment he imagined himself in her bed, his body wrapped around hers. *You're really dreaming now,* he admonished himself as he turned and nearly fled down the walk.

He barely avoided a collision with a bulky figure weaving down the walk. At first he assumed the man was drunk, not an uncommon sight in Tombstone, but closer observation revealed the man was only dead tired, possibly hurt.

"Can I help you? Jonathan reached out to put a hand on the man's arm, but he angrily jerked away.

"Leave me alone!" he snapped and stomped on down the street in the direction of town. "I have to see the sheriff," he muttered to himself.

Jonathan couldn't have said why he followed the man, perhaps it was the mention of the sheriff that intrigued him. But he was soon standing in the shadows outside the Bird Cage Saloon, watching while the man went inside. He waited, hoping the man would reappear.

Long minutes dragged by. The double doors swung open and two men came out. Jonathan tried to maneuver closer, but he was able to hear only snatches of their furtive conversation. He was sure they were discussing Nate Laramie and the woman who had ridden out of town with him. No mention was made, as far as he could tell, of Indian Joe. Had Laramie's friend not reached them in time to help?

The sheriff's voice rang out sharply as the two parted to go their separate ways. "We'll ride out at dawn. Don't be late, Wallace."

"Sure thing, sheriff. This time we'll get him, sure!" The second man's voice was thin and frightened, though he was obviously making an attempt to sound sure of himself.

"Shut up!" the sheriff cautioned. "Now, get on home and rest up. Be ready to ride hard!"

"Yes, sir!" The bigger man shuffled off down the street, leaving the sheriff standing alone, the garish light from the Bird Cage Saloon making his face look more evil and cold than it did ordinarily, Jonathan thought, as he watched from the shadows. He could see the resolve in the man's hate-hardened eyes, black eyes that glittered with a deadly purpose.

Jonathan didn't know what had happened to Nate Laramie and the woman, or to Indian Joe, who'd been sent by Rachel to help them. Nor did he know what the sheriff was plotting for sure, but he knew enough. He would follow the sheriff and Wallace when they left town the next day and do what he could to help Laramie and his mysterious female companion when the inevitable showdown occurred.

Deciding it would be best not to worry Rachel Foster further by this new knowledge or his own plans, Jonathan hurried back to his hotel room to prepare for the next day's adventure.

Agitation showing in his wrinkled face and in every line of his portly body, Lucien Moran strode up and down the wooden walk that lined Allen Street, looking for Sheriff Potts.

He'd arrived in Benson on the late stage and had hired a horse for the ride south into Tombstone. Unaccustomed to riding horseback and already worn out from the hard travel of the stagecoach, he was frustrated and irate and in no mood to search the two-bit town for its two-bit sheriff!

Moran told himself he should have known better than to get involved in a scheme that included the likes of Tombstone's leading citizen and sheriff! The man's beady black eyes should have been warning enough. But he had been desperate, and felt there was no other way to appease his creditors and save his home and his belongings, so he'd gone along. Now he was in too deep.

He had to have the sheriff's help to get his daughter back. Nothing could happen to Sadie — he wouldn't let it! He would do anything to get her home safely.

Where was that damned sheriff, anyhow? He had followed his trail from bar to bar and finally to that despicable Bird Cage Saloon. He'd never seen anything like the decadence of it. He shivered to think of his Sadie being held in a place like this Tombstone — and by men like the ones he'd seen this night!

It was nearly four A.M. and the revelry and carousing had, if anything, increased as the night progressed. Didn't these people ever sleep?

The bartender at the Bird Cage wouldn't tell him where the sheriff lived, so he decided he would wait on the steps outside the jail until daylight. Surely Potts would show up then, or someone would come along who would take him to the sheriff's house.

He sat down and leaned his fatigued and throbbing head against the jail's outer wall. Soon he was dozing, his hat pulled down over his face.

His breath puffing small clouds of vapor in the chilly air, the sheriff made his way toward his office quietly, leading his horse. It was still before dawn, but he wanted to be out of Tombstone and on his way after Laramie before anyone knew what he was about. He needed to retrieve some extra cartridges and the Colt pistol that was in his desk drawer, then he'd meet Wally on the edge of town.

He almost stumbled over the substantial body that reclined beside the stairs to the jail and his office. "What th . . . ?" he swore softly, and the bulky shape moved in reply.

Rising awkwardly to his feet and pushing his hat back into place, Moran squinted at the sheriff. They recognized each other instantly. The sheriff could not conceal his surprise and dismay at finding Moran there.

"What are you doing here?" he demanded, his voice harsh.

"I've come for my daughter."

"You've *what?*" The sheriff almost shouted, caught himself, then shoved Moran inside his office. The older man collapsed into the nearest chair.

"It's been a long trip and I'm very tired, so don't *push* me, Potts. I've come for Sadie and I'm not going back without her." Sweat beaded his upper lip and forehead, even in the icy-cold room.

The sheriff sat down behind his desk, steepled his fingers under his chin, and returned Moran's stare. "I don't know what in hell you're talking about," he said slowly.

"This!" Moran shoved a cable across the desk. "It was sent from Tombstone. Somebody has my daughter, and I want to know who. You're the law here, Potts. You'd better get her back for me."

"Now hold on, Moran. I don't know anything about this. I haven't seen your daughter. There have been no strange women in town. If there were, I'd know about it." He struggled to suppress the smirk that he knew wouldn't set well with a man so worried about his daughter.

"Well, if this cable says she's here, she's got to be around somewhere, doesn't she? I think this has something to do with the 'Silver Lining' thing. I don't know how I ever let you talk me into a shady deal like that. I want out!"

"It's too late, Moran. You're in too deep. The damage is already done. One man's dead—and another soon will be."

"You talking about Laramie? Did you know he paid me a visit in St. Louis and demanded his mine back? I refused, of course. But when he left he was very angry. Could he be the one who sent this? Do you think he has my Sadie?"

The sheriff hadn't known that Laramie knew about Moran's connection to the mine, and he was surprised to learn of his visit to Missouri.

"You didn't tell him anything, did you?"

"No! of course not. And I refused to cooperate with him in any way. That must be why he followed the stage she was on and kidnapped her. So all of

190

this is your fault, Potts."

Sheriff Potts was not pleased with the additional complication. He'd already found it difficult to deal with Nate Laramie, and now it seemed the outlaw had the upper hand again.

But not for long. There were ways of dealing with men like Laramie. And Dan Potts knew them all.

He and Wally would make quick work of Laramie and get Moran's girl back, if Laramie had such a captive. Then everyone would be happy.

"I'm going after Laramie now," he informed Moran. "He's ridden up into the Dragoons. Don't worry. I'll bring your daughter back. Just give me twenty-four hours."

"No! I'm coming along!"

"No way, Moran. You'd just slow us down."

"I've already got a horse! And I rode it all the way in from Benson," he boasted, not mentioning how sore his rear end was from that few hours' ride. "I'll stay right with you, you'll see, Potts. You can't leave me behind! Besides," he said, eyes narrowing in understanding, "I wouldn't be surprised if you couldn't use an extra gun when you catch up with this Laramie!"

The sheriff would never admit his fear of Laramie to anyone, but Moran's arguments led him to reconsider. He *could* use a little more help in a showdown—Laramie was a good shot and a tough man in a fight. And if he did have Moran's daughter, the man had good reason to want to go along.

"Okay." He opened the middle drawer of his desk and scooped up extra ammunition and his ivory-handled Colt .44. "Let's go."

The two men waited on the edge of town for almost a half hour. There was no sign of Wallace. "Never could trust that man," the sheriff muttered.

"Looks like it's just you and me, Moran."

"I'll hold up my end," the Easterner promised, patting his firearm and urging his mount into a slow lope, the best he could do, determined to keep pace with the sheriff and his big stallion.

They said little more as they headed across the prairie that sprawled up into the foothills of the mountains. The warmth of the sun as it climbed ever higher into a clear blue sky soaked through the remaining thin layer of snow, melting it until the trail was clear of its cottony blanket.

Higher and higher into the mountains they climbed, the two mismatched allies in search of a dark-skinned cowboy and a young woman with flaming hair.

Chapter Thirteen

The next morning, the outlaw and the lady each steered a path clear of the other, as wide as was possible in the tiny one-room shack. They seemed determined that their eyes not meet, that they not discuss their new intimacy and their changing relationship, that they avoid touching each other, even by accident. Unable to control his baffling emotions and the tension in the small room any longer while she was near enough to touch, and knowing there was no way they could leave the shack for a while, Laramie stomped outside. At least he wouldn't have to be so damned close to her!

He puttered around, doing everything he could for the horses. He got them fresh hay and fodder, cleaned the stalls, even brushed down their coats until they shone. It didn't take nearly long enough.

The sun was trying to peek out and the day promised to be a beautiful one, even though the air was still frosty. Rifle in hand, he tromped about in the snow. After a while, he spied a rabbit and fired, hitting it cleanly. They would have fresh meat for dinner tonight! He skinned and cleaned it, thinking all the while, unable to keep his mind off Sadie, unable to forget soft, golden skin and open

193

arms. "Damn!" he cursed, losing the battle.

Taking the rabbit inside, he said gruffly, "Sadie, get your coat on and come outside. I have an idea."

As anxious as he had been to get out of the four confining walls and giving in to her unreasonable desire to be near him, Sadie snatched her coat from a hook, slid her arms into it, and buttoned it up quickly. In no time she had her boots on and was happily following him out the door. Whatever he had in mind would be better than sitting around inside, baffled by his sudden change of mood.

"It's time you learned to shoot," he announced.

"Really? And you're sure you're up to the challenge?" She was smiling, thrilled to see that he was interested enough in her to try to teach her to shoot.

"Of course. You should be able to defend herself without having to resort to hitting someone over the head. Not everyone would stand still for that!" Now he was smiling, too.

"You admitted yourself that it worked pretty well, Laramie." He did not answer, and she went on, "But I would definitely like to learn to shoot. So, let's go!"

"Now, this is the way you hold a firearm," he said, demonstrating with the rifle braced against his strong shoulder. He sighted down the long barrel and squeezed the trigger. A deafening roar made Sadie's ears ring, and she saw a can strategically placed, spin off to the snow-covered ground.

"Pretty impressive, but you *have* had a lot of practice, Laramie."

"Think you can do as well, tenderfoot?" he challenged.

194

"With enough practice, I'm sure I can do even better." She thought of all the abilities of Rachel Foster and of how much he seemed to admire the widow. She made up her mind she would show him what Sadie Moran was made of today.

He handed her the firearm and stood back, arms crossed, to watch. Her first efforts were, as expected, clumsy and ineffectual. How could such a dainty shoulder brace a heavy gun and bear the brunt of its powerful kick? He would have to help her. He moved up behind her.

As he put his arms around her to steady her arms and the gun, he realized his first, colossal mistake of the morning. He hadn't thought about having to be this close to Sadie Moran to give her shooting lessons. The feel of her body snug up against his was almost more than he could stand. He cursed vividly.

"That's the way to hold it. Now you try it," he ordered gruffly, backing away.

Closing her eyes, Sadie pulled the trigger and staggered backward, bumping into the hard wall of his chest, the only thing that kept her from crashing to the ground. His hands still on her arms, they both looked to see where her shot had landed, since the can still sat untouched on the post where he'd put it. A dull splash drew their attention to the well, where the bucket was no longer attached to a rope now dangling uselessly in the air.

"Nice shot, Miss Moran. But what has my well ever done to you?" His voice was shaking with barely restrained mirth.

Sadie tried to hold on to the frown that had been her first reaction, but a dimple scored the side of her mouth, and soon her warm brown eyes

195

were sparkling and she was laughing along with him. "I told you I might have to practice a little."

"A little!" he hooted. "My dear Miss Moran, you could practice from now until the turn of the century and you still wouldn't be able to hit the broad side of that barn at twenty paces!" His words mocked her, but his eyes didn't. There she saw humor and affection, or did she only imagine it? "And please be sure and warn me," he went on, "so I can hide all my valuables before you make another attempt."

She whirled and looked at him pointedly, her eyes moving below his waist. "Then I suggest you depart for the cabin in all haste, Laramie. Or I just might start shooting again right now!"

Hands raised in surrender and a wide smile on his lips, Laramie backed toward the shack as she advanced, her small feet disappearing in the over-sized tracks his boots had left. She continued to threaten him, though she was smiling, too, until they were both inside, shaking the snow off and removing their coats and boots. She stood the rifle up in the corner and he sighed with exaggerated relief.

"Relax, Laramie. If I ever shoot you, it will be because I fully intend to."

"That's a comfort." He chuckled and turned to build up the fire. They both stood near it warming themselves and saying nothing further for the longest time. At last she strode over to the cot and climbed up in the middle of it, pulling her long legs up under her, still enjoying the warmth of the crackling fire. He pulled the straight-backed chair around and straddled it. He was as near to her as he was to the fire, and they could hardly avoid

196

looking at each other.

"I should have let you try again. No one learns to shoot with one shot," he apologized.

"Tomorrow," she promised, eager to try again.

He felt his admiration for her growing with each passing minute and hardly knew what to do about it. She was a tenderfoot from back East and should be the representation of everything he despised. Why, then, was he so drawn to her, so solicitous of her welfare, so bemused by her wit and her fetching good looks? If he didn't know better, he'd swear he'd gotten hold of some loco weed!

A companionable silence wove its way round the two of them like a silken spider's web, gently pulling them ever closer together and breeching their walls of defense.

Sadie had never felt so vulnerable, nor had she ever been so content, satisfied to sit quietly in the presence of another person. Surprisingly, she found herself beginning to trust her kidnapper and to have other feelings for him that were not so clear cut.

As he sat across from her now with the glowing light from the stove dancing across the dark planes of his rugged face, she thought she'd never seen a more handsome man. Her heart beat a tricky little rhythm when she looked at him, and it left her winded.

And, she told herself, he'd looked after her safety in both small and big ways since he'd made her his captive. First, the encounter with the snake. Then those three awful men. She shivered. He'd truly been wonderful in the clearing, coming so gallantly to her rescue. But afterward he'd been angry, and he'd made her so angry, she'd shouted right back at him. His anger had been mostly at the men and at the danger she'd thrown herself into. She could understand that now as she hadn't been able to before.

She also thought she understood Nate Laramie considerably better than he understood himself. He'd tried to present himself as a rough frontiersman, nothing more. But she had discovered an intelligent, caring man under that exterior, and she was not fooled. She wanted to know more, much more, about this man.

"Sadie?" His rich, questioning voice was the one that broke the silence.

"Yes, Laramie?"

"Cactus would have shot me if you hadn't hit him the way you did, and I never said thanks." A sheepish grin softened his features, and his blue eyes lit with the humor she found so appealing. "So thanks!"

She tried to frown but gave up the impossible effort, her lips curving upward and her own eyes dancing with pleasure. "A little late, Laramie, but your apology is accepted."

His smile was now doing funny things to her stomach, and as his eyes held hers, her heart raced, pumping blood wildly through her veins. She wanted to shout, to laugh, to cry, to sing, but most of all she wanted to throw her arms around him and pull him close, so close, and maybe never let him go.

Once again, though, he made the first move. It was not the crushing embrace she longed for. Instead, the back of his knuckles brushed her cheek in the lightest of caresses. It was a feather stroke, not an embrace at all, but her heart and body seemed not to know the difference.

"Laramie . . ." Her voice was ragged, filled with a longing, a desire so powerful it swept away every rational thought.

"Anyone ever tell you how very beautiful you are in firelight, Miss Moran?"

"No."

No one had ever told her she was beautiful at all, she realized. And she was unaccountably glad the words had been spoken first by him.

"Really? I knew people from Missouri were stubborn and hard-headed, but I never knew they were blind as well."

His hand moved to lightly stroke the tumbling chestnut curls, and he seemed awed by the feel of her silken hair beneath his touch. He sighed. "Beautiful red-gold fire. I've wanted to do this since the first day I saw you."

Sadie thought that at this moment nothing could give her more pleasure than the touch of his hand.

But she was wrong.

His hand fell to her shoulder and slid down her arm, still light, still stroking, still kindling an answering fire inside her. She placed the palm of her left hand lightly against the taut skin of his cheek, delighting in the feel of him, in awe at her response to him. His hand tightened on her arm, and he drew her toward him. She came willingly, anxious to feel more of the same sensations that now spiraled through her uncontrollably.

In one soft cry of acceptance, she put away her ladylike inhibitions, the claims of civilization, and dashed any lingering doubts that would keep her from accepting what he offered.

His lips moved across hers, first softly, like the

wings of a butterfly, but then with increasing hunger and demand. He wanted her. And she'd never wanted anything so much as to lose herself in the wonder, the mystery, the passion of his embrace. Her arms went around his neck and his encircled her in return, pulling her against him so that she felt every sinew, every straining muscle, and the constant, strong beating of his heart.

Even as Sadie gave in to the insistence of her body's commands, Laramie waged a battle with himself. He'd never experienced anything so wonderful as the feel of the soft curves of her body molding into his, or the answering desire he'd seen in her eyes before his lips claimed hers. And he'd never wanted anyone so fervently — never desired anyone so desperately. His body clamored and swelled with his need.

Harshly, he reminded himself that Sadie Moran was an innocent, a lady, gently bred and reared. She deserved so much more than a randy coupling on a cot in a mine shack!

Hands that had been exploring enticing curves and satiny skin fastened themselves lightly on her arms and very gently set her away from him. Her eyes, still smoky with passion, showed her confusion, but she said nothing.

"I'm sorry, Sadie," he said softly.

She sat back on her heels, but her eyes never left his as she studied him. "You're afraid of me, aren't you, Laramie?"

"No," he answered too quickly. But was he?

He was surely becoming uncomfortable with his aroused response every time she was near him. He cursed roundly at himself. She deserved more than a drifter, a cowboy on the wrong side of the law.

Yes, he admitted, he *was* afraid, afraid of what she was doing to him, and afraid of what he might do to her.

"I've never been afraid of anything—or anyone—in my life," he replied, but he knew that what he said was the truth only as it applied to his past.

"I've been afraid lots of times," she admitted with surprising candor. "I was afraid when you came charging out of the mountains that day and stopped the stage. And I was afraid when you spoke my name and put me up on your horse. And I was afraid of what you might do after I tried to shoot you." She stopped and smiled at him, longing to see his previous good humor return. "But I'm not afraid of you now, Nate Laramie. I don't think I'll ever be afraid of you again. I don't care what you say—or what you do. You're a good man, a gentle man, a loving man. Whatever has brought us here was not of your choosing, and I think you must have had very good reasons for what you did, for what you're doing."

"Sadie—" He wanted to tell her she was all wrong. He wanted to tell her he didn't deserve her trust. But he couldn't. Nor could he explain any of it to her. And yet he knew that when he did what he had to do, she would hate him.

"Talk to me, Laramie."

"When I was a little boy," he said, "I thought my life would always be happy and filled with people I loved. Mama and Papa were kind and wonderful, and I loved them very much, just as they loved me. We did everything together—the three of us—we fished, watched the stars at night, went to church meetings in the wagon. I never missed having friends my own age. The two of them were all the

201

friends I needed."

Sadie listened, pleased that he would share his past with her, intrigued by the picture of him as a young boy, but fearful of where the story might lead.

"One day, Mama took sick. She was gone before sunset. There was nothing we could do but sit there helplessly and watch her slip away from us." Tears shimmered in his blue eyes as he recalled the tragedy of his childhood.

"Papa was never the same after that. He'd saved some money, he said, but it would never do him any good. He wanted to send me East to school. I didn't want to go! I wanted to stay there with him, in my home, the only home I could remember. I wanted things to be the way they had been. But he wouldn't hear of it. He said he'd wasted his life and I mustn't waste mine.

"When I came back with the degree he wanted for me, he was gone, too. I never got to see him again, hold his hand one last time, tell him goodbye. And he never saw the educated son he'd sacrificed so much for."

He stopped talking, added some more wood to the fire, and poured each of them a cup of coffee, handing her a steaming mug as he continued. "For a while I couldn't seem to get my mind on anything. I drifted out West, first to Texas, then California, New Mexico, and finally Arizona, looking for something to care about. That's where I met Jeffrey Foster. He became my best friend and changed my life around. We had some good times! Even after he fell in love with Rachel and settled down to have a family, we were always close. He was the brother I never had. He was my family."

"What happened to Jeffrey?" Sadie asked quietly.

"When the silver boom first hit Tombstone, lawyers and investors flocked in. They were responsible for a new scheme every day, practically every hour. We got word a syndicate wanted to help us get our mine operational for a small percentage of the take. It was Eastern money, but the sheriff was the company's local representative, and it all seemed perfectly legal. They would provide financing for a new vertical shaft, and they claimed we'd be shipping close to two hundred tons of high grade ore per month.

"Not knowing what kind of men we were dealing with, we had to agree. We could never have gotten it out of the ground with the resources we had between us. Soon the mine was humming—there was a hoisting works and a new shaft house, and this mine office was built.

"The 'company' was more interested in profit than the welfare of the men. It was indifferent to deteriorating working conditions. Unexplained disasters began to occur. First, there was a fire in the timbers that shored up the mine, causing a cave-in. We found out it was deliberately set.

"Jeff began to suspect they were trying to get us out of the way and take over complete operation of the mine. He was taking a pack train of burros hauling bags of silver ore to Tucson where he planned to investigate. He got to Tucson all right, but he never made it back. It was called a freak accident, but I knew it was a lot more than that. Whatever Jeff found out, he paid for with has life. I've never doubted that. It's my fault Jeff's dead. I could have stopped them. I could have saved him! But I let him go. I did nothing, Sadie, and now

203

he's gone, too."

"It wasn't your fault, Laramie. None of it was your fault."

"I should have gone along. But I let him talk me into staying at the mine. My misjudgment cost my best friend his life."

"Did you ever think that if you had gone along, you'd probably be dead now, too? You did the right thing, the sensible thing, to stay here and look after things."

"No." The hard light in Laramie's eyes convinced Sadie that Jeffrey's murderers would have had their hands full had his partner been along, but she said no more.

"They tried to get to me a few times after that. But then I guess they gave up on that and decided they'd use all their power and influence to legally steal the mine. They almost got away with it. But there is a document that proves the mine still belongs to Jeffrey and me, the original deed."

Her face brightened. "Well, surely, if you can get your hands on that paper, you can reclaim your mine and settle all this? And you can clear your name and start to live a normal life again?"

"Yes," he said, frowning, his eyes clouded with new worry. "If I can get that paper, all this will be over." He stopped talking, realizing he'd said too much.

Sadie was moved by his story. She had seen him hurting as a boy, and then as a man. She wanted nothing more than to reach out to him, to stroke away the worry lines from his face, to hold him close to her. Something in his face told her he wouldn't welcome that. Her eyes filled with tears.

Laramie wanted no part of the sympathy he saw

dawning on her face and wondered why had he ever told her so much about himself.

"I'm going to see to the horses and then I'll give you another lesson, that is, if you still want one?"

She understood that he had changed the subject so suddenly to relieve the tension steadily building between them, and agreed readily.

"I'll be ready," she promised.

While he was outside, she decided to get the gun and have him show her how to load it before they went out for target practice. She knew he had some extra ammunition somewhere.

Looking around, she saw the leather pouch he always carried with him. Probably that would be where he'd keep extra shells. She opened the flap and reached inside. Instead of the cold lead of the ammunition she expected to find there, her hand fell on a crumpled piece of paper. Pulling it out so that she could get to the bottom of the pouch, she saw that it was an envelope and was postmarked St. Louis, Missouri.

Thinking it odd, and drawn by the familiar handwriting, she held it out in front of her. What was he doing with correspondence from her home town? Her fingers trembling, Sadie could not resist opening the brown envelope. A single sheet of foolscap fell out. She unfolded it and, recognizing her father's wobbly script, began to read its contents.

"Mr. Laramie," she read. "Regarding your recent inquiry about the silver mine located outside Tombstone, Arizona, I'm afraid I can be of no help to you. The papers in my possession . . ."

She got no further. The paper was rudely snatched from her fingers and Laramie stood looming over her, furious, his blue eyes icy.

"What do you mean, going through my things?" he shouted, seeing a knowledge in her eyes that hadn't been there before, along with new doubts and suspicions.

"What does it mean, Laramie? What do you have to do with my father? What does he have to do with you? That's why you kidnapped me, isn't it? To get to my father." Her eyes were cool now, accusing, completely lacking in the warmth and laughter that had filled them earlier.

"It was you, wasn't it?" she demanded. "You were there in my home the day I left for Tucson. I heard you arguing with my father." She looked up at him where he stood silhouetted in the doorway and saw again the angry stranger who'd rushed past her in the hallway that day.

Why had she never connected the two events until now? She hadn't gotten a very good look at that man, but there'd been something about him that had intrigued her, something that had aroused her compassion, pulled at her heart, even then.

"You heard me say I was catching the stage to Tucson and you followed me, didn't you?"

He didn't need to answer. She already knew the truth of what she'd spoken. It was in her eyes and in the proud, determined lift of her shoulders as she faced him.

"You'd do anything for that mine, wouldn't you?" she demanded.

Her inner struggle was clear on her face. "You wouldn't hurt my father, would you, Laramie?"

His gut twisted in pain. Her accusation was much too near the truth. What he planned to do — what he *had* to do — would indeed hurt her father.

206

Maybe not physically, but it would ruin him financially and would permanently damage his reputation.

Laramie had been coming to the slow realization that Sadie Moran cared at least a little for him, but he was buffaloed by the knowledge that struck him now with the blow of a fist while he looked into her accusing eyes. He cared for her, too!

He'd gone soft in the head to have such unacceptable feelings for his own captive. What a damned fool thing to do! How could he have let it happen to him?

"Yes!" he yelled back at her, his anger at himself manifesting itself outwardly in hostility toward her. "I've told you from the beginning that this was not a Sunday social, that I was serious about doing what had to be done. Surely you knew I didn't take you off that stage just for your good looks, as appealing as those might have been. Your father wouldn't listen to reason — or to the pleas of a desperate man that he do what was right. He knew only too well what he was doing when he practically threw me out of his home that day."

"It was my home, too," she said softly. "And he *is* my father. I won't listen to you say bad things about him, and I won't let you hurt him."

"No. I've said too much already. This business will soon be over and you'll be back home where you belong."

"And my father?"

He didn't answer.

Sadie told herself that Laramie was the one at fault here, surely not her father. She'd been mistaken to think she saw a softer, more caring and honest side of her kidnapper. He'd just been leading her on, getting her to care for him, so she wouldn't want to get away, so she would be his captive in mind as well as in body.

How easy she'd made everything for him! Well, no more. She would fight him if she had to, and she would get away from him. And she'd do it soon—before he could hurt her anymore, and before he could get to her father through her.

Laramie watched the emotions track across her beautiful face. He saw first her hurt, then her anger and determination as she made the transformation back to Lucien Moran's well-bred daughter. He could no longer trust her to stay with him, and he knew she would no longer help him. She probably regretted ever nursing him back to health.

At her first opportunity, she would run straight back to her father. He would have to watch her every moment—treat her as his captive, not an equal, much less a friend, as he had begun to do. She would always side with her father against him, even if her father was dead wrong! Why had he ever thought it might be different?

"We'll leave as soon as it's light," he said. It was time to return to Tombstone, to end this business once and for all.

But Sadie had other plans.

Chapter Fourteen

Laramie awoke to a brilliant sun and a blinding headache. He rubbed the back of his head, fingers gently probing a sizable goose egg.

"Ouch!" he roared, and was immediately sorry when the noise reverberated through his aching head. "What th' hell?"

The room was empty. Sadie was gone. His mind at first refused to accept the fact. How had she gotten the better of him? It was obvious she'd hit him with something. But how had she managed it?

He tried to remember. He'd been sitting up in the chair, determined not to sleep, determined to keep a watchful eye on his captive. Now that she knew her father was involved, there was no telling what she might do.

Then his eyes had roamed over her tempting body curled in a deep sleep under the quilt. Her steady breathing lulled him. Soon he found himself relaxing his guard, remembering. He thought of the night before, when he'd been next to her under that same quilt; he remembered the time he'd kissed her so thoroughly and she'd responded, making his heart leap. He thought of her hands moving tenderly over his wounded shoulder and

209

heard in his imagination the sound of her soft, warm laughter.

And then he must have dozed off!

He reached down for the heavy skillet that lay innocently upended beside his chair. Her weapon, no doubt. At least she hadn't decided to try shooting him again, he thought, with a wry smile. She might have missed and hit him!

No, he knew that this time, if she'd wanted him dead, she could easily have killed him.

"You should have finished the job, Sadie Moran," he said into the silence. "Because I'll come after you and I'll catch you. You will be my prisoner again." *And this time, I'll never let you go,* he thought.

The rifle still leaned against the wall where she'd propped it up yesterday after her shooting lesson. He was surprised she hadn't taken it until he reached for his holster and discovered it was empty. She'd taken his six-shooter instead!

"Damn you, Sadie!" he shouted, grabbing the rifle and his coat and charging out the door. He threw open the door to the makeshift barn where the horses had been and cursed even more colorfully. She'd not only taken his gun and taken one of the horses, but she'd turned the other one loose so he couldn't follow her easily.

"You're one crafty lady, Miss Moran. But I'll find you yet. You haven't seen the last of Nate Laramie!"

He started off down the trail on foot. Before long, the deep snow was over his boot tops and soaking into his legs and feet. He could not go far like this. He faced the fact that he might never catch her in time, might never see her again. That thought brought to his heart an unbearable agony. For a little while he had dared to harbor such an improbable hope, to dream of a life that could never be.

Sadie had left the mine shack and an unconscious Nate Laramie behind her at dawn, certain she'd done the right thing, under the circumstances. It had been almost too easy. Laramie had fallen asleep, probably because he'd trusted her too much. She winced, feeling again the jarring crunch of the skillet as it cracked against the back of his head. She'd tried not to hit him too hard, but she'd had to be sure he was out cold with the first blow, or he could have overpowered her and she would never have gotten away from him.

She had saddled one of the horses, finding it a little easier than her last experience with Nate's big, yellow horse, but still it had been a hard task. All the while, as she worked and even as she mounted up, turned the other horse loose, and started off down the narrow trail, she expected to hear "Sadie . . ." and to have him come rushing after her angrily, putting a stop to her flight. Her perverse heart had her almost wishing he had.

But the stillness of the morning was undisturbed, bringing her an astonishing torrent of unhappiness. Nate Laramie had somehow become a part of her life, almost as necessary to her as breathing. It was harder than she'd ever expected it to be, riding away from him. It was as though she'd left the best part of herself back in that shack with him. But

211

he'd left her no choice.

Her discovery that his plans for revenge included blackmailing her own father had driven her into action. She forced herself not to look back, but nudged the horse she was riding on down the trail, leaving Laramie farther and farther behind her.

She would ride back into Tombstone and prevail on Rachel Foster to allow her to stay with her until she could wire her father for money so she could return home. He'd be so glad to hear she was unharmed—and free.

Uncertainties clouded her mind. She *was* doing the right thing, wasn't she? He had been blackmailing her own father, and she had no idea what else his plans might include.

She shrugged her shoulders, trying to put troubling thoughts of the handsome, enigmatic Laramie out of her mind. It would be a relief to return to her former life and erase all thought of that brooding cowboy from her mind.

Then she recalled, without wanting to, the look of hurt on his face when he'd shared his past with her. Now she had left him as surely as everyone else he'd ever cared about. At least, for a while, she had thought he cared about her. She had even dared to hope something good and wonderful could grow between them. But she'd been such a fool.

Laramie's feet throbbed from the wet cold until they grew numb, but still he plunged ahead. He had to catch up with her before she reached Tombstone, although he couldn't have explained why that was so important to him. What could he say to her? His mouth twisted. He had never said enough to her, and yet he'd always said too much.

Sadie Moran had burrowed her way under his skin, made herself a part of his life, and thoroughly claimed his heart. With blinding, painful insight, he realized how much he'd come to love her. But now it was much too late for that. She was gone!

She had left him, fleeing into the arms of civilization, into the arms of her father, who was still, in spite of everything, his enemy.

Could he have done anything differently? What if he'd told her how he felt about her? What if he'd told her everything? It wouldn't have mattered ... her loyalty to her father was so strong, it would have outweighed any feelings she might have had for him.

Why was he running after her, then? Kidnapping her had proven to be the biggest mistake of his life. Not only had it *not* accomplished what he'd intended, but it had brought him a whole new set of problems, worse than the ones he'd had before.

He sat down on a rock, his head lowered, deep in his unpleasant thoughts, defeated.

"My friend, today you need help of Indian Joe, yes?"

Laramie's head snapped up. He hadn't heard a sound, but his Indian friend stood only a few paces from him. "How do you do that?" he demanded.

"Your people would say—much practice." The Indian smiled. "Sometimes is best to move with no sound. Live longer."

"Yes. It's good to see you, Joe. But why are you here?"

"Golden-haired woman ask me to help you."

"Rachel!"

"She say you in much trouble, but until now, I not agree. Woman with flame-colored hair maybe trouble, but not kind Laramie need help with, eh?"

"I'm not so sure about that, Joe." Laramie rubbed the lump on the back of his head.

"She much woman, no?" Joe asked, still grinning.

"Yes, she's very much woman!" Laramie agreed.

"I bring your horse—the short one! I ride with you to stop this woman. Sheriff and stranger ride this way."

Any horse, but especially his own Shorty, sounded like a gift straight from heaven. Laramie thanked his friend, but refused his offer to go along.

"This is my fight, Joe. I'll handle it."

"White man too proud to take help from red friend?"

"No. You know it's not that. I've had this show-down with Potts coming for a long time. I need to do it myself. And the woman—well, she's my problem, too." But he was not so sure that he'd be able to handle her, he thought with a grimace. In fact, he'd been handled by her pretty well, if the truth be known.

"I stay out of your way." The Indian nodded in understanding.

Laramie clasped his hand. "Thanks again, my old friend." He didn't even ask how Indian Joe had come to have his yellow horse. The ways of the Indian were unknowable, but he was as good a friend as a man could have. He lifted his hand in a final salute, riding off down the mountain.

He thought he might still be able to catch Sadie before she reached town, even though she'd gotten a good start on him, while he'd been forced to walk.

"Let's go, boy!"

Sadie felt sure she'd ridden at least half the distance down the mountain when she heard the steady hoofbeats of more than one horse on the trail up ahead of her. She reined her horse into a stand of trees off to the side, fearful it might be the sheriff and the man called Wally returning to finish the job the three men had started. She didn't trust Tombstone's sheriff, especially since she now knew what caliber of men he employed. Breathless, she waited, mentally begging her horse to stand still and not make a sound.

Two men rode into sight. One in a white hat rode tall and easy in the saddle, as though he'd spent a lifetime on horseback. The other, a little heavier, hat falling down over his eyes, bounced about uncomfortably, his arms flapping.

"Father!" she cried, urging her horse out of the safety of her hiding place. "Is it really you?" But she knew it was, had known almost since her first glimpse of the two men. It had just seemed so strange to see him here. And he'd looked so out of place. "What are you doing here?

"I've come for you, child," he puffed. "Are you all right? He didn't hurt you, did he?"

"No, Father, I'm fine. But how did you know where to look for me?"

"A cable. He sent me a cable, saying he had you. I came as quickly as I could. I would never have left here without you, Sadie, never!"

"Laramie telegraphed you? I never knew."

"See there, Moran," said the sheriff. "It *was* Laramie. I knew it had to be him. Where is he?" he growled at Sadie.

She saw the evil hatred in the depths of his small, black eyes and shivered. No matter what Laramie had done, he didn't deserve to be in the clutches of this man. She would never help Potts find her kidnapper.

"I think he's a long way from here by now," she lied. "He set me free and took off. Said something about Alaska."

The sheriff's expression said he wasn't quite ready to buy Sadie's story, but he looked puzzled, too, as though unsure why she would lie to him.

"I think we'll just have a look-see up at the old mine shaft, if you don't mind riding on a little further?"

Moran seemed to have mixed feelings about further pursuit, now that he had his daughter back, and Sadie claimed she was very tired and could hardly wait for a bath and a decent, soft bed. But the sheriff would not be deterred.

"You can wait here, or you can come with me, but I'm going up after him." The bloodlust in his eyes made Sadie suddenly fearful for Laramie.

"We'll come along," she said with determination. "Won't we, Father?" But she had already remounted and turned in behind the sheriff's big

216

horse.

Grumbling, Moran managed to haul himself back up into the saddle. They had left him no choice in the matter.

As they rode, Sadie hoped fervently that Laramie would be long gone by the time they arrived. She had no desire to witness a confrontation between these two deadly enemies. But she couldn't let the sheriff ride off after him alone. He would sneak up and ambush Laramie and claim he'd been escaping, or something. The sheriff was a liar and possibly even a murderer, if what Laramie had told her was true. But was it? Why should she take the word of an outlaw against that of a territorial sheriff?

As though following her train of thought and determined to convince her of Laramie's guilt, the sheriff spoke. "I'm very relieved to find you in good health and good spirits, Miss Moran. When your father told me you'd been taken prisoner by Laramie—well, frankly, I had my doubts we could reach you in time to save you. He's a ruthless and quite dangerous man."

"Really, sheriff? He didn't seem so to me. As a matter of fact, he actually saved my life on a couple of occasions. And I'm sure he meant me no real harm." What could she be thinking, defending the man who'd kidnapped her? But the words had spilled out of their own accord in an automatic response to the sheriff's crude remarks.

"You are a forgiving, long-suffering young woman, to speak so kindly of a man who stole your freedom and blackmailed your father."

Sadie heard the sarcasm rife in his words and did

217

not respond. Someone had to stand up to men like Sheriff Potts, and if Laramie was such a man, he could not be all bad.

"At least, you've come back to us safely," interjected her father, eager to change the subject which had veered close to something he didn't wish discussed in front of his daughter. "And that's all that matters now."

"Is it, Father? Then why are we going *up* the mountain, rather than back toward Tombstone?"

"It is my duty to bring Laramie to justice for his crimes," the sheriff said, his voice as hard as the frozen ground beneath their horses' hooves.

"What crimes exactly, sheriff?"

He seemed taken aback by her question, but rebounded quickly. "Well, first, there's kidnapping, and then there's the more serious charge of murder."

"Whom is he supposed to have murdered?"

"Jeff Foster. He murdered his partner so he could have the Silver Lining all to himself."

"But it didn't work out that way, did it?"

His black eyes narrowed to slits and moved over her insolently. Still, he tried to conceal the fury there that he was trying to control.

"No, it didn't! He was a cheat, and he lost it all! But I'm really surprised he would say anything to you about all this. Just what else did he tell you, Miss Moran?"

Sadie berated herself for revealing as much as she already had to Potts and decided to tell him nothing more. She did not trust him, even if he was the law, or what passed for the law in Tombstone, Arizona. They rode on silently.

The words she'd read in her father's letter jumped into her mind. "The papers in my possession . . ." She looked over at her father. He had to be involved in this somehow. Could he hold the key to Nate's getting back his mine? She couldn't wait to talk to him alone—to make him tell her exactly what was going on here. She would demand the truth from him.

"If I didn't know better, ma'am, I'd have to think you were siding with a criminal, maybe even trying to protect one."

"Sadie, would never do such a thing!" her father huffed, but his brows knitted together in a worried frown as he stared at his only child. Sadie did not look at him, but her worried eyes continued to search the trail ahead as they came nearer to the mine shack.

How could she warn Laramie? If she called out, the sheriff would know for certain his suspicions about her sympathies were correct. She'd seen the hateful gleam in his eye, and she had no idea how he would respond if she crossed him.

Perhaps she could delay their arrival somehow and give Laramie additional time to get away . . . but how? She was sure nothing she tried would work for very long, but the shack was probably less than a mile away. She had to move quickly.

"Ohhh!" she moaned, the back of her hand flying to her forehead. "I suddenly feel so dizzy!" She fluttered her eyes and plunged on, hopeful she could at least convince her father with her charade.

The sheriff simply stared at her, his gaze hooded by heavy lids.

Sadie swayed in the saddle, seeming to be in imminent peril of slipping to the ground. With a stifled curse, Potts threw himself to the ground and reached for her, catching her smoothly as she slid off her horse.

He couldn't be held up by a damned fainting woman, but neither could he afford to turn Moran against him just yet. He needed to get his hands on the papers Moran had—then Laramie would never *see* his mine again. But if the girl convinced her father to hand those same papers over to Laramie, he would be ruined.

Did Moran have the papers on him? The thought was intriguing, and he was a little gentler as he deposited Moran's daughter onto a smooth boulder. Since Moran had gotten the cable from Laramie demanding the deed to the mine, he would almost surely have brought it with him. If he didn't have it on him now, he would have left it in his hotel room. Either way, Potts felt it was almost in his grasp. But first, he'd have to do something about Moran and his troublesome daughter.

Not able to bear the man's disgusting hands on her a minute longer, Sadie opened her eyes, blinking. "I think . . . I think," she said haltingly, "that I feel a little better. If I could have a drink and perhaps rest here for a moment?"

"Of course," the sheriff agreed a little too readily and unfastened his canteen, holding it out to her. "You drink this, and you and your father stay right here. It's not far up ahead. I'll take care of Laramie, then be right back and we'll be on our way back to town."

"No!" Sadie protested. That was not at all what she'd intended. "I'm fine, really. We can go on

220

now."

"I insist," said the sheriff in implacable tones. "You stay right here, Miss Moran—and you, too, Moran. I'll be back very soon."

Why did his promise sound like a threat in Sadie's ears?

He was on his horse and out of sight before she could protest further.

Her mind whirled. She had to do something. "Laramie!" she cried out after three or four minutes had passed. "Look out!" Her voice echoed through the hills, but she couldn't be sure if he would hear her warning, or if he could get away in time. She could only hope.

Laramie was not as far away as she thought, but had been observing them from a short distance away. He had been close behind Sadie when she met up with the sheriff and her father. Then he had followed as the three made their way toward the mine shack, wondering if Sadie had told them where to look to find him.

He heard her voice ring out in warning and had his answer. His heart jumped. She didn't want the sheriff to ambush him, had even tried to protect him.

From his vantage point, Laramie could still see Potts as well as Sadie and her father. Her words had reached the sheriff's ears too, and he pulled up, as though undecided about what to do, whether to go on, or to go back to the Morans and silence Sadie.

Puzzled, Laramie watched as the sheriff dismounted and circled around, making his way back toward the father and daughter. What was he doing? He couldn't mean to harm them, could he?

Moving closer, the sheriff threaded his way quietly through the brush. As he went, he slid his gun out of its holster. There could be no mistaking his intentions now. He drew aim on the elderly Moran, who sat beside his daughter. Apparently, he planned to kill Moran. If he did that, he would undoubtedly have to kill Sadie, too!

Laramie knew he must do something to prevent Potts from murdering the two of them.

"Stop right where you are!" he shouted, standing up in the stirrups.

The sheriff whirled and fired before Laramie could react, sending his rifle spinning wildly out of his hand. Now he faced his adversary unarmed.

At that moment, Moran walked up beside the lawman, a small derringer gripped tightly in both his pale hands. "Need any help here?" he offered weakly, not having any notion what had really occurred between the two men, or what the sheriff had been about to do.

Potts shook his head impatiently, waving Moran away. "You're under arrest, Laramie!" His harsh voice rang out, echoing back from the rocky hills that towered above them. "And you'll hang for the cold-blooded murder of your partner before sunset tomorrow!"

Laramie stood tall, shrugged slightly as though to say the sheriff's words had no meaning for him. His blue eyes drilled into Sadie who had now joined them.

Why didn't he argue? Why had he revealed himself to Potts? Why didn't he fight? Why didn't he protest his innocence? He couldn't have killed Jeffrey Foster! They were best friends. He couldn't have! Could he?

The sheriff's spiteful words still rang in her head. "That man is no good. He killed his partner. And he planned to kill you and your father. He'd do anything for what he wants. The damned 'Silver Linings' is an obsession with him. Always has been. Always will be. He won't let it go til he swings from a rope."

Her father, by his silence, had agreed. Could they both be mistaken about Laramie? Or had she been so thoroughly tricked—hypnotized by twinkling sky-blue eyes into thinking Nate Laramie was more than a murderer and kidnapper? She just didn't know anything anymore. She didn't understand herself, much less anyone else. Her wide brown eyes mirrored the confusion in her soul.

Laramie stood stock-still while the sheriff yanked his arms behind him and snapped handcuffs over his wrists. It was obvious he would do nothing to save himself, though she knew he could have easily overcome the sheriff and her father, if he'd tried. Why didn't he? What had happened to his strength? his will?

None of this made any sense, and Sadie's mind reeled from her efforts to figure it out. After the long, pointed stare that had so unsettled her, Laramie refused to look at her again. It was a long, long ride back into town.

Jonathan Lee had put in a long, hard day since

early morning, trailing the sheriff and the portly stranger up into the mountains. He had been relieved when the surly Wallace had not shown up, but puzzled by the sheriff's new companion. Now his muscles ached from the unaccustomed riding and he had come off without anything to eat. He was ravenous.

He was just a little bit proud of the way he'd been able to keep his presence a secret, knowing he would be in a better position to help Laramie if the sheriff had no idea he was anywhere around.

When the beautiful redhead had joined the two men, he had been shocked. Her affectionate greeting to the older man indicated a close relationship that made him wonder exactly what was going on, and just how many things were going on that he didn't know about.

After a short discussion, the three had turned back up the mountain trail, probably still in pursuit of Laramie. Jonathan then observed Laramie's sudden appearance and challenge of the sheriff, but it happened so fast, he hadn't been able to do anything except watch helplessly. He couldh't help but wonder what had caused Laramie to so foolishly put himself in jeopardy at the sheriff's hands. It seemed unlike the Nate Laramie he thought he was coming to know.

He drew a deep breath of relief when the sheriff fastened on the cuffs, rather than shooting him down. They would still have a chance even with Laramie in custody, as long as he wasn't dead.

Jonathan wove his way down through a stand of thick trees and through a deep arroyo, meeting up with the party well down the hill. He wanted it to appear as if he'd just ridden up from town and had seen nothing of what happened.

"Ho there, sheriff!" he called. "What's going on?"

"Mr. Lee," the sheriff acknowledged, his voice chilly and edged with suspicion. "You're the last person I would have expected to see up here. Out for a Sunday afternoon ride? A constitutional, perhaps?"

"As a matter of fact, something very like that," Jonathan lied. "Tombstone is beginning to seem a bit small and provincial for my taste. I felt the need for some fresh air and a change of scenery. But I'm surprised to find you out in the hills—and in the company of such a beautiful young woman." He removed his hat, bowing in Sadie's direction.

"Ma'am," he said politely, "I'm Jonathan Lee, on the governor's staff and in Tombstone for an extended visit."

He turned his horse around and fell in step with them, apparently determined to join them.

"A long visit?" Sheriff Potts asked sharply. "I was surprised you didn't leave when the governor and the rest of his staff did, Mr. Lee."

"Jonathan, please. I had my reasons for staying on for a while, sheriff. I hope there's not a problem with that. Tombstone seems like a right friendly place and a good town in which to make one's fortune rather quickly, if what I hear is true."

"You should be careful about believing everything you hear, Jonathan, and even the things you see may require a closer inspection. Tombstone is a tough town, and it takes a special kind of man to survive out here. Some are better suited for the

225

softer life of the big city," he said pointedly.

Jonathan showed no offense, but smiled broadly thoroughly enjoying his word games with the sheriff. "Sometimes a man's gotta stretch himself though, wouldn't you agree?"

Thinking he'd like nothing better than to see this Easterner's neck stretched out at the end of a rope along with Laramie's, the sheriff didn't answer, but fell back for some words with Moran.

Jonathan manuevered his way until he was riding close beside Laramie and they could exchange comments without anyone overhearing.

"I'm sorry," he whispered. "I came along to see if I could help, but I was too late."

Laramie looked long at Jonathan Lee, his blue eyes dark and troubled. "I'll be all right," he said, "but Potts tried to ambush Moran and his daughter back there."

So that was why Laramie had revealed himself and dared the sheriff to shoot him, Jonathan realized. He had been protecting them!

"He may try it again. Keep on eye on them for me, Mr. Lee?"

"I sure will. But please call me Jonathan. We have a mutual friend, Rachel Foster."

Laramie noted the softening of the man's eyes when he mentioned Rachel's name and recalled how smitten the handsome stranger had seemed with her at the governor's reception. Something was going on.

"She's more than a friend to you, Jonathan?"

There was a sheepish smile and then the admission, "Yes, a lot more, I'm afraid."

"She's a good woman."

"Yes.

A bond of instant friendship developed between the two very different men who shared an affection and admiration for the widow Foster.

The others had ridden up close behind them, and there was no chance for further conversation as they entered the outskirts of Tombstone.

Chapter Fifteen

Rachel had dressed with the greatest care that Sunday morning in her best dress, a linsey-woolsey fabric in a soft rose color. Her golden hair was pulled up and away from her face in soft, fat curls. She laced up her good shoes and called to the boys to hurry and put on their best.

It was nearing noon, and she had a few last-minute things to do before they would be ready to receive their expected guest. She was filled with anticipation for this luncheon with Jonathan Lee. She'd been able to think of nothing else since she'd blurted out her invitation the night before.

The table, covered with a cloth of snowy linen, was set with her mother's china and silver and her few remaining unbroken goblets. She hoped she hadn't overdone it as she stopped to place a hand-embroidered napkin beside each of the four places. She wouldn't want Jonathan to think she was putting on airs, nor would she really want him to know how important this occasion was to her.

Careful not to smudge her good clothes, she reached to stir the bubbling stew pot that hung over the fireplace on a long handle. A pot of chicken and dumplings smelled delicious and was

228

ready to serve. In an iron skillet that sat on three legs, golden brown cornbread steamed. A fresh pie sat on the window ledge close by, and its fruity aroma hovered in the air, making her glad she'd put up some berries the previous spring.

Rachel had been up and about, making her preparations since before dawn, but she was so excited she took no note of fatigue. This was something she'd wanted to do, and she'd worked hard to be sure every detail was perfect.

She walked into the sitting room, rearranged a vase, and plumped up a pillow on the sofa. It was a warm and comfortable room, and she could envision Jonathan sitting there, his long legs stretched out in front of him and that wonderful smile on his face.

"Boys!" she called out. "Come here and let me see you." Their young faces, too, reflected anticipation, and each had done a good job of getting ready. Clean faces sparkled, and their hair was slicked back neatly. She straightened Timothy's suspenders and stood back for inspection.

"Two better-looking fellows I've never seen!" she avowed, her hands on her slender hips and a wide smile on her lips. "You make your mother so proud. Now, come here and give me a kiss."

Timothy raced over and threw himself at his mother. She lifted him up and he planted a sloppy kiss on her cheek. But Christopher held back.

"Aw, Ma," he said, his cheeks pinkening with embarrassment. She'd noticed that ever since Jonathan Lee had come into their lives, Christopher had been trying to be like him, more of a grownup.

"Even a man can still kiss his mother," she said kindly, leaning over. He pecked her lightly on the cheek and then, self-conscious, backed away, his hands thrust deep in his pants pockets.

A sound out front had him whirling away and running over to the window. But in a minute, he turned back toward her, showing his disappointment. "Shouldn't he be here by now, Mama? He said twelve o'clock, didn't he? I heard the clock chime, and he's still not here!"

"It's only a few minutes past, Christopher. He could have gotten tied up in town. I'm sure he'll be here soon. Tell you what . . . dinner's all ready. Let's go out and sit on the porch and wait for him."

Christopher, needing no more encouragement, rushed out the door, Timmy at his heels. She reached for their jackets and her shawl and joined them. "Here. Put these on. It's still chilly, even though the snow is all gone."

The snowfall had been a freak one for Tombstone in October and had quickly disappeared. Cool, dry air had begun to dry out the streets, leaving only a few muddy holes for the townspeople to avoid as they made their way home from Sunday services.

The streets emptied of their midday traffic, and soon all was quiet again. The clock inside struck one and Rachel jumped. She hadn't realized so much time had passed. What could have happened to Jonathan? He'd seemed like such a nice, honest man and had acted as though he were truly interested in her and the boys. Maybe he'd decided he wanted nothing more to do with a widow and her two sons.

She lifted her shoulders, gave her head a slight shake to clear it of troubling thoughts, and tried to keep her voice from revealing her own disappointment when she said, "Let's go on and eat, boys. Apparently, Mr. Lee has been held up."

Rachel rose, opened the door, and went inside, Timmy trailing behind her. But Christopher sat where he was, not moving. "I'm not hungry," he said. From the sound of his voice, he choked back tears with great effort.

"That's all right, Chris," she said. "Maybe you'll feel like eating a little later. I made the chicken and dumplings just like you like them." But he'd helped her pluck the chicken and he knew every detail of the lunch she'd so painstakingly prepared.

She fixed a plate for herself so Timothy would eat, but she had a hard time swallowing. They ate in silence, and she sent her youngest son back onto the porch while she cleaned up. She could hear his childlike voice trying to cheer up his older brother.

Tears filled her eyes. It hurt that Jonathan had stood her up and had not bothered to show up or send word, but what was hardest to take was how much Christopher had built him up, only to be let down so hard by the man he so admired.

"How could you?" she whispered into the empty kitchen.

It was almost three when she rejoined the boys on the porch. Christopher sat huddled in a corner, still wearing his coat, even though a bright sun had made the day pleasantly warm.

"Come here, Chris," she said, patting the seat on the porch swing beside her. "Sit with me. Let me help you take your coat off."

He accepted her help without comment.

"There, isn't that better?"

He nodded.

The silence grew. What else could she say to this small boy to relieve his pain and his disillusionment? She put her arm around him and he leaned his head on her shoulder, willing to accept the comfort she offered.

"Why, Mama? Why didn't he come like he said he would?"

"I don't know, Christopher. But until we know better, what do you say we give him the benefit of a doubt? Perhaps he had good reason."

"Do you really think so?" His face brightened. "Do you think he still might come?"

"Maybe," she said, but her own doubts were very strong. "Why don't you take little Timmy inside and help him get ready for his nap?"

"Okay, Mama!" He jumped up, anxious as always to please his mother. "But I'll be back out in just a few minutes, and we'll keep watching for him together, won't we?"

Another long hour had passed and Christopher was out back tending to his horse when Rachel noticed a small group of riders heading into town from the direction of the Dragoons. At first hopeful it might be Nate and Sadie, she was disappointed to see that the riders were all on horseback. There was no wagon.

Still curious, she studied them as they drew closer. Sheriff Potts' white hat stood out in the small crowd. He was the only man in Tombstone she'd ever seen wearing a white hat. Beside him rode a heavyset older man. And just behind them was a slender female with bright auburn hair. It had to be Sadie!

Then she recognized Nate Laramie—could she be mistaken, or were his hands cuffed behind him? "Oh, no!" she cried out.

Only when they were almost at her house did she see that the other man in the party was Jonathan Lee. What was he doing with them? Had he been in on the sheriff's plan from the beginning? Her mind tumbled, seeking explanations, acceptable solutions to her questions, but finding none.

Jonathan tipped his hat and smiled apologetically, but it was apparent he wouldn't be stopping to speak to her. Mr. Lee obviously had business with the man she most despised in Tombstone—Dan Potts!

Jonathan saw the surprise and the hurt in Rachel's eyes. It hit him with the force of a rockslide—she thought he was working with Potts! He saw it when she looked at him. And he thought of the meal she must have prepared and the way she and Christopher would have been waiting and looking for him. Would she ever understand? Would he ever be able to make it up to both of them?

He had to stay with Moran and Sadie to be sure the sheriff didn't try anything else, so he couldn't even stop to try and explain. He had probably been the world's biggest fool, and he just might have lost someone who could come to be more important to him than his life.

"Damnation," he said, under his breath.

A big crowd had gathered in front of the jail to watch the proceedings, anxious to get a look at Sheriff Potts' newest prisoner. Many showed surprise that it was Nate Laramie, an honest, hardworking man, a man who'd never been involved in the drunken revelry or shootouts so commonplace in Tombstone.

But others more knowledgeable were aware of the bitter feud that raged between the two men and were not surprised to see the sheriff use any means at his disposal to put Laramie out of action. Still others breathed a sigh of relief that the previous owner of the Silver Linings would be out of commission and no longer a threat to them. He'd been getting too close to the truth, endangering the security of those who were a part of the "company."

Rachel stood on the fringes of the noisy crowd and wondered why she'd come. There was clearly no way she could help Laramie by being here. Jonathan was no longer in sight, though she didn't know what she would have had to say to him—or he to her—if he had been. Eyes wide, she watched Laramie hustled inside without a struggle or a

234

backward glance. Was there no one who would help him?

One by one, the men standing around her began to drift away. She had to do something. She couldn't just stand there and let this happen.

Someone bumped her elbow and a feminine voice said, "Sorry." She whirled and found herself looking into the world-weary but kind eyes of Lily Delgado, the sheriff's "woman."

"That's all right, Lily," she said, accepting her apology, but her hand grasped the older woman's arm before she could move away. "Do you understand what's happening here?"

"Leave it alone, Mrs. Foster. You shouldn't even be here, a nice lady like yourself." There had never been any real friendship between the two women, but each had been kind to the other on more than one occasion and they respected each other.

"I know he's your friend," Lily went on, "but there's nothing you can do here."

"He plans to hang Nate, doesn't he, Lily?"

"Yes."

"And he'll never get a fair trial—not in Tombstone and not with Judge Donovan on the bench." Rachel spoke aloud facts that were indeed known to Lily. She didn't answer, but still looked steadily at Rachel.

"We have to do something, Lily." Rachel had to get the other woman's help somehow. But could she be persuaded to go against the man she loved and help Laramie? Rachel had an idea.

"Have you thought what will happen to the sheriff—and to his career—if he does this? He's

235

obsessed when it comes to Nate Laramie and he doesn't think clearly. It will ruin him, Lily. His career will be over. And when it's proven that Laramie was completely innocent—as it will be—he could even go to jail himself."

She paused to let the words sink in. Though Lily had been concerned and even worried before, it was clear she hadn't considered the ramifications of the sheriff's actions that Rachel described to her. Knowing how much the other woman cared for Potts, in spite of what he was, she was almost sure Lily would do anything she could for him.

"What are your plans? What do you want from me?" Not completely convinced, still Lily seemed willing to listen.

Rachel outlined a desperate plan of action. She had no idea whether they could carry it out successfully. But she knew she had to try.

By the time she was finished speaking, Lily had made her decision. "You know he'll never forgive me for this if he ever finds out I had a part in it."

"He'll never learn it from me, Lily. I promise. And remember, you'll be doing the best thing for him—you'll be saving him from himself. You don't think you'll have any trouble getting him away from here later?"

"Nah. He'll come . . . but give me a couple of hours, at least."

Rachel hurried away, not at all as sure about her plan as she'd appeared to Lily. It was risky and dangerous for everyone involved.

Lucien Moran rushed his daughter away from the scene outside the jail. She'd been through enough, and he wanted to protect her from any more ugliness. He had rented adjoining rooms at the hotel before leaving Tombstone with the sheriff, hopeful Sadie would be with him when he returned.

They would spend this one last night in Tombstone and then be safely away from the despicable city and its less-than-civilized inhabitants. If he very carefully controlled his thoughts, perhaps they wouldn't linger on the innocent man locked up in the Tombstone jail.

At least, Moran knew Laramie was not guilty of murder, but he *had* kidnapped his daughter, and that was surely enough to put a man behind bars. Sadie hadn't seemed too happy to see Laramie arrested, and briefly Moran wondered about that. Apparently, the man had not mistreated his captive. He'd questioned Sadie closely on the ride back and had been relieved at her answers. "No, Father," she had assured him, "he didn't hurt me. He didn't *do* anything to me."

"Well, we'll just let the sheriff handle this one," he muttered to himself as he turned in. Sadie still moved about in the next room, but soon put out her light and all was quiet. Moran fell into a deep, peaceful sleep.

Her father's loud snores soon drove Sadie from her hotel room. But the noise was only the last straw—the four walls had been steadily moving in on her in claustrophobic fashion ever since they'd checked in. She longed to be back in the cave, or even the rickety line shack, but she didn't want to think about that. She was supposed to be getting a few hours sleep before they left for Benson early the next day. Her father seemed anxious for her to be away from Tombstone as soon as possible, probably wanted to protect her from the harsh realities of a hanging.

A hanging. No! If Laramie was telling the truth and was innocent, surely the court would rule in his favor. Even out here a man wouldn't be hanged without a fair trial, would he? The evil hatred in the sheriff's obsidian eyes flashed through her mind and she wondered. He acted as if he thought he *was* the law, or that he was somehow above it. Would an innocent man be safe in his hands? She had reason to doubt it. Still, it was none of her business, as her father had said. It was enough that she was safe and they would soon be on their way home.

When she looked up, she realized with a start that her steps had led her unconsciously to the alley behind the jail. *He* was in there. Laramie was a few feet away behind those bars. What was he thinking? What was he feeling? Did he hate her as much as his eyes had declared? Did he think she'd betrayed him to the sheriff?

She walked a little closer, stopped and held her breath as a shadow moved past the window. He was pacing. She could see him now, but was sure he couldn't see her in the blackness of the alleyway.

A frown scored his high forehead, and he ran his fingers through his thick, black hair in that fa-

238

miliar gesture she'd seen before, leaving his hair mussed. He seemed not to notice, nor did he slow his movements, back and forth, back and forth. He hadn't seemed to care about his fate before, but now she could see that he did. He cared very much.

Her hands twisted together and Sadie barely restrained herself from calling out to him, from going to him.

She heard the hauntingly familiar depths of his voice. But he had turned away from the window, toward the door of his cell. His voice spoke not her name, but another's.

"Rachel," he said in rebuke. "You shouldn't have come here."

"I had to, Nate. I can't believe what's happened, what they're trying to do to you." Rachel's clear voice carried through the night air and, by listening carefully, Sadie managed to hear every word. "We have to get you out of here. You know what judge he's lined up to hear your case, don't you?"

"Judge Donovan," he said flatly.

"Yes, the judge Sheriff Potts carries around in his pocket. They'll see you hanged, Nate. I know it! Jonathan will try to contact the governor, but he's back East again, and it may be too late by the time he reaches him."

Laramie's chuckle was bitter. "I can't see him lifting a finger to help me, in any case. Don't worry, Rachel. I'll get out of here . . . and when I do, he'll pay."

"No, Nate! When will this end? You have to let it go, and get on with your life."

239

"Never. Not until you and the boys have what's rightfully yours."

Just then, a deputy interrupted their conversation and told Rachel that she would have to leave.

Sadie stood in the shadows for long minutes. Watching him pace the cell and listening to him talking to Rachel, she had made up her mind. Nate Laramie deserved her help and her love. She would not turn her back on him. She would do whatever it took to help him escape and clear his name.

Rachel turned toward home, her mind full of her plans for bringing about Laramie's release. Though she hadn't had a chance to explain it to him, she was sure it would work. She would get the doctor's wife to watch the boys so she'd be free to put all her efforts into freeing Nate. It had to be done before this night was over.

So intent was she on her thoughts, she did not see a tall figure lounging in the shadows in front of the hotel. When he stepped out in front of her, she bumped into him, coming to an abrupt halt.

"Ooomph!" she complained.

The man laughed softly. "The same thing young Christopher said the time he ran into me head first!"

"Jonathan!" she exclaimed in surprise, instinctively keeping her voice low. "What are you doing here?"

As she waited for his answer, all her earlier doubts and fears where he was concerned came raging back. She stiffened.

"I'm doing something Laramie asked me to do, Rachel. I know it looked bad for me this afternoon, but I've only been trying to help your friend, I swear! And, I'm sorry, so very sorry, about lunch. I had no time to let you know. I'll make it up to you and the boys, I promise you that . . . if you'll let me, that is."

Rachel's trusting nature convinced her to believe him instantly and unreservedly. He was still her ally, and Nate's as well. "We have to get him out of there tonight, Jonathan. Sheriff Potts will hang him tomorrow!"

"I know, Rachel. I've been trying my best to come up with a plan that will work. But you mustn't involve yourself in this. It's much too dangerous."

"You know me better than that, Jonathan. If there's *anything* I can do to get Nate out of jail, I'll do it. I cannot just go home and sit there idly and allow this to happen."

"Of course not."

"I have a plan, Jonathan, and you can help me. Lily Delgado should be bringing the sheriff through those doors in the next hour or so," she said, pointing down the street in the direction of the jail. "And when she does, here's what you do." She whispered her plans to Jonathan Lee, who listened carefully and nodded a couple of times before she was done. They parted, going their separate ways in the darkness.

Chapter Sixteen

"Time to do us some fancy celebratin', sheriff!"

Dan Potts was surprised to see Lily at the jailhouse since she had never come there before. But her happy grin and pleasantly round body that threatened to spill out of her gown added impetus to her words and he found himself wanting very badly to go with her.

"Lily, you know I'd like to, but I've got important business here. We've got Laramie behind bars, and I'm going to be sure he stays there. You run along. Maybe I'll join you later for a few minutes."

Seeing the disappointment in his face, she stood her ground, not content to listen to any of his excuses. "Laramie's locked up good and tight, now, isn't he, boys?" she questioned the deputies.

"Sure is, Miss Lily! No way he's gettin' outta here. G'wan, boss. Have yourself a little fun." Wally urged the sheriff to go, thinking to catch a few winks in his absence. Sam Jenkins, the deputy who had filled in for Lucas, shook his head in agreement.

"Now, you see there, sheriff. You got some good men here and they'll take care of things til you get back. Come on along, no more argument out of you!"

He wavered for a few seconds longer between what he saw as his duty and the insistent call of the pleasures of the flesh. "Aw, hell, Lil. I never could say no to you, now could I?"

With a suggestive smile, he snatched his hat off a nail behind his desk, stood and held his hand out to Lily. He sent an exaggerated wink in the direction of his men. "I'll have to be back here in an hour," he said, but they both knew he'd never been able to leave her in just an hour's time.

"Sure thing. One hour. Now, come on with you. Let's go!"

Arm in arm they walked over to the door, which he opened with a flourish, allowing her to precede him. He hummed a bawdy tune as they strolled along the wooden walks. The arm that went around her ample waist was soon straying upward, and he filled his hand with her breast, causing her to cry out in mock alarm.

"Think of my reputation," she rebuked him, laughing lustily. "And control yourself until we get to my room." Her eyes told him that once they were alone, she was his to pleasure him in whatever way he desired.

The sheriff chuckled and walked a little faster, all thoughts of Nate Laramie temporarily exiled from his mind.

Sadie knew what she must do. Whatever Laramie was, and whatever he might have done, she

243

could not leave him to the mercy of the sheriff. She remembered she still had Laramie's gun and that she had slipped it under her bed earlier, not knowing what else to do with it. Now she would use it to help him.

She flew back across the street, up the hotel steps and noiselessly let herself back into the room. Moving quietly, but having no great fear that she would awaken her father, who was a heavy sleeper, she slipped the gun out of its hiding place and dropped it into the pocket of her jacket.

Retracing her steps in haste, she once more stood outside the narrow window of the jail cell.

"Laramie," she whispered and held her breath, waiting. No movement from inside. Was he asleep?

"Laramie," she called out again, careful to keep her voice low so as not to arouse the guards.

A shadow loomed large in the window. She stood facing him, but he said nothing. Holding the gun tightly in two trembling hands, she held it out to him. For long seconds, he did not move, but his eyes held hers. Neither of them spoke.

At last, he reached through the bars and lifted the gun from her hands.

"I have a horse for you. It will be waiting out back." She didn't mention that she had gotten two horses, including the one she'd "borrowed" from her father. She tried not to think how hurt and angry he would be when he discovered what she'd done.

"Why are you doing this?" Laramie's blue eyes

raked over her, showing no pity, ruthlessly seeking the motivation behind her actions.

Because I love you more than my life, she wanted to say, but didn't. This was not the time for words of love.

"Hurry, Laramie," she urged, fleeing out of his sight, back into the dark night.

Laramie felt the comforting cool weight of his Colt revolver where he'd stuck it under his shirt, snugly inside the waistband of his buckskin trousers. After Sadie had handed it to him through the window, he had quickly spun the chambers to be sure it was still loaded and then had hastily thrust it out of sight.

He paused briefly to wonder what had brought her to do such a thing. It was the last thing he would have expected of Sadie Moran. Safely back in the custody of her father, he'd assumed she would have been as anxious as Moran to put Tombstone behind her forever. She had to know that by helping him, she put her own father in jeopardy. Yet she had done it anyway!

His heart hammered and not entirely from the excitement of the impending action. She cared for him — Nate Laramie! She had to! There was no other answer to explain her actions. First, she had called out to warn him of the sheriff's ambush, and now she'd brought him the gun. She had come when he needed her. Maybe — he dared to dream again — maybe she even loved him?

Laughter and loud voices sounded in the outer

office of the jail. He wasn't sure what was happening out there, but could have sworn he heard a woman's voice among in the conversation.

When one of the deputies brought his dinner tray, he would make his move. It had long been dark, so surely someone would be coming soon.

He didn't like the idea of Sadie being alone for long in the dark alley, and he was anxious to collect the horse she'd promised and be on his way.

The thought that he might never see her again brought him intense pain, but he'd always hold to his heart the knowledge that she'd cared enough to help him escape.

Quiet pervaded the jail. Were the deputies eating? Would they ever bring him his dinner? Or maybe they'd already eaten and dozed off. If Sheriff Potts was still out there, it was a sure thing he'd never sleep. Laramie suspected, though he couldn't be sure, that the sheriff might have left. If so, he couldn't expect him to be gone long, and it would be considerably better to make his move during his absence.

"Hey! How about some dinner back here?" he called loudly, trying to initiate some action.

"Keep yer shirt on, Laramie. It'll be here soon. Your widow friend—" Wally snickered suggestively, "promised to come back with something real soon."

Rachel! He didn't want her involved in this. But how like her to be so thoughtful. She had always been there for him. He reflected on the differences between his feelings for Jeff's widow, which were protective and affectionate, and the

246

wild, tempestuous longings and the fierce anger the feisty Sadie Moran aroused in him. If she hadn't come into his life, he might have settled for a life with Rachel and the boys, had even considered it, in fact. But now he could see what a mistake that would have been.

With a rustle of her full skirts and a basket of food in her arms, Rachel Foster swept into the jailhouse for the second time that evening.

"Evening, gentlemen," she said, smiling at the two deputies. On the desk between them, she set out a big crock of homemade soup and some fresh, steaming cornbread. "Nothing like soup on a cold night, now, is there?"

The eyes of the deputies widened with pleasure, and their mouths were all but hanging open in anticipation.

"Thank you, Mrs. Foster!"

"Yes, ma'am. Thank you! This sure looks tasty!"

Each took a soft linen napkin she offered, tucked it into his shirt front and sat back down to devour the delicious meal she'd provided for them.

"No trouble at all. Now, may I take this small bowl in to your prisoner? I'm sure he must be quite famished by now."

"Sure nuff, ma'am. You just go right on in there and fix him up good and proper." They hardly glanced at her, so intent were they on digging into the feast she'd brought. They were more accustomed to their usual fare of hardtack biscuits and strips of dried beef.

"This here's like Christmas and Thanksgiving all rolled into one!" said Sam as he gobbled down a whole slice of cornbread in one mouthful.

Rachel watched them with a satisfied smile, then hurried back to where Laramie still paced in his small cell. "Here, Nate. Eat quickly. We've a plan to have you out of here in a few minutes."

He took the bowl and large hunk of linen-wrapped bread thankfully, realizing just how long it had been since he'd eaten.

"You sit down and eat that while I tell you everything," she instructed, and he did as she said without comment.

"The sheriff's gone. I don't think he'll be back for some time," she said with a soft, knowing smile, quite certain of Lily's ability to keep him entertained. "I've provided those two unsuspecting deputies with a very special dinner. When they've eaten their fill, they'll no doubt become *very* sleepy." Again, she smiled and Laramie smiled back, amazed at her as he always was, but grateful for anything that would get him out of a very bad situation.

"As soon as they're out cold, Jonathan and I will be back to get you out of here. Then he'll go find the U.S. Marshal who's a friend of his, and the real truth will come out. You'll be free. But until then, we have to get you safely away from Tombstone and out of the reach of Sheriff Potts."

He slipped the gun out from under his shirt and showed it to her. "Sadie brought this a few minutes ago," he explained. "She said she'd have a horse waiting for me in the alley."

Rachel's surprise showed clearly on her lovely face, but was followed by the dawning of a new understanding. "She's in love with you, Nate! I should have seen it before."

"I don't know so much about that. She cares enough to try and help me out of this, I guess. But I can't let anything happen to her—or to her father."

Rachel saw his love for Sadie Moran written plainly across his handsome but troubled face. She wondered why she hadn't realized it before.

Jonathan strode through the doorway, hearing the prisoner's last words. "I'll look after them for you, Laramie. Now, let's get you out of here. The boys out front really enjoyed your home cooking, Rachel," he said with a chuckle. "They should sleep until morning."

He tried several keys on the ring before he found the right one. "Aha! that's it!" he exclaimed, throwing the door open wide. Rachel told Jonathan about Sadie and the horse as they hurried out the back door and into the alley.

"Nate," she whispered, "there's a ranch house up in the Whetstone Mountains. It belongs to Sarah and Benjamin Weaver. Do you know it?"

"Yes."

"Ride there quickly, then. They've gone to California for several months. It's empty and will be safe. They won't mind, I'm sure of it. They're good people and always willing to help someone in need. I'll ride out there in a couple of days and bring you some more supplies. Now hurry!"

Laramie disappeared into the darkness after

shaking Jonathan's hand and giving Rachel a quick hug.

Sadie sat astride, clad in the same men's trousers Laramie had dug out of a trunk for her — had it been only days ago, and not the years it seemed? She clutched the reins of a second horse in her hand, her heart pounding with a heavy dose of fear, mingled with a growing excitement. She hadn't told him she would be riding with him, but there was no way she'd let him leave without her! Whatever happened now happened to both of them, whether he liked it or not. She didn't care where they went or what he did, as long as they were together. And she knew, deep in her heart, that he must feel that way, too.

Out of the black depths of the night came the sound of heavy, muffled footsteps. Sadie's breath caught in her throat. What if her plan had failed and the sheriff was coming to lock her up, too?

"Sadie."

The soft, blessedly familiar voice came from directly behind her! Laramie hurried to the other horse, taking the reins she handed him and threw himself easily into the saddle. "It seems that I have to thank you again."

"Later!" she said and wheeled her horse, heading out at a gallop for the edge of town. Laramie's mouth fell open, but he had no choice but to fall in behind her.

In the darkness, any shape or movement could represent an enemy, a threat to his new-found freedom. No words could be exchanged between them until they'd left Tombstone well behind them. He was alert for any sounds of pursuit, though he expected it would be at least an hour or perhaps several before the alarm was sounded. After they had ridden for several miles, the lights of town began to fade and he slowed their horses to a trot. He moved up beside her. Grabbing her reins, he brought her mount to a sliding stop. His did the same. He jumped from the saddle and pulled her down to him, his strong fingers fastened around her waist. They stood toe to toe. His blue eyes snapping with angry fire, he demanded fiercely, "What do you think you're doing?"

"Helping an outlaw escape?" she asked, a crooked smile on her lips, hoping against hope to see a similar response on his face.

"This is not funny, Sadie." He did not smile. "You can't come with me. I'll be more of a fugitive than ever. I'll have to move fast, and I'll always be on the run. It's no life for a woman. Besides, you would just slow me down." He spoke firmly, but he could not believe what it was doing to his heart to talk to her that way.

"You know better, Nate Laramie. You're just saying that. The first time we were together, you kidnapped me and I had no choice. But this time, I can make up my own mind. I already have! I'm coming with you whether you like it or not, Mr. High and Mighty!

"I'm taking you back, Sadie."

"No!

"Don't argue with me. It's too dangerous."

"I'm not leaving you, Laramie."

"Why not?" His eyes challenged hers in the same way his voice did. They were questioning her, demanding answers.

As their eyes locked and held and sparks flashed back and forth, he saw something in those honey-brown depths he'd never expected to see in a woman's eyes again. Was it possible that Miss Sadie Moran was really in love with him? His blue eyes probed, so desperate was he for the right answer to that question. But he was also terrified of discovering the truth.

If she did—God help him—feel something that strong for him, what was he going to do about her then? For he couldn't allow her to go with him, and he wasn't sure he could take her back. The trusting look in her eyes squeezed his heart in an unbearable way and he muttered angrily, turning away from her.

Sadie's eyes never left the wide slant of his shoulders. She knew he fought an internal war with himself and that her future, *their* future, depended on its outcome. What could she do? If she touched him, would he pull her to him or turn away? Could she bear his rejection if he did that? She hurt so badly now, she didn't know if she could stand any more pain. But she couldn't—she wouldn't—leave him out here alone. There was no way he could make her go. Just when she'd found the one true love of her life, she wouldn't let him be taken from her.

Nate Laramie was good and kind, and as much a man as any woman could want. He'd taught her so much, she thought with a smile—not just to rope and shoot, but he'd taught her about commitment, about devotion and loyalty, and about how to respond to a man's touch.

Her body quivered as she recalled the incredibly satisfying sensations of his caresses. He was a wonderfully gentle but exciting lover and had awakened her body to a thousand new sensations. She had learned to love in his arms, in every way it was possible to love another person.

And now he wanted her to leave him, just forget everything that had happened between them and move on.

"No way, Laramie," she said, her voice firm but husky with feeling. "There is no way I'm leaving you now. We've come this far together. I'm with you to the end. We're going to see this thing through. You can't make me leave you."

He whirled around and rammed his fingers through his already ruffled hair in agitation.

"Sadie . . . ." He tried to make her name a threat, but it came out more as a strangled plea. "Sadie, please go back now." His strength to leave her was ebbing away, but he made one last desperate attempt.

"I got you into this. You had no choice about that. But now I'm offering you a way out. I'm giving you back your freedom and the life you had before. Your father is waiting for you. Go to him, Sadie. Leave me alone. This is my fight, not yours."

He was wrong. Somewhere along the way, his battles had become her battles, too . . . his cause, hers. She thought of her father then, and her heart went out to him. Misguided, he'd used bad judgment and done some foolish things, but she knew he loved her and his only concern now was her and her freedom. He didn't know Laramie, and Sheriff Potts had convinced him that her captor meant to harm her. But Sadie knew better.

Laramie had never wanted anything that was not rightfully his, the mine that had been stolen from him and his partner. And his own good name. No . . . she wouldn't abandon him now. The sheriff and his men were set on killing him. They would shoot him down in cold blood or lynch him without a second thought. She was the only thing that stood in their way, and she was not about to leave his side, not now, when he needed her more than she'd ever dreamed of being needed by anyone.

Sadie stood a little straighter and looked him in the eye, her gaze clear and unflinching.

"Wrong again, Nate Laramie! This is *our* fight!"

She was back in the saddle before he could stop her. Laramie stood looking up at her in the dim light of the moon. A posse would be after him before morning, and he didn't have time to argue with a hard-headed, irresistible woman. He would have to get them safely to the ranch, then he'd find a way to get her back to town, back to her father, and safely out of this mess. For in spite of every wonderful thing she'd just said, he couldn't let her stay with him and risk her life.

254

Dan Potts thanked his lucky stars for sending Lily Delgado his way. Always, in her arms, he'd been able to block out the world and forget his troubles for a time. Tonight was no exception. She'd been true to her word and had done everything in her bag of loving tricks to please him.

He felt a pang of real regret that she was not the kind of woman he could make his wife. No, he could enjoy Lily as often as he chose, but when it came to the selection of Mrs. Dan Potts, he would have to pick a woman like the widow Foster, someone genteel and respectable. Lily had always known that as well as he did.

"I have to go now, Lily," he murmured, his voice muffled against her soft flesh.

He was mildly surprised when her arms tightened around his neck, refusing to turn him loose. "No, you don't. There's still one more thing I have to do for you before you leave." Her voice was husky and provocative, and he felt his flesh grow hot and tight again.

Her hands on his shoulders pushed him gently onto his back and held him there. Then her head moved lower, her lips dropping kisses and her tongue teasing down the line of his muscled, darkly furred chest, across his taunt midriff and lower still. Potts groaned his approval and abandoned momentarily any thoughts of leaving Lily's embrace. "Ahhh!"

Her hands caressed and stroked even as her mouth and tongue continued to work their magic on him, bringing him back into the throes of ecstasy yet again.

Lily found the task not unpleasant and would have prolonged it for selfish reasons even if she weren't desperately trying to keep the sheriff away from the jail for Rachel.

But Potts, his passion thoroughly spent this time, was stubbornly bent on leaving. She knew she had done all she could. She could only hope it would be enough.

As he stepped into his pants and bent to pull on his boots, the sheriff found himself becoming more and more concerned about his prolonged absence from the jail. His deputies, though unquestionably loyal to him, were not always the brightest of men, and Laramie was quick and intelligent, with more than one friend in Tombstone.

He grabbed his shirt, slipped his arms in, and shoved the tail into his pants. Then he belted on his holster and tied it around a firmly muscled leg. Lily was holding his hat out to him and his jacket lay over a chair by the door. His badge shone in the light of the dim lantern she'd lit after becoming convinced of his unwavering determination to leave. She put herself in the way of his exit and claimed one more lingering kiss before allowing him to push past her.

"Be careful, Dan," she said, her voice soft as he strode out into the darkened hallway.

His name from her lips echoed in his ears as he left her. Had she ever called him anything but "sheriff" before? He didn't have time to consider the import of that startling fact, but hurried down the stairs, out onto the wooden walk, and

256

down the street in the direction of the jail.

Everything appeared to be normal from the outside. Yellow light spilled out the windows, and all was quiet and peaceful, perhaps a bit too quiet. Usually, there would be sounds of laughter as the men on duty joked or played cards. It was not until he stepped inside that he became aware of the muffled sounds of his deputies' loud snores.

"What th' hell?" he shouted. They did not move. He pulled one of them up by the hair of his head and, disgusted, dropped his head, which thumped against the desk.

"Drugged! Damned fools let themselves be drugged!" He was shouting furiously, already knowing what he'd find when he went through the door to the cell. Just as he expected, the heavy door with its thick bars stood open wide, the keys still dangling uselessly in the lock.

He ground his heel into the floor as he swung around and strode back out to the office. The sight of his unconscious deputies infuriated him, sent his temperature rising and hot color flooding into his face.

Black, angry eyes didn't miss a single detail—he noted the empty soup bowls and the snowy linen napkins. Supper had not been delivered by the saloon as usual. Who, then? His mind whirled as he tried to come up with answers. What woman would do anything for Nate Laramie?

Rachel Foster, of course! It had to be! His anger building, he made his way directly to her house, unmindful of the late hour, and banged loudly on the front door. He'd force the truth out of her and he'd *make* her lead him to Laramie! Then they would both pay for what they'd done to him!

The Foster home was completely dark and still. He pounded harder. After a few minutes, the door swung open a crack and a gray head covered by a lacy nightcap peered out at him. "Shush yourself, Sheriff! What in the world is wrong with you? The boys and Mrs. Foster are sound asleep!"

But, contrary to her words, Christopher appeared at her side. His eyes wide, he assumed a protective stance that said louder than words that he would defend his family and his home, if he had to.

"Go back to bed, Christopher," she told him, her voice gentle. "I'll handle this."

"No, ma'am," he disagreed, his childlike voice polite but strong. "My Mama says I'm the man of the house now."

She smiled and patted his head. "Of course you are, dear."

The sheriff was fighting his growing impatience. "What are you doing here, Elizabeth?"

Elizabeth's husband, the doctor, had been an influential citizen in Tombstone, and the sheriff knew better than to do battle with the revered widow, who stood now effectively blocking the door of the Foster home, denying him entrance. "Where is Ra . . . er, Mrs. Foster?"

"She's quite ill, sheriff. And she asked me to come over and tend the boys while she got some much needed rest."

"I have to see her."

"Oh no, you don't! She is finally asleep, and I will not allow you to disturb her! Come back tomorrow afternoon, Sheriff Potts. Now, goodnight."

She stepped back and pushed the door closed, but his hand slapped against it, not permitting it to close. "You tell the ailing Mrs. Foster," he said, his voice with a hard, sarcastic edge, "that I know about her part in all this, and that I will find Laramie and bring him back. And they will both be sorry!"

He turned away then and stomped off the porch. Not ruffled in the least, the diminutive Elizabeth Connors slammed the door firmly and put her arm around the shivering lad beside her.

"Don't let him upset you, Christopher. He makes a lot of noise, but your mother and Mr. Laramie are a whole lot smarter. He won't do anything, you'll see. It will all be okay."

Christopher looked up at her with a tentative smile, his fears calmed somewhat by her words. "You're pretty smart yourself, Mrs. Connors — what you said about Mama bein' sick an' all. But do you really think she'll be back soon?"

"Yes, any minute now, Christopher. Any minute. I did hate to lie, but never mind, it was for a good cause! Let's have us a nice cup of hot chocolate while we wait for her, what do you say?"

"Yes, ma'am!"

The sheriff, angered further by his encounter

with the doctor's wife and frustrated in his attempt to get the truth from Rachel, made his way back down Allen Street, daring anyone to get in his way. He was oblivious to the rowdy, boisterous voices spilling from the open doorways of the Oriental saloon and the Alhambra. He ignored a brawl occurring in the middle of the street as two drunken miners cursed and shoved each other, a small crowd urging them on, anxious for some excitement, thirsty for blood.

His steps sounded loudly on the planks as he neared the Cosmopolitan Hotel, where Moran and his daughter were staying. The beautiful Sadie Moran had shown an unusual sympathy and interest in her kidnapper. Was it conceivable she might even do something to help him escape? It was certainly a possibility he couldn't discard without looking into it. Since he hadn't been able to get his hands on Rachel Foster for now, he would just go check on Sadie Moran, and he would make her tell him what she knew.

He banged on Moran's hotel room door. Sleepy and disgruntled and still in his nightshirt, Moran responded to the summons, but asked cautiously before opening the door, "Who's there?

"It's me, Potts! Open this door, Moran!"

A bolt slid back noisily and the door swung inward. "What do you want of me, Sheriff? It's been a long day, and my daughter and I are trying to get some sleep here."

"You haven't seen Laramie, then?"

"No! Why in God's name would I? Isn't he still safely behind bars in your most excellent jail, sheriff?"

Noting the look of intense fury on the other man's face, Moran assessed the situation, coming instantly awake. "He's gone then? Broken out of jail and gotten away from you? Well, at least Sadie's safe here with me."

Or was she? Both men made the same inference at almost the same moment, and they headed for the connecting room.

It was empty and the bed undisturbed.

Beating the sheriff to the punch, Moran demanded, "How is this possible, Potts? I thought you were in control in Tombstone, and you can't even keep one criminal under lock and key for twenty-four hours! Not only that, but your carelessness has put my daughter in peril once more. I'll have your job for this, and you will never wear a badge anywhere west of the Mississippi again — or east of it either, for that matter. You find her and bring her back — unharmed! Do you hear me?"

"Your meaning is perfectly clear," the Sheriff ground out from between clenched teeth. That damned Laramie had made a fool of him again! "The posse is gathering even as we speak." He spun about on his heel and strode out through the door. "I'm sure you'll want to go along," he flung back over his shoulder.

Moran had never dressed so quickly or so carelessly, and he was rushing down the stairs, shirt unbuttoned and coattail flapping, minutes after the sheriff's departure. A few doors down the street, he ducked into the livery for his horse.

"What do you mean, my horse is gone?" he demanded of the blacksmith.

"It was your daughter, sir. She rode out of here over an hour ago with both horses."

"Was someone with her?" Moran was turning red in the face, but trying his best to maintain some calm.

"No, sir. She was alone, so far as I could tell. Riding one of the horses and leading the other, she was. I thought it a mite strange, but she said you'd sent her after them, that you planned an early start back to Benson tomorrow."

Moran was flabbergasted. What could this possibly mean? The horse would have been for Laramie, but he could not believe Sadie would help the man willingly. He must have had something on her, threatened her in some way. But how? And where could they have gone?

"Well, rent me another one. The fastest you have available. I'm riding out with the posse."

In the blacksmith's humble opinion, this city slicker would not be able to control his fastest horse, but the glitter of the gold coin in the man's hand and his angry, impatient demands convinced him to do as he said with no further argument.

The posse galloped out of town within the hour, Moran riding beside the sheriff, desperately fighting to control his high-spirited mount. They rode off in the direction of the Dragoons and had covered a good deal of ground before they began to question and then to doubt strongly whether Laramie had indeed gone that way.

Moran heard the discussion between the sheriff and his best scout while they tried to second-guess their quarry. After a heated discussion, they turned back in the opposite direction, tracking toward another distant range of mountains.

"Do you know what you're doing, Potts?"

"Leave my job to me, Moran. Just keep your mouth shut and you'll have your daughter back before dawn." The sheriff's control over his emotions was tenuous at best.

The treacherous terrain slowed their pace, and Moran had the opportunity he'd been wanting to speak to the sheriff of his plan.

"I've decided," he began, taking a deep breath, "that it's a time I made things right. Tomorrow, once we have my Sadie back, I'm going to the judge with the real deed to the Silver Lining. Then this whole matter can be cleared up and my conscience will be clear. I'm ready to take my medicine, whatever it may be."

Potts was livid, his face fiery red with his fury. "But . . . but you can't *do* that, Moran! It will be the ruin of us all. We've worked too hard—done too much."

"You're right. We have done too many things on the wrong side of the law—and too many people have been hurt or killed. Now my daughter is in danger *again*. It's just not worth it." He let out a long, weary sigh.

"It's worth a bloody fortune! Can you really turn your back on that?"

"I think so. If I can just get Sadie back safely, nothing else matters anymore. I'm sick of the whole thing. I never expected it to go so far."

"I never expected it to go so far," the Sheriff mimicked. "But you couldn't wait to get your hands on that tidy little package of $10,000 for coming in with us, could you? Then you didn't care much about the particulars. And now that it's gotten a little sticky . . . well, that's just too bad, Moran. You're in this for keeps. Don't you even *think* of trying to get out of it anymore."

Wisely, Lucien Moran said no more.

Chapter Seventeen

Several hours' hard riding brought Laramie and Sadie well to the northwest of Tombstone, nearing the Whetstone Mountains. The Weaver ranch could not be far ahead. There had been no sign of any pursuit, and Laramie thought he might be safe there for a few days while he made plans. He could go out West and start over, but he found the thought depressing and hastily discarded it. There could be no starting over, no future for him anywhere. He knew that as well as he knew anything.

Nestled in a thicket of trees, its white adobe walls gleaming in the moonlight, the sprawling ranch house seemed to reach out to them in welcome, providing a welcome place of refuge for thcir weary bodies.

They rode slowly into a manicured courtyard and dismounted. "It feels good to have the earth under my feet," Sadie said with a tired sigh, as she handed her reins over into Laramie's outstretched hand. His fingers brushed hers and his touch sent her head reeling, making her wonder if her feet were truly on the ground.

She swayed slightly, and his strong arm was around her waist instantly. "Are you all right?" he asked, his deep voice full of concern for her.

"Yes," she said, but she thought, *I'd be better if you weren't quite so near.*

"Sure?" he asked, reluctant to release his hold on her.

"Quite sure," she murmured, stepping away, wondering what could have possessed her to ride out here with him.

"I'll tend the horses and then we'll see if we can find a way inside." His face was inscrutable, his voice firm, but unrevealing. What was he thinking? Would he be glad to be rid of her? Did he wish she'd stayed in town like he'd said? She had surely been ten kinds of a fool not to! Maybe she should go back in tomorrow.

The door proved to be unlocked and swung open easily when Laramie pushed on it. He went in first, took a long, careful look around, and then motioned for her to follow. The interior was quiet and bathed in soft golden moonglow from a skylight overhead.

"It's beautiful," she breathed, her footsteps ringing on the Mexican tiled floor as she followed him across a spacious living area. "Just the kind of place I've always dreamed of."

Laramie turned and looked into her face, aglow with pleasure. Her brown eyes sparkled, and her lips curved into a smile that made his heart skip a beat.

"There's so much I don't know about you," he said.

266

She smiled serenely up at him, but her heart was doing crazy somersaults in her chest. Did he want to know more about her? Had he any idea of the effect he was having on her?

"Sadie." His voice wrapped itself around her like an embrace. He stood so near his sweet breath touched her face. He smelled of tobacco and leather—wonderful, intriguing smells—not at all like someone should who had just broken out of jail. She was intoxicated by the sound of her name on his lips, by the nearness of his body to hers, by her own escalating reaction to him.

"Sadie. Thank you." His hand reached to caress her cheek, his thumb lightly stroking across her chin. She ceased any attempt at breathing, spellbound as she was by his touch, his voice. She was incapable of speech.

She trembled and her eyes filled with tears. He was thanking her for rescuing him. Thank God he was safe! He wouldn't be hanged tomorrow! The relief that swept through her made her knees wobbly. She hardly had time to wonder at her own weakness before he'd swept her off her feet and securely into his arms, her head cradled against his chest where his own heart pounded none too rhythmically.

"Sadie . . ." he said once more. "My love."

Could she have imagined the whispered endearment or had he really said it? *My love!* She hadn't until that moment dared to believe, to hope that he might return the love that had been building steadily in her heart for him, that she was at last willing to acknowledge to herself.

"Nate."

Nate! She'd called him Nate! Her use of his given name for the first time went through him like a double-edged sword, tearing him apart with the tenderness it implied and at the same time bringing healing in the form of a rich contentment he'd never felt before. Until now, he'd always been simply "Laramie." He had gotten used to it, even liked it, really. But the way her soft voice lingered over the single syllable of his first name was very special and in his mind marked a substantial change in their relationship.

He levered himself down onto an overstuffed sofa, still holding her close and placed a kiss on the top of her satiny hair.

"You smell wonderful," he murmured.

"Lilac water."

"Yes, that, too. But *you* smell wonderful, Sadie. I want to inhale you, to touch you all over. I want to love you. God help me, Sadie! I want to make love to you!"

"I need you, too, Nate, as I've never needed anything before. I love you, Nate Laramie."

"And I love you." His lips claimed hers, searing her with unquenched desire. Their passions, once ignited by words of love, flamed out of control.

They would have this one night, if they had no other, and it would be worth any price. It would be theirs for a lifetime.

"Well, love me then. Love me, Nate."

Her arms fastened around his neck and pulled his head down to hers fiercely. Her soft lips moved beneath his and her tongue made tentative forays into his, teasing, tantalizing, beckoning, promising. He responded in kind, taking possession of her lips, her mouth, wanting more than anything to make her wholly his, for this moment and for always.

Without relinquishing the kiss, he stood up with her in his arms and strode in the direction of an arched doorway, inexpressibly glad to discover an oversized bed waiting on the other side of it.

Holding her firmly in one arm, he reached down and flipped back a quilted spread. Ever so gently, he deposited her on top of the sheets, leaning over her, reluctant to release his hold on her even long enough to remove his hampering clothes.

"God! Sadie! You're so beautiful. You take my breath away!"

"I'm not breathing too easily myself, or had you noticed?"

He had.

He was, in fact, awed by the extent of her response to him, by the love shining from her eyes and by her ardor, which seemed equal to his own. His eyes lingered on the unsteady rise and fall of her chest, and his hand sought to calm the rhythm by caressing and stroking the smooth roundness, by filling his hands with her. She only breathed faster and he grinned down at her. "That doesn't help?"

"No," she sighed, over the hammering of her heart. "But who needs to breathe?"

A much stronger need was coiled tightly, like a rattler poised to strike, deep in her stomach. It was terrible, awesome, and wonderful. Nothing else mattered, except this man and this night in his arms. She felt she had lived all of her life for this, and she opened herself completely to the joy she knew he was capable of bringing her.

"Maybe," he said, his voice low and seductive, "if this were looser, you could breathe more easily."

His fingers began to move down the row of buttons of the man's shirt she wore, and it fell open, revealing perfectly shaped globes of ivory skin. His breath caught in his throat.

"Having trouble breathing yourself, Laramie?" she asked with a satisfied laugh as she shrugged out of the shirt and pulled him down to her.

"Wait!" she laughed, pushing him away again, urgently wanting to feel him closer to her, to feel his skin on hers. "Wait! Here!"

Small but agile fingers worked loose the buttons on his heavy shirt, and she pushed it impatiently back off his shoulders. Eagerly, her fingers ran through the thick, curly mat of hair on his chest.

With a muffled cry, he lowered himself over her, fitting himself to her until every inch of her bare skin was covered by his. She felt warm and womanly next to him, and the heat rose even further in his loins, demanding that he take her, make her fully his.

His hand slid between them and worked his belt buckle free, then unfastened his breeches. He lifted himself on one arm and gently tugged her trousers down over slender hips until she lay before him nude, except for the pants around her ankles, her alabaster skin glowing in the moonlight.

"Are you cold?" he asked, sitting on the edge of the bed to remove his boots, but his eyes never left her. He tossed his boots, one at a time, onto the floor. Standing, he dropped his buckskin trousers and stepped out of them.

She looked at him, enthralled by his masculine beauty and his obvious need for her.

"No." She laughed. "I'm very warm, in fact."

Gently, he pulled her boots off and dropped them down beside the bed. Then he caressed her legs as he slid her trousers off over her slender feet.

Her eyes were dreamy and unfocused, but each movement he made, his slightest touch, impacted on her. She moved in response, then in total abandonment as she gave herself over to the sensations swirling through her.

She thought if he didn't stop his tender torment she would surely die, but she knew she was dead if he did stop.

"Don't stop!" she entreated. "Nate! Oh, Nate! Don't ever stop loving me, please."

"I won't Sadie, my love. I won't ever stop. You're mine and you'll always be mine. Say it. Say you love me."

"I love you. I do! With all my heart. . . ."

Her words were smothered as once more his mouth consumed hers. He kissed her deeply and she kissed him in return, putting her whole heart into it. His hands still stroked the length of her hip and down her legs and back up to brush the sides of her breasts now nestled into his chest.

Her hands trailed down his muscled back, massaging and exploring. She loved the feel of him, his strength, his smooth, warm skin. He was her whole world as they lay there more one than two. Her legs wrapped around his instinctively and she felt an insistent nudging between her open thighs. She was ready for him and arched her back, reaching up to him, welcoming him.

He thrust gently, but she was having none of it. She urged him on with her hands, which slid down his back, dropped below his waist, and pulled him to her, holding him as close as she could. They moved in a true unison known only to lovers, delighting in the sensation.

She was more than ready when his love exploded inside her, bringing her to a height of passion that was very much akin to pain, and she cried out once.

"Did I hurt you?" He tried to pull away, his eyes full of concern for her.

"No! Oh, no! You would never hurt me. You never could. I loved it! And I love you for always."

"Yes, for always." Tonight, it was enough that they said the words. Tomorrow would be soon enough to prove if they could really ever be true.

They lay content in each other's arms, surrounded by a comforting cocoon of their mutual satisfaction, of their love. Before the night was over, they would sample the same sensual pleasures again, more than once. Each time their joy and delight seemed to increase and become harder to contain. They reveled in touching, in feeling, in caressing, and in the discovery of new wonders.

Fulfilled in a way she'd never been before, and perhaps never expected to be, Sadie lay still in his arms. The knowledge of her love for Nate Laramie swept through her with a delicious but bittersweet pain. Though she knew now how much she cared for him and how much she would willingly sacrifice for him, there were problems, impediments to their relationship, even to their lives, that loomed large in the predawn semi-darkness. She wondered if they'd ever be able to overcome them and whether they could ever have any kind of a life together.

As though reading her thoughts and sharing her doubts, he spoke into the darkness, "You have to go back, Sadie. I couldn't bear it if something happened to you. You're in danger here. I can't keep you safe."

The admission was for him the hardest thing he'd ever had to say, but the odds against them were insurmountable. And it was true: he couldn't protect her from the dangers, and they could never run far enough to escape them.

"No!" she cried. "I won't leave you! I can't!" A vision flashed into her mind of bullets tearing into the chest where her head now rested. Or his beautiful, much-loved body suspended above the ground by a rope, booted feet dangling in the air.

Tears flowed from her eyes unnoticed until they traced their way down her face and dropped onto his bare skin. "You know I'd go to the other side of the world for you. Please let me stay with you, Nate. I'm not worried about being on the wrong side of the law. I never thought much of the 'law'

273

in Tombstone, anyway!"

"Sadie," he said, his voice infinitely soft and tender, his hand under chin lifting her head so he could look directly into her exquisite, sad brown eyes. "Don't you see? I'll never allow you to be hurt. And you can find only hurt with me. I have no life, no future. Even if I get away from Potts, there's nowhere—*nowhere*—for me to go." His eyes were turbulent and filled with raw pain, the same pain that now made it impossible for her to speak.

Hungry mouths and bodies fused in a futile attempt to allay their growing fears and the unseen demons that pursued them. Breathless, she pulled away at last. A picture of his life on the run filled her mind. He'd be an outcast, hunted every day of his life. He would never have any peace. She couldn't let him do that to himself. They had to make a stand now and settle this thing. He was not guilty, and she would help him prove it.

"Let's go back, Nate. I'll help you, and I'll make Father help. We'll clear your name and see that you have a fair trial. We can put all this behind us."

It was a desperate plan, doomed to failure, and they both knew it. He said nothing.

"No," she said, shaking her head in resignation. "Of course you can't go back. They would kill you before anyone could stop them, wouldn't they?"

An imperceptible nod of his head acknowledged the truth of her statement.

"All right, then," she said quietly, her feelings resolved. "I will go back tomorrow. You can go on running alone. Without me along, you'll be able to

274

get away. I'll do everything I can—in Tombstone, in Tucson, in Washington, if necessary—and I know I'll be able to prove your innocence. I'll never stop trying. I love you, Nate." She kissed him.

"We still have tonight," she said, her lips only a whisper, a breath away from his. "Just for this one night, we'll be together. Then I'll go, if you still want me to."

Want her to! God! did he want to cut off his right arm? It was all he could do not to take her up on her generous offer of herself and run away with her, as far and as fast as they could.

Maybe to Alaska . . . ? He could do some prospecting there. Maybe he'd make another rich strike and they wouldn't have to worry about anything anymore.

No, it could never work. He kissed her again, knowing he loved her too much to take her with him. He loved her too much to endanger her safety.

They slept only with the arrival of the dawn, the quilt drawn up to their chins, still wrapped in an intimate embrace, arms and legs entwined. Until the time came, they would put thoughts of leaving out of their minds.

"I've sent a rider north to find the marshall, Rachel, but, it could be days, maybe a week or more before he finds him and gets him back here." Rachel and Jonathan had watched Laramie and Sadie ride out of town, satisfied that they'd gotten away

275

without being seen and that they'd done all they could for them for the time being.

"And that may be too late for Nate."

"Yes, *if* the sheriff catches up with him. But Laramie's smart, and you gave him a good place to hide. They should be safe there for a while."

"I hope so."

He pulled her into his arms and felt his heart jump when she came willingly and laid her head trustingly on his shoulder. She felt so good, so right, next to him. He never intended to let her go again.

"What about Moran?"

"He rode out with the posse. He should be safe enough."

"You know what they'll do if they catch Nate, don't you, Jonathan?

"Yes, but we just have to hope and believe he's covered his tracks and is safely hidden."

"Yes. Did you know Sadie's in love with him?"

"Moran's daughter?" he asked, caught by surprise.

"Mm-hmm. I could see it in her face. And why else would she help him."

"That's true. She brought him a gun and a horse, and she rode out of town with him." He found himself wishing that someday someone might care for him that much. No, he corrected himself, not someday . . . *now,* and not someone . . . *Rachel!* That his tender feelings for her had turned to love occurred to him, even while they talked of Sadie's love for Laramie.

Wanting time to sort out his new feelings before

speaking of them to Rachel, he put his hands on her arms and took a step back. "I'd better walk you home now. We don't want the boys to worry any more than they already have."

"All right," she agreed softly, her eyes still searching his.

Christopher's excited voice rang out as soon as they entered the house. "Mama! Mr. Lee! You should have seen Mrs. Connors talk back to the sheriff! She was really somethin'! And he was so angry, but then he left and she made us some cocoa and we been sittin' here talkin' and waitin' for you!" The words rolled out of his mouth in his exuberance to see her home safely. "Where'd you meet up with Mr. Lee? What'cha been doin'?"

"Whoa there, Chris. We'll answer all your questions. Just slow down a little bit. Maybe you could get your Mama a cup of that chocolate while we catch our breath?"

"Sure 'nuff, Mr. Lee!" He jumped to the task, anxious to please and eager to be a part of the grown-up activities swirling about him. "Would you like some, too, Mr. Lee?" he asked Jonathan.

"Sure would. Thanks."

Rachel hugged Elizabeth Connors. "Thanks so much for being here and for what you did with the sheriff."

"He had no business comin' here like that and demandin' to see you—a nice widow-lady like yourself. Don't think he'll try it again soon, though. I purely did put him in his place."

She laughed, remembering the sheriff's nonplussed countenance when she'd denied him en-

277

trance to the Foster home in no uncertain terms. "Said he was gettin' up a posse, though. Sure hope your Mr. Laramie has a good place to hide out till this blows over!

"He'll be all right," Jonathan broke in, but his words were directed as much toward comforting Rachel as they were to the doctor's elderly widow.

"Where is he, Mr. Lee?" Christopher asked, excitement still quivering in his high-pitched voice.

"Well, now, son, I really don't know exactly," he replied truthfully. "But I'm sure he's in a safe place by now, and a long way from Tombstone."

Rachel spent a restless night worrying about Laramie and Sadie, having heard the sheriff and his men ride out after them sometime later, but she couldn't help being glad he'd escaped and feeling a measure of pride for the part she'd played in it.

With Potts out of town, and off in the wrong direction, it should be safe for her to ride out to the ranch the next morning with the supplies she'd promised, and she could make sure Nate and Sadie were okay.

Sunrise found her humming as she loaded her buggy with a few small boxes of staple goods, along with some home-cooked food and a gallon of fresh water, just in case. She remembered to throw in a couple of handmade quilts as well.

Mrs. Connors arrived to look after the boys. When Rachel spoke with Christopher about her plans, she was purposefully vague, knowing he'd want to go along if he knew her destination. Mrs. Connors wisely directed his attention to helping her with a project she'd brought along, and Rachel was able to get away without too many more questions.

Gathering up her skirts, she climbed up into the buggy and guided the good-natured horse out of the backyard and into the road leading out of town toward the northwest.

Anxious to be safely away, she urged the horse into a trot, unaware that a horse and rider were racing to catch up with her until a man's voice alerted her to his presence.

"Just where do you think you're going, Rachel Foster?" he demanded.

Rachel pulled back on the reins, recognizing the voice of Jonathan Lee. She'd known how vehemently he would object, and had hoped to get out of town without his knowledge.

"Morning, Jonathan," she said pleasantly.

"Morning, yourself. Now, would you mind answering my question?"

"As you can see, I have some supplies. And I'm on my way out to the Weaver ranch to deliver them."

"And you knew I wouldn't let you go alone, so you didn't bother telling me. Why not, Rachel? I thought we trusted each other. I would have gone in your place."

"I know that. And I do trust you, but I've asked far too much of you already. You've been very kind to help me and Nate."

"It is not kindness that led me into helping you," he replied, his voice serious. "I happen to like and respect your friend. And I feel a strong amount of affection for one Rachel Foster, as well."

He was smiling now, and she was inexpressibly glad that he was no longer angry.

"I'm really sorry, Jonathan. I should have told you," she admitted. Why don't you tie your horse on behind and climb in, if that suits you?"

"It sure does; that suits me just fine," he affirmed, doing as she suggested.

The day seemed a little brighter with him beside her, and she felt a lot more comfortable with the the trip ahead of her.

She told him honestly, "I'm glad you caught me."

"Me, too, Mrs. Foster. Me, too!"

He took the reins from her and slipped an arm around her shoulders. "There's almost nothing that's not more pleasant if it's shared by two. Hyah!" he yelled to the horse, picking up the pace, although he was in no big hurry to reach their destination.

It was mid-afternoon when they finally reached the picture-perfect Weaver ranch. It seemed much too quiet. There was no sign of any of the animals outside, and no sounds came from inside.

"Is something wrong?" she asked.

"I don't know. Maybe they decided to hide out somewhere else."

"Or something's happened to them." Rachel was alarmed and frightened that the sheriff might have been there ahead of them, that her ideal hiding place had instead proven to be a trap.

"You stay here," he cautioned her, handing her

the reins and stepping lightly down from the buggy. "I'll go have a look around."

The revolver in his hand should have reassured her, but somehow it didn't.

"Be careful, Jonathan."

"I will. If there's *any* sign of trouble, you hightail it out of here as fast as you can. Promise?"

He untied his horse from the buggy and let the reins fall to the ground, knowing his horse would stand there until he needed him.

"Promise?" he repeated.

"Yes, I promise." She didn't want him to go in there alone, but had no idea how she might stop him. "Be careful," she whispered once more.

Jonathan worked his way across the front courtyard, making cover of the lawn ornaments and the well, anything he could use to keep himself hidden from the house. If Laramie had been in there, he would have heard them coming, recognized Rachel's buggy and horse, and been outside to meet them.

If he wasn't inside, then someone else could easily be there, and, he was not taking any chances. The sheriff of Tombstone had been eager to be rid of Jonathan Lee ever since he'd made his first appearance in town at the governor's reception. It was wise to be cautious around an unscrupulous man like Dan Potts.

Jonathan was close enough to one of the front windows to have a peek inside. Nothing seemed out of place, and it appeared peaceful and deserted, but he eased his way around back just to be sure. Slipping inside, he checked out each of the eight large rooms in the house. It was empty.

Then where were Laramie and Sadie Moran? Were they in danger? Out back again, he checked the barn before returning to Rachel, who had remained obediently exactly where he'd left her.

"No one here," he told her. "But I didn't see any signs of trouble. And their horses are still in the back. They probably went for a walk. It *is* a nice day, isn't it?"

Rachel smiled down at him. "Yes, it is. Help me down?"

He did, but was careful about how long his hands lingered around her waist. They loaded their arms with the parcels she'd brought and took them around to the the kitchen door.

"Let's go back out and take a look around for them," he suggested, after they'd unpacked the boxes.

They walked around the spacious grounds of the beautiful house and sat at last on a bench built beneath the yawning spread of a paloverde tree.

"How did you manage to get away without young Christopher?"

She chuckled. "It wasn't easy, but with Mrs. Connors on my side, he didn't really have a chance!"

He laughed. "She can be quite formidable, huh? As can a certain young woman I know."

"Formidable? No one's ever described me in quite that way before, Mr. Lee." She laughed. "And I'm not sure whether I should be flattered or offended."

"Well, perhaps no one else knows you quite as

282

well as I do, Mrs. Foster," he said with a wink that took her back to the first night she'd met this remarkable man at the governor's reception. She wasn't sure she knew him very well, though. It seemed he talked very little about his past or his reasons for being in Tombstone.

"I'm glad you didn't leave with the governor," she said.

"Me, too."

"But why *did* you stay on, Jonathan? It wasn't just because of Nate's troubles, was it?"

"No," he answered honestly. "I had my reasons. A job I'd been assigned to do required that I stay here. And," he continued, "I stayed because of a certain fascinating blonde who practically knocked me off my feet!"

Her eyebrow raised, she looked to see if he was still joking with her. "You're teasing me, aren't you?" she accused him.

"No! I'm quite serious. Of course, the blond I'm talking about is only about three-and-a-half feet tall and almost literally knocked me off my feet when he ran into me at the livery!"

"Christopher! Why, Jonathan Lee, you're impossible! You lead a girl on in the most unforgivable way."

She started to get up, but he took her hand and pulled her back down beside him, saying, "No, I'm not leading you on, Rachel. And this is no joke."

He kissed her and by the time he was through, neither of them was laughing, but both were happier than they'd been in a long, long time.

"I think I'm falling in love with Christopher's

283

mother." His eyes twinkled as they held hers. "Is it possible she might care for me a little, too?"

"It is just possible, Jonathan Lee, it is just entirely possible."

"We have to discuss this further, but right now, I think we'd best be about the business of searching for those two elusive friends of yours!"

The brilliant sun had begun its stately ascent into the blue sky that morning when Sadie awoke by Laramie's side. The night they'd spent in each other's arms was not something she would soon forget. It was not something she'd *ever* forget. Now he slept peacefully, and she studied his face for a few moments, drinking in every feature, before slipping from the bed. She found her shirt where she'd discarded it the night before and slid her arms into it. It fell below her knees, and she didn't bother putting on her pants or her boots.

Barefoot, she walked through the house, enjoying the polished beauty of the oak furnishings, the colorful braided rugs, and the paintings with a definite southwestern flavor that decorated the walls. It was truly a lovely home. She couldn't imagine why anyone would want to leave it, even for a short while. But she was glad, so glad they had!

For a moment, she tried to pretend that none of this nightmare was real, that this house was their own home—hers and Laramie's—and that they could be happy and safe here. She stepped out onto a covered portico and breathed in the fresh

284

mountain air. A perfectly glorious day was promised by the cool, dry air and brilliant, warm sunshine. The birds and the trees seemed alive with
color and song.

At that moment, she understood Laramie's love
for this dazzling Arizona and began to share it.
The red rock cliffs stood in stark relief beyond a
rolling green mesa. No sign remained of the snow
that had swept through the Dragoons, making the
two of them prisoners in a hillside cave. She
smiled.

It had been interesting, being there with Nate
Laramie, but it would have been even more interesting if she'd known him then as she did now.
She'd had no idea of the passionate wonders
awaiting her under his quilt, or she might have
crawled under sooner. And if she had, they might
still be in that cave!

Her happy laughter was melodious, infectious.
Laramie awoke instantly at the sound of it. He
stretched and yawned widely.

Then she was standing there in the doorway—
bare, slender legs and feet, her shirt carelessly buttoned, hinting blatantly at what he knew was
underneath! She was the most beautiful woman
he'd ever seen, and God help him, he loved her
with a passion he hadn't thought possible.

"Sadie Moran, you are a witch, a very cunning
witch." He spoke gruffly, but there was no rancor
in his voice.

"And are you completely under my spell now?"
she asked, moving toward him across the room like
a hungry cat stalking its prey, her eyes hypnotiz-

ing, mesmerizing.

He felt himself grow hard and held out his arms to her. She tumbled across him, covering his face with kisses, raking her nails softly up and down the length of his arms before trailing them down his chest and along the lean line of his hips.

"Yes," he murmured, pinning her against him so that neither could breathe comfortably. "Yes! I admit it! I am absolutely under your spell. I'd do anything you say."

"Anything?" she demanded, her voice husky with aroused passion. "There *is* one thing. . . ."

"Ahhhh!"

She reached for the quilt and pulled it over their heads with a happy sigh. "Mmmmm."

It was well past noon before they gave a thought to breakfast.

"How about an omelette and ham and biscuits?" she asked as he trailed her out into the well-equipped, spotless kitchen.

"You're not that much of a witch, lady."

"No. Maybe not. Let's see. No eggs. No ham—wait! Isn't that a smokehouse out there? Make yourself useful and see about bringing in some meat. Then you can start a good fire, Laramie, and maybe I can find a big pot or a skillet, or something."

He bowed to her commands with a crooked smile and moved into action. Sadie watched him through the window as he lifted a heavy bolt and dragged the door open. Her eyes lit up when he strode back out with his arms full, closing and bolting the door carefully behind him.

They would have a good breakfast after all.

"Have you forgotten that this outlaw has my daughter for the second time, Sheriff? And there's no telling where he may be taking her, or what he plans to do with her," Moran insisted, trying to keep his seat in the saddle as his excited mount danced beneath him. "Why are we stopping here?"

He wanted nothing so much as to feel the ground under his feet again, but he was determined they keep doggedly on the trail of Laramie and Sadie.

During the long day, the scout had found and lost their trail several times, and it seemed there was still some question as to which road they might have taken.

"Well?"

"The scout needs a closer look, just to be sure, and we've been riding hard for hours. The horses need rest. You look like you could use a little stretch yourself, Moran. I know you're unaccustomed to the saddle."

Realizing he had no choice, but muttering his disapproval, Moran dismounted awkwardly. His knees were stiff and his legs wobbly, and the damned animal he'd been riding sidled away from him, pulling at the reins he was grasping tightly in his fist.

"Let me have him," the sheriff commanded. "Go sit down for a minute."

The scout returned and held a whispered conversation with the sheriff. It was obvious to everyone

287

that they had lost the trail once more. Laramie had outsmarted them again.

Anger hovered over the sheriff like a black thundercloud, and even Moran knew better than to say or do anything to antagonize him further.

"We'll camp here for the rest of the night," he barked, "and start out fresh again early tomorrow morning."

"Not me!" Moran said quietly. "I'm going on! If you won't come, I'll go on alone. My daughter's out there! I know she is. And I will find her."

"And just what will you do if you accidentally run into them, Moran?"

"I . . . I'll take care of Laramie, and I'll get Sadie back," he said, with a good deal more bravado than he felt.

"Sure, and I'm the King of England!" scoffed the sheriff. "You'll do nothing but get your fool self killed, or you'll get lost out here and no one will ever find you!" The thought was imminently pleasant to an irate Sheriff Potts, and he allowed the very determined Lucien Moran to ride out alone without further comment.

No meal Sadie had ever eaten, regardless of how carefully prepared, had ever tasted as good as the very simple breakfast she and Laramie shared. All of her senses were heightened to an exquisite level — colors appeared more vivid, foods were more flavorful, aromas more tempting, even the twittering of the birds in the trees outside held a sweeter sound for her. Laramie had turned her

288

world upside down and then set it upright again—but everything had changed. It was all more splendid than she could have imagined.

The sparkling white flash of his teeth in happy smiles was much more frequent this morning, and she knew he must be feeling some of the same thrilling joy that filled her to overflowing.

In a night of passionate, repeated lovemaking, they had shared their souls and opened up to each other. Surprisingly, neither had been hurt by the other, as they had feared. When their eyes met, a new silent understanding and closeness passed between them.

Sadie had never been so happy in her life. She never wanted to leave this place, or his arms. If by wishing she could make it so, it would be, and they'd stay here forever.

"Come with me. I have something to show you." His blue eyes twinkled with mystery, and his smile and outstretched hand urged her to join him.

"Okay, but I really think I should put my pants and boots on first, if we're going outdoors."

He was obviously reluctant and allowed her time to dress only by thinking ahead to what he was planning for her. "Well, hurry up, then, while I clear this away."

He kissed her thoroughly, turned her around, and pushed her through the doorway, watching her until she was out of his sight.

Efficiently, he cleared away their dishes and washed and dried the plates and silver, stowing everything away exactly where it had been. He wiped off the oak dining table, and was waiting

289

for her when she reappeared.

"Mmmm. Think I liked you better the other way."

"You're a lecherous man, Nate Laramie."

"Yes," he agreed, licking his lips.

She smiled and lifted herself up on her toes to receive another long, lingering kiss.

"We'll never get there, if we don't stop this," he groaned, breaking away reluctantly.

"Get where?"

"It's a secret. But you will like it, have no fear, Miss Moran."

He took her hand and led her out into the courtyard, through the gate, and up a narrow trail that wound into the mountain looming up steeply behind the house.

They had walked nearly a mile when he turned off the trail, leading her into a thick grove of trees. She ducked beneath the branches he carefully held aside for her. Below them, white rocks glistened along a riverbed and they followed it until it disappeared around a bend.

"Close your eyes."

She did. He led her up and around the bend. "Now stand right here." He positioned her just so, then said, "Open your eyes now, Sadie."

She did. Her eyes widened at the magnificent beauty of the place. Just below them was a very deep pond, with water so clear she could see massive boulders at the very bottom. A breathtaking waterfall cascaded down from far above their heads.

Laramie watched her delight, inordinately

pleased with himself for bringing such a look to her face. He knew he had to find a way to put an end to the feelings growing between them, but wasn't sure he possessed the strength. He had been hit hard, sometime during the night they'd spent together, with the knowledge of just how much he loved this Sadie Moran. His captive had turned the tables on him and kidnapped his own renegade heart. He felt that he must leave her a way out of the relationship, a relationship with no future, no matter how much he tried to fool himself.

He wasn't good enough for her. What kind of life could he offer her? With him, she'd never have any security. And there were so many things to keep them apart. She hated Arizona; he doubted he could live anywhere else. She was a city girl; he a cowboy, wanted by the law. She had led a sheltered life; he had hardly had a shelter for most of his life.

On the other hand, when she'd fought beside him, she'd hardly seemed like a sheltered city girl. And she had never complained or held back from doing what needed to be done. She had the grit of a pioneer woman, and she could do anything she set her mind to. But what made him think she'd ever set her mind to making a life with him, way out here in the Arizona territory? She was much too smart for that, much too smart to love someone like him.

And there's the little problem of the sheriff and a posse, he reminded himself. He would not allow himself to dream any longer dreams that could never come true. The sooner she was gone from him, the better. He had to do whatever was necessary to see that she returned to Tombstone and to her father, and it must happen quickly, before he lost completely the will to send her back.

The troubled look on his tanned, rugged face almost wiped the happy smile off hers as Sadie struggled with herself, not wanting him to know the direction her own thoughts were taking.

"What is it?" she asked.

"Nothing. I was just thinking you should have shot me when you had the chance."

"Nate Laramie! You're a bigger fool than I ever thought you could be! What could possibly be going on in that thick skull of yours?" She backed away, a glint in her eyes. "Besides, you'd better be careful what you say. I'm a much better shot than I was back then!"

The music of her laughter brought a reluctant smile to his lips, but did nothing to remove the doubts that plagued him when he thought of her. He was a drifter, with nothing to show for his life. And there was a part of himself, deep inside, that had withered and died a long time ago. He was less than a whole man. He doubted he would ever be whole again.

Still, when she smiled and looked at him like that, it was all he could do to keep from sweeping her into his arms and holding her there forever. She was sunshine to his shadow, innocence to his world-weariness, honor to his dishonor, sweetness to his impotent anger. Had two people ever been less alike? Could he ever love anyone more?

Sadie saw both the love and the terrible turmoil

in his eyes. Determined that they enjoy their interlude in this beautiful, secluded spot, she challenged, "Let's take a dip!"

"What? Sadie, it's cold! And that water's icy."

"Yes," she said, with a slow, sultry smile, "but we can warm each other."

Grinning, he began stripping off his clothes and splashed into the crystal clear water ahead of her.

"Brrr!" he said, shivering, but he reached up eagerly to catch her when she jumped into his arms.

Laughing, he staggered back, lost his balance, and fell, taking her under the water with him. Choking, gasping for breath, they broke the surface of the water as one.

"When do we start to get warm?" His lips descended to claim hers and their bodies pressed together tightly.

"Any minute now," she promised as her hands stroked down the length of his smoothly muscled shoulders and back. "Aren't you feeling any warmer yet?" she asked innocently as her hand crept around to caress the hard length of his desire. "Yes, it seems you are."

"Sadie Moran! You really *are* a witch! You can make a man hot in icy water. C'mere!" he gasped, pulling her closer. "I think you can stand a little warming yourself!"

"Ahh! yes!" she moaned, and he slipped inside her, cushioning her body against his, supporting her weight easily. They moved in the wonderful age-old rhythms of love, mindless of the chilly waters that swirled about them.

The sun had climbed higher in the sky and

added its warmth to that of the quilt he'd brought along that they snuggled under after their brief swim.

"That's one way to get you under my quilt," he chuckled.

"I don't think you'll have any more trouble with simple persuasion," she countered, snug and happy in his arms. "I'll join you under a quilt anytime, Nate Laramie. And I'll stay there just as long as you'll let me. I never knew how much fun could be had underneath one. I thought they were just for keeping out the cold, silly me!"

"Well, that, too," he murmured, his lips nuzzling her ear and sliding down the column of her neck. "Not cold now, are you?"

"No, I don't think I'll ever be cold again. And I like it right here."

His lips moved over the swell of her breast. "Me, too," he whispered against the softness of her skin. "And here—and here—and here."

The banked fires in her responded to his caresses and were soon flaming hotly. "You've brought out the wanton in me, Laramie."

"Where is that particular streak, Miss Moran? Is it here? No? Here?"

"Ohhh! You're torturing me, sir! Yes! Yes! It's there—and there—and there!"

The quilt fell away, but neither of them noticed, even as the afternoon sun did its work, warming their bare skin with its golden rays.

Tombstone seemed a world away. The only realities were the gentle lapping of the water, the rustle of a soft breeze through the tops of the trees, and the azure sky overhead.

Sadie lay on her back, hands clasped behind her head, and looked up into eyes the same clear blue as the sky, eyes that were smiling down at her with a tenderness and love that made her heart lurch.

"Only what's happening here and now — that's all that matters, Nate."

"Yes." His hand stroked her brilliant mass of hair and his eyes held hers, as though he would enter her soul, have her every thought open to him.

"There's only today, only you and me and this beautiful place," she said. "I'm so happy you brought me here. I wish I could stay here forever, right here in your arms."

"Yes." He aligned his body beside hers and pulled her tightly against him. She felt the urgency of his need when his lips brushed across hers and all else was forgotten.

From atop a bluff not far away, Jonathan and Rachel were witness to a portion of the romantic scene before they turned away in embarrassment. They had followed the trail leading up to the mountain from the house until they happened upon the idyllic spot where Laramie and Sadie had thought themselves to be alone.

"I think they might prefer to be left alone. What do you think?"

"I agree," she said, a becoming, rosy blush sweeping up over the classic contours of her face. "Let's go."

Quietly they slipped away, back the way they'd come, leaving the two lovers luxuriating in each other's arms, still unaware they'd been observed. Jonathan tied his horse to the back of the buggy again, and they climbed back in, making a hasty, good-natured exit.

Chapter Eighteen

Moran made his solitary way through the desert, following a roadway at times indistinct and overgrown, cursing himself for being a fool for leaving the sheriff and his small posse. He knew nothing about the country through which he was riding, and less than nothing about how to capture an outlaw, if indeed he ever caught up with him!

But he did know he had failed Sadie too many times in her short life to let her down now. He had never been able to fill the empty spot left by her mother's death, and he hadn't been much of a father. He'd neglected her and done things to imperil her future, though he'd always thought he'd been acting with her best interests in mind. If only he could find her and get her back home to St. Louis, he'd spend the rest of his life making it up to her.

He'd made up his mind that as soon as he was back in Tombstone, he'd go straight to the judge and settle matters about the Silver Lining. He'd never felt good about that deal, but he hadn't realized how wrong it had been until recently. Sadie had explained to him about Jeffrey and Rachel Foster and what the loss of his mine and his friend had done to Laramie as they had ridden side by side down out of the Dragoons. No wonder the man had become an outlaw—and a kidnapper. The shady dealings of the "company," comprised of himself, Sheriff Potts, and several other powerful businessmen, had driven him to it.

But what was Laramie doing with Sadie now? Had he grabbed her again as his insurance, or had she gone willingly this time? That possibility brought him up short, and a sharp pain stabbed into his chest. Had she run away with the outlaw, even taking his horse and without saying a word of good-bye to him?

A blazing red sun settled down, sliding out of sight beyond the purpling mountains. His heart told him he'd find Sadie if he kept on following the road leading into the Whetstones. Shadows lengthened, and he worried about what he might discover if he did catch up with his daughter and Laramie.

"No! Nate! It's almost dark." Sadie laughed merrily while sliding slender legs into the wide trousers and rolling them several times around her waist so they didn't drag the ground. "Let's go back to the house. I'm starving!"

"Me, too!" His hawklike brows lifted suggestively, telling her food was far from his mind. His hands encircled her bare midriff and pulled her back into him for one more long kiss.

Walking back to the ranch house, they argued heatedly, their disagreement marring the blissful day they'd just spent in each other's arms.

"I'm taking you back tonight, and that's the end

298

of it."

"I can go alone, Nate. It's not hard to find the way. If anyone were to see you, they'd take you back to be hanged, with no questions asked.

"I don't plan on getting caught, Sadie, but I will absolutely not allow you to go back by yourself."

He cared enough about her to endanger himself for her! Her heart found new hope in the fact. But she couldn't let him do it. She'd do anything in order to keep him from putting himself in such a dangerous spot. Drastic measures appeared to be in order.

She began to devise a plan even as they neared the house. Before she could carry it out, she would have to convince him she'd had a change of heart about letting him take her back to Tombstone.

"You're a stubborn, hard-headed man, Nate Laramie. And there's just no arguing with you, is there?"

"Nope!" he agreed with a self-satisfied smile. "So let's get ready to ride."

"All right, we'll do it your way, but at least let me fix us something to eat first. I'm still starving!"

He laughed, relieved that she had capitulated and eager to please her. "So what'll it be?"

"Didn't you say you saw some beef out in the smokehouse? That sounds wonderful. We could barbecue some and have some of those new potatoes . . . Her mouth watered, but she knew if her plan went well, neither of them would be enjoying the feast she described this night.

"Come on, let's go take a look in there." He couldn't have played into her hands any better. She walked beside him around back of the house, still holding his hand.

She stood back while he opened the door, though. "It's too dark for me in there. You choose something and bring it out, okay?"

"All right, ma'am," he said, walking inside without suspecting what she had in mind for him. He whistled happily.

Sadie stepped back, leaned against the door, and shoved it closed. As quickly as she could, she dropped the heavy bar into place. A look of total horror crossed her face. She couldn't believe what she'd done to him.

Neither could he.

At first, his voice was incredulous. "Sadie? What's happened? Are you all right?"

When there was no answer, he became more concerned, his voice growing louder. "Sadie? Answer me, please. What's going on?"

"I'm sorry, Laramie," she said, just loud enough for him to hear, and then turned away and ran toward the barn. She had become more proficient at saddling a horse with the practice she'd had lately, and handled that task without too much difficulty. The hard part was leaving him behind.

Riding out under the archway that marked the entrance to the Weaver ranch, Sadie heard thunderous blows falling on the sturdy wooden door of the smokehouse and heard his angry shouts.

"Sadie! You come back here and open this door! Let me out of here! Stop this foolishness right now!"

But it wasn't foolishness, and she could not stop. She'd done what she had to do, though he would never understand or forgive her. It was the only way she could keep him from endangering himself by riding back to Tombstone with her. She tried to close her ears to the sounds of his angry curses followed by a pleading tone of voice even harder to ignore.

"We can discuss this, Sadie. How can you do this to me?"

She nudged her horse with her knees, urging him into a canter, anxious to be out of range of his voice. There was not a part of her that didn't long to fly back, open the door, and throw herself into his arms. She knew there was a chance, a good possibility, in spite of what she'd said, that they would never see each other again, never hold each other, never make love again. Still, she'd had to leave him.

If she could convince her father to help, maybe they would have a chance to clear Laramie's name. But Lucien Moran was a proud and stubborn man, and she wasn't sure she really had a chance of enlisting his aid.

An owl hooted eerily from a branch somewhere overhead, and Sadie jumped in alarm. While she'd been torturing herself with thoughts of Laramie, it had grown suddenly quite dark, and the slightest sound was now magnified tenfold.

Laramie was right. She was a fool! She hadn't realized what it would be like in the desert alone after dark. Why hadn't she at least waited until morning?

But she knew the answer to that. Even if she had been able to persuade Laramie to wait that long before taking her back, she feared she would never have been strong enough to leave him had she spent one more hour, much less one more night in his arms.

Her body longed for the comfort of his caress even as her heart pined for words of love she would probably never hear again. How easy it would be to turn and ride straight back to him. How precious the extra hours she could spend showing him how much she loved him!

But if she did what she wanted most in the world—turned around and went back—she'd be doing the unthinkable. She would be a danger, a very real danger to his safety, and a threat to his life. He could ride farther, faster, and much easier without her.

It might take him a few hours, but she was sure he would be able to escape the smokehouse. She could send Jonathan back just to make sure. Then he could be on his way to somewhere far away. She harbored a small hope the sheriff might even give up the chase if she were back safely, especially if she could get her father on her side.

She must hurry to reach Tombstone or the posse before they got to Laramie. But in the darkness, it was so difficult to make out the trail she slowed her horse even further, terrified he might step in a hole and stumble, or that she'd lose her way altogether. Picking her way along when she wanted nothing more than to race across the miles separating her from town was necessary, but very hard.

The moon arched into the midnight-blue sky, its welcome light a beacon allowing her to move along a little more quickly. Strange noises continued to plague her and kept her nerves in a constant state of agitation. Tombstone was still miles away, but she found herself imagining she could see the glow of lights from the frontier town, its frayed edges spread in haphazard fashion across the desert plateau.

Sadie stopped by a spring, a small pool surrounded by cottonwoods and willows, to water and rest her horse, though in all likelihood, she was considerably more tired than he. Her legs stiff from being in the saddle for so long, she dismounted and squatted to scoop up a refreshing drink for herself.

She was not quite certain exactly when it happened—nor exactly which of the night sounds alerted her to the unsettling knowledge that she was no longer alone. Something had stirred out there in the darkness, something foreign to the peaceful calm of the night.

Could it have been a bird, or some other desert creature? No . . . it was an alien sound: the steady clop-clop of a horse's hooves soon became recognizable and grew louder as it moved in her direction. Since she'd ridden off the trail a bit to reach the pond and was hidden by the tall trees, it was possible the rider would pass by without ever seeing her. She held her breath, hoping that might happen. What if it was the sheriff? And what if he kept on going up this trail which led straight to the Weaver ranch—where Laramie might still be locked helplessly in the smokehouse?

But it could also be one of the prospectors who roamed these hills at will, or any of a number of other people, she tried to tell herself.

Still, her eyes were glued to the space where she'd first be able to see the approaching rider. She dare not even blink for fear of missing him. She thought she heard only a single horse, but there could be more coming behind him.

After a few minutes of very tense silence when she stood immobile, afraid to move or make a sound, a horse and rider moved into sight. The horse was dancing and pulling against the bit, and the heavyset rider seemed to be doing everything he could to maintain some control over his spirited mount.

Her eyes widened.

"Father?" she whispered, astonished. And then she shouted, "Father!"

The horse shied and almost unseated a very startled Lucien Moran.

"Sadie?" he cried out, turning his mount with great difficulty in her direction. "Sadie, is it really you?"

"Yes, Father."

"What are you doing out here? Are you alone?" he asked, eyes darting about fearfully, as though expecting Laramie to emerge from behind one of the tall cactus plants at any moment.

"Yes, Father. I left Laramie back in the mountains."

"Are you all right? He didn't hurt you?"

They both remembered when he'd questioned her the same way before, but her answer had not changed.

"Of course. I'm fine. But you look exhausted. Come over here by the stream and we'll talk while you rest."

He hugged her hard after he managed to dismount, then flopped down with a groan. She sat by his side. Neither seemed to know where to start or what to say to bridge the gap that separated them. So much had happened that needed to be sorted out.

"Did you run away from him, then?"

"Well, yes, I . . ."

"I'm so glad, Sadie. I was afraid — afraid you had gone with him willingly."

"I did, Father," she admitted, speaking softly. "I had to help him escape. He's an innocent man. Nate Laramie has never killed anyone. And Sheriff Potts would have hanged him without a fair trial."

"But you left Tombstone, and you even took my horse, without saying a word to me. Why didn't you come to me, Sadie?"

"I was afraid you wouldn't understand, afraid you'd go to the sheriff, afraid you'd try to stop me. I love him, Father."

Moran admitted to himself that her accusation was true. That was exactly what he would have done. And he would have been wrong, just as he'd been wrong all along, wrong about Sheriff Potts, wrong about Laramie, even wrong about Sadie.

He didn't deny what she said. Instead, he asked, "So why have you left him now?"

Sadie explained the reasons that had driven her to lock Laramie in the smokehouse. "He would have endangered himself to protect me, Father. I couldn't let him do that. I have to find a way to prove he's innocent of Jeffrey's murder, and that his claims about the mine are true. I need your help."

She looked at him, her big brown eyes sad and pleading. "Can I count on you? Will you help me,

Father?"

The time had come for Moran to make a decision, to stand for something he believed in for a change. His daughter was giving him that chance. Could he do it? Was that strength lying dormant somewhere deep inside him? It had been so long since he'd done anything good, anything honorable.

"I'll help you, Sadie," he promised. "What can I do?"

Sadie could hardly believe her own ears. He'd said he'd help her! With the two of them working together, they could surely get Laramie out of this mess.

Excited and so happy she was near to bursting, she jumped up. "First, we have to get back up there and let him out of the smokehouse. And then we'll take him back to Tombstone and get this mess cleared up."

It was late afternoon and several hours had passed when Indian Joe suddenly appeared beside the buggy in which Jonathan and Rachel rode, making their way back toward Tombstone. It was as though he'd come from out of nowhere, as though he'd been patiently watching and waiting until he was needed.

"Sheriff and men come this way. Ride fast. Soon, they find Laramie and his woman," he said after the briefest of greetings.

"That sounds like trouble. It may be that Laramie will need our help more than ever before this night is over. Can you make it back to town alone, Rachel? It's not far."

306

"Of course." She wanted to argue and say she would go with them, but she understood that she would be no help, would instead very likely be in the way. Besides, she needed to get back to her boys.

"We go, then, Mr. Jonathan Lee."

The Indian never spoke another word. Jonathan could just as well have been riding alone, for all the conversation they shared, but he found the silent Indian's presence a decided comfort in spite of that. He was a good man to have on one's side. Laramie was fortunate to have his loyalty.

They retraced as quickly as they could the same path he and Rachel had followed earlier. But this time as they neared it, the ranch was far from silent.

While they were still some distance away, they heard sporadic popping sounds that could have been gunfire. Concerned, they kicked their mounts into a gallop. But as they rode hard toward the sounds, the noises increased in intensity. Jonathan feared they would be too late.

Laramie, certain Sadie was no longer out there or anywhere nearby, had soon ceased his shouting and pounding on the door. Dejected, he dropped down on the hard-packed dirt floor in the darkness. Why had she done it? Had he misjudged her all along? Could it all have been an act, everything that had happened between them? But if so, what had been its purpose?

He heard again her whispered words of love and could almost feel the satiny length of her curves against him. She couldn't have been lying about that, too, faking her response to him.

"Why, damn it, why?" He smacked his fist into the wall beside him in frustration and the pain felt surprisingly good. She'd said she was sorry—he was sure he'd heard her parting words correctly. Sorry for what? For leaving? For locking him in? For not loving him?

He tried to recall their earlier argument word for word. As he thought about it, something began to make sense. She'd been adamant against his escorting her back and then had suddenly, without explanation, changed her mind. He'd thought at the time how unlike her that was.

Of course! She'd been fooling him—planning to trick him and ride out alone. But she'd done it for him! She had locked him in this infernal smokehouse for his own protection. The knowledge gave him new desire to find a way out and go after her. He ran through a disturbing list of things that could happen to her in the desert alone, none of them pleasant.

He felt about him in the pitch black of the cubicle for some sort of lever he might use to raise the heavy bolt. Several times he bumped into huge slabs of meat hanging from the low ceiling, but he found nothing. He'd be damned if he'd wait for the light of morning, when he could have a good look around. That might be too late for him to help her.

Dropping to his knees, he groped about, reaching into dark corners, frantic to find something, anything, he could use to secure his freedom. Too much time was passing and he was getting nowhere.

He stood, crossed over to the door, and threw his shoulder into it with all the strength he could muster. It didn't budge or make even the smallest sound, but his shoulder throbbed from the effort. The opening along its edge was not nearly wide enough to get his hand through, and the finger he managed to slip into it was not nearly strong enough to raise the bar. He still needed a tool of some kind and went back to his search.

A sound reached him. Had someone spoken outside the door? He couldn't believe his ears! It was Sadie's voice! She'd come back for him!

"Laramie! Don't worry. We're here. We'll have you out in just a minute." She was coming closer, even as she spoke to reassure him.

He stood back, impatient. Footsteps sounded. The bar creaked as it was raised. The door swung open slowly, and he strode thankfully out into the fresh night air. He was glad she'd come back.

Once he'd understood why she'd locked him up and gone away, he'd been willing to forgive her everything. Now he only wanted to hold her, feel her sweet lips against his. He took a step toward her, holding out his arms, but stopped in his tracks when he noticed the man standing in her shadow.

"Moran!" he exclaimed in shock. "What are you doing here? Sadie, what is the meaning of this?"

"I met him on the trail, Lar . . ." she started to explain, knowing she had to convince him quickly that her father intended no harm, that, in fact, he had agreed to help him.

"How convenient!" Laramie interrupted, taking a step backward, suddenly painfully aware that he was unarmed. "And do you both intend to turn me over the the sheriff now?" His eyes met and held hers. "Your first loyalty has always been to him, hasn't it? I can see I've been a fool ever to trust you." The hurt lay just beneath the anger in his eyes, but she saw it and was wounded by it.

"Wait! Laramie! You don't understand. Father wants to . . ."

"Stop right there, Laramie! Get your hands in the air!" A harsh command broke the silence, and Laramie found himself looking into the business end of the sheriff's deadly black revolver.

His eyes swept the clearing, taking note of the sheriff and the two deputies who surrounded him, each mounted and each with a gun pointed straight at his heart!

Taking in the situation in a single glance, he turned his blue eyes, now frigid with contempt, on Sadie. He had been right in the first place. She must have planned this all along. It didn't matter that she'd made love to him and pretended she cared.

She'd only been playing with him; it was all simply an exciting game to her! Her supposed help in his escape had been a front, probably part of a plan of her father and the sheriff to spring him, so they could hunt him down and kill him. That way nothing embarrassing would come out in a public trial. It had all been a setup! Of course, Moran had been in on it, and had convinced his daughter to play a small, but very effective part.

He felt his suspicions confirmed when Sheriff Potts ordered him up on a horse and directed one of his men to tie his hands behind his back.

"All we need now is a handy noose, right, Sheriff? And you'll have what you've wanted all along. I'll be out of the way for good, and the 'Silver Linings' will be all yours—yours and your friends'—and no one will be around to stop you or to ask questions. Really clever of you to use my own 'captive' against me. But tell me, how were you able to convince her?"

He looked pointedly at Moran and at Sadie, who was once more seated on her horse. His anger was so strong, it was like a living thing. "I guess it's true what they always say—blood is thicker than water, eh?"

Sadie flinched from the harsh, angry words directed at her. She could understand his feelings. She knew what it looked like, and she knew just as certainly that he would always despise her now. She'd never be able to convince him she'd left as she had because she loved him, nor would he accept the truth that she'd had no part in bringing the sheriff.

It was all over.

She watched in horror as the sheriff proceeded, evidently about to do exactly as Laramie had predicted. A noose was tied to a sturdy tree limb and lowered around his neck.

"Father! Help him! He saved my life! You can't let them kill him!"

Her father sat still as a statue in the saddle beside her. He was quite obviously powerless, much too weak to stand up to the sheriff and his armed men. If there was a way out of this, Sadie saw with a sinking heart, she would have to find it alone.

"Sheriff Potts!" she shouted. "You can't do this!

It's murder. I'll see to it that the whole town hears about it."

"Will you now?" His laughter was harsh and threatening. "Your father would be an accessory. Could you watch him go to prison with me?"

"You can't get away with cold-blooded murder!"

"This is not murder, Miss Moran, but execution." His emphasis on the last word sent chills through Sadie's body. The man was demented. She had to stop him!

She kicked her horse into action, racing it across the distance that separated her from the sheriff. Hurling herself out of the saddle, she caught him by surprise and knocked him off his horse. She landed on top of him and he grabbed her arm to throw her off, but with the nails of her free hand, she clawed his face, leaving bloody tracks.

"She-demon!" he growled in a low whisper. "It might be more fun dealing with you than I'd thought."

They rolled over and his body pinned her to the ground. He now held both her wrists, and though she thrashed violently, there was no doubt his superior strength would win out.

"Sadie!" Laramie's strong voice rang out in alarm and warning.

"Shut up!" ordered the deputy, who held the end of the hanging rope. "If you don't want something awful to happen to you *and* the little lady, that is!" To be certain Laramie didn't say any more, Wally tied his handkerchief tightly around Laramie's mouth, turning his continued protests into muffled, angry grunts.

Sheriff Potts hauled Sadie to her feet and

dragged her out of sight of Laramie and the others.

Bound and gagged, Laramie watched the struggle between the sheriff and Sadie before they disappeared from his sight, his anger intensifying along with his fear for her. He began working the knotted rope that secured his wrists. The hemp was strong and the knot tightly drawn, but he kept twisting and pushing against it, rubbing his hands back and forth, back and forth, until, gratefully, he felt the rope begin to loosen.

The burly man who guarded him had turned his attention in the direction the sheriff had disappeared with the struggling woman. He grinned lewdly and licked his lips in anticipation.

"Who d'ya spose'll be next, Sam?" he asked his companion, remembering how her soft body had felt under his when he'd attacked her up in the Dragoons.

"Not you, you horny old bastard. The lady'll want somebody with some looks, some charm, and some experience!"

"I shore don't see nobody like that around here," he retorted with a loud guffaw, and spit a stream of tobacco over his shoulder. "Reckon she'll just have t' take what she can get!"

Sam laughed loudly and turned away to answer nature's call.

Hands free of the bonds at last, Laramie yanked the noose up and over his head. With the speed and strength born of natural instinct and driving need, he lunged at the deputy beside him. They both tumbled off the far side of Wally's horse and rolled across the hard ground, pummeling each

313

other, seeking for some advantage.

Grunts and curses marked their combat as dust flew and arms flailed in the air. It seemed they would go on like that all night, until the larger man's head hit against a boulder with a crushing blow.

Hearing the scuffle, the man called Sam, glanced back over his shoulder, fastened his pants hurriedly, and turned back, lunging toward the fighting men. Before he could make a move for his gun, Laramie was on him and hit him a stunning blow on the side of the head. With an angry grunt, he toppled over backward and lay quite still.

Laramie could still hear Sadie's muffled protests. His mouth twisted in agony. He covered the distance between them in quick, impatient strides. The sight of Sheriff Potts' black-clad, muscular body covering Sadie's stabbed into him, and his face contorted with renewed fury.

"Turn her loose, Potts!"

The sheriff muttered, raised himself off the ground, and found himself looking down the barrel of his own rifle, cocked and ready and resting against Laramie's shoulder, the light in his eyes avowing his willingness, even his eagerness to use it on his adversary. The sheriff's heart beat loudly, and fear made his dark features appear to shrink as he saw only too clearly the spot his lust had gotten him into this time.

Holding up one hand, he showed his willingness to bargain. "We can talk this over, Laramie. I ain' hurt the girl. See?" He motioned at Sadie, who was now standing behind him.

"Move away from him, Sadie."

Before she could take a step, the sheriff's strong arm went around her neck in a viselike grip, and he slipped a knife out of his belt and held it to her throat.

"Now it seems I have a little more to bargain with, eh, Laramie? You wouldn't like to see her tender skin slashed, her blood dripping onto the ground, now, would you?"

Laramie's gun was trained on Potts, but he didn't have a chance of hitting him without risking hurting Sadie in the process. He knew that and the sheriff knew that.

Moran had pulled out his derringer when the sheriff first grabbed Sadie and had yelled for him to release her. In a split second he made the decision to do whatever it took to protect his daughter. He had never shot anyone before, but he was sure he could do it now, if he had to. But when his high-spirited horse began dancing all around, threatening to bolt and run at the slightest provocation, the elderly Moran had been forced to channel all his energies toward controlling the beast. He hadn't been able to get a good shot at the sheriff or either of his men.

One of the deputies, groggy but conscious, lurched to his feet and scrambled across the yard to pick up his gun. He fired at Laramie, who whirled when the shot whizzed past his ear and fired back in a reflex action.

Moran's horse at that moment decided to leave the entire noisy fracas behind. Bolting for the gate, the animal brought Moran directly into the middle of the exchange of gunfire.

The sheriff, having lost his advantage, threw Sadie to the ground, retrieved his own gun, and joined the battle going on around him.

Bursts of rapid gunfire continued, a sharp, acrid smell permeating the smoke-filled air. The awful concussion of rifle and pistol shots seemed endless. Sadie sank to the ground and closed her eyes, hoping to make the awful scene end, helpless to do anything more for Laramie, her father, or herself.

A scream rent the air, followed by another. The sounds reverberated in Sadie's head. She looked up to see the sheriff grab an elbow that was spurting blood. One of the deputies fell, a circle of red staining the center of his forehead. She saw the look of consternation on Laramie's face as he stood, smoking gun in his hand, his eyes turned toward Sadie's father.

As though in slow motion, Sadie watched in horror as her father slid from his horse.

"Father!" she cried out, attempting to run to him.

"Not so fast, Miss Moran," the sheriff said, the rifle in his good hand pointed at her, indicating to Laramie to throw down his gun. When he saw he had no choice without endangering Sadie, Laramie complied.

Sadie ran toward the crumpled body of Lucien Moran. "Father!" she cried.

With some difficulty, she rolled him over and saw the vivid stain over the pocket of his shirt. His eyelids flickered, and she knew he still lived.

"It'll be all right. We'll get a doctor," she promised without considering the impossibility of carrying it out. "Just lie still."

He struggled to sit up, but she gently held him

316

down. "No, you're bleeding. Please lie still."

"Sadie," his voice was thready and weak, but his hand reached for his breast pocket. She helped him when she saw he was determined to retrieve a piece of paper. "It's the deed, Sadie. It will clear up everything. Give . . . to . . . Laramie . . ."

"I will, Father."

"Be happy, daughter. I've been . . . weak . . . one. You . . . strong . . . like your Mama. I love you."

"I love you, too, Papa!"

She hadn't called him "Papa" since she was a child. Apparently comforted by her words and the knowledge that she loved him still, he breathed his last and lay still.

"No! Papa! Please don't die!" But even as she spoke, she knew her words were to no avail. Her father had died in her arms.

She had the deed that would set Laramie free and clear his name, but one look into the sheriff's black eyes was enough to convince her she'd never be allowed to use it. His gun was now aimed directly at Laramie's heart. He would pull the trigger before she could do anything to stop him.

But the sheriff was taking his time, enjoying putting an end to his enemy, hopeful that he might even make Nate Laramie squirm a little before he died.

"So it comes down to this, after all? Just you and me, and the young lady, of course," he said, glancing suggestively at Sadie. "Miss Moran helped you escape and tried to stop a lawful hanging. There's nothing to keep me from shooting her down right after I've had my fun with you." The

317

only reason he hadn't taken care of her already was because he still lusted after her and was hopeful of getting into those men's trousers she wore so beguilingly before he finished her off.

"Oh yes, there is, Sheriff Potts! Put the gun away!" Jonathan Lee's voice rang out.

"On whose authority?" the sheriff snarled, black eyes glancing in the direction of the new threat.

"Mine. As a representative of the U.S. Marshall's office."

Jonathan flashed his star, hidden on the inside of his coat pocket. "You can take any complaints you have about Laramie or about Miss Moran up with the judge — in court tomorrow! But until then, he will be in my custody."

Jonathan had ridden out into the open with Indian Joe by his side. Both of their rifles were aimed at the open-mouthed sheriff.

"But he *deserves* hanging! He killed his partner and now Lucien Moran, as well. You can't mean to help him, Mr. Lee."

Jonathan had ridden up after the smoke had cleared and bodies already littered the clearing and had not seen what had taken place.

He looked to Sadie for denial or corroboration of Potts' accusations, but her eyes were distant, almost as though she wasn't aware of what was happening around her.

"Every man deserves a fair trial, Sheriff," Jonathan said, still observing Sadie with sympathy, but keeping a trained eye on Tombstone's sheriff as well. "We'll help you with the bodies and escort you and your prisoner back to Tombstone."

His strong voice and the silent but well-armed

318

Indian Joe were enough to make Potts stop and think. He shrugged his shoulders, seeing the futility of trying to fight all of them. He could still see Laramie hang if he played his cards right.

Jonathan found a wagon in the barn, and he and Laramie did most of the work of loading the bodies onto it while Indian Joe watched the sheriff. Sadie sat in unnatural silence.

There was a minimum of conversation on the long ride back to town. Laramie allowed his gaze to stray in her direction once or twice as he rode alongside the wagon, then lost himself in his own sad thoughts. She despised him and blamed him for the death of her father. No wonder she wouldn't look at him.

And she was right to feel that. Even if it hadn't actually been one of his bullets that had struck her father, he was the one responsible for Moran's being there. It was he who had set in motion the events that had ended this night in tragedy.

Chapter Nineteen

Eunice Marie Clark arrived in Tombstone on the morning stage, a needlepoint carpetbag in each hand and a determined gleam in her deep gray eyes. She had come on an important mission and did not plan to leave until she carried it out.

Inquiries regarding the whereabouts of Miss Sadie Moran led her eventually to a windswept hillside where a funeral had just been conducted.

She bustled up beside a tall, handsome gentleman and two middle-aged ladies, who stood back, well away from the few other mourners. "Oh, my! Oh, my! I'm too late! Poor little Sadie! It just doesn't seem fair."

"You know her, then?" the man asked, his deep voice concerned and hopeful.

"Indeed I do! Indeed I do!" she exclaimed. "I'm her Aunt Eunice from Tucson. Such a terrible thing to happen to her!"

"Yes, it is." His voice now held another element she couldn't quite make out. She only knew he was someone she would want on her side rather than against her, and without asking, knew he was on Sadie's side and that she was lucky to have him for a friend.

She wanted to question him further, but at that moment Sadie turned and caught her eye. Recognizing her niece from a photograph Lucien had sent her not so long ago, Eunice picked her way through the rocks, sagebrush, and cactus, skirting the simple white crosses that were chronicles of violent death, until she reached Sadie. She gathered the younger woman into her more-than-ample arms. "Sadie, child! It's me—your Aunt Eunice!"

"Aunt Eunice! But how did you know? I just sent a wire off to you this morning—about Father's death." Sadie stepped back and looked her over. "Are you all right? Should you have made the trip?

"Yes, dear. I'm fine, really. I've been trying to get down here to see just what was going on ever since your father wired me he was coming to Tombstone, but that sharp-eyed watchdog he hired to look after me was hard to escape! As soon as I got rid of her, I set out straight away on the first available stage! I'm feeling much better, as you can see."

Sadie *could* see. As a matter of fact, to look at her aunt, one would think there'd never been anything seriously wrong with her. She certainly looked robust and happy now. Laces and ribbons adorned her bright, colorful dress and wide-brimmed hat. There was not a speck of dust on her black high-top shoes.

"I *am* sorry for my inappropriate appearance, child. But I had no idea. Your poor father! They said in town he'd been murdered. How perfectly dreadful! But I'm sure you don't want to talk about all that now, do you? Tsk, tsk," she clucked, placing a comforting arm around Sadie's shoulders.

Lucien Moran's funeral had been simple. Sadie had watched with dry eyes as her father was lowered into the hard-packed earth of Boot Hill Cemetery, her tears already long spent and a numbness now in control of her emotions. Too much had happened too fast, and she could no longer cope with any of it. She wouldn't allow herself to think about it, to hurt any more.

So she'd drawn back inside herself, until her aunt's presence and sympathy brought back her feelings of grief and confusion anew. She lay her head on the older woman's shoulder and wept for what was gone, and for a future that looked more and more hopeless with each passing minute.

Rachel stood back, allowing the two of them some time to share in their mutual loss before introducing herself and insisting Sadie and her aunt come back to her house for some light refreshment. Sadie was about to refuse when Eunice spoke up. "Haven't eaten a bite since I left Tucson, and that's been quite a spell, I can tell you!"

Rachel smiled. "You surely don't look like someone who's been traveling for hours. Why, you seem fresh as a daisy. Sadie, I think I can even see a little family resemblance."

Sadie started to protest, having seen nothing of the sort, and honestly not sure she was pleased, but she decided it would be unkind.

"All right, Aunt Eunice," she agreed, "we'll stop at Rachel's for a few minutes."

"I knew you'd see it my way, dear. Come along with you now. Give an old lady a hand, will you?"

Old lady, indeed! Sadie thought, but obediently took her aunt's arm and guided her across the road to Rachel's house.

"Lovely. Why, it's quite lovely, Mrs. Foster. You've done *such* a nice job, a young widow like yourself, with two young sons, too!"

While Rachel served sandwiches and Sadie nibbled politely, her Aunt Eunice ate hungrily, yet managed to keep up a steady stream of conversation all the while.

"Haven't seen Sadie here since she was knee-high to a grasshopper, and a right pretty little thing she was, too! I've always wanted her to live with me, felt like she needed a mother, you know, but Lucien would never hear of it. Such a stubborn man! Sorry, didn't mean to speak ill of the dead, my dear," she apologized quickly. "Felt like it was time for you to visit your only aunt, though, so when I took sick, I immediately sent for you." She laughed. "Course I made such a speedy recovery, I was well almost before you received my wire!"

"Aunt Eunice, why didn't you let us know?"

The truth dawned on Sadie, and she demanded, "Did you do it on purpose?"

"No, not really, dear. I did have a touch of the ague when I wrote, but I knew it was the only way he'd ever let you come. And I wasn't even sure that desperate measure would work. You must be quite a headstrong young lady yourself to have convinced him to let you leave St. Louis!"

Her laughter had a tinkling, happy sound that caused Sadie to forgive her instantly for the subterfuge. Her intentions had apparently been good. Sadie was coming to like her devious, lively aunt more and more in spite of herself.

"I had planned such good times for the two of

us." Eunice Clark sobered as she considered the recent tragic events. "But I am so sorry for what's happened, that poor Lucien had to die that way. Is it my fault, do you think? Did my little scheme to bring you out to Arizona send him to his death?"

She seemed so contrite and ready to take the blame that Sadie hastened to reassure her. "No, Aunt Eunice, you couldn't have known. All this trouble started a long time ago. Father did some things he shouldn't have. He got involved with some unscrupulous men." Sadie's eyes filled with tears, and her aunt was instantly by her side with an arm around her.

"He wasn't a bad man, though," Sadie went on. "He just made a mistake. And he was trying to make things right when he died. He promised to help me clear Laramie, and he gave me the original deed to the Silver Lining."

"What, dear? Wait a minute! You've lost me completely! What's the Silver Lining? And who is this Laramie? Clear him of what?"

Rachel hastened to explain the dishonest business deal involving the sheriff and Moran, the murder of her husband, and Nate Laramie's plan to recover the mine that had so far brought nothing but trouble.

"So that explains why he kidnapped you. I am beginning to understand. I'll just bet that handsome man I spoke to at the funeral was this Mr. Laramie."

Sadie nodded. She had noticed him there, along with Lily Delgado and Mrs. Morrell from the boardinghouse. But none of them had approached her, and they had disappeared before she'd had a chance to seek them out.

"He cares for you more than a little, Sadie."

"No, Aunt Eunice. He doesn't care anything for me. I was a means to an end for him. He was kind to me at times, and he even saved my life, but it's all over now."

The betrayal he'd felt when he came out of the smokehouse was all too obvious. And then, he'd said nothing after her father died. He no longer cared for her, if he ever had.

But Sadie's aunt knew what she'd seen and heard in the man's voice and in his eyes. She saw in her niece's eyes the same overwhelming love, in spite of how hard she was trying to hide it.

"We'll see. We'll see," she said, turning her attention to Jonathan. "Mr. Lee, what brings you out to this wilderness? Are you *really* an assistant to the U.S. Marshal? How very exciting!"

Rachel was glad to have the chance to talk privately to Sadie while her aunt spoke with Jonathan. "Stay a little longer, Sadie. No one really needs to be alone at a time like this," she said. "Friends can help, if you'll let us. I know." The brief frown and flicker of pain her eyes reminded Sadie of the loss that her friend had suffered, a grievous loss, and not so very long ago.

"Oh! I *am* sorry, Rachel. It seems it's easy to forget what others have gone through when your own troubles are foremost in your mind. I'm being selfish; please forgive me."

The hug the two shared was spontaneous and full of warmth and shared grief. They felt a new closeness and comradeship developing between them.

"Don't keep things bottled up inside, Sadie. You have to deal with your feelings. I know how hard all of this is for you."

"I'll be all right, Rachel, really. I just need a little time to sort it all out."

"Wouldn't it be easier if you let Nate share it with you? I know how much you care for him."

"*Cared* for him. It's all over, Rachel."

"No, I don't believe that. You can't turn something as special as the two of you had off just like that. You're hiding from what you feel about him. Why? Are you afraid?"

"Of course I'm afraid!" she cried, instantly chagrined at her outburst. But Rachel smiled, glad to see signs of life returning to her friend, and the little burst of color that crept back into Sadie's pale cheeks.

She *was* afraid, Sadie admitted to herself, afraid that she would have to see him again, terrified that she might never see him again. The last time she'd seen Nate Laramie, she'd been sure there was contempt, perhaps even hatred in those vivid blue eyes.

"Have you talked to him?"

"No. He'll never understand. It's no use." He would never believe now that she hadn't betrayed him, even if she could get him to listen! She might as well get on with her life. She had her pride, too, and she might be able to salvage the bit of it that remained. "I have my ticket for St. Louis, and I'll be leaving on tomorrow's stage. Laramie will have what he's really wanted all along, his mine, and I'll be back home where I belong."

"You don't really believe that. You are more important to him than the Silver Linings is, or ever was. He loves you, Sadie. And you belong here with him, not back in Missouri! I'm surprised he hasn't told you that himself!"

Rachel reprimanded herself for being so bossy — it wasn't her usual way — but two people who loved each other were about to throw it all away, and she had to do whatever she could to prevent it.

"I've never heard him say anything like that." Sadie's voice was lifeless once more. "He never wants to see me again. He hasn't said a word to me since Father died."

"He came to the funeral."

"Yes, to pay his respects to the dead, I suppose. It had nothing to do with me, I'm sure. He just stood there still as a statue, watching me. He knows it's all over."

Rachel knew that Laramie was a fighter, and she knew he loved Sadie very much. What she didn't understand was why he wasn't coming after her, why he was holding back and allowing someone he loved to walk out of his life. It wasn't like the man she had known.

The women soon said their good-byes and, with a heavy heart, Sadie walked with her aunt back to the hotel where they were both staying.

"Do you think we might sit and visit a bit, Sadie?" her aunt asked, when they were inside the lobby.

"Perhaps later, Aunt Eunice. I'm so tired, I need to rest before the trial this afternoon. If you'll excuse me, I think I'll go on up now." She hugged her aunt and added, "But I'm so glad you're here."

"I am too, dear . . . I am, too. Sleep well and I'll see you later, then."

"Thank you."

Eunice Clark cloaked her feelings as the attractive young woman walked away from her, up the stairs and out of sight to her room. It really *had* been a long day, and it wasn't over yet. She still had work to do. She hadn't come all this way for nothing, no indeed, not this time!

Gathering up her long and heavy skirts, she turned for the door and disappeared outside. When she returned, she would have a nice, long talk with Sadie before she left on the morning stage. She was hoping that by the time she was finished, Sadie just might choose not to leave at all.

Sadie wore the same black serge dress she'd borrowed from Rachel for the funeral when she appeared in court later that afternoon. Though Eunice had thoughtfully brought along her trunk from Tucson, there'd been nothing in it suitable for a funeral—or a trial.

Her pulse raced as she heard the heavy door slide closed behind her. She paused to look around the austere courtroom, the same room where the Earp brothers had appeared a few days before to explain their role in the gunfight at the O.K. Corral, a violent, scandalous event that had rocked the populace of Tombstone. Polished wooden benches were separated by a wide center aisle and jammed with curious townspeople. The jury box on her left was empty, since this was to be only a hearing. Swinging half-doors at the far end of the aisle opened to the judge's raised and oversized desk. Several men stood behind two tables facing the judge's bench. Laramie and Jonathan, his star now in plain sight, were on the left, and Sheriff Potts and two men she didn't recognize were on the right.

She tried to avoid noticing the slope of familiar shoulders, and the line of Laramie's long dress coat that she had seen on one other occasion, the night of the governor's reception. When he turned back toward her, the light blue of his eyes vivid against his sun-darkened skin, she forced herself to look away.

Sheriff Potts carried his arm in a sling, but his black eyes shone as hateful as ever. The judge was sober, shrouded in flowing robes that signified his respected position in the court. With his thick mane of white hair and curling mustache, he was quite forbidding.

Sadie remembered Rachel's words to Laramie, about the judge being in Potts' pocket. So, he was not lawful at all. Here was a man who would choose for himself and his interests, rather than for what was right. How did she think she could ever make him understand Laramie's side and set him free? It was probably every bit as hopeless as Laramie seemed to think.

Still, she had to try. It was her last chance to help him. She could not stand back and watch him hang for things he hadn't done. He hadn't asked for her help and probably wouldn't welcome it, but he was going to get it anyway! She squared her shoulders and stepped forward into the crowded room. Rachel scooted over and made room for her in the front row, just behind where Laramie stood. It was not the seat Sadie would have chosen for herself, and she was painfully aware of how close she sat to him. She could, if she dared, put out her hand and touch his shoulder without moving.

The time would come when she would step forward, be sworn in, and tell what she knew about the deed and her father's death. She could only hope it would help. Aunt Eunice had listened quietly as she told her what she planned to do in court and agreed with her wholeheartedly. Sadie had been able to convince her not to come along only by insisting there was nothing she could do to help.

The sheriff stepped forward to make his charges against Laramie, charges that included claim jumping, the murder of his partner Jeffrey Foster, and kidnapping. Last, he played his ace in the hole with the statement, "And I accuse Nate Laramie of the malicious murder of one Lucien Moran!"

An audible gasp was heard throughout the courtroom.

Sadie jumped to her feet and cried out, "No! That's not true!"

"Young lady," the judge admonished her, "do you have testimony or evidence to present to this court? If so, you may be duly sworn in. If not, I warn you to be seated and be quiet, or you will be held in contempt."

"I do, Your Honor. None of what Sheriff Potts has said is true, and I can prove it. I have new evidence showing legal ownership of the Silver Lining, and I myself was a witness to the death of Lucien Moran, who was my father." As soon as Sadie started to speak, the courtroom quieted to a complete, expectant silence.

"Come forward, then, and take the stand. Bailiff, swear her in." He glanced at Potts, giving him a chance to stop her, but the sheriff was in hushed conference with the man next to him and said nothing.

"State your full name, please."

"Sadie Moran."

"What is your business in this matter, Miss Moran?"

Sadie pulled out of her pocket the original deed to the Silver Lining and carefully unfolded it. She glanced down at it, then over at Laramie, who looked puzzled but interested. She looked back up at the judge before beginning.

"Your Honor, Nate Laramie is neither a thief nor a murderer. Nothing he has done merits a prison sentence, much less a hanging. His partner in the mine, Jeff Foster, *was* murdered, that much is true, but by others who were attempting to steal the mine, not by his partner, who was, incidentally, his best friend. This document, the original deed, which was in my father's possession until yesterday, should prove Laramie's legal claim to the mine and show that he had no cause to kill his partner, though others did have such cause!" She looked directly at Sheriff Potts as she said those last words.

"As to the second charge of murder, that is even more preposterous. I was there. Sheriff Potts viciously attacked me and threatened to kill me. He would have shot Laramie down in cold blood, except that he was able to free himself and fight back. Nate Laramie was protecting me as well as himself when he fired at the sheriff. My father . . ." Her voice broke and she brushed away a tear

331

before concluding, "My father, Lucien Moran, was caught in a crossfire. It was an accident that he was shot, and Laramie is not in any way responsible for his death. I suggest to you and this court that the wrong man is on trial here, and that your questions should be directed to Tombstone's sheriff. As to the kidnapping . . . I believe that I am the principal party involved in that, and it is not my wish to press charges." She looked at Laramie as she said the final words.

The judge studied the document she handed him. He would have liked to deny the veracity of the deed she'd presented him, along with Laramie's claim to the mine, just as he would have chosen not to drop the murder charges against him. But Jonathan Lee, assistant to the U.S. Marshal stood steadfastly by Laramie's side, determined to see justice done at all costs.

"What do you have to say, Sheriff Potts?"

"It's all prefabricated hogwash! Not a word of truth to it!"

"Do you have additional evidence or witnesses to corroborate your own story?"

"No, sir, Your Honor. Not at this time." He looked down momentarily, but his attitude was surly. "Are you going to take the word of this woman—" he pointed at Sadie, who had resumed her seat beside Rachel, "over the word of a duly appointed official of this city?"

"I'm afraid I have no other choice," he said, glancing up at Jonathan. "This court will have some questions for you as well, Sheriff, regarding the falsification of the Silver Lining claim and the murder of Jeff Foster, but we'll take that up at a later time. The case against Nate Laramie is hereby dismissed." He handed the deed over to Laramie, and exited quickly into his chambers.

Laramie stood to Jonathan's left, more handsome than Sadie had ever known him to be, but solemn and distanced from her, as though they were already separated by the miles she would soon put between them. He showed no emotion as he accepted the deed, proof of his renewed joint ownership of the mine.

Rachel sat on a straightbacked bench listening to Sadie's testimony, hands folded in her lap, aware of the tensions and the raw pain in the courtroom that had nothing to do with the proceedings. She knew Nate Laramie enough to feel his suffering. Though his face was stoic, she knew that his emotions were in turmoil, just as Sadie's were. They were both stubborn and proud and badly hurt, and they could do something they would regret for a lifetime. But what could she do?

She heard the gavel fall, ending the session, and stood as Laramie shook hands with Jonathan and turned and walked back to her.

"Here, Rachel. The mine is yours now," he said, holding the deed out to her. "I only wanted to get it back for you and the boys—and for Jeff."

"No! Nate!" she cried, refusing to take it, twisting her handkerchief in her hand. "It's yours, too. Half of the Silver Lining belongs to you. It always has. I won't hear of anything else. Jeff would have wanted that, and you know it."

His eyes darkened with renewed distress, and it hurt Rachel to see it.

"We'll run the mine together, Nate. Partners forever, remember?" she said.

"No, Rachel." His voice had the sound of finality. "I'm leaving Tombstone. There's nothing for me here." He smiled then, and Rachel's heart lurched to see a little bit of the old Laramie returning. "The manager of the Silver Lining is a good, dependable man, Rachel, and he'll see to your interests. Think maybe I'll go to Alaska and try my hand at finding the gold stuff. Maybe one day there'll be a 'Gold Rush' mine with my name on it?"

"Oh, Nate! Please don't go like this!" Tears filled her blue eyes and she flung her arms around his neck.

"I have to, Rachel," he said into her ear, his arms around her.

Neither of them saw the abject misery in Sadie's face as she observed them, nor did they notice her hasty exit from the courtroom. She fled through the hall, down the stairs, and out into the street, aware of nothing except that she had to get away from them. She couldn't stand to see them together like that.

She'd heard enough of the conversation to understand that he planned to leave Tombstone and was giving the mine to Rachel. Why? Hadn't that been what he'd wanted all along? To get the mine back, clear his name, and make a new life for himself in Arizona? He would *never* be happy in Alaska! Why was he doing this?

Why do people go to such lengths to make themselves unhappy, she wondered as she made her way back to her hotel. There was no packing to be done, since her trunk had never been unpacked, and the long hours until her departure the next morning stretched out in front of her. Just before sunset, she'd visit her father's grave to say her last good-byes and then turn in early and hope she'd find relief in sleep, though she didn't hold out much hope for that.

Rachel and Laramie walked out of the court-house together. He escorted her home, since Jonathan had stayed behind for a conference with the judge. She'd given up arguing with him about the mine, at least for now, but she had to make one more attempt to get him and Sadie back together.

"Remember when we had a picnic over there, just the three of us — you, me, and Jeff?"

He looked over at it and shook his head. He remembered: it had been the day they'd made their official claim to the mine, and youthful spirits had been so high, dreams had seemed only a heartbeat away. A smile tugged at the corners of his mouth.

"That was before you learned to cook. As I recall, Mrs. Morrell was responsible for the fried chicken and potato salad." He mused, "I don't know when any meal ever tasted so good."

The breakfast he'd shared with Sadie at the ranch jumped unbidden to his mind, and he just as quickly blocked it out, determined not to think of her.

"That was the day Jeff and I decided we'd build this house. We were all so happy then," she said, her voice wistful, her heart full of good memories. "But those times don't have to be gone for good, Nate."

"For me, they are. Jeff's gone, Rachel! We can never have him back again." Though he spoke

335

softly, his voice was ragged. But Rachel knew his pain was not entirely rooted in the past.

She took his hand. "Yes, that's true. But *we're* still here. And we still have our friendship. The boys love you like a father. And there's Sadie and Jonathan," she added, looking to see what his response would be.

For long seconds, he stared down at her, then seemed to realize what she was saying. "You're in love with Jonathan Lee?" His eyes brightened and a genuine smile softened his features. "I'm really glad for you, Rachel. You deserve happiness, and he'll make the boys a fine father. I have to admit I was surprised to learn of his secret connection with the marshal's office, but I was awful glad when he showed up at the ranch. I owe him a lot."

"Wait just a minute! He hasn't even asked me yet, so don't be too free with the congratulations," she protested. But she smiled and added, "But I think he will soon. And I plan to say yes. Maybe I'll even beat that man to the altar!"

They had reached the front gate of the Foster home and he bent to undo the latch, glad for the chance to hide from her the turmoil her revelations had stirred in him. When he looked back up at her again, his face was composed and his eyes were warm.

"I hope you'll be very happy together."

"And you and Sadie?"

"What about her?"

"I know you love her. Have you stopped to think what your life will be like without her? There's nothing worse, believe me, than to be without the one you love. I don't want that for you."

Of course he'd thought about it! He'd thought of little else since he'd watched her father die and had seen her looking at him, her eyes full of hurt and pain. He wasn't sure he could even live without her, but he had no choice.

In his own mind, regardless of what Sadie had said in court, he knew he had been the cause of her father's death. Even if he hadn't actually pulled the trigger, he had set up the events that brought it about. Everything that happened had been his fault. He was an outlaw, and he'd done nothing to be worthy of a lady. He could never bring her anything but unhappiness.

"She's going home, where she belongs. What else is there to say?"

Sadie wasn't the only one who was afraid, Rachel realized as she watched him. Nate Laramie was afraid, too, desperately afraid of opening up and loving again, of being hurt again. It was safer for him this way. And if blaming himself made it easier, then that's what he seemed determined to keep on doing.

Though Rachel tried arguing with him further, she could not seem to get through to him, and she knew that time was running out for them.

"Invite an old friend for dinner?" he asked, after they were inside the parlor.

Rachel was taken by surprise, but quickly extended a cordial invitation. "You're always welcome at my table, and you know it. Jonathan will be joining us. Is that all right?"

"Of course."

Suddenly, Laramie wished he'd kept his mouth shut. Seeing two people who cared for each other sharing a meal was more than he'd bargained for tonight. Finding no polite way to back out without hurting Rachel's feelings again, he was stuck.

"Sadie's all alone until she leaves tomorrow. Her Aunt Eunice plans to retire early, so I'm sure she won't be company for her. Don't you think we should include her, too?"

How could he disagree when he wanted more than anything in the world to be with her tonight, in spite of anything that had happened? On the other hand, it would be decidedly uncomfortable for both of them, to say the least.

Rachel continued as though he'd agreed with her unreservedly. "Will you go over to the hotel, then, and invite her for me while I throw a few things together?"

"Rachel . . ." His voice held a warning. He was beginning to get an idea of what she was up to.

"Go on now, Nate. Quickly! It's almost dinner-time!" His protests fell on deaf ears as she shooed him out the front door.

He walked fast through town, hoping the brisk evening air would fill his lungs and clear his mind. It was the time of day he loved best of all, but he only glanced at the red and gold of the sunset over the mountains to the west. He was reminded too vividly of shining hair in that same flaming golden color. He shook his head, trying to rid his brain of her image, but it wouldn't go away. She filled his mind and his heart, even after all that had happened. Would he never be free of her?

The agony of sitting across from her at dinner was something he dreaded and longed for at the same time.

At the hotel reception desk, he asked for her, feeling his heart and spirits droop when he was told she'd stepped out a few minutes before and hadn't said when she'd be back.

He waited on a wooden bench on the boardwalk outside for almost an hour before he gave up and started back for Rachel's. By the time he got there, his disappointment was well hidden, but the meal had lost its appeal. Still, the conversation was lively, the boys happy and talkative as usual, and Jonathan and Rachel working hard to keep a lively mood to the evening.

Nate's few smiles were reserved for Christopher and little Timmy. Rachel could only imagine what he was going through, but her kind heart went out to him and to Sadie.

On her return from Boot Hill, Sadie walked near the Foster home and heard the sounds of laughter pealing from the kitchen window. She had never felt so alone.

Then she saw Laramie standing there in the semi-darkness of Rachel's front porch. How she longed to run into his arms, tell him everything was all right, tell him how much she loved him!

But she remembered how distant he'd seemed in court. He didn't want to talk to her. Even after what she'd done, he hadn't said a word of thanks. Not that she'd expected any, of course. But somehow, she had hoped that by standing up for him, she might be able to make him see how much she cared for him, and realize that she'd always had his best interests at heart.

It hadn't been enough. Her pride would not let her do more; she feared his rejection too much.

She walked by quickly on the far side of the street, hoping he hadn't seen her.

Laramie made his apologies early after dinner, needing some time alone. Outside, he paused on the step and breathed in deeply. The tensions inside him had built at a steady pace all day, until they had become almost unbearable. He was a free man, and that felt good. Sadie had testified in his behalf and, he admitted, that felt good, too. Why, then, did he feel like he'd lost everything that was important to him?

He'd recognized her desire to tell the truth, to set the record straight, and he would have expected no less from someone of her character. But she still had never looked at him or acknowledged any feelings she might still have for him. Her eyes continued to tell him it was all over. In his heart he knew the same thing, had known it since the moment her father died in her arms.

Laramie lit his cigar and stood motionless, lost in his troubling thoughts. He had as little to offer her as ever, but he should at least express his appreciation for what she'd done in court. It hadn't been easy for her, he could see that. Maybe he should talk to her once more, if just to say "Thank you."

He could hardly believe his eyes when he saw her in the dim light, making her way hurriedly back toward the lights of town.

Laramie tossed his cigar out into the road. He watched her walk away, his eyes narrowing into slits as he warred with himself. Should he just let her go, without saying anything more to her? It might be the kindest thing he could do for her. But something inside him insisted that he speak to her at least one more time.

When he had made up his mind to go after her, she was already out of sight, so he rushed down the Fosters' front walk and headed toward town. He would catch up with her, try to make things right. He'd tell her that he did appreciate what she'd done for him.

It was a simple decision, and there was no reason it should excite him so, but his heart was hammering against the wall of his chest. He had not walked far before he caught sight of the slender figure just ahead of him, on the other side of the street.

"Sadie?"

She whirled, obviously surprised to find him behind her. He didn't think she looked pleased and was almost afraid to approach her. He knew he couldn't stand it if she refused to listen to him or rejected his thanks. But he had committed himself now; there would be no turning back.

"Laramie? What is it? Is something wrong?"

"No, nothing . . . what are you doing out so late alone?"

"I really hadn't much choice. I had to visit Father's grave once more before I left, and there didn't seem to be an escort available."

He couldn't see her face clearly, and he wasn't sure if her words were meant as a rebuke, or if it was her gentle way of teasing that he'd grown to love so much.

"I came by earlier," he blurted out, "to invite you

341

to dinner at Rachel's."

"I'm sorry I missed you."

Did he dare to believe her voice held the sound of honest regret?

"I'm sorry, too."

A long silence followed his apology. Sadie tried to calm her racing heart and figure out what was behind his words. She knew she longed to read more into them than he was saying, and tried to restrain herself. Chances were, he was only being polite, doing the right thing. If he wanted anything more, he'd surely say so, wouldn't he?

"I wanted to thank you for what you did in court today. I was so proud of you in there. I know it took a lot of courage. You didn't have to do it, Sadie."

"Of course I did. I couldn't let them punish an innocent man." Her voice was soft and sweet. "Anyway, you're more than welcome. But I would have done it for anyone."

Of course she would. He was fooling himself to think there had been anything else to it. But there was one more thing he had to say, before she was gone and it was too late.

"I'm really sorry about your father."

"It wasn't your fault, Laramie, just as I said in court. You have to stop taking the blame for everything that happens. That kind of thinking has torn you apart, and you can't go on living that way. Don't you see? You must put all guilt and hatred behind you, be willing to live again, free yourself from the past. You have to be willing to forgive yourself."

Not ready to face the things she was saying, he

abruptly changed the subject. "Are you leaving in the morning?" *Please don't go!* his heart pleaded with her.

"Yes." *Beg me to stay!*

"Have a safe trip." *My heart goes with you.*

"Thank you. I hope you'll be happy, Laramie." *But I can never be happy, not without you.*

They had reached her hotel and seemed to be able to say nothing more, so they said goodnight, perhaps for the last time.

Chapter Twenty

Later that evening, Sadie was to have another troubling conversation, this time with Aunt Eunice, who knocked on her door after she had retired for the night.

"I'm so sorry to bother you," Eunice apologized as she entered. "I know how tired you must be, but there are some important things we must discuss before you leave tomorrow."

"What kind of things?" Sadie asked, wrapping a robe around herself and sitting on the edge of the bed.

"About your father and what's been happening here in Tombstone."

Sadie really needed someone to talk to and soon found herself pouring out her heart to her aunt, who proved to be a good and sympathetic listener.

"Why did he do that, Aunt Eunice? He must have known the mine deal was all wrong from the beginning. Did he want money so badly that he'd set aside his morals, his integrity, to get it, even stoop to stealing what rightfully belonged to someone else? I don't understand. Father was a good man, wasn't he?" The question was a plea for help, and Sadie's wide, brown eyes showed her distress all too plainly.

"Oh yes, my dear! Your father was a *very* good man. But . . . now, you sit right down here on the bed and listen. I have some things to tell you."

Sadie's mind raced through a catalog of possibilities of what her aunt might be about to reveal, but shook her head. She simply hadn't a clue. All her life, she'd thought she understood herself and her past, but now her life seemed a stack of wobbling building blocks about to come crashing down around her.

But knew she had to face it. The things she'd learned about herself from Laramie over the past weeks had made her stronger, more able to do that. She stiffened her spine for the blow, sitting up straighter.

"What is it, Aunt Eunice? You must tell me everything."

"I know, my dear. I know." Her aunt's face clouded, and she seemed to drift away. "I found out the full extent of your father's problems only after I arrived here in Tombstone. It seems that he had been having difficulty for some time. His debts had mounted steadily over the past several years, because of circumstances that were really out of his control. He began to feel helpless and was at the end of his rope. He was about to lose the house and what was left of his business. He was afraid he'd lose you, too. So, even though what he did was very wrong, it was the action of a truly desperate man who felt he had no other way out. He never meant for any harm to come to you, my dear. That would have been the last thing in this world he'd have wanted. I don't believe he knew the whole story about Potts and the mine. He would never

345

knowingly have been involved in murder."

Gentle hands fell on Sadie's shoulders, encouraging her to face her past. Big, solemn gray eyes were soft with caring, overflowing with tears and with love.

"I know, Aunt Eunice, but he was wrong, wasn't he?"

"Yes, I believe he was."

The two women studied each other for long, silent minutes. Sadie struggled with her feelings. How was she to know the truth anymore? She felt as if her whole life was a patchwork of lies. The edges of reality were so smudged, she could no longer make them out. She had always thought her father could do no wrong, and now he'd tumbled off that lofty pedestal. But he was her father, and she'd never questioned his love for her.

"I know all of this is very troubling for you, my dear, but don't you think you might put all this behind you and make a new start? I know it's a tremendous shock to lose a father, and especially under such circumstances . . ."

"Yes, it is. I don't know," she continued, shaking her head, "I just don't know. And I'm so tired, I can't think anymore." Her shoulders slumped with an exhaustion that was mental as well as physical.

Sadie remembered nothing more until she awoke the next morning, in her gown and under the covers of her hotel bed. Someone had helped her get undressed—her robe was laid neatly over a chair—tucked her in, and left. Aunt Eunice, of course.

The one thing she knew for certain was that she would be boarding the morning stage and going back to settle Lucien Moran's affairs in St. Louis. At least for that little while, she could put the troublesome vision of Nate Laramie out of her mind, Lord willing.

Eunice was waiting for her outside. She smiled tentatively. "I had them bring down your trunk, and here's your handbag. They made it to Tucson, even when you didn't." Beside her stood Sadie's calfskin trunk, which hadn't been opened since before she left St. Louis.

"Thank you, Aunt Eunice."

Was that all there was to say? It seemed to be all she could muster, even though the hurt in the other woman's eyes was not well masked.

"You're still going, then?"

"I have to."

"Are you sure? You have a home with me, if you want it, if you ever want it."

"I know . . . thank you. But I have to go."

Unaware of the subject of their midnight conversation, Laramie watched the two women, puzzled by their restraint. Sadie was heart-stoppingly beautiful, even in the somber colors she wore out of respect for her father. Her complexion, a paler than usual shade of ivory, accentuated the lustrous copper of her hair that tumbled about her head in charming disarray.

He wanted to run across the street, throw her up over his shoulder, and ride away as fast and as far as they could go, into the sunset, and never let her go. But he would never take her anywhere again — not against her will.

Sadie seemed bent on leaving, having turned her back on him and all they'd meant to each other. He didn't know how to combat the defenses she had built up against him or the ones he'd raised to protect himself from her.

He'd told her he loved her, but his plot for revenge had finally killed her father — and, in the process, any love she might have had for him. He'd seen it in her face. He couldn't bear to watch her leaving town, though, so he turned and strode away in the direction of the livery stable.

Sadie saw him go, and with him any hopes she might have had for happiness, admitting to herself that she'd been fiercely wishing he'd come after her and plead with her to stay. But she'd been right when she had told Rachel it was all over between them, and she was right to be leaving Tombstone and Nate Laramie far behind her.

Eunice Clark stood in the middle of the street until the dust had settled from the departure of the stage, straining for one last glimpse of her niece, tears streaking down her cheeks. She knew Sadie was making the wrong decision, but it was hers to make, not an interfering aunt's.

Why hadn't she just stayed in Tucson, where she belonged, instead of coming down here, meddling in other people's affairs? she asked herself. But the answer was simple: this was her niece, her only flesh and blood, and she'd had to do what she could. Was it all over, then?

No . . . not if she could help it. She couldn't go after the stage very well by herself. But she knew just the person who could!

She entered the dark, musty stable as though she'd been there countless times before, though, if the truth be known, she'd never been in such a place in her whole life. She had watched Laramie disappear inside and had made up her mind to talk to him no matter what.

After her eyes became accustomed to the dim interior, Eunice could make out huge, looming shapes in the stalls. There seemed to be no one inside. Stopping to listen, she heard from somewhere in the back the sound of iron striking iron . . . someone was working back there. She would go and see if whoever it was could help her find Nate Laramie. Lifting her skirts, she walked with a determined step across the straw-covered dirt floor, wrinkling her nose and being careful where she walked.

Before she reached the back, she became aware of a crooning sound off to her left, almost as if someone were singing to a baby. She turned to her left and found herself much too close to a large, yellow horse. Kneeling down by the animal's front legs, Nate Laramie was rubbing on some ointment and speaking softly to his horse.

"It's all right, Shorty. Just a little scratch," he was saying in a gentle voice. "Have you fixed up in nothing flat!" He pivoted on his heels when he realized he was no longer alone.

"Mrs. Clark?" he asked, looking up in some surprise. "What are you doing here?"

"I came to see you, Mr. Laramie. Sadie's gone . . . and I need to speak with you."

He didn't ask why, but hastily finished what he was doing, stood, and wiped his hands on a rag. He walked out of the stall.

"Perhaps we should walk outside?" he suggested.

"Certainly," she said with a relieved smile. "Thank you."

Once they were out in the sunshine, she began without preamble. "Mr. Laramie, if you don't go after her, you're not the man I think you are!"

He smiled. "Not one to hide your feelings, are you, Mrs. Clark?"

"Please call me Eunice. And no, I certainly am not. Particularly when it concerns someone whom I care about a great deal. Now, I love Sadie, Mr. Laramie . . ."

"Nate," he interrupted.

"Nate. As I was saying, I love her very much. And I don't like to see her hurt. She did not want to leave here, and she did not want to leave you. I can't believe you're so blind you couldn't see that! I know you love her, and I don't know why you're not going after her right this very minute!"

"You're partly right, Eunice . . . I *do* love her. I have for some time, but she knows that and she chose to leave anyway. So you see, she had to want to leave. It's best for her that I don't try to stop her. I took her off a stage once before—against her will. I vowed I'd never do anything like that again, and I won't." He ran wide, tanned fingers through his already tousled hair.

"You're a stubborn, foolish man, Nate Laramie."

"Your niece told me the same thing, more than once," he said with a soft chuckle, thinking back to those good times they had spent together.

"Well, she was right about that much, at least! Now, since you love her and she loves you, I see no reason why you shouldn't ride out of here right this minute and bring her back. Do you?" Without giving him a chance to say anything, she hurried on, "You're also a coward, Nate, and it's time you put the past behind you and went on with your life. And it wouldn't hurt Sadie to do the same thing. I *know* she loves you. She told me so, just last night." Eunice Clark inhaled deeply. She could

350

hardly believe she'd said all that to such a fierce-looking man.

"She said that?"

"Yes, in those very words," she lied, praying, *Lord, please strike me down for stretching the truth a bit to help these two young people!* Something outlandish had to be done to get them back together, and she was just the one to do it!

He seemed to be considering what she'd told him, yet he made no move toward his horse.

"I'm going back to my hotel, Nate. But if you're as smart as I take you for, you'll ride out after her and you won't come back without her!"

He said nothing as she walked away, her head high and her step brisk and determined. He admired her pluck, and she'd surely given him a lot to think about. Was she telling the truth about Sadie's feelings? Even if she was, he was not sure he could do as she suggested.

Only one other person was making the relatively short trip to Benson, where the stage would be picking up several more passengers for the long haul back to Missouri. Sadie had dreaded the trip for many reasons, but in a way, leaving Tombstone now was almost a relief. At least for the moment, she didn't have to battle with herself about what she should or shouldn't do. She'd made a decision. Regardless of whether it was a wise one, it was done. But it was hard to put the last image she had of Laramie and of her aunt—standing there on the street—out of her mind.

Purposefully, she struck up a conversation with the other passenger in order to distract her from that train of thought. Thankfully, this elderly woman was much more talkative than the folks she'd shared a stage with on her other journey, and talking with her helped to pass the time.

The coach had not yet reached Benson when she saw a cloud of dust off to their left and realized someone was in pursuit of the stage. Sadie looked out her window, then looked once more, feeling as if she'd already been here, had already played out this particular script. Apparently, they were about to be robbed.

But the other time, it had been Nate Laramie, who'd meant her no harm and had so drastically changed her and her life. Would she go back and change all that, all they had shared, if she had the chance? No, not on your life, she thought with a measured smile.

It was an experience she never wanted to forget; she only wished it could have worked out differently. They could have been happy together; somehow she knew that. And they could have built a wonderful future on the foundation of their love.

A man's shout carried clearly through the open window. Perhaps this time she was in real danger and about to be attacked and robbed, but for some reason she remained calm and untroubled. The woman with whom she'd spent the past hours visiting was not taking it quite so philosophically, however, and seemed nearly ready to faint.

"Oh me! Oh, my!" the lady exclaimed, fanning her reddening face with her scented handkerchief. "Whatever is happening to us?"

"It's all right, I'm sure," Sadie hastened to reassure her, sticking her head out the window, ignoring the woman's hand that was tugging on her arm, trying to keep her inside.

A yellow horse in a long, hard gallop was narrowing the distance between him and his dark-clad rider and the stage, though the driver had now whipped up the team to their top speed. The rider lay low along his mount's neck, urging him on. Sadie's heart slammed against her chest and she didn't dare to believe her eyes. It was Laramie!

The driver, fearing a holdup, reached for his rifle.

"Stop!" Sadie yelled up at him. "I know that man. He means us no harm."

He gave her a hard stare, checked behind them to see that the man had no weapon in his hand. "Okay, lady, if you say so." He pulled up, slowing the team, but his reluctance was obvious.

Shorty was now even with the window of the motionless stage. "Howdy!" The rider acknowledged the driver with a smile and a friendly greeting. "Sorry for the hurry. Hope I didn't trouble you too much. But would there happen to be a Sadie Moran on board?"

Pulling herself out of the viselike grip of the older woman, Sadie opened the door and stepped down.

"I am Sadie Moran." A ghost of a smile brushed her lips and color was high in her cheeks. Her brown eyes sparkled with life.

"Then you'll please come with me, ma'am. I believe we have some unfinished business." His voice was gruff, but for her ears alone, as he whispered urgently, "There's no life for me without you. Will you come with me, Sadie?"

She gave him her hand and a brilliant smile. He had his answer, even as he pulled her up in front of him and felt the welcome warmth of her body

353

against his.

"Have a pleasant day, folks!" He grinned, tipped his hat at the open-mouthed passenger and driver, and spurred the big yellow horse into a gallop across the desolate Arizona territory.

"Well, I never!" said the little old lady, adjusting her spectacles so she could see the couple a little better as they rode off into a dazzling middday sun.

Chapter Twenty-one

An immense load had been lifted from Sadie's shoulders and flung to the four winds the moment she had seen him and realized who was stopping the stage. She had never been so happy in her whole life. He'd come after her! She didn't know why — or even where he was taking her now.

It didn't matter. If the big, foolish man only knew — she'd willingly go with him anywhere on earth. She never intended to let him go again.

They raced across the desert prairie, the wind whipping through her long hair and stinging her eyes, but she leaned back against his wide, warm chest and felt the steady rhythm of his heart and was more content than she'd ever been. She felt secure in the curve of his strong arm. She heard his sigh as he lay his cheek briefly on the top of her head and knew she was at home at last, in his arms, right where she belonged. Whatever their problems, they could be all worked out.

A few hours later, he drew his horse up in front of a very familiar-looking shack, jumped to the ground, and held up his arms for her.

"Welcome back," he said as she slid down off the horse and into his embrace. His smile was chased away by a worried frown. "I was afraid you wouldn't be glad to see me, afraid you wouldn't want to come with me."

"Well, maybe I'd have thought it over a bit more carefully if I'd known where you were taking me," she said with a happy smile.

"Why, Miss Moran, I thought you'd developed a certain fondness for this place. I know it's not quite as nice as the ranch—or even the cave—but I did remember to bring the quilt." His blue eyes gleamed with mischief. "Do you know anyone who might be cold enough to be willing to share it with me?"

"It *is* getting a bit chilly. I'd imagine that after dark it could be downright cold in that cabin. Wouldn't you think so?"

"I would, indeed." His eyes were saying outrageous things to her and his lips moved over hers to repeat the messages coming straight from his heart. His arms wrapped themselves around her as though he'd never let her go.

In mutual understanding, she waited while he put the horse in the barn and they went inside together, just as they had once before. Neither seemed to notice there was no fire and that a layer of fine dust covered the sparse furniture. Their eyes were only for each other.

"I thought I'd lost you! Oh, God! Sadie!"

"Laramie, come here." She held her hands out to him.

He walked toward her slowly, his eyes probing the depths of hers, seeking and finding answers to all his unspoken questions. With a muttered curse at his weakness where she was concerned, he swept her into his arms.

"You belong to me," he breathed, his body im-

356

printing its demands against hers, straining to be closer still, to feel every sweet inch of her. He had denied himself and her for the last time—he had no strength left for that.

"Sadie, love, be mine."

"Yes, oh God, yes, Laramie!"

Eager hands reached for the buttons on his shirt as if she couldn't wait to plow her fingers through the thick, silky mat of hair. She indulged herself, running her hands across his chest, delighted by the harsh, uneven beating of his heart, a pounding that spoke of his escalating desire and his love for her.

His arms tightened around her, meshing her to him, and she wrapped her arms around his neck, pulling his head down, claiming his lips with a deep, possessive kiss.

He relished her in the role of aggressor and was content to let her set the pace for their lovemaking as long as she didn't tarry too much! For his loins throbbed with his fervent need for her. He had to make her his or die from the torment.

She backed out of his embrace, her lips pearly still from their kiss and her exquisite brown eyes filled with love and longing for him.

How could such a woman love the likes of him? But that warm, caring look that burned with banked desires could mean nothing else, could it?

"Sadie, are you sure? Say the word and I'll take you back to St. Louis myself. All the things you said to me last night were true, though I couldn't admit it then. I'm trying very hard to turn loose the past, and I'll do my best to make you a good life, but I still don't have much to offer a woman like you. I'd understand if you didn't want to stay with me."

"You're a silly, stubborn man, Nate Laramie. And you're wrong, so very wrong. You have so much to offer. I love you. I'll always love you. And nothing—do you hear me—*nothing* you can say or do will make me leave you again. So, just . . . you . . . hush!"

The awareness of her love for him swept across his face like a prairie twister, contorting and changing its contours—leaving a new calmness and peace behind, smoothing out the lines of worry and hurt.

"Love me, Laramie."

And God help him, he did. In a blinding flash, he saw as clearly as it was possible to see how very much he loved this woman. He would give his life for her, he knew with a calm certainty. The feeling was so satisfying, he wondered why he'd been so gun-shy of it all these years. He was still not sure what kind of life he could offer her, but right now all she was asking was himself and his love. There was no way under heaven he could deny her that.

He had waited too long, denied his feelings for her too many times, held himself carefully away from her far too much. His body ached to take her, thrust into her, filling her with his seed and himself. He couldn't offer her moonlight and flowers, but he could do everything possible to make their lovemaking special, make it something she would remember with pleasure and, if he was lucky, with longing.

He slipped the blouse down over her shoulders and made love to the woman he was claiming for his own.

Sadie awoke to the pleasant warmth of a crackling fire and the even more pleasant sounds of his happy serenading as he splashed noisily in the round, wooden tub. He didn't notice when she slipped out of bed, tiptoed over, and took up his rifle that leaned against the wall.

"Come out of there, Laramie!" she called, brandishing the gun at him in a threatening fashion.

"Not on your life, Miss Moran."

"Wouldn't be the first time I've seen you stark naked," she laughed.

"No?"

"No. You remember the day I modestly handed you a towel? Well, it wasn't before I'd had a pretty good look at the merchandise! And I decided something right then and there, Nate Laramie."

"What was that?" he asked, on guard and not moving from where he sat immersed in the sudsy water, his knees drawn up to his chin, arms crossed protectively in front of them.

"I decided that one day I'd make *you my* prisoner, outlaw!"

"And you've done a right fine job of doing just that, Miss Moran! A right fine job!" He laughed heartily.

Then he stood up slowly, unashamed, water sluicing off his beautiful dark-skinned body and splashing onto the floor of the shack where they'd spent the past night lost in each other's arms.

With a slow, seductive smile, she lowered her eyes and saw with some satisfaction that she truly had his undivided attention. She tossed the unloaded rifle aside and stepped into his arms, unmindful of the water that dampened the front of her blouse and seeped through the layers of her heavy skirt and petticoats.

"Don't you think it's about time you made an

honest out of me?"

"I was about to insist on that very thing," he murmured into her hair.

He was the shelter, the haven, the home she'd search for all of her life. He was everything and so infinitely dear to her.

"I love you, Nate Laramie," she whispered, and his answering avowal was swallowed up in the hungry joining of lips and bodies.

Much later, they sat quietly talking, working through all the things that had happened to a new and abiding love.

"When you let the stage roll out and keep on going, I knew for sure it was all over. Why did you decide to come after me?"

He didn't mention his conversation with Eunice which had, after all, been only the catalyst that had pushed him into doing what he'd known all along he would do.

"I watched you leave, and I was so afraid," he answered quietly. "I went out to the Silver Lining and sat there alone for a long time, thinking about the past and the future. Your Aunt Eunice is right. I have been a stubborn, foolish man and a cowardly fool."

"She said *that?*" Sadie asked, amazed that her aunt would say such a thing.

"Well, yes . . . she said exactly that." He grinned. "She is really something. I guess spunk runs in the family."

"Go on with what you were saying," she urged softly.

"Well, I could see that I've been hiding in the past, afraid of the future. I was so afraid of being hurt that I couldn't reach out to you, even when our love was the only thing that made any sense in this life. And I'd carried a load of guilt around with me ever since my partner died. I was finally able to see that it was all over. I'd done everything I could to make it right. And I had stupidly let my future ride out on the last stage without lifting a hand to stop it. I'd lost everything and everyone I'd ever loved, and I was about to lose you, too. But this was different. I was *letting* you go, and not doing anything to stop you. Finally, I saw that the things that had happened to people I'd loved were not my fault, just as you tried to make me understand. My parents — Jeff — none of it was my fault. Even your father's death. You didn't blame me, but it was harder for me to stop blaming myself. I had to stop feeling so guilty and trying to make up for it all. The mine didn't matter anymore, even Potts didn't matter. *You're* the only thing that matters to me, Sadie. And it *would* have been my own damned fault if I'd let you go out of my life without a fight! I just couldn't face the future with that regret. I knew I had to get you back, or at least I had to try. I love you, Sadie. More than my life, more than my past, more than anything else in this world."

"And I . . . I had to know if you really loved me — if you'd really let me go. But I was afraid, too, so afraid I'd lost you. I just wanted to run and run, but I realize now I was doing the same thing you've been doing. Together we can face anything, Nate. I want to go back and start all over."

"Mmm! But right now I have something I'd like to tell you, if you'll join me under this quilt for a little 'private discussion'?"

"I will indeed!" she exclaimed, falling into his arms, willing to let her body do all her talking for

361

the time being.

Awakening to the first gossamer rays of an early November morning, Sadie decided she'd finally learned the meaning of the word *bliss*—it was utter and complete happiness in the arms of one dearly loved.

The man who shared her bed and in whose arms she'd spent the long, glorious night was everything she wanted in a man. He was good and honest and loving, a man who could be depended on in a crisis, strong in the tough times, gentle in easier times. She knew he would always be there for her and she would never have to worry about the depth of his love for her. It would be her one constant in an uncertain world.

He had not been troubled during the past night with awful nightmares, as he had so many times before. She felt they were over for good, that he'd finally made peace with his past.

He slept peacefully now, his hair rumpled. She reached to smooth back an errant lock that had fallen over his forehead. His eyes blinked open and the smile began there and spread to his full lips.

"Good morning, ma'am."

"Good morning, sir."

"Been awake long?"

"Not long. Sleep well?"

"Like a baby."

She smiled. "Good! Me, too."

"Are you happy, Sadie?"

"Mmm. Deliriously. You?"

"Yes. This is a feeling I've simultaneously searched for and run from, all my life. Now I can't imagine what would possess a man to do that—run from happiness, that is."

"Some men tend to be a little stubborn and maybe a little foolish."

She smiled at him, flashing that intriguing dimple that he found so fascinating, and his heart took an unexpected tumble.

"I love you, Sadie Moran."

"And I love you, Laramie."

"Come here and show me how much."

"I'm not sure you have the time."

"I have all the time in the world for you, my love . . . all the time in the world."

Dan Potts watched the sun break from behind the sloping hill beyond the decrepit shack, his black eyes narrowing in anticipation of the final confrontation he planned for Nate Laramie and his lovely lady friend.

They deserved no better than what they were about to get for what they'd done to him. His career was ruined—the marshal had already taken back his star and stripped him of his office. Charges were being brought against him for the theft of the mine and for the murders of Jeffrey Foster and Lucien Moran. Even his Lily had turned her back on him, claiming to be sickened by his behavior, and his former deputy Wallace had hightailed it out of town like a jackrabbit the minute trouble started.

He pushed the white hat lower over his face, his eyes riveted on the small cabin. His patience was soon rewarded by a wispy curl of smoke that snaked up from the rear. It quickly grew larger and blacker, becoming a cloud that crept up over the roof and around the corners. Tiny fingers of flame scorched and burned the wood, breaking into a gratifying flame that promised to rapidly engulf the wooden shack.

Potts threw his head back and laughed, a banshee howl of deranged glee.

Laramie wasn't sure which brought him out of his contented cocoon of sleep: the crackling of the fire, the acrid, stinging smoke, or the distant, howling laughter. Instantly, he was on his feet, dragging Sadie from the bed and casting about for a way out of the burning trap the cabin had become. He rushed over and shoved the door, which was already beginning to burn, only to find it securely fastened from the outside!

The fire was burning unnaturally fast. With a normal fire, they should have been given some warning; it would have taken a few minutes to catch hold. Something was very wrong. In a flash of intuition, he had his answer. This fire had been set!

Laramie cursed himself—he'd been so lost in his consuming love for Sadie, he'd let down his guard, and his carelessness could well cost them their lives.

Sadie pulled on her clothes and shoes as fast as she could, and stood ready to follow his lead.

He was at the single window from where he was able to see the sheriff sitting astride his horse, a few hundred feet away, watching the cabin intently.

He yelled, "Potts! This is between you and me. Let the woman go! I'm sending her out the window now."

"Not on your life, Laramie! *No one* leaves here

364

alive—except for me, of course." More of that eerie, insane laughter followed.

Laramie turned back into the room. The door was blazing, and soon the entire cabin would be an inferno. They had to make a move and fast, or they'd burn up along with it.

By now, the blaze would have burned through the ropes that more than likely were responsible for binding the door closed. He could probably kick it open, but they would have to run for it through the flames, and then deal with the sheriff once they were outside. But at least Potts seemed to be have focused his attention on the window, not the door, which he obviously considered impassable. They might have a chance if they could catch him off guard.

"Bring that bucket of water over here," he told Sadie, grabbing the quilt off the bed. "Douse this down good."

She did. He swung the quilt over her head. "That will protect you from the fire. When I have the door down, make a run for it!"

"But what about you?"

"I'll be right behind you," he promised, directing brutal kicks at the bottom hinge of the door until it gave way and was tilted wildly to one side. He grasped the chair, swung as hard as he could, and landed it with a punishing blow on the top of the door, which fell outward. He gave Sadie a shove toward the opening.

"Go on!" he ordered.

"No! Not without you!"

"Go, now! For God's sake, Sadie! Move!"

"No! You get under here with me and we go together or I'm not moving from this spot." She coughed, having gasped in the hot air that seared her lungs.

"All right!" He grabbed his rifle and ducked under the edge she was holding up, pushing her in front of him, sending them hurtling through the doorway.

Sadie could hardly breathe. Her lungs felt as though they were filled with molten lava, and the wet, soggy quilt was suffocating her. They crashed onto the smoldering wood that had been the door and the splintered chair and rolled across the hard ground. Laramie's arm was around her but when he pulled her to her feet again, throwing off the quilt, his other hand held his rifle. Expecting an ambush, he searched the horizon for the sheriff.

A cloud of desert dust marked a rider's hasty retreat.

"Coward!" Laramie flung the words into the wind. "Damn you, you coward!" And then, to Sadie, "I'm going to get Smokey and go after the son of a bitch!"

"No, Laramie! Let him go!" she cried as she ran behind him toward the barn.

"Not on your life. He meant to kill us both. You will never be safe as long as the bastard lives." The muscle in his jaw twitched angrily. The man had tried to kill Sadie—twice! He wouldn't live to try it a third time!

"Nate, please. Let the marshal go after him. They're probably looking for him right now. Take me back to Tombstone and you can ride after him with the posse. Do it the right way this time, for me?"

When he stopped what he was doing and looked at her, she knew she'd gotten through to him and a

366

feeling of immense relief swept through her.

"All right, lady. We'll do it your way, this time!"

When she smiled, he knew he'd done the right thing and that he would do almost anything she asked if she'd only smile at him like that!

He hugged her tightly and said, "Let's get out of here!"

"Anything you say, boss man!"

"Sure!" he laughed, pulling her up behind him.

When they reached the rise where Potts had been minutes before, they saw the reason for his hasty departure. A large posse was in hot pursuit of the lone rider. In all likelihood, he would be apprehended shortly.

Laramie and Sadie watched them with a shared feeling of satisfaction.

"Looks like our ex-sheriff will get what's coming to him at last, eh, cowboy?"

"Looks like!"

"And it looks like they don't even need your help."

"Looks like."

"And it looks like I'll have you all to myself for a few minutes longer, at least until they come back."

Before Laramie could answer, she heard another voice, one with a familiar midwestern accent.

"Appearances can be deceiving, ma'am."

When they turned, they saw Jonathan Lee riding toward them. "I sent the others after Potts. I was afraid you all might need my help. Appears I was wrong."

"Appears like," Sadie said with a smile.

"You have an uncanny way of riding in just when you're needed lately, Jonathan Lee!"

"Timing. It's all in the timing," he said, smiling

back at them. "What, exactly are the two of you doing way out here again, if I may ask? I thought Miss Moran was safely on the stage, on her way back to Missouri."

"It's a long story, Jonathan. We'll write you about everything after we get back to Tombstone," Sadie said.

"Changed your mind about leaving, did you, Sadie?" Jonathan asked with a wink.

"Sure did. A lady's entitled to do that, isn't she? Of course, I had a little help." She looked at Laramie. "And I do detest a long stagecoach ride! Do you think Rachel could put me up for a few days while we plan a wedding?"

"I'm sure she can—and will! And congratulations!"

Before long the posse was galloping back in their direction. When they came nearer, the three friends could see that Potts was not with them.

Alarmed, Jonathan questioned one of the men. "Doc, what happened? I didn't think you'd have any trouble catching up with him. You didn't let him get away, did you?"

" 'Course not," the man answered nonchalantly. "Seems Potts had other ideas. He come up to a deep crevasse and just kept on going, right over the edge, at a dead run. Wasn't nothing any of us could do, 'cept watch! Sure looked like he knew exactly what he was doin'!"

"Maybe he did," Jonathan replied. "There really wasn't much left for him to live for. It's all over, then. We might as well ride back to town. Coming, Laramie?"

"We'll be right behind you," Laramie called, but his attention was turned in the direction of the

368

woman seated behind him on Shorty. No words were necessary between them. They both knew that all books were closed for good, all accounts paid off in full. The past could be allowed to fade into history, where it belonged.

He kissed her one quick, victorious kiss and spurred his horse into motion.

Chapter Twenty-two

Eunice Marie Clark helped her lovely niece into a cream-colored satin dress, styled hurriedly by a local seamstress. She slipped it down carefully over her head without mussing a single strand of her elaborate coiffure. Red-gold hair was piled on top of Sadie's head with care, and secured with sparkling rhinestone and pearl combs, tendrils allowed to escape only if they were intended to do so.

Rachel had spent all morning fussing over a hairstyle that had to be perfect, and Eunice was not about to be the one to mess it up. *Let Laramie do that,* she thought with a chuckle.

"What are you laughing at, Aunt Eunice?" Sadie questioned her, looking back at her happy face reflected in the mirror.

"Oh, nothing, dear. Just thinking of your handsome husband-to-be!"

"He is that, isn't he?" she agreed, fastening around her neck the beautiful single strand of matched pearls Laramie had given her as a wedding present. When she'd wondered at their beauty and how he'd come by them, he'd murmured something about Indian Joe and left it at that.

"A little headstrong, perhaps, but surely good-looking enough to make up for it! Imagine him holding up the stage and taking you off for the *second* time! That's really quite romantic."

"Yes, imagine that!" Sadie's eyes searched the blue-gray eyes of her aunt. "You wouldn't have had anything to do with that, I suppose?"

"Me, darling? Certainly not! I never *dreamed* of the little scheme he had in mind. Worked like a charm, though, didn't it?" she asked, with a big smile.

"Yes, it did. I am so glad he came after me. I thought I'd lost him forever." Her eyes were dreamy, her happiness locked deep inside.

Rachel knocked and entered the upstairs bedroom, where Sadie and Eunice were making their preparations for the afternoon wedding.

"Sadie, you're not going to be late for you own wedding, I hope?"

"Of course not. Just look at all the wonderful help I'm getting. I'm almost ready, Rachel." She fastened pearl drop earrings on her ears, and they all admired the results.

"I have an early wedding present for you." Rachel disappeared and was back in an instant, in her arms the most beautiful handmade quilt Sadie had ever seen.

"It's from Lily Delgado. She said maybe it would make up a little for all the trouble Dan Potts brought you both. She also said," Rachel added with a smile, "that she hopes the two of you will be very happy under it!"

Their happy laughter pealed through the house and reached the ears of Jonathan, Christopher, and Timothy, who were waiting impatiently below in the parlor.

"What do you suppose they're up to now, Christopher?" Jonathan asked with a mock frown on his face. "Women!"

"There's just no telling, Mr. Lee."

"I think you could start calling me Jonathan, Chris. We men have to stick together, don't we?"

"Sure do . . . Jonathan! We sure do!"

Jonathan leaned down and picked Timothy up in one arm, his other hand reaching for Christopher's. It was thus they stood when Rachel entered the room first, and the sight brought her heart a joyful leap.

"Here are my men!" She knew she'd said the right thing when she saw Christopher's happy grin.

"Hi, Mama! Ohhh! Miss Moran, ain' you the purty one!" he added, seeing Sadie just behind his mother in the doorway.

"*Isn't* she the pretty one," his mother repeated, correcting his grammar.

"She sure is!" he said in awe, and everyone laughed. "She sure is! Will you look like that when you marry Mr. Lee . . . uh, I mean Jonathan, Mama?"

"She will be very beautiful, Chris," Jonathan assured him. He walked over to kiss Sadie on the cheek and give her his good wishes. "You do look lovely," he told her.

"Thank you. Jonathan, how can I . . ." she began.

"Sadie, it's not necessary. Laramie would have done the same for me, or for Rachel. He's a good man. He'll make you a fine husband."

She kissed him back and turned her attention to the boys. "My! don't the two of you look handsome. I'm so glad you agreed to be my attendants."

Both boys wore new suits and had fresh haircuts, and their small chests puffed out at her words of praise.

The wedding was a simple but elegant affair, the bridegroom tall and stunningly handsome in a long-tailed black coat and snowy white shirt, the bride a vision of loveliness in satin and pearls.

Wedding vows were repeated fervently, in hushed voices replete with promises they both intended to keep for a lifetime. Bright blue eyes met and held warm, brown ones flecked with bits of amber and gold.

Once Jonathan handed Sadie over to her bride-groom, their hands had clasped so firmly, it was as if they would never let go. An overwhelming sense of well-being made their feet feel like dancing, their hearts like singing.

". . . pronounce you man and wife!"

The minister had finally said the words! Sadie turned to face her husband, both their hands still clasped between them.

"Mrs. Nate Laramie," he whispered, before his lips brushed hers. He put her arm in his, and they turned to face a happy group of friends. Applause broke out when the parson announced, "I present to you Mr. and Mrs. Nate Laramie."

Sadie turned to Rachel, who stood by her side and hugged her hard, then bent to embrace Christopher and Timothy, while Laramie shook hands with his best man, Jonathan Lee. On their way up the aisle, Sadie stopped beside Eunice to present her with a flower from her bridal bouquet and kiss her affectionately.

"Mrs. Sadie Louise Laramie. Has a nice sound to it, doesn't it?" They were stealing a few minutes alone, after they were outside the church and before their guests began to file out.

"A very nice sound. And now may I please kiss

373

my bride?"

"Nice of you to ask my permission. I don't re-member you ever doing that before, Laramie!"

"Don't you think that now we're married, you could call me Nate—or Mr. Laramie?"

"Certainly not! You'll always be just plain 'Lara-mie' to me!"

"I guess I should be grateful. It's better than 'out-law' or even 'cowboy'!"

"Which would certainly be inappropriate, since Jonathan made you one of his official deputies." She laughed. "He sure is an improvement over Tombstone's last sheriff, isn't he?"

No one had been sorry to see Sheriff Potts stripped of his office, and Jonathan Lee, who had been working undercover for the U. S. Marshal, was a popular choice to take his place. He had been welcomed with open arms by the citizenry. It was thought he would surely bring peace and a new dig-nity to the town, things that had been sorely missed for some time.

"Jonathan's a good and honest man, and I'm glad he and Rachel have announced their wedding plans. Speaking of weddings, do we really have to go to that danged reception? I have a much better idea how we could spend the evening."

She playfully slapped his arm, reprimanding him. "All of our friends will be there. Rachel and my Aunt Eunice have spent hours making plans and yes, we do have to go! But," she added, "I'm sure our guests will understand if we don't stay too long. After all, it is our wedding day."

"Come here and show me, Mrs. Laramie!"

"As you wish, Mr. Laramie!"

The whole town of Tombstone seemed to have turned out for the wedding celebration held in the

374

town hall, and a spirit of gaiety spread through the invited guests.

Eunice Clark flitted about the crowded hall, checking on the punch and cake, making sure that all went smoothly.

"What are you thinking?" Sadie's voice interrupted her activity. "I'd like you to come and stand in the receiving line with us."

"I was thinking that I'm looking forward to the future as I haven't been able to in a long time," she said, taking Sadie's arm. "There's that big, handsome man you married, and he's starting to look a bit impatient. Can't imagine why!" Her soft laughter brought Sadie a good feeling that lingered through the greetings to their guests, the cutting of the cake, and the first dance with her husband.

In Laramie's arms, though, her thoughts were only of him. "Do you realize this is the first time you've ever danced with me?" she asked, with a nudge in his ribs.

"A big mistake on my part. You belong in my arms."

The music swirled around them and they relished the moment, unaware even when they were joined by other dancers and the floor filled.

The merriment continued for hours longer—a heavily spiked punch was being enjoyed by the adults. When the party began to wind to a close, the bride and groom were no longer in their midst. No one knew how long they'd been gone, but their smiles revealed that they did know *why!*

Gauzy light from a silvery moon cast a halo about a few of the puffy clouds that lingered near it. Night birds called and a soft breeze ruffled the tops of the trees in the courtyard of the Weaver ranch where Nate Laramie sat with his new bride.

Looking up into the breathtakingly beautiful sky, Sadie pointed out the illuminated clouds and said, "Look, Laramie! What do you see up there?"

He slowly turned his eyes away from her to look up to where she pointed. He stared into the heavens, pulling her close to him, snug against his side and his heart, enclosed by his protecting arm.

"It looks like a cloud, Sadie, a cloud with a silver lining!"

"Yes," she sighed. "We've found it together, haven't we? Our silver lining? And it makes everything worthwhile!"

"*You* are my silver lining, my love, and you will always be the one who lights up my nights, the one who makes my life worth living."

"I love you, Nate Laramie! And I don't think I'll ever be afraid again."

"Nor will I. Not as long as we have our love and each other." He paused. "And as long as we make sure you never get your hands on a gun again!"

"I wouldn't suggest hiding any firearms under a floorboard, then! You should be ashamed for trying such an old trick on me, Laramie. You thought it would work because you'd gotten your hands on a city girl who didn't know any better."

"Guess you showed me, didn't you?" He grinned, remembering how she'd looked sitting with the loaded rifle on her lap when he peeked in the window of the shack.

"And you—you let me go to all that trouble to saddle Shorty and ride out of there, knowing all the time you were going to stop me before I got very far."

"Yup. But while I watched you, I knew that I was

really the one in trouble."

"You did?"

"I sure did. Now, how about trying out that new quilt Lily made for us?"

"Best idea you've had in quite a while, Laramie!"

Epilogue

"Rachel Marie!" Christopher shouted, "you come back here. Your mama says it's time to wash up for dinner!"

A peal of enchanting laughter was his only answer as the three-year-old child lifted up her skirts and scooted out of the courtyard without a backward glance.

"Catch me if you can, Christopher!" she called back to him over her shoulder.

"I can!" he shouted, and took off after her at a run, thoroughly enjoying the chase.

Rachel and Sadie stood in the doorway of the ranch house, watching their children with proud and happy smiles.

"The boys love her so, Sadie."

"Yes, and she idolizes them . . . has ever since she was big enough to crawl. They're like big brothers to her."

"I wonder how they'd all feel about another addition to our family?" Rachel asked.

"Rachel!" Sadie's eyes widened. "Oh! that's wonderful! I know how you've wanted another child. What does Jonathan think?"

"What does Jonathan think about what?" he

asked, coming around the side of the house, Laramie by his side.

"About having a son or a daughter?" Sadie filled in the rest of the conversation for him.

Jonathan picked up his wife and whirled her around in a circle, a delighted smile spreading across his face. "I just couldn't be prouder!"

"This calls for a celebration!" Laramie said, thumping his good friend on the back. I think I have a bottle in the cellar. Sadie, if you'll get the glasses?"

"Sure thing, boss man!" she replied, heading for the kitchen. Rachel followed along with her to help.

"I'm so glad you and Nate were able to convince the Weavers to sell you this place. The Laramie Ranch. Has a nice ring, doesn't it? It's just perfect for you!"

"Yes. You know, I fell desperately in love with the place the night Laramie and I rode out here for the first time. It felt like home then, and it still does. I suspect it always will."

"I hope so. I like having you so close and being able to see you all regularly. I wouldn't want the three of you to ever leave here."

"If we have our way, we'll grow old and die right here. No cause to worry!"

They both laughed, enjoying their friendship. Sadie set out crystal glasses and a decanter for the four of them; for the children she added a cool pitcher of juice and tall enamel glasses. Rachel helped her arrange them on a carved wooden tray.

Jonathan and Nate were discussing business matters regarding the Silver Lining mine the two families now owned and operated jointly when the women came back out with the glasses.

"We've made some good investments with our profits, so even if the pumps can't keep up with the water that's coming in and the mine has to be closed, we still won't have to worry," Jonathan was saying.

"I know. I hate it for the workers' sakes, though. They depend on salaries we may no longer be able to provide," Laramie said, a worried frown on his face.

"Every week a few more men leave town, some going down to the copper mines in Bisbee, and some as far away as the gold mines in Alaska, but they're finding new jobs. Anyway, there's nothing we can do about it. We've tried everything we can to keep the mine operational."

"Lily's doing a good job for us in accounting and payroll, isn't she?"

"Sure is. I think there'll be a city clerk's job open for her when the mine closes for good."

"Great! Now, how about that toast?" Laramie said, raising his glass, filled with light, bubbly liquid. "To Mr. and Mrs. Jonathan Lee and their growing family! Congratulations, you two!"

"Hear! Hear!" Sadie added, holding her glass high.

Christopher came tearing back into the courtyard, Timothy at his heels as usual, and the chubby-legged Rachel Marie bringing up the rear.

"Children! Come over here and join us in a toast."

Rachel Marie climbed up on her daddy's knee and threw her pudgy arms around Laramie's middle. "Daddy! I love you!" In her most serious voice, she continued, "Do you think I could have a new brother or sister of my very own?"

"How about it, Laramie?" Jonathan demanded, with a raised eyebrow.

"Well, honey, I guess I'd have to talk that over with your mother."

"Well, do it, then, Daddy! Okay?"

They all shouted in laughter.

"Guess we should be getting on back to town," Rachel said, smiling at Jonathan. "Does it seem like we've been through this before?"

"What?" asked Sadie and Nate in unison.

"Well," Jonathan explained, "one other time we came out here and our presence was not too welcome, so we made a hasty retreat!"

"When was that?" Sadie asked.

"The day we brought supplies out here when Potts was looking for you two."

"We never saw the two of you or any supplies . . ." Laramie began.

"No, I believe you were otherwise engaged over by the pond."

Sadie and Laramie looked at each other, then at Jonathan and Rachel. A sudden dawning of understanding was simultaneous.

"You didn't . . ." Sadie began.

"Well, not really," Rachel hastened to add, "but we saw enough to know it would be best if the two of you were left alone."

Sadie's face was a becoming pink, and even Laramie looked a bit flustered.

"We never went into the kitchen when we came back," Laramie filled in. "I even spent some time in the smokehouse, if I remember correctly." He looked at Sadie. "That's something we never talked much about."

"Uh, I think we'll get on back now," Jonathan

381

said. "See you in town soon?"

"Yes, we're coming in on Thursday to pick up Sadie's, Aunt Eunice. She'll be coming on the Tucson stage. She can't stay away from her only grandniece for very long!"

"She's doing well, then?" Rachel asked.

"Very well! She's in the best of health, and she does enjoy spoiling Rachel Marie," Sadie told her.

"When you come in to town, plan to have dinner with us, will you?" Rachel asked, herding her two boys up into the buggy.

"We sure will!"

A few minutes later, the buggy pulled out of the front gates, leaving Rachel Marie and her parents alone in the lengthening shadows of late afternoon.

"Aunt Eunice is coming! Aunt Eunice is coming!" the child chanted, dancing around the two of them. "Will she bring me something?"

"Doesn't she always? Now, I think it's about time for a bath, some dinner, and then bed for you, young lady. Come along."

Nate Laramie watched his two women walk toward the house, a look of inexpressible pride and contentment on his tanned, handsome face.